Blues with Ice

by

Tin Larrick

Copyright © Tin Larrick 2017

First published 2017 by The Obscure Cranny Press

Dedicated to the memory of HST… 80 this year, and needed more than ever

PREMISE:

Being on the road is not like reading *On the Road*.

Discuss.

PROLOGUE

Marie and I met at the raggedy, grime-caked comprehensive that we both attended back in the day. It was a rough, horrifying place, and I was exposed overnight to the desperation of drugs, violence and the thin line of self-destruction that seemed to separate those who had some vague idea about what they wanted their future to hold and those that were just hell-bent on surviving until the next day. Curiously, where I was concerned, the two categories seemed to be interchangeable.

Mature beyond her years, Marie didn't seem to have any of these identity crises. She was studious, sensible and took no truck with any idiots. It's very easy to maintain the values you were brought up with while you're still in the bosom of your family; once you leave, however, that world outlook is severely tested. So, while I was pusillanimous enough to drift from one rough crowd to another, Marie held firm to such a confident extent that nobody messed with her. Not everybody liked her, but they respected her. The same could not be said for me.

The one beacon of hope in the bleak trenches of this bleak institution was my discovery of the school drama club. Twice a year – at Christmas and at the end of the summer term – a full bells-and-whistles production would be staged. They were properly done, as well, with auditions, rehearsals two evenings a week – more as opening night got closer – stage production, costumes, music – the whole nine yards.

Marie was into it as well – but then, of course she was. My maiden outing in a speaking part was *The Voyage of the Dawn Treader* – I was Caspian to Marie's Lucy. It was all very exciting for me, and during the early days she sternly told me off more than once for larking about during rehearsals.

During one of the show's evening performances, her voice betrayed her on stage, and her line disappeared in a hoarse croak. She cleared her throat politely, winked at the audience and tried again, starting with "What I MEANT to say was..." and carried on. She didn't miss a beat, but best of all was when she caught my eye and smiled, her skin glowing under the hot stage lights.

That was when I was 13, and she was 15. By the time we'd gone through *Dick Tracy*, *The Box of Delights*, *Cinderella* and had progressed to Molière, at the ages of 16 and 18 respectively, I was desperately, hopelessly in love. In love in that almost-ethereal, totally-unattainable, never-gonna-happen, she's-way-out-of-your-league kind of way.

We had co-starred in a summer production of *Le Médecin malgré lui* – Marie as Martine to my Sganarelle – and I was acutely and painfully aware that, following the final show, Marie would be leaving school and heading to university after the summer break, leaving me to eke out another two years gazing at my navel and cleaving kudos from 'A' Levels that, in our town, would be utterly useless for anything other than more studying. I envied her fleeing our grey industrial hometown, I craved the free-thinking wing-spreading she would no doubt undertake, and to cap it all off I was inconsolable that she was going.

When you're a kid and people tell you your schooldays are the happiest days of your life, most of us tend to scoff or laugh or groan. Then, when you grow up, you think about it a little differently.

What they mean, of course – although they might not know it – is that you are *emotionally involved* in whatever it is you are doing. If somebody talks about having had a great night out, they mean that their emotions, their feelings, were awakened and invested. When you are younger, your feelings tend to be that much more alive than when you are older, when they can sometimes seem dormant for months or even years at a time, and you can stagger through great chunks of your existence feeling more or less numb, lurching towards some inevitable end point based on the dregs of what you thought you were striving for back when you had some concept of the future.

As a grown man, I haven't quite conceded the point *per se*, but on this basis there is no doubt that those balmy nights rehearsing and performing various attempts at amateur dramatics were, in fact, among the best of my life. While I admired Marie from afar – she being in a *serious* relationship with the school cricket captain – there were burgeoning romances with girls my own age, and from audition to curtain, every single emotion seemed to be fully engaged at every waking (and often sleeping) moment, alive and raw and electrified. There was the excitement of performing, the thrill of applause, the horseplay, the occasional fight, the laughs and the trepidation of discovering cautious kisses and borrowed cigarettes.

The final night of *Le Médecin malgré lui* coincided with the last day of term before the summer holidays. It was a hot and sticky July evening, and the heavy topcoat, wig and thickly-caked foundation of my French aristocrat's costume proved decidedly uncomfortable (although being tirelessly tended to by the make-up ladies every time I stepped into the wings did rather kindle the illusion of stardom).

By the time we had finished the bows – Marie hanging off my arm like the dutiful wife she was portraying – there was a kind of electric euphoria in the air. The run was over. The tension that had built steadily since the first audition had dissipated, and we were alive with the satisfaction of a job well done and an unrelenting urge to celebrate.

This took the form of the director leading us all en masse to our local pub ('local' was actually relative, but it was the teachers' favourite and the nearest one that catered for our kind of people) where the cast and crew did gifts, speeches, drinks and whiled away the evening listening to the band.

The pub was way, way out in the sticks – which might have explained the tolerance of artisan babbling – and the garden at the back tapered away down a grass verge to a riverbank where, in the summer, kayaks and small fishing boats would idle lazily downstream towards the sea. On the other side of the pub was a disused railway line sprinkled with bluebells and forget-me-nots that hadn't been operational for thirty years. It was so far out that utter inebriation was needed just to make either the walk home or the exorbitant cab fare bearable.

It was there, lying on the grass in the dark, listening to the ripple of the water, the strains of *Liars' Bar* and *Rotterdam* drifting outdoors from the pub band, the evening still warm from a day incubating in the July sun, that the virginal, sixteen-year-old Alex Gray found himself. Lying on his back, looking at the clear navy blue sky, wondering at the intoxicating smell of the eighteen-year-old woman beside him, whose head was resting on his chest.

I don't remember what we talked about, other than it was everything. I do remember, however, Marie lifting her head to look at me. Her face was in shadow, the edges of her hair like electric filaments in the glow of the outdoor terrace lights. She touched me on the cheek, said "You've still got some make-up on your ear," and pushed her lips against mine. She touched my tongue with hers, and I might have lost her forever, lost her to a yawning summer cut free from the social network of school to hold us together, lost her to university and adulthood and the big world beyond this one, but I didn't. From this magical night onwards, she was mine, and I hers.

*

Many years later, the pub burned down. The Beautiful South broke up. Marie graduated and went to Canada. I laid felt roofs by day and played blues guitar in pubs with names like *The George* and *The Bull's Head*. Doing this for a year seemed like a long time. Doing it for two didn't seem any different. Doing it for three… well, by then, I'd forgotten the start of it.

One day, Marie came looking for me.

She found me.

I wished she hadn't.

ACT ONE – VEGAS

CHAPTER ONE

DEATH ROW AIRPORT

The light over the mirror in the airport gents' was harsh and tinged with blue. I touched the skin under my eye. It was soft and tender still, but the swelling had gone down and the eye had opened a fraction.

Hoping my unseemly appearance wouldn't cause any consternation when I attempted to board, I splashed some water on my face and exhaled heavily at my reflection. I picked up my flight case and hauled my duffle bag from the tile floor, slippery as it was with a sheen of water and god-knows-what. I slung the bag over my shoulder. It was easily big enough for me to climb into and close the drawstring over my head, and it was packed tight with the contents of my entire life.

I slugged it out with the bag for ten yards or so, then gave in and dropped it heavily onto a trolley. I stood my flight case vertically against the bag, where it stood like a mottled grey tombstone adorned with flight labels, and pushed it towards the departure lounge of Terminal 3, Heathrow Airport.

A ten-hour flight to Los Angeles is unfun for most people, unless you can sleep your way through it - preferably aided by Jim Beam miniatures. If you're 6'2" and in cattle class it's even less fun, so when I saw I had a window seat at the front of the line that allowed me to stretch my legs out by the bulkhead, I was pleasantly surprised.

I had kicked off my shoes and was flexing my toes on the carpet when a woman sat down next to me in a cloud of perfume and swish of brightly-coloured silks.

She was short, inching towards forty and very pleasant to look at, with a deep suntan and shiny dark hair tied back with a diamante butterfly.

She also had an extremely small baby in her arms.

Great.

At that moment, the babe was sound asleep, but I knew what these things were like.

She turned to me and made direct eye contact in a manner so bold that I realised she couldn't possibly be English, almost daring me to deal with the elephant in the room. Or, in this case, the sprog in the cabin.

"I'd hate to see the other guy," she said, brightly. The accent was Australia, or possibly New Zealand. My ear for antipodean dialect was not all it could have been.

It took me a second to work out that she was talking about my eye.

"Oh, this," I said, touching the tender area spreading from the socket down towards my nose. "This is what happens when you try to play Cajun blues in the Dog and Duck."

She sat forward suddenly as the laugh escaped her like a gunshot. The sound was like a silver spoon chiming the edge of a crystal whisky tumbler. It was as loud as a bell, and I fired a nervous look down at the baby as it stirred in her arms.

"Yeah, Skip James had his problems," I said, nevertheless encouraged by her reaction, "but I'm pretty sure angry blokes with bulldog tattoos and Liverpool shirts never gave him a kicking on the banks of the Delta."

"Tell me about it," she said, the back of her hand over her mouth as she alternated words with laughter. "I thought we had boors in Oz, but you English, wow. Some of you make us look enlightened."

"How long did it take you to work that out?" I said, thinking: I've seen the word 'boors' on the printed page, but I've never heard anyone actually use it in conversation.

"Four months. I've been staying with my sister in Chiswick – you know, show off the wee one…" – here she held the sleeping cherub aloft in both arms like the Olympic torch – "…and now I've had enough. I'm going home. The plan was to stay for six months, but I thought I'd spend the last two soaking up some Californian rays."

"Why not?" I said.

She tilted her head slightly.

"Mind you, you *sound* English, but there's more to you than that, no? Full of Eastern promise, you are."

I could have parried the flirtatious serve-and-volley with an equally sharp cross-court backhand, but instead, totally instinctively, like some primitive natural selection-and-elimination motor function, my eyes dropped to her ring finger. There was a fuck-off great rock there, barely held in place by a shiny gold band. It was only for a split-second, but I'm pretty sure she saw me looking.

"You play the blues?" she said, her laughter winding down.

"Every day," I said, smiling.

"And we're on a flight to LA," she said. "You off to seek your fortune?"

I didn't answer. She'd needled me. She was at least fifteen years older than me, and I suddenly felt like a silly kid with dreams of being a rock star. The fact that I was pretty much exactly that didn't seem relevant.

I stared at the bulkhead in front of me. She gently touched my forearm with her elbow and leaned forwards, trying to catch my eye. She was smiling, teasing, her eyebrows raised.

"I just like playing music," I mumbled.

The smile got wider. She nudged my empty shoe with her foot.

"Christ," she said. "What size are *they*?"

I shrugged.

"What's your name?" she said.

"Alex," I answered. "What's yours?"

If she'd said 'No names,' then a world of smoky promise and whispered desire in anonymous airport hotels in nameless stopover cities where time has no meaning might have opened up. Then again, I might have thought that if she'd answered 'Veronica.'

As it was, something else happened.

The kid woke up.

Ten hours later, the Ruby Tuesday commenced its descent into LAX, and the images on the back-of-seat multimedia screens were replaced by images of flowers and other vegetative grotesques in the wild. It was one of those accelerated stock footage films, where the entire blooming cycle takes place over a few seconds. I suspected that these films were probably intended to perform a sedative function during takeoff and landing, but as my stomach lurched I felt that somewhere between conception and execution these good intentions had been hideously lost.

A murmur of quiet applause rippled through the cabin as the undercarriage thumped the tarmac. I smiled to myself; the relief was palpable. During the long wait at the airport my bored mind had made the connection that 'Heathrow' is only one letter away from 'Death Row,' but otherwise I was not and never have been excessively nervous about flying. That's not to say it isn't stressful – despite brilliant white smiles, frilly service and conversations that strain to be casual, crashing and burning always seems to be the thing everyone is trying furiously not to think about.

I helped 'Veronica' (I never did find out her name) with her bags from the overhead locker and she rewarded me with another devastating smile. The child had remained awake for much of the flight, necessitating her more or less constant attention, and, when I wasn't sleeping, our conversations had remained superficial.

I couldn't offer her my number, because I didn't have one and didn't know where I was going to be staying. There was a brief window of opportunity where she could have given me hers, but the collective courtesy of passengers allowing an attractive woman with a baby out into the aisle did not extend to me, and we were quickly separated by a phalanx of sweaty travellers all brittle with tired irritability. She was ushered to the front of the plane with the other infant-bearing passengers for whom 'priority' was just a daily label; a flash of brilliant silk as she lingered with the cabin crew for a moment, and then she was gone.

Disembarking, I noticed the smell first – a smell of hot weather, and the way another country's tarmac smells when it gets hot, and the way the aircon smells as it tackles the heat. A thousand hot English summers would never smell like this – it's just something about the climate, something about the fact that good English weather always feels just a heartbeat away from an ice storm.

The first native face I saw was an LAPD officer with a sniffer dog sticking its crude snout into the crotches and bags of the tired, shuffling passengers. For the sake of a possible career move, I sized up the uniformed brute and weighed odds. Doubtful – he outsized me by about six inches and fifty pounds. He gave me a cursory nod and I looked past him through the window of the boarding tunnel, where giant Fords and Lincolns and Buicks were slinking across the airfield. I'd never met a famous person in the flesh before, but right then I knew how it felt.

After being fingerprinted and photographed I collected my bags and made for Customs. The officer on the gate raised an eyebrow as I strolled towards him.

"Anything to declare?" he asked, nodding at my flight case.

I thought – just a cut-price epiphany.

"You got a job back home in England?"

"I'm a computer engineer," I lied.

"Then you can afford to do a lot, pal," he laughed.

My lag-addled brain didn't really grasp the meaning of this, and so I nodded and walked out into the arrivals terminal.

As I sloped off, I was quietly grateful that my dad talked me into a return ticket, though I would never have admitted it.

I recalled the conversation.

He said – just get a return ticket. Just in case.

I'd said – Dad, I'm not planning on coming back.

He said – I know, I know, but if you haven't got a visa, they won't even let you in the country with a one-way ticket. It's just a safeguard, and if it doesn't work out, you can come back.

His hand on my shoulder.

A few weeks before, in the planning stage, the immigration red tape was really getting me down. It had taken all the fun out of it, when I read a journal by some guy who had hopped on a plane to New York and got a cash in hand job doing removals, where rich women in the Hamptons were tipping him more than he knew what to do with. *He* didn't come back.

No doubt the details had been stripped away for the sake of a good read, but it was enough for me. I felt rejuvenated, and went back to basics. No plan, no red tape, just my stuff in a bag and a plane ticket. The rest I would work out as I went. Did Kerouac have a visa? Shit, no. He never really left the country, of course, but you know what I mean.

As I slithered into the arrivals terminal and looked at the bank of courtesy telephones, I remembered I had nowhere to stay, and my heart sank. My feet hurt, my head itched, my eyelids were sagging, and suddenly my decision to render 'adventure' synonymous with 'spontaneous improvisation' didn't seem quite so hot. I could see Dad's face. That silent I-told-you-so, the wincing smile.

The best I could manage was a Motel 6 on Century Boulevard for sixty-five dollars a night. I reserved one night with the idea of sleeping well and then sketching out a strategy the following day. I hauled my stuff out to the pickup point and waited for the shuttle. The warm air of the Californian afternoon on my skin somehow seemed very final, as if to say *you're here now, you're breathing the air, there's no going back*. Somewhere behind me the plane I arrived on was thinking about leaving again.

After half an hour a shuttle arrived and drove me into Inglewood. I tipped the driver, stepped off and looked around in a daze. A shimmering heat haze hung over Century Boulevard; dusty broken signs offered Liquor, Mex Food To Go and Live Nuds. I wondered briefly what a nud was, then pulled my bags inside and checked in.

The girl on the desk mimicked my 'Cheers' with a giggle, and I took the lift up to the room. As functional as it possibly could have been, with a view of Century Boulevard stretching out to the east.

I showered, then checked Camille. After ten hours in the subzero cargo hold, she was hopelessly out of tune and in dire need of attention. I tinkered with her for twenty minutes or so, then stashed her under the bed. I lay down, star-shaped and wide-eyed like a week-old baby, my mind in a whirl, an edge of panic lurking just offstage. Then sleep took me, so sudden and heavy it was like being anaesthetised.

Around four the next morning I was wide awake. The liquorice-red neon HOTEL sign from the Best Western opposite glowed through the crack in the curtain. I stepped onto the warm balcony and gazed at the lights of Los Angeles, the amber lights of Century Boulevard dwindling to a point in the distance. From a billboard across the street Oprah grinned at me. The flat white concrete balcony wall was cool on my arms, and one thought was prominent in my brain.

What the hell am I doing here?

There was only one logical answer.

It was time to call Marvin.

CHAPTER TWO

ON THE PITH

I woke up suddenly when the panic-worm did double-time and made an entrance stage left into my consciousness. I sat bolt upright in bed with a huge intake of breath, my heart pounding in my chest, the oxygen raw in my lungs.

I had, after all, only paid for one night, and was convinced I had slept through the 11:30am check-out time. I switched on the television and channel-hopped until I found CNN and discovered with relief that it was only 7am.

I took in the news with a kind of slack-jawed osmosis. The newscasters, Ric and Patti, reported on the night's mayhem without batting their well-powdered eyelids. A car had wrapped itself around a traffic signal last night four miles away in Redondo, practically slicing the driver in two. A bunch of gang bangers had unloaded their carbines at two LAPD officers somewhere in Watts.

They went international. After a steady NATO aerial bombardment of the wrong targets – a refugee convoy, the Chinese embassy – the war in Kosovo would be over imminently, they said. With the indictment of the Serbian president for war crimes, it was only a matter of time…

I couldn't take it. I switched it off and rolled over. As a child, my parents had never espoused the idea that smashing things up to get your own way actually worked, but then they didn't know everything.

After taking a shower and sucking some water straight from the tap, I checked the telephone on the bedside table and saw that local calls were free. I tried to call Marvin. When the call wasn't accepted, I called reception.

"I'm trying to ring a friend of mine," I explained. "The call isn't being connected."

"*Ring*? What do you mean?" the girl asked, giggling again. She presumably slept under the desk.

"Ring? Call? On the telephone?" I said, perplexed.

"Oh, *right*. Where does your friend live?"

"Los Angeles."

"*Where* in LA?"

"Oh. I'm not sure. Hollywood, I think."

"That's why you're not being connected. You're in Inglewood – only calls to Inglewood are free. There's a charge for Hollywood. Try area code 323."

"But it's all Los Angeles, isn't it?"

The girl giggled again, and I hung up. I tried Marvin again, but the call still wouldn't connect.

I was packed and ready to go in half an hour. I left the Motel 6 on foot, hauling my guitar and bags down the scorching sidewalk of Century Boulevard. I made a mental note to learn the art of travelling light – my gear weighed a tucking fun.

At that precise moment, as I walked, I had no plan at all, other than to find somewhere cheaper to stay. And to my relief I found somewhere, less than two hundred yards down the street. Marletta's Motel was only twenty dollars a night plus tax.

My heart sank as the door popped open. What a dump. No phone, no cable, no plug in the bath, no towels, a funny smell, and a hole at the bottom of the door that was shaped suspiciously like a shotgun blast. Still, you get what you pay for, I suppose, and as the water was hot, the aircon worked and the bed was comfortable, I didn't mind too much. At least there were no roaches. That I saw, anyway.

I sloped down the street and tried to call Marvin from a phone box. This ostensibly simple task turned out to be more difficult than first presented – the machine ate all of my change, but before I could call the operator to protest or break into the machine to get my money back, I realised that the box was nothing less than a lethal greenhouse. The sweltering heat began to cook me alive through the glass, and I gave up.

Eventually the survival instinct kicked in, and I formed a careful decision to find something to eat. I left the motel on foot and – after a slightly abortive start whereby I was shepherded to the correct bus stop on the *other* side of the street by a concerned citizen who clearly realised I did not want to end up in Watts or Compton – caught the bus to Hollywood via the LAX Transit Center. I tried Marvin again while I waited for the bus, and this time managed to get through, but no one was home. I left a droning message.

After getting off the bus somewhere along Santa Monica Boulevard, I tried him again, and he finally answered – half-asleep and hungover.

"What are you doing?" Marvin asked.

"Christ, not a lot. Surviving, I guess."

"What am I doing, what am I doing?" he mumbled. "I can meet you for lunch?"

"Sure."

"Great. Call me later, we'll talk details. I'm ruined."

The sun was harsh, and my neck roasted as I headed north up Fairfax, past Sunset and Selma, before turning west into the relative shade of Hollywood Boulevard.

The area was residential (with umbrella and hat shops conspicuously absent), and appeared to consist mainly of rental apartments aimed at, I guessed, Hollywood wannabes. I made a mental note to remember it. I had the pleasure of a couple more nights at Marletta's; beyond that, I didn't know where I would be sleeping. With a return flight six weeks hence that I fully intended not to use, committing to something that made this idea vaguely feasible seemed like a good start. There was an A4 flyer advertising studios to rent tacked to a nearby telegraph pole, with phone numbers cut into tabs along the bottom of the paper. I tore one off.

I caught another bus west, and as I noticed the Capitol Records building appear on the skyline, the trappings of urban Hollywood started to pop up in every direction. I hopped off at Mann's Chinese Theater, and bought a gallon of OJ at a café opposite. I sat at a table outside and watched the tourists scamper excitedly around each other, hoping for a glimpse of…. somebody. Not me, that was for sure.

My thirst quenched and the sun held at bay by the buildings, I tried Marvin again, figuring a couple of hours must have gone by since I spoke to him. It was probably more like forty-five minutes, but in any event he answered with decidedly more clarity of purpose than when I spoke to him earlier, and he told me to sit tight and he would be along, pronto.

I guessed I still probably had the best part of an hour before he arrived, and so attempted to seek out the base of the Capitol Records building, with some vague dreamlike idea of marching in, indefatigable, slamming down a demo tape on the desk of some fat piggy-eyed executive and leaving him slack-jawed at the wonder of how such an unremarkable device could hoard such a bounty of talent.

I didn't succeed in finding it – and didn't really try hard enough – and so returned to mooch up and down outside Mann's, trying to ignore the ego that was demanding fantasies of red carpets, flashing bulbs, limousines and the elusive concept of mass adulation. Towering above me was a hundred-foot billboard image of John Travolta in his latest film, and all of a sudden the gulf between *here* and *there* seemed nothing short of insurmountable.

"Alex, dear boy. Fantastic to see you!"

He was already pumping my hand before I had fully registered him, decidedly less groggy than earlier.

Nine months in California had done him the world of good. In a black sport coat, white T-shirt, jeans and canvas shoes, he had somehow gone from being plain lanky to tall and lean, like a college football Tommy Lee Jones. His face was all sharp angles at cheek and jaw, like a Christmas tree biscuit, while his previously milk-white skin was edged with tan. Last time I saw him the brown curls had been cut tightly to his head in a public schoolboy baize; they had now grown out over his ears with thick sideburns to match. The specs were gone, the five-day stubble looked the money and he even looked like he'd had his teeth done. Good job too. They weren't all that.

"I'd hate to see the other guy," he said, still pumping my hand.

"Yeah, me too," I said, trying not to roll my eyes. "I might get a matching pair."

"I see you found the nerve centre," he said, looking around at the tourists. "Keep your wits about you. So what's been going on? You finding your way around okay? When did you get here?"

"Yesterday, I think. Actually, it might have been the day before."

"Lag, huh? It's a bitch. You need to tough it out. Don't sleep… dear boy, you look beat. Let's eat. Come on."

I must have been swaying or something, for he guided me up Hollywood Boulevard to a solid Italian restaurant called Miceli's. We were ensconced in a booth by Toni, a second generation Italian waitress who couldn't have been a day over one hundred. The leather was cool on my skin. Marvin ordered a beer, while I, unable to face the prospect of embarrassing Marvin by having my fake ID sniffed at, opted for cola. Marvin eyed me with something approaching pity and ordered a couple of extra beers for himself.

"Where are you staying?" he asked again, following up with "My God! Gangsta!" when I described the motel in Inglewood.

Marvin, in his quest for details, pumped me on my itinerary, my activities to date, the logistics of my being and punctuated every answer with 'Mm-hmm? Mm-hmm? Fantastic. Fantastic," with his fist propping up his chin. Eventually it started to feel like an interview.

I didn't recall our last conversations being quite so stilted, but then it occurred to me that we hadn't spent any time in one another's company while sober – a fact that helps one paper over the cracks of meeting someone you don't actually know very well. This point Marvin

26

may have recalled himself as he discreetly slid one of his beers across the table to me.

Twenty-five to most people is just a kid – unless you're a twenty-year-old adrift in a strange country and the twenty-five-year-old knows his way about with enough funds to eat somewhere like Miceli's without batting an eyelid. I ordered chicken marinara – my first proper meal in what felt like weeks, and, washed down by Coors, I started to feel decidedly less tightly wound.

"This place…" he said, chewing carefully on a piece of peppered steak, and waving his fork around to indicate Los Angeles in general, "…this place is everything they say it is. The big lie is that the fat line in the sand between success and failure doesn't exist. It does, of course, but failure *here* is nothing like failure in, say, Swindon."

"What do you mean?" I said, not really following.

"What I *mean* is, everything is relative. Look at me. Less than a year ago I was signing on in the rain at Thanet dole office. Now I'm here, doing what I love. In the scheme of things I'm an absolute nobody, but, shit, you should see my house. You should see my *office*. And last week at some launch party I was actually within sniffing distance of Carmen Electra's breasts."

A more demonstrative barometer of achievement was difficult to imagine at that particular moment.

"So what about me?" I said. "You're saying I could make a go of it here?"

"Ah, shit, yeah, man," he said, dropping his fork. It clanged on the plate. "Remind me. What's your gig?"

"Music. Blues."

"Right, yes, yes, yes. I remember now. You gave us some covers last year at that hovel in Wales. You were pretty good. You got a band, or is it just you?"

"Well… just me, really. I have a couple of mates that come in now and then to help me lay down some tracks for the demos, but…"

"Good. So, blues. Much of a market for that where you are?"

"Hardly any. I might get lucky with a theme night here and there, but there's not a lot of call for it. The only thing I seem to get with any regularity is a kicking," I said, touching my eye.

He nodded in sympathy.

"Exactly my point. But here, you only have to walk down the street and you'll find a blues club. Your kind of place, your kind of people, and they'll put you on. Hey, you got a copy of your demo? I don't know too many people in the music biz, but it's all interchangeable at some point upriver. I'll ask around."

"Really? That would be… oh, shit, they're all back at the motel."

"Fortune could grab you by the balls any second, man. Keep at least one copy with you at all times."

He opened his jacket, where I saw a rolled up wad of white paper tucked into the inside pocket. He raised an eyebrow and grinned.

"What's that?"

"My latest script."

"Wow. Can I read it?"

"Of course you can, but not this copy. This pocket is never empty." He closed his jacket and drained his beer. "It's still a lottery, see, but you only need three numbers to win the jackpot, not six. Get it?"

I certainly did.

Intense was a word that pretty much defined Marvin from the inside out, and the combination of rich food, beer, jetlag and a day's walking in the baking sun probably started to render me rather dull company.

My conversation descended into rehearsed-sounding holiday soundbites, but what else could I say? That I was here to Seek Meaning? That I was on a deeply important self-imposed quest to avoid sliding into institutional narcolepsy in adulthood? That's what I wanted to say, but I couldn't get the words to surface. What I *didn't* want to say was that, so far, I had spent most of my brief time in California deeply regretting the decision to come at all.

Marvin settled the bill while my wallet was in my hand, waving it away with a flick of the wrist.

Outside, I shielded my eyes from the sun. Marvin suggested a constitutional to work out the bugs, and we walked up to the Yamashiro restaurant, high in the Hollywood Hills, and I took in a glimpse of the city and the Hollywood sign shimmering in the heat. LA didn't really look much like a city to me, more a patchwork of conflicting areas stitched together at random. Which, of course, it more or less was.

Marvin began to tell me about some new gizmo that was supposedly going to revolutionise home movie entertainment. Called a DVD, it was indistinguishable from a normal CD, but you popped it in your player and got sound and picture you could only dream of. It wouldn't degrade over time and there was no more fast-forwarding or rewinding tape, either – at the touch of a button you could leap to anywhere in the film.

"I like my tapes," I said. "I bet they'll cost a fortune, anyway."

"VHS is only good for sea defences," he said. "Throw them out."

I started to properly flag, and so Marvin told me to get some rest and call him in the morning. He had to work that night anyway – whatever *that* meant.

"And get the hell out of Inglewood, pronto," he said, shaking my hand.

We parted ways and I headed off to Western Avenue. I hopped on a bus and watched the glitz of Hollywood flit by like a movie reel, and as the crude designs and breadline of Inglewood started to appear after only a few blocks, my eyes closed and oblivion took me.

A shrill Californian voice jolted me awake sometime later, still on the bus, and, fortunately, with my possessions intact. I wiped the drool from my chin, looked around and saw a small ginger man in a white string vest and stars-and-stripes pantaloons talking excitedly to a girl that looked like a Baywatch extra. Or so I thought. He might have been talking to the door.

She looked completely out of place until I realised the bus was nosing into the outskirts of Venice Beach. I got off the bus, as did the Baywatch extra and the small ginger man, who appeared at my flank pulling a tartan shopping trolley along behind him. He ended up walking alongside me for the best part of a minute. It seemed silly not to say something.

"Alright," I muttered. "Going to the beach?"

He turned around, raising suspicious eyebrows as he did so, then he saw me and grinned, showing bad teeth.

"Yeah, but I'm gonna get the next bus. That dumb bitch is walking. It's like, a whole mile," he said in a nasal accent, indicating the Baywatch extra, who had allegedly made a pass at him on the bus. He introduced himself as Marcello, and then uttered something else about the Baywatch extra that I didn't understand, but it included the words 'shaving,' 'lesbian,' and 'lipstick,' and was accompanied by a gesticulation on his part that went equally misunderstood.

I shook hands with Marcello.

"You like beers?"

"Of course," I replied.

"Well hell, let's go get some beers. I just need to stash this in, like, some bushes or something," he said, indicating his rather cumbersome shopping trolley.

We began to walk, and the logistics of buying alcohol began to filter through my decision-making process. A friend of mine, Barry, who fancied himself as both an entrepreneur and a corporate terrorist had recently acquired a laser printer and laminator. Neither were domestically common in 1999, and he had provided me with an extremely convincing fake driving licence prior to my trip. However, I was terrified of using it.

"Erm, how hot are they on identification in Venice Beach?" I enquired.

"What'd you say?" he shouted.

"ID. I'm, er, only twenty."

30

"Don't worry, man."

We stopped at a 7-11. Marcello told me to wait outside, and he went in, dragging his tartan trolley behind him.

Three minutes later he came barrelling out in what didn't take me long to realise was an escape attempt, although the trolley, now fully laden with stolen beer, was proving something of a drag on his momentum. As a consequence, the enormous, roaring security guard was making good ground on the departing thief.

The parking lot outside the store was on an incline that led away down to the road, and the trolley got caught up in Marcello's legs. He performed an acrobatic but doomed attempt to avoid going arse-over-tit by vaulting the trolley as it overtook him, and he ended up sprawled on the hot concrete as bottles of beer smashed around him.

He was not to be deterred, however, and by some fluke of momentum and gravity, he managed to roll up onto his feet and keep going. He didn't look back, and somehow managed to outrun the guard.

In fact, the security guard had given up by the time he reached the scene of disaster. Broken glass lay everywhere, and rivers of chilled amber liquid flowed down to the road. The trolley was a mess of mangled tubing and torn tartan.

The guard looked at the carnage and scratched his head. He would be coming back shortly, no doubt, and so I discreetly sidestepped around the edge of the building and cut through some bushes at the rear of the store to the road on the other side.

The brief drama over, my thoughts returned to Barry as I walked. Our friendship had a discernible and predictable shelf life. The fork in my own particular road presented two choices, and both of them – the bohemian aspects of a grafting musician, and the institutionalised rank structure of the contingency options – appalled him. As far as Barry was concerned, capitalism was divine, and if you couldn't afford it, it didn't matter, as long as you *had* it. Wall Street was his Mecca. He was a year older than me, and I knew that before long he would tell me it was time to get serious.

The sun was like a heavy iron skillet on my neck as I sauntered through Muscle Beach, sucking on a vat of Coke. I took in street theatre, buskers, dancers, tattooists and tattooed, stoners and the remnants of Pride 1999. A flyer for a website called MARINE STUDS was thrust into my hand, and as *Subterranean Homesick Blues* played out of an unseen PA system somewhere up ahead, I felt the camera on my face.

I turned as the camera went *click-FLASH*, and then the photographer disappeared among the crowd.

"Hey!" I called.

I barely got a glimpse of him, but I saw the string vest and stars-and-stripes pantaloons, and realised it was the unusual shoplifter named Marcello. He would have stuck out like a sore thumb – had he been anywhere else in the world other than Venice Beach.

I considered pursuing him, but left it too late and he disappeared. I stood still for a moment, wondering what the hell was going on, then told myself that behaviour of that nature was probably *de rigueur* in this part of town.

After discovering that the concrete bunker housing the beach toilets contained nothing so novel as doors on the cubicles, I sought refuge in Borders. I bought a bagel, a cappuccino and a copy of *Smoke,* and sat down at the counter.

I skipped over the feature on Dennis Franz's favourite cheroots, and instead pored over the classified section while absent-mindedly – and liberally – dousing my coffee with the contents of a chocolate powder shaker. *Bon Jovi tribute band seeks Sambora lookalike.* I checked my reflection in the mirror above the counter. Hmm, perhaps not. I sipped the coffee as I read, and descended into a paroxysm of hacking coughs as I realised that the chocolate powder was, in fact, cinnamon.

Chastened by the experience, and mortified by the histrionic sympathy I consequently attracted from one or two deeply concerned Angelenos, I rolled up the magazine and sloped out to the street again.

I eventually reached the Santa Monica Promenade, by 4th

Street, and that was where I saw him.

Rosco Dunhill III. Even now I don't know if that was his real name. He was beater than anybody I'd ever seen on either side of the pond. He looked and sounded like BB King would have looked and sounded if he had lived in a skip and chewed thumb tacks for the best part of fifty years. He was massively obese, wearing a Cadbury-purple T-shirt the size of a parachute and dirty elasticated track bottoms. His face was speckled with black-and-white stubble embedded in his leathery skin like the remnants of a shrapnel blast, and his guitar was held together with gaffer tape and the flight decals that adorned its war-torn body.

Some Romo throwback with a blond mullet and denim drainpipes who had been performing ill-advised harmonies on an earlier Temptations number asked him if he knew *What a Wonderful World*. Careful analysis of the gestures and facial tics that followed led me to deduce that old Rosco would love to play it, but it extended beyond his repertoire.

I saw my moment. My guitar was the sole reason I'd taken this bloody trip, and I'd be damned if it was going to be the reason I went home.

I left my seat, leaving a layer of skin on the hot painted bench, and introduced myself to Rosco. I offered to show him the chords, and he seemed more than happy, which was good because I suddenly realised he might get sore at some stranger poking his nose in where it wasn't wanted.

I had to change the key a bit, because I'm a baritone and this guy was out and out bass. F major, A minor; *I see trees of green, red roses too...* D minor... *I see them bloom...* and...

I couldn't remember any more.

I muttered something by way of an excuse and then sat down again. I heard some kid laugh loudly from behind me. I didn't look round. Romo smirked. Rosco shrugged, then got on and bashed out a howling version of *I Asked For Water (She Gave Me Gasoline)*.

After establishing that no one was looking at me, I stopped wishing that the San Andreas Fault would have a wobble and swallow me up, and I stretched out and laced my hands behind my head, gazing upwards at the blazing California sky. By now, Rosco Dunhill III had quite a crowd around him as he bawled his wounded words. The late afternoon sun seemed to bleach the pigment out of the sky, turning it pale blue like when you slurp the colour out of the ice in a vivid summer cocktail.

The afternoon stretched lazily over the bulging cluster of people swarming over the promenade. The glistening bodies basted by the heat were sluggish and made me tired just to look at them. Occasionally a wisp of breeze would drift in from the Pacific to cool the glowing flesh, but I could smell the hot concrete, hard on my tired feet, and felt an urge to join the excited throngs clamouring for the shade.

It was at that moment that I got a chance to redeem my crushed ice-breaker with Rosco. In front of his amp (*woke up this morning*) was a canvas bag containing copies of his own album, *Bladder Washout Blues*, for five dollars apiece, as well as all the proceeds of the morning – which, as far as I could see, had been bountiful.

Next to the stack of CDs was a flat wooden box with a glass front, about half the length of a shoebox. Mounted inside it on a bed of red felt was an assortment of dollar bills and coins, arranged in a pattern. On the glass was a small printed label that I couldn't read.

As I patted my hot hair, I sensed swift, sudden movement coming from the north end of the promenade. I looked up to see two young skate punks sprinting past Rosco's stage, pausing only to steal the bag in front of his amp.

Rosco stood up in a fury, dropping his already-battered guitar to the ground. He yelled "Hey!" but attempted no pursuit, because to all those who bore witness it was obvious that striving to haul his three-hundred-pound carcass along at anything more than a casual saunter would be nigh impossible in this heat.

But the perps, in order to execute their escape, had to run

directly in front of the bench upon which I was perched. Not out of concern, indignation, sympathy nor any other altruistic trappings, but something more like a reflex and therefore utterly involuntary, I stuck my leg out. Had any more substantial movement been required, I would not have budged an inch. Not because I was scared, ambivalent or even unpleasant, but because I was, at that moment, a stranger in a strange land, and the instinct is not to draw attention to oneself.

But all this went unsaid, because it turned out to be such a deft interception. The first delinquent blundered straight into my outstretched calf, his crony thumped into the back of him, and the two of them went sprawling along the hot cement of the Santa Monica Promenade. I picked up the bag, dusted it off and handed the spoils back to a seething Rosco Dunhill III.

He ignored the bag in my outstretched hand, instead choosing to haul himself a skate punk off the ground to castigate. With a meaty paw he administered two or three open-hand slaps to the face of the quivering individual, peppering his onslaught with expletives. These barked reprisals were mostly unintelligible, but I managed to pick out "yo' momma", "punk" and "bitch". Suitably chastised, the urchins scurried off, encouraged by good riddances from the disapproving crowd.

Rosco returned to take the bag from my hand. I looked at him expectantly.

"I owe you thanks, little man," he growled in a gravelly monotone.

I shrugged.

"You like to play music, huh?"

"I guess."

He nodded approvingly.

"Come to the club tonight."

'The club' implied a certain familiarity on my part, because I doubted it was the only one in Los Angeles. I raised my eyebrows to further prompt him.

"The Mint on Pico Boulevard, a block east of La Cienega. Saturdays I play a set before Harry Dean Stanton's band."

I managed to find the tongue I'd always had before I left England.

"I'll be there. Thank you."

His left eyelid twitched involuntarily at the sound of the unfamiliar accent.

"You English?"

"Yes."

"Been in LA long?"

"Flew in yesterday."

"Got a guitar with you?"

I nodded.

"Bring it. I'll show you thanks."

He turned and walked back to his tiny stage. I looked down at the stack of albums, and read the printed label on the box of dollar bills. It said *MY BLUES*.

I looked up again at Rosco. He was well into *She Likes To Boogie Real Low* before I decided to move.

The interaction had proved rather liberating. After leaving Marvin I had planned to go back to the motel and sleep for a few hours, and had quietly fretted when the impromptu bus-nap meant I had overshot my stop and ended up here. Something to do with endorphins, maybe (whatever they were), but the thought of dozing on the beach for an hour or so was suddenly extremely appealing, and a spontaneous decision I might not have entertained in my post-arrival funk.

So I did. I took off my shirt, lay down on a bed of sand as warm and soft as, well, my bed, and fell asleep listening to the waves and children playing and wondering if there was such a thing as a bottle-nosed endorphin.

The slight drop in temperature from late afternoon to early evening stirred me, and, in something of a daze, I negotiated my way back to Marletta's. After the events of the day, it suddenly seemed like the place to not be at all costs.

I took a long shower. When I emerged, I looked at my dripping wet torso in the mirror, and performed a handful of ridiculous poses. Could I get on Muscle Beach? It didn't take me long to conclude that I most definitely could not: although the colour wasn't far off, the shadows were in all the wrong places.

I shaved, pulled on a white T-shirt and jeans, and covered the ensemble with my black Joseph overshirt. I felt almost instantly better, especially when I left Marletta's and felt the balmy night on my skin. The temperature had dropped to a comfortable twenty degrees, and the lights of Century Boulevard marked my journey to the street. The night was a clear navy blue, and no less than eleven aircraft were hanging in the sky as they converged upon LAX, like fat fireflies looking for a light.

CHAPTER THREE

GOUJONS OF SOUL

Camille was a beauty, the love of my life. Sleek and curved with a shiny ebony body, she truly was a work of art. This custom 1958 Les Paul mapletop reissue featured triple Floyd Rose humbuckers, rosewood fingerboard, a mahogany neck and a warm lilting sound that could transport you to the basements of the French Quarter and the banks of the Mississippi Delta in a heartbeat. The moment I'd seen her hanging up behind the counter of Earl's Emporium in the Lanes, I'd fallen in love. Every note brought to mind rusty Packards, hot neon in rain-slicked streets, shrimp gumbo, syrupy bourbon rolled around Lucky Strikes and sweat-soaked clothes sticking to your body – and, if you were lucky, maybe someone else's.

Being too poor for a cab I had allowed myself plenty of time to negotiate the criss-cross of public transport that I anticipated needing to get to The Mint. Despite this, I still arrived in mid-LA with a couple of hours to spare. I had nothing else on my itinerary besides my serendipitous encounter with Rosco Dunhill III, and it was proving difficult to keep a lid on the excitement in my belly.

I was twenty years old, and when I flew to LA I left four application forms in the bedroom I was renting from my parents. One for the army, one for the navy, one for the Metropolitan Police and one for a management consultancy that Barry had slipped into the mix. My solemn vow – if I didn't make something of out of my trip to California, I was going to have wise up and bring one of them to bear. With my scheduled visit to The Mint looming ever closer, it was increasingly difficult to ignore the smouldering embers of hope that were whispering to my innards that I might not have to make that choice. My hands felt good. The nerves felt good. If he invited me to play, if I could just *feel* it, tonight might prove definitive, one way or the other.

To keep my brain from going into existential overdrive, I stopped at a diner on La Cienega for coffee and apple pie. It was a small place with faded linoleum and yellow vinyl booths. The counter was laden with pastries and slabs of ice cream in various colours, lined up in rows like a child's xylophone. An extractor fan above the till whirred like a hair dryer.

I noticed a computer on a desk by the double swing-doors that led into the kitchen. The handwritten sign on the wall above the monitor was blowing in the draught of an unseen fan, and it took me a moment to realise it was for public use. I paid the man five dollars and sat down at the screen.

I wedged Camille under the desk, between my seat and the wall, and logged into the machine. This was 1999, a strange vacuum where the technological potential of the twenty-first century had yet to be realised, the whole thing on hiatus anyway while the globe panicked quietly about the millennium bug. The concept of email was still comparatively new; web-based email – the idea you could send *and* receive mail from any machine in the world – was positively mind-blowing; that is, if you disregarded the screen loading line by line, as slow as an egg timer.

The dial-up whirred and clicked painfully, and I had settled into a kind of vacant trance by the time I had logged into my Hotmail account.

When I did, the vacant trance was replaced by a kind of slack-jawed shock, although to the casual observer the difference would have been negligible.

There were four new emails. Two were junk, one was from my mother – sent, I noted, before I'd actually arrived in Los Angeles – saying the kinds of things that mothers say to their itchy-footed offspring, and the fourth was from Marie.

DATE	FROM	SUBJECT
JUN 8	CAROLE GRAY	hi son
JUN 9	Microsoft Team	Important Upgrade
JUN 9	Marie Clement	ANY CHANCE?? X
JUN 11	Furniture Plus	Sale ends Monday!

Still catching flies, I opened the email, only dimly aware of the butterflies in my stomach.

Hey my gorgeous boy!

You missing me?

Well, my year's sabbatical in Vancouver draws to a close, and I'm heading home soon. The idea sucks beyond belief, and I have no idea what I'm gonna do when I get there, so I'm gonna take the long way home.

I'm coming down to California, spend a few days, then head for New York for a few days before I fly home. Don't know yet how I'm going to get to NY, but it should be fun finding out! Aren't you going too? Maybe we could hitch together.

If my calculations are correct, you've arrived in LA by now. If you're around, want to come get me??? My flight gets into LAX at 9pm on June 12th – Delta 198 from Seattle. I've got no plans, no reservations, no nothing, so you might have to ride to the rescue.

Be there or be square!

Luv ya,

M x

I logged out of the machine, thinking – if this escapade had taken place a couple of years earlier, I would have been almost completely untraceable in LA except for postcards home. As it was, technology had made me utterly discoverable. [How little I knew…]

I stood up and looked at my watch.

Holy shit.

9pm on June 12th.

That was now.

Not only had I heard from a woman that I had not really expected to hear from again this side of the Apocalypse, but I was very suddenly faced with the reality of seeing her in the very near future.

I had staggered about a hundred yards south on La Cienega in a total daze when I realised that I had left Camille in the diner.

I swore aloud and ran back, panic rising in my sternum. The diner had been half-full – although, at that moment, I was feeling like more like a half-empty kind of guy – which was more than enough for it to have wandered out unnoticed.

I burst in and ran over to the desk with the computer.

No dice.

Camille was gone.

God-shitting-DAMMIT!

I whirled around and scanned the diner, my heart bouncing like a hard-boiled egg in a cement mixer. There were around twenty people sitting at the various tables. No furtive glances. No sweaty brows buried in newspapers. No vans screeching to a halt outside. No masked culprits sprinting for the getaway van, my beloved under their arm. No tell-tale signs of thievery at all. They were all chewing, slurping and conversing in utter contentment.

I walked past all the tables, conspicuously checking under seats and around legs. In a city where personal space and interpersonal etiquette is as sensitive as day-old sunburn, it didn't take long for me to draw some enquiring comments. I politely explained – as politely as utter dread and horror will allow – that I had left my guitar behind, and someone had half-inched it. I actually used the word 'half-inched' on a young couple sitting by the window; foolishly, because the conversation got rather off-topic, focusing instead on my cute accent, rhyming slang, what I was doing in California, blah blah blah and all things British – including, I imagined, our bad teeth and world-renowned impatience.

I questioned the man behind the counter and got only a vacant shrug. I turned it up a notch, and he reciprocated in kind with defensive belligerence. He couldn't help, and, thanks to my manner, probably wouldn't have done even if he could have. I thought about leaving him a hundred bucks to ask around, but it wasn't much, I couldn't afford it, and I had no guarantees he wouldn't pocket it and then instantly forget about me.

In the event, not one single person could help me. The proprietor did at least point me in the direction of Beverly Hills police station, where I filed a report. I thought I had done a pretty good job of examining the scene, but when the desk sergeant asked if the diner had CCTV, I couldn't answer. These were the days before you couldn't turn a street corner without a video camera in your face, and, in my view, it was a bit of a specialist line of enquiry.

The desk sergeant did not share my view. It didn't sound like anyone would be going down there to check, either. I did have some photographs of Camille, but not about my person. The one distinctive feature, should she ever appear in a pawn shop window, was the small inscribed plate under the neck joint which read:

A – NEVER GIVE UP – M

Yes, appropriately enough, I wouldn't have had Camille without Marie. I might not have had Marie without Camille, come to that.

For good or ill, Marie was intertwined with every mournful blues lick that ever smoothed out of Camille's slinky body – in part because she had bought her for me.

When I first discovered the joys of earning my own personal full-time income – joyful because I was still living rent-free with my parents – Marie had already become a diligent saver and a thrifty spender with one eye firmly on future rainy days. Her occasional shows of generosity were reserved for those she genuinely loved, such as her parents and her sister, and I guess I was pretty chuffed when I found out I was in that circle too.

So when she offered to buy Camille, on the spot, without a burning need to rush home and check the accounts ledgers first, it was a definite first for me. I was quite speechless. My parents had been

42

generous enough, but spontaneous bursts of expenditure had more or less ceased when I hit double figures. I could have bought Camille for myself, but not without some serious financial jiggery-pokery, and probably not before someone else swagged her out of the shop window first.

Marie knew how much I had to have her, and, despite a comparatively short relationship at that point, she knew how difficult it was to come by decent mid-range left-handed guitars. [I'd once tried to do a Hendrix by inverting the strings on a budget imitation Stratocaster, but had only succeeded in nearly drilling my hand off when I tried to swap the strap nut.]

But despite being at least two-parts pragmatist, her encouragement that I pursue music was unfailing. It was never qualified by contingency plans of a career in dentistry – all she ever said was *You're really good, keep on going, never give up* or derivatives thereof. She used to like me playing and singing to her, and we even wrote a couple of songs together, so maybe the nub was that we just had different ideas of what success looked like.

So, really, it was her fault I ended up on a building site with serious consideration being given to joining various starched institutions that amounted – at twenty years old, anyway – to selling out my soul for eternity.

I sat down on a bench at a bus stop on La Cienega, my head in my hands, in an effort to slow my spinning brain. Bizarrely, I started to focus on the fact that the arrival of Marie's flight would clash with my visit to The Mint – maybe she could come too? maybe her flight would be late? maybe… before remembering that without Camille, there seemed precious little point in going at all, unless I intended to bus tables.

I clawed my hands down my face and groaned at the sky in despair. From feeling completely out of my depth, to chancing upon a tiny crack of opportunity, only to fill said crack with the cement of my own idiocy. All in the space of a couple of days.

I was tempted to ignore the email. I was tempted to reply, telling her to shove her casual let's-meet-up-after-a-year plan. I was tempted to get on the next flight out of there, and THEN reply to the email, telling her – just to twist the knife – that it was her email that made me fly home early. I was tempted to walk out across La Cienega in front of the next bus.

I knew I wouldn't do any of those things. I couldn't leave without Camille, and I knew that I couldn't resist seeing Marie again, no matter how hazardous it would prove to my health.

I hadn't heard from her in over a year. She hadn't even arrived yet, and she had already thrown my world into turmoil.

CHAPTER FOUR

BUTTERFLY

In my moping ill humour I told myself I wasn't bothered either way, but it was impossible not to get butterflies when Marie walked through the arrivals gate. Maybe I was just relieved to see a friendly face, or maybe it was because she looked utterly, utterly fantastic.

"Hi, Alex," she breathed, kissing me on the cheek. "Long time no see."

The perfume was different, too. But, I swear, it wasn't just the perfume I could smell.

A little over a year earlier, I'd said goodbye to her as she got into her father's car and set off for Heathrow. She'd wanted me to come along as well and see her off, but I'd fudged my excuses and made 'We're not together any more,' come out as 'I've got to get some new shoes.'

So off she went. When she left me standing in the road and boarded the Air Canada flight to Vancouver with her degree in her pocket and a gap year working in a ski resort beckoning, she'd looked her usual self. Big green eyes. Tiny nose. The smile that scythed through me the first time she fired one in my direction. Shiny red-edged brown hair falling straight down almost to her waist. A propensity for denim. Slightly bookish maybe, but cute as hell.

So, fourteen months and what looked like nine thousand crunches later, when she sauntered through the arrivals gate with a spiky blonde bob and a pierced navel, I did a bit of a double take – by which I mean I had to scrape my jaw off the floor.

The funny thing was, I was half expecting it. At the start of her trip, we'd spoken every couple of weeks. A few months in, she'd phoned me, drunk, in the middle of the night, to tell me in detail about a little lesbian experiment she'd dabbled in with one of her fellow chambermaids.

My silent reaction had doubtless spoken volumes. Shock was there. A little bit of envy too, I guess. But most of all was the simple fact that I couldn't believe it. No way my studious little girlfriend would have tried something like that when we had been going out. Not only that, but I couldn't believe I'd missed it, and for the first time it hit me that I really had been left behind, in all senses of the phrase.

With all this in mind, I only took solace in the fact that I was convinced I didn't still have feelings for her.

I took her suitcase and we hopped a cab back down Century towards the motel and my shitty little room. She talked nineteen to the dozen in the taxi, telling me about the blast she'd had and the seemingly endless list of new mates.

I shifted uncomfortably as the cab arrived at the crapheap motel. Marie didn't bat an eyelid – she bounded over to the door and opened it with her arse.

I went out for coffee and bagels and let her unpack. When I returned the place was alive with the sound of her hair dryer and the assorted detritus of someone who was making themselves very much at home. I quietly set down the coffee, looking, I imagined, not unlike a rabbit in headlights.

She emerged from the bathroom, singing, and sat on the edge of the bed in only her towel.

"Rub my shoulders, darling," she said. "The flight was a bitch."

I silently obeyed, adding the pink heart tattoo on her left shoulder to the growing catalogue of surprises.

In the mirror, I could see she'd closed her eyes, and I leaned down to kiss her neck. My hands slipped around her front, and I shook my head in wonder at the hard ridges that now passed for her stomach. Unable to stop myself, I took her breasts in my hands, and she let out a little gasp.

And then wriggled away. She propped herself up against the headboard, half a smirk on her face, her hand resting on her knee, a bracelet dangling from her wrist, the towel only just about on.

"Alex… I didn't tell you. I have a boyfriend. In Canada."

Ouch. I rolled back on the bed – the *other* bed – and clamped my legs together, totally unsurprised.

"What's his name, what does he do and how old is he?" I said, staring at the ceiling.

"Funnily enough, his name is Alex. He's twenty-seven, and a professional snowboarder."

"Oh, *great*," I said.

"Don't feel bad," she said. "You're still sexy as fuck, Alex, but I don't cheat."

As it seemed to be a day of unending surprises, I produced my pack of Marlboro Lights and lit one up. As far as she knew, I was still a lifelong non-smoker. As far as *I* knew, so was she.

But somehow I wasn't surprised when she leaned over, removed the cigarette from my mouth, took a long drag and then replaced it between my lips. I could taste her lipstick on the butt.

Let's talk about the chronology, briefly. Officially, we'd split up a year or so *before* she went to Canada. She'd gone away to uni while I finished my 'A' Levels – I'd taken Drama, English and Media Studies, so on completion I was, naturally, totally unemployable, and landed a dead-end roofing job in the town we'd spoken so long of escaping. (I could tell you the name of it, but it could have been anywhere; towns like it are interchangeable the world over.) The relationship managed about eighteen more months of this and then, inevitably, failed.

But we kept in touch, and hooked up whenever she came home to visit her parents. Whenever this happened, we'd end up in bed. Neither of us met anyone else serious, so although the party line was that we'd split up, nothing was different, really.

Until now. She'd met someone else on her post-grad gap year, and all bets were suddenly off. The fact that it was a professional snowboarder seven years my senior was just garnish. I, of course, was still single. The building trade gets you the odd fumble on a Friday night after last orders, but precious little else.

And I realised that my conservative recollections of her were both inaccurate and slightly unfair. She was far from boring; there was a spark about her that seemed to grow as university beckoned. Not only did my clumsy teenage brain find the dichotomy between her serious side and her zest for life to be something of a paradox, but also that attempts to reconcile it were painfully erotic.

There was the house party for Dan Wylie's eighteenth, where Marie, after more than a handful of vodka collinses, led me into the bathroom, pushed me against the sink and sank to her knees. I recalled her free hand brushing her hair back over her ear, and the memory of the bathroom light catching her gold teardrop earring will take as long to fade as the sun will to implode.

There was the time we missed our train home from London, and killed time until the next one in the (long-since defunct) Molly O'Grady pub in Victoria Station. We only had time for one drink, but it was enough slavish intoxication for Marie to drag me past the concourse toilets and through a fire exit into a deserted atrium under construction. It was pretty eerie; the dust sheets that hung off everything were like ghosts, but Marie, undeterred, yanked down her jeans and climbed onto a workbench, pulling me towards her by the belt.

The security guard that emerged through polythene curtains to disturb us was kind enough (as he pointed out the CCTV camera). It gave me some heart that if I ever did succumb to the pull of a 40-year uniformed career, I might not end up the goosestepping, clodhopping institutionalised brute that I was terrified of becoming.

There was the midnight trip home from a gig in Middlesbrough, where a sudden, penetrating blizzard of Siberian snow began to fall on the otherwise-empty motorway.

'Fall' is the wrong word – not least because it was totally horizontal, firing at the car like Exocet missiles. The headlights ensnared every white-jacketed projectile, lighting them up like blinding laser beams. The effect it had on my vision was extraordinary – like the Millennium Falcon shooting into hyperspace. My eyes were helpless to do anything other than try to focus on each individual one at once.

At one stage, an owl flew fast and low across the windscreen, so close it made Marie yelp. Its white underside flashed even brighter than the snow – it was impressive to the sober mind; to the chemically-affected, it would have been positively portentous.

Driving was thus completely impossible, but it was settling so incredibly fast that I didn't have a choice – within minutes lane markings had vanished under thick snow like cotton wool; the verge followed suit and the central reservation wasn't far behind.

(Marie got her practical streak from her old man, a wily old two-ton know-it-all with a Victorian work ethic; he'd seen the forecast and insisted we take his Range Rover for our trip north. He irritated me sometimes, but I thanked God for his pragmatism the night we went to Middlesbrough. Plus he let me drive it.)

So we had no choice but to pull over into the first Travelodge we saw; by the time we had parked and got inside it was up to our knees. Properly besieged and with nothing else to do, we embarked on a night of activity that was probably illegal in some U.S. states.

I guess that's the proper marker of adulthood – when snow starts to fill you with dread instead of glee. At eighteen I was more or less ambivalent about it, but that night with Marie gave snow a whole new meaning, and by the morning I was so sore that the thought of sitting bare-arsed in an untouched blanket of the white stuff was quite appealing.

So if, when she left for Canada, she had a spark labelled 'naughty,' then when she walked into the arrivals hall at LAX, it was a flame that consumed her.

So I sucked on my cigarette, trying desperately to think about cabbage, and instead decided to damp the fires of mordant passion by telling her about Rosco, the Mint, and latterly, about Camille.

She listened patiently. Naturally, she was upset – more so than I was expecting, actually. She didn't fly off the handle, however, and was more sympathetic than anything.

"Did you report it to the police?"

"Yeah, but nothing will happen, unless it turns up in a fence's garage sometime in the next century."

"Better that than it being found and left where it is."

"It's pretty identifiable. It still has the engraving on it."

"It does?"

"Of course. Why wouldn't it?"

"Wondered if you might have prised it off."

I stared at her.

"Did you go to the club?" she said.

"Of course not. I don't have a guitar."

"You couldn't have got another one? Hired one or something?"

"Can't afford it. I've only been here a few days and I'm already bleeding money."

"Maybe he would have lent you one."

"Oh yeah – great first impression. Besides, I doubt he'd have one. Southpaw, remember?" I said, giving her a Bill-and-Ted burst of air guitar. "I didn't have time, anyway. I came to get you."

"Well, let's go now," she said, standing up.

"Now?"

"Sure. It's still early," she said, and I detected for the first time the tiniest edge of a North American accent.

"It's nearly midnight."

"You can't pass up something like this. Come on. I just need to dress."

She held out a hand. I took it and stood up. We were only a few inches apart.

"We'll never get a bus this time of night."

She snorted. "We'll get a cab."

To my disappointment, she dressed in the bathroom, while I quietly panicked over the cost of a round-trip cab ride from Inglewood to Pico and back.

Marie emerged in a cloud of something sweet-smelling that I didn't recognise, but that I knew I somehow wouldn't forget. She was wearing skinny denim pedal-pushers and a white baseball vest with pink piping – that pierced navel on display again – and we went out into the still-warm night.

By the time I'd worried myself into a corner over the practicalities and etiquette of splitting the cab fare, Marie had already paid it.

We stood on the edge of the sidewalk and looked up at the cool green neon strands of the Mint's sign, the night air warm on our skin, the pulsing red dots of downtown LA rising up in the east.

There was a poster of Rosco in a glass case near to the doors, and a deep thumping coming from within that suggested to me the blues element of the evening might have been and gone.

On the poster, underneath Rosco's photograph, was a picture of his guitar, the Mint, and the printed box of dollars with *MY BLUES* printed on the glass that I had seen in Santa Monica. I wanted to know the story behind it.

I walked up to one of the doormen. I was tall enough to directly address his bow tie.

"Hi. I'm, er, looking for Rosco?"

"You a friend?"

"Not exactly. He told me to meet him here."

"You want to come in, pal, you'll need to put on some shoes and pay the cover charge."

"I don't want to come in," I said, aware of Marie coming up behind me. "I just…"

The doorman noticed Marie, and his manner thawed a little.

"Sorry, folks, he ain't here," addressing – in this order – Marie's breasts, navel and face. "He did his set and left. Got a residency starting at another club."

"Oh, okay," I said, disappointment sinking in my chest like a cold water balloon. "I don't suppose you know where?"

A gaggle of five or six rich looking young people appeared in a flurry of perfume, smoke and good cheer, anxious to secure our man's attention and thus entry.

"You don't suppose.... what?" he said, deep furrows appearing on his brow.

"Where's he gone?" Marie said.

"Las Vegas," he said, and turned to his palm-greasing new friends.

Marie and I stepped back and shuffled to the kerb to find an obliging taxi. I asked her if she wanted a drink, but she looked suddenly tired.

"Let's get something and take it to the motel," she said. "We need some rest if we're going to Vegas."

CHAPTER FIVE

BINDWEED

Still not fully adjusted to the time difference, I woke up early, the dry taste of an A/C hangover in my mouth, and pulled on some jeans. Marie, whose north-south sojourn had left her body clock largely unaffected, was sleeping soundly. The thought of peeking under her duvet to see what she was wearing to bed these days was almost irresistible, but I managed to banish it.

Am I some kind of perv? I thought, as I jaywalked across Century to the little Mexican coffee stand. Maybe I was, maybe I wasn't, but something told me it wasn't tartan pyjamas any more.

I left breakfast on her bedside table and went out to call Marvin – miraculously, he answered. Quite a lot had happened since I saw him. I gave him the condensed version – which, for some reason, omitted Marie.

"Vegas? Brilliant! You read my mind," he exclaimed.

"I can't go to Vegas," I said.

"Sure you can. Why the hell not?"

"I need to find Camille."

"Mate, I fear the ship has sailed. How are you going to do that?"

"Posters, trawl the pawn shops, put out some ads, that kind of thing."

"You'd need to offer a reward. Is she insured?"

"Yeah, back home," I said, trying to ignore the glow I felt from his using the gender-specific term. It felt like he'd joined my club, rather than the other way round. "I could use the claim money for the reward, I guess."

"Claim clams, eh? Well, be in charge of yourself. Use my home number on your posters," he said. "You have twenty-fours. I'll sort out logistics – transport, maps, shit like that – you sort out your posters and all that, then we'll hit the road and go find the man that wants to groom you."

"Marvin... there's a detail."

"Go on, bloke."

"My girlfriend... my *ex*-girlfriend. She's just rocked up. From Canada. Can I bring her?"

Silence on the line. He was obviously angling for a lads' weekend.

"Marv, I'm sorry to dump it on you. She's been in Vancouver for a year, and she wanted to hook up on her way home. It's months since I told her about LA. I didn't think she'd remember. If it's a problem, don't worry."

"Why not?" he said. "All life is drama. She like to gangbang?"

He meant it as a joke, of course, but as I walked back to the room, I just had to wonder.

I did as instructed, and spent the day making posters, calling the classified pages and working systematically through a list of pawn shops in the Hollywood and mid-LA area. Marie helped me, and I took Marvin up on his offer of using his home number on the ads, which was actually pretty helpful, given my largely nomadic existence. I put my Hotmail address down too.

I balked at the thought of offering a reward that I didn't actually have, but Marie persuaded me otherwise.

"We'll cross that bridge when we come to it," she said. "She's insured for, what, a thousand? Offer five hundred dollars reward, then you might get her back and have a few bucks left over."

I had never made an insurance claim before, and imagined it to be a bureaucratic process that would no doubt be complicated by having to orchestrate it all from California through a series of expensive telephone calls.

Then the settlement cheque would be posted to my home address; my parents would have to cash it and then wire me the money. They would probably advance me the settlement if I asked them, but I couldn't stomach the conversation that I knew would ensue:

- *Alex needs some money.*
- *Already? How is he?*
- *Not good. Camille was stolen.*
- *What?? He's only been there five minutes. How the hell did he manage that?*
- *He left her in a café.*
- *Oh, that careless boy.*

"Hon?"

"Huh?"

"Did you hear what I said?"

"Sorry. Yes. Marie, I'm sorry."

"What for?"

"Being so careless. Losing Camille."

She squeezed my hand and smiled.

"Don't worry. We'll get her back."

It was a tiring but productive day – albeit I was probably just giving ideas to some of the more dubious pawn shop proprietors – and I felt a little better when we crashed out back at the motel.

The following day we checked out – the thought of being baseless again creating a small pit of anxiety – and, saddled with bags like a couple of pack horses, rode the bus to Marvin's place. The local advantage of my having had a few days' head start on Marie was palpable, and I'm sure I earned a couple of brownie points for negotiating the public transport system without incident.

Just as well, really. As we were on the bus it became apparent that Marie was now a head turner. Shit, this was new ground. Appearing that I knew what I was doing allowed me to maintain at least some semblance of dignity.

Marvin rented a little white stucco house on South La Jolla, a leafy suburb off Fairfax. Incentivising him had obviously caused his hit-and-miss reliability skills to misfire a little less, for he was waiting on the immaculate front lawn with a large holdall when we arrived.

The wheels of our cases rumbled on the smooth sidewalk as we rolled up. He grinned at us, hands jammed into the pockets of the ubiquitous black sport coat, thumbs poking over the edges.

Camille's absence was still a source of some dismay for me, but as we arrived my neuroses took a back seat. This was something to do with the quietness of the street, the sunlight filtering through the abundance of green and the pristine white Chrysler convertible at the kerb.

I introduced Marie to Marvin, and my recollection that she used to be a little apprehensive around new people was clearly well out of date. This was only a sideways observation, however, because Marvin was pumping my hand and holding some keys in the other.

"I can't drive, dude," he smiled, turning my hand over and dropping them into my palm.

This was an unexpected surprise, but it felt right, and I knew Marie wouldn't want to drive. I was an average roofer, an average writer, an above-average guitarist, and – at twenty – an average drinker, but the one thing I could do with confidence, verve and no trace of humility was drive. Even the prospect of driving from one foreign – and frankly, where the traffic was concerned, nuts – city to another foreign city filled me with a kind of excited dread.

We slung our stuff in the trunk and headed south on Fairfax towards Interstate 10, Marvin performing some kind of perfunctory navigation in the passenger seat with maps that were drowning him. Marie sat in the back, and the three of us slapped on sun block in a kind of rotation. Marie applied some to my neck, while Marvin attempted to put it on my calves, which was a little weird.

Between us we had Springsteen, Dylan, Steely Dan and Sinatra, with some Elvis for our approach onto the Strip. To my relief – but not surprise –

Marie sat forward, yacking away to Marvin, and I was happy to leave her to it. I kicked off my sliders and drove barefoot, the perfect sky and palm fronds blipping over the car. The freeway stretched to a point in front of us as we left LA behind, and I started to feel fucking fantastic – free, confident and chilled in a way that I hadn't since my arrival.

The temperature started to climb as we hit the Mojave a couple of hours later, and I found myself craving a cold beer. It hit 117° outside Baker, just as the traffic started to clam up. In the gridlock, Marvin leapt out of the car and ran to the side of the highway to take pictures of us, the car and the desert. When the traffic started to pick up Marvin started to trot alongside.

"Marvin! What are you doing? Get in the car!" I yelled.

He was approaching something of a sprint before conceding defeat and running back to the car. He eschewed the door – through style or necessity, I wasn't sure – and instead vaulted the sides of the Chrysler, landing awkwardly in his seat to a cacophony of angry horns from behind us.

The traffic began to move freely again, and we raced through miles and miles of barren desert and scrubland, which was punctuated periodically by huge advertising billboards standing in total isolation.

Privately, I wondered if the inside of my mind looked similar.

We swept past a colossal motor graveyard; several miles of wire fencing containing the burnt-out husks of dead automobiles. In the furthest corner was an ancient red London bus lying on its roof, and I wondered how the hell it got there.

After a while Marvin likened the top-down Mojave experience to sitting in front of a hair dryer. This was not a creative analogy – this was exactly what it was fucking like. On the experience of being barbecued alive in the open air, we eventually admitted defeat and pulled over so Marvin could put the top up. On the road again, Marvin cranked up the A/C, mumbling that the car rental guy said not to do this in case the engine overheated.

Marie leant forward and tapped me on the shoulder.

"If we break down, how long before we die?"

I thought about it.

"Five… maybe *six* minutes?"

We crossed the state line into Nevada in the early evening, and almost immediately, the pleasure mine appeared on the shimmering horizon. *New York, New York* belted out of the stereo as we began our approach.

Marvin thought it would be good to put the top down again, but the idea of doing this at eighty miles per hour was not a good one, and any sense of wonderment we might have had as we descended was undone by the need to hold the roof on.

But Vegas pulled us towards its bosom, and, in a kind of dream, we cruised in. Landmarks from movie history sprang up in every direction – they shot *Fear and Loathing* and *Diamonds are Forever* in our hotel; *Swingers* was shot over *there; Rain Man* over *there*. Once again, I felt like I was finally getting to meet a childhood hero in the flesh, sucked towards the centre of an intangible fame.

Marvin had indeed booked us rooms at Circus Circus, and my anxiety about what my share of the car and hotel costs was going to amount to was banished by the sea of glitz spreading out before us. We parked, checked in, dumped bags and soon I was spinning on the spot on the Strip.

Vegas, baby. In with a bang, jazzed up, neon tripping down the Strip, still one-hundred-degrees-plus many hours after dark. Chemical enhancement was totally unnecessary – I was blitzed by Caesar's, Venice and Bellagio's. Hot winds licked at my face – could this be real? Would we come back as BOYS?

The first stop was the huge and rather suggestive pink cupola of the Adventuredome, and the myriad rides, rollercoasters and sideshows contained therein. Given the surroundings, to describe them as 'amusements' seemed a trifle prosaic, but that's how they would be billed if they were on Southend Pier. The crazy mirrors seemed strangely appropriate, although my wide-eyed, rather wan expression was still apparent despite my bulbous cranium and mile-long chin.

By the time we reached the rollercoasters, Marvin became animated, and his natural enthusiasm went into overdrive. The source of Marvin's excitement was the Big Shot – a vertical rapid ascent ride at the very top of the tower that filled me with a kind of nameless dread – and the High Roller – a rollercoaster just under the 'Shot whose tracks encircled the top of the tower like Medusa's snakes and which appeared marginally less horrendous than the other one.

The cost of a ride was steep, but, before I could argue the perverse logic of using even more of my meagre budget for what would undoubtedly be a thoroughly unpleasant experience that could be replicated *gratis* by driving off the freeway at ninety miles an hour, Marvin had already bought tickets for all of us. To my surprise and horror, Marie – surely too practical for such frivolity – was suddenly and massively up for it.

I actually thought I was going to die. The rollercoaster was what I imagined a plane crash would be like, while the other one just made an acute attack of labyrinthitis seem like a breeze. I'm sure it would have been even worse had I opened my eyes. Behind my G-force-battered head I was dimly aware of Marvin roaring and Marie shrieking.

Afterwards, I supported myself on a wall with one hand and doubled over, trying to shrug the cold sweat from my body and soothe my troubled stomach.

Marvin came over and clapped me on the back.

"Fantastic!" he shouted, having broken his rollercoaster cherry, aged twenty-five. "Excellent effort, people. What we need now is a drink."

I retched. Even the lift back down the tower seemed too much, and I felt my gullet rise and then sink again. I grabbed for Marie's hand.

"You big wuss," she said, smiling.

"Help me," I said.

Things perked up when we exited the lift. I managed to straighten up to see that both Marvin and Marie were also pale and sweating, and I felt a little better.

Thinking some fresh air might help stop the onset of *mal de debarquement*, we hauled ourselves outside and walked down to the Riviera, Marie being remarkably tolerant of what amounted to Marvin and I performing a near-verbatim recital of *Casino*.

We did the rounds of the tables. I ordered a stiff one from a pigeon-lovely cocktail waitress with the longest legs I had ever seen. She passed it over – no *mention* of a charge, let alone ID – and wished me luck, the sentiment not quite reaching her eyes.

I started small on the slots, barely daring to look up and see the karma king waiting to give me the heave-ho; that constant honky-tonk of slots, chimes and the unmistakable murmur of people being sucked dry.

After a couple more free measures of bad scotch, I decided to brave the roulette table. Sitting alongside limp-wristed geckos fluttering chips across the baize, my head went into some kind of nosedive. I bet all my cash, minimum stake every spin to prolong the agony, and lost the fucking lot inside six minutes.

I carried my whisky over to the slots, and, before the horror could really kick in, somehow managed to win back exactly what I just lost. That must be Vegas, I thought, as a shower of silver coinage clattered into the large plastic cup in my hand. The waitress was still hovering in my field of vision, and so I ordered another one, leaving her a couple of dollars as a tip.

We compared notes. Marie had also had a slice of beginner's luck, albeit she wasn't carrying around a cup of quarters like a wandering hobo. In any event, she treated us all to dinner. Or perhaps it was breakfast. I had no idea, and before long we were outside again.

We passed a parade of shops set back from the road by a

parking lot, where, sandwiched between a diner and a K-Mart, was a pawn shop.

It was dark and uninviting, and quite obviously closed. Through the iron bars, the window display was unlit, but the daylight was reflected in the record players and television screens – and the shiny surface of an electro-acoustic guitar.

She was a beauty, a real Southern steamboat delight of a Casino. It was too dark to make out the exact colour – maybe maple or light red – but to my amazement she was a lefty. She was a little rough around the edges, but to me that just meant there were some stories there. I peered past the display into the shop. It was too dark to see much, but there were only one or two other guitars hanging up.

The price tag said two hundred dollars. I shouldn't. I *couldn't*. At the death, I had just about broken even on the slots, but if I hadn't, my budget would have been halved, and I still had the best part of six weeks to eke out in this befuddling country that refused to love me like I loved her.

But it's an investment, said a voice from the sound chamber. The six-week-long budget was intended to sustain me at minimum stake, with the expectation that I would be set up for something more permanent by the end of it, with my blues generating some equilibrium, if not necessarily a profit.

That ain't gonna happen without una guitarra, said the voice. *Buy her or go home now.*

What about Marie?

"She's handsome," said Marie's voice at my shoulder, a second or two after her scent reached my brain.

"The Casino? Yeah, she is," I said, not turning around.

"Few miles on the clock. You gonna buy it?"

"I don't know. Maybe I'll come back when they're open. I'm not sure I'm ready."

"You mean like when your rabbit dies, you don't want to replace it straightaway?"

"I never had a rabbit."

"Come on. Your friend wants to buy souvenirs."

She hooked her arm through mine and we crossed the street. We started out in a determined fashion to find Rosco, but without any real plan or method, we quickly decided that more beer and a refrigerated interior would be far kinder to the constitution, and so all squeezed into the back of a taxi instead.

We found a quiet corner in one of the apparently plentiful lounges at the MGM Grand and made ourselves at home on huge black sofas that enveloped us completely. I lay my head back and the world finally started to slow down.

"Right," Marvin said, springing up onto his seat and spinning round so he was on all fours. "Where's the bar?"

As he scanned the room, I saw a pretty girl passing by, a huge ice box containing bottles of Budweiser strapped to her chest.

"How much?" I asked.

"One dollar a bottle, sir," she smiled.

"Fuck!" shouted Marvin, spinning back around to face the source of this good news. "*How* much?"

"Jesus, will you stop yelling?" Marie said, covering her face.

"Sorry, dear," he grinned. "And as for *you*, dear," he said, addressing the Budweiser girl, "…a dollar a bottle means I would get thirty bottles for thirty dollars, yes?"

"That's correct," she said, still smiling and totally unfazed by Marvin's countenance. She must have seen all manner of loonies in here.

"Then thirty of your finest Buds, please," he said, pulling cash from his wallet and slipping it into her palm.

She only had twenty-two in the box, but such orders were clearly not uncommon, and she returned shortly afterwards with the balance.

I watched her go. She had hair the colour of cornsilk, and was pretty in a way that was incongruous to her surroundings. In the space of five seconds I fell into a fantasy about being alone on a ranch with a

Kansas farm girl, where insatiable passion was absolutely necessary simply in order to survive the relentless boredom. The daydream evaporated when I realised Marie was watching my eyes.

Marvin arranged the beers neatly on the table, the tip of his tongue poking out the side of his mouth in concentration.

"Ten for *you*, ten for *you*, and ten for *me*," he said, flicking the cap off a bottle with some sleight of hand that I couldn't replicate.

"Well, cheers, everybody," he said, clinking our bottles.

I drained mine in one, and felt instantly better. I started on the second just as something that sounded like Thelonious Monk began to play from somewhere, and I sank a little lower in my seat.

"That's a boy," Marvin said, beaming.

"I need to win some money," I said.

"This just goes to show how the human physiology works," he said.

"What do you mean?" Marie asked.

"The drinks are either dirt-cheap or free because they don't want you to spend your money on the *drinks*. They want you to spend it *gambling*, because the more lubricated you are, the more you'll spend, and the harder it is to stop. Drink up."

"Oh, great," I said.

"Mate, if you're short of cash, I can sub you."

Before I could answer, he dug in his pocket and pulled out a bundle of cash. He dropped it on the table in front of me.

"You'll need to get it changed up, of course," he said. "But the house is very accommodating when it comes to currency."

It was a wad of sterling as thick as a brick, neatly wrapped in a white paper band.

"Jesus, did you rob an armoured car or something?" I said.

"This is the land of opportunity," he said. "The American Dream is there for the taking."

"How much is here?" I asked.

He shrugged.

"A little shy of ten grand."

I stared stupidly at the money.

"I can't take this," I said. "I'd never be able to pay it back."

"That's not thinking very positively," he said. "You will. Consider it an investment in your talent. You use it to get yourself set up, and then pay me back six cents vig on the dollar once your income goes past, say, thirty grand a year. Besides, you could win it all back tonight."

Marie was watching this exchange with a wary eye, or maybe she was still thinking about the Kansas Budweiser girl. I had no idea what thirty grand a year even looked like. It seemed like a lot of money to make, especially from making music. I looked at Marie. Marie stared at me. The air-conditioning had caused goosebumps to spring up on her tanned shoulders.

"Fuck it. Thanks, I think," I said. I stood up, excitement starting to trickle through me at the possibilities that suddenly seemed to be opening up like budding flowers.

"You can afford to just lend someone ten thousand pounds? Just carry it around with you in case someone needs it?" Marie said, as I made to go. "What is it you do again?" She wiped her mouth with the back of her hand and set her beer back on the table.

I looked back at Marvin, mid-step. He was smirking, his eyes narrow. I turned again and resumed my purposeful journey.

A splutter of laughter stopped me.

"Mate, I'm sorry. I'm sorry," Marvin said, guffawing. He stood up and grabbed my wrist. "I just had to see what you'd do."

"What do you mean?" Marie said.

"It's *fake*. It's prop money."

"It's what?"

"Prop money. As in, you use it as your props. Film, TV, stuff like that."

I flicked through the bundle.

"Jesus. It looks so *real*. Not that I've seen many fifty-pound notes."

"That was a rotten thing to do." Marie sat back and folded her arms under her breasts.

"Madam, I wasn't going to actually let him *cash* it. It was just a joke," Marvin said.

"What is it you do again? Besides having fun at other people's expense, I mean," she said.

"I work for a film production company. In Santa Monica."

"Very glam. Doing what? Making the tea?"

"When I want one, yes."

The first time I had encountered Marie's withering unimpressed schoolteacher routine all those years ago, I had folded like a pack of cards. That had been many years ago, however, long before we got together, when I was thirteen and still larking around in drama club. Marvin, however, was completely unfazed, and simply grinned.

He produced a couple of business cards and slid them across the table. They were professionally done, with a graphic of a 1940s Boeing-Stearman biplane swooping across a blue banner that ran the length of the card, under which MARVIN PRICE, PACIFIC JETSTREAM PRODUCTIONS, SANTA MONICA was embossed.

Marvin repocketed the fake cash while I examined his card. I watched it into his pocket.

"It's so real," I said again. "Could we… you know? Would they be fooled?" I indicated the casino cage with my head.

"Very unwise," Marie said.

"Not to mention completely illegal," said Marvin.

For less than the time it took for ten thousand pounds cash to bounce in and then out of my life, Marvin looked worried. Maybe he had something else up his sleeve, or maybe Marie was just a little too by-the-book for him. Either way, I began to worry that they didn't like each other. She certainly didn't seem to like him.

As if thinking the very same thing, Marvin opened another beer and put it in front of her. She said nothing, but drank it without protest, and the beer mellowed the atmosphere considerably as the evening rolled on.

My eyelids slowly began to get heavy. There was a lull in the conversation, and just as I was about to doze off I felt something cold. I looked down and saw Marie's bare toes pressed against my leg.

"Got to be siesta time," I said. A silver ring on her middle toe was catching the light.

"Are you kidding?" Marvin was incredulous.

"The journey and those bloody rides have done for me," I said, standing up. "The fear has used up all my energy."

"This is an outrage. You, sir, are to accompany me to a titty bar…"

Marie stood up beside me, and Marvin's protests petered out.

"Actually, it's not a bad idea," he said, a look of sage understanding crossing his face. "We can regroup tomorrow. It's going to be a monster session. Lock up your accountants, and all that."

We took a cab back to the hotel, Marie pressed up against me in the back. Her breathing was heavy and slow, and my heart started to throb, the adrenaline like liquid electricity in my chest. She hadn't drunk all her ten beers, of that I was fairly certain, but she'd had… enough.

Back at the room I took a shower. I was towelling myself dry when there was a knock at the door.

"Alex? Are you decent?" Marie's voice was playful.

"No."

"Then let me in."

I inhaled, my pulse doubling.

"It's open."

She pushed the door open and stood in the doorway. She was wearing a diamante choker and six-inch heels.

And nothing else.

"No one ever got an erection quite like you, Alex," she said.

She led me to the bed and kissed me deeply on the mouth, her lips roving over mine with a heart-thumping, almost violent enthusiasm that – I remembered now – alcohol had a tendency to generate.

"Your body looks..... leaner," she whispered. "More sinewy."

"The perks of physical labour," I said, between gasps.

"And you got another tattoo," she said, sucking on my lower lip, her hand moving over the new design on my shoulder, which showed a silhouette of a long-legged woman blowing a sax in a city forest of skyscrapers under a crescent moon.

"You're not the only one full of surprises, Marie."

I didn't tell her who'd done the inking.

She kissed my neck. Her breath was hot, and loud. The room started to spin and I fell back on the bed, Marie's painted pink fingernails drawing white lines on my stomach as her head moved south and her lips roamed my body.

Then she suddenly stopped and stood up, conflict in her eyes.

"Sorry," she said, and I got a brief glimpse of the girl I grew up with.

She grabbed some clothes and disappeared into the bathroom.

CHAPTER SIX

JUNE HAVOC

Stone cold broke, stone cold sober, I stepped out alone into Vegas, this Siegel brainchild of one-night stopovers for GIs. Stitched onto a barren desert like a cold turkey stretch of mindfuck, Vegas is that corner of your head you could unlock if you allowed yourself to go far enough. It sits, unassuming, on the black landmass, a twinkling lesion of stardust promising indescribable fairy magic, an all-cash advance with no down payment, and then the karmic debt collectors come knocking as you're sinking down into your shoes. My God, it's in the desert for a very good reason.

Unable to face the inevitable resultant awkwardness and unwilling to debrief what had just happened – although some might say *debriefing* was a moot point, I weaved my way along the Strip in a light-headed funk, sinking hostile whiskies as I went, swiped from glass-eyed cocktail waitresses who cursed my departing back – nothing in this town was *really* free. They prepared them on the rocks whether you liked it or not – two parts whisky, eight parts crushed ice, and the taste was so diluted that it was barely drinkable. There was enough liquor seeping between the cracks of the mini glaciers in my glass for me to feel it, however, and I decided that I needed to start working towards my original design and find Rosco while I still just about had command of my faculties, especially if the liberal attitude towards serving statutory minors was to continue.

My legs were heavy and tired – something to do with the poundage of coin still in my pockets, probably – and I felt hollow inside. Fourteen minutes under a cold shower after *coitus interruptus* with Marie hadn't helped much. Given that, at that particular moment, I would have sliced and diced my own mother for the chance of shagging the arse off her, her moment of doubt seemed, well, a trifle unfair.

Whoever said there is no sex like sex with an ex was probably right, but Marie was a double-edged sword. There was the instant that nostalgia and memories were unleashed into the present the second flesh met flesh, but in Marie's case there was also the painful desire to explore her new body, and the murderous curiosity of how her new-found confidence, disinhibition and general enthusiasm for life would manifest themselves in bed.

More grotesque analogies appeared in my brain, each one more extreme than the one before; each one intended as a barometer, an illustration of my want. For the chance to press up against her naked body, I would have gladly:-

- Indulged in cannibalism.

- Sprinted naked through downtown Vegas.

- Dined out on tree grubs.

- Spent a month in a Siberian gulag.

- Abandoned a sinking ship full of kittens to its fate.

Maybe I was a sex addict. Maybe it was as simple as that. Gambling wasn't really on my radar – although my novice attempts in Vegas had already led me towards the slippery slope, it was still done with the wry smile of the ain't-it-quaint observer – and I'd never really bothered with drugs enough to make an informed decision. My alcohol consumption was about the same as most twenty-year-olds, although working in a lot of high places had led me to curb it pretty quickly during the week.

There was nothing subtle or understated about the conveyor belts that drew you into the casinos under red-carpet tunnels of oyster-bed lights, fountains and spouting stone cherubs. They appealed to your weaknesses in a way that meant you couldn't resist, even though no good could possibly come of it. It's like telling an alcoholic his next drink will make him rich and successful and irresistible to women – we know it's a lie, but we do it anyway. If anyone *were* in any doubt – or tried to kid themselves of the fact – the dark, piss-lined alleys and spewing dumpsters that marked the casinos' exit doors brought it all home. Lotus flowers don't take rejection well.

Hoping for another stroke of luck like I'd had earlier on the slots – the fact that the more sensible among us would have called it a *near miss* notwithstanding – there was a grey perforated edge of overbite desperation in my brain. How could anyone survive in this frenzy for longer than a week? It was Stockholm syndrome on a mass scale. I bet everything, right down to the last dime in my pocket, and…

Blew.

The.

Lot.

Above the chirp and rattle of slots and roulette, and beyond the dead-eye croupiers, I could hear the man upstairs laughing.

The genie was well and truly out of the bottle, and conservatism at this stage was just a bad joke, like putting on your seat belt after you'd crashed. Resigning myself to the fact that I had failed on all counts and that I would be getting the next flight home as soon as I got back to LA, I withdrew a substantial amount of cash from an ATM that didn't even *ask* for a PIN, and tried to ignore the poster above my head:

HAVE YOU GOT A GAMBLING PROBLEM?

CALL 1-800-567-2421 NOW!

I snatched the cash from the drawer and stuffed it into my pocket. Half the problem, said my drunk brain, is that American money doesn't even feel real.

I allowed myself to be sucked into Bellagio's and started sprinkling cash around in an entirely non-strategic way – roulette, blackjack, slots. I even had a pop at poker and baccarat, just for a laugh. My cavalier attitude earned me a very small audience and extra attention from the waitresses – anyone mad or rich enough to not care had to be worth a second look. That car crash fascination, again.

Then something odd happened. The heavy celestial

pendulum of Luck swung out of the heavens and back into my neck of the woods. I started to win. Chaos started to pour over me like hailstones.

It was like a snowball rolling down a hill. I won back a few bucks at poker, and then switched to blackjack, where things continued to improve. By the time I had taken root at the roulette table, I was seeing exponential returns.

I even started to lose count. After about an hour, I made a rough calculation that I had just about broken even on my total budget, but it didn't stop there.

I began to get a good routine going with the waitresses. Drinks appeared at my elbow in a streamlined fashion – they appeared, I replaced the empty with a five-dollar bill, they were replenished. When I was about five hundred up, the waitress's hand stayed on the glass.

"Hope your luck holds, sir," said a voice.

I turned my head and saw the Kansas Budweiser girl at my elbow, only this time she was in her nightlife cocktail waitress get-up and she was toting liquor and not cheap beer.

She smiled, and held my gaze.

"I'm Sam," she said.

"You are? I'm, er, Alex."

"I'm pleased you're doing well."

"That makes two of us," I said, shifting in my seat so I was fully facing her.

"No more bets," said the croupier.

"I finish at 5am," she said.

"You do? That's great…er, what time is it now? I haven't a clue."

"A little after one," she said, and laughed.

I picked up a napkin. The croupier was holding his pen out, not taking his eyes from his work.

I went to write my phone number, but then remembered I didn't have one. I wrote my room number instead, wrapping the napkin around a fifty-dollar bill, while the old Alex Gray looked down at this new high-rolling maverick and shook his head, wondering who he was trying to kid.

She held up the napkin, and then slipped it into her bra.

"You're doing well. I'd better not distract you."

"Keep them coming," I said, and she wandered off.

I kept playing, my levels of intoxication becoming ever more saturated until I couldn't tell the value of one chip from another. When I was up by what I estimated in my addled state to be about two thousand incredible dollars, I got the most bizarre sensation of fear and panic, as if I had just walked into the blinding glare of an oncoming Cadillac. I began to take huge gasping breaths as the adrenaline pulsed in my chest, and very suddenly I slid off my stool and headed out to cash out my winnings, only realising how drunk I was once I started walking.

I was straight enough to hear the girl congratulate me, however, and she handed over twenty-two hundred and fifty dollars. I shoved the bundle into my pocket, and, realising my faculties – or lack thereof – made me an easy roll for some professional street hustlers, I made straight for the lifts.

The room was dark – or as dark as it was going to get in a city with the world's largest electricity bill – and, using the outside neon to guide me, I put a chunk of the cash into the little metal safe hidden in the wardrobe, keeping some in my pocket to walk around with.

Marie was asleep in one of the beds. Her breathing was slow and deep. I staggered to the bed – and nearly collided with the electro-acoustic Casino from the pawn shop window. It was leaning up against my bedside cabinet with a note inserted between the strings: *Déjà vu! X*

I picked it up and strummed it quietly. It had a nice, clear ring. I put it down and removed some of the cash from the safe, and tucked it under her pillow. It's funny how when you have nothing in your pocket you can think of nothing else, but when you've got a few bucks you get used to it pretty easily.

For a second the temptation to curl up beside her was strong, but I was exhausted and steaming drunk, and there was clearly still no indication that we were anywhere other than Inglewood's one-bed-each rule.

I lay down on the other bed, listening to the rumble of traffic and laughter, the red neon from the street pulsing on the ceiling like a heart monitor.

CHAPTER SEVEN

MR WETBACK

My sleep must have been deep and uninterrupted, because it felt like only minutes later that there was a heavy knocking at the door. I sat up suddenly in bed, my head throbbing with yesterday's Budweiser and the increasingly-familiar dehydration of the aircon being on all night.

"Come on, people, time's-a-wasting!"

Jesus, it was morning. The sunlight was blinding on the white walls, and even with the air-conditioning on I could feel the baking heat of the day outside. I could practically smell it. I looked over at Marie's bed. It was empty, and I could hear the shower going.

I opened the door. Marvin beamed at me. The knocking had been heavy because he had been kicking the door with his foot, his arms laden as they were with croissants, coffee and a paper sack full of water bottles. I would later come to regard this image of him kick-starting the day as something of a motif for my West Coast shenanigans, but right then his fizzing energy left me rather envious.

"About time," he said, pushing past me and dumping breakfast on the table. "I can't believe you went to bed before me and you're *still* not up. Where's your good lady?"

I didn't immediately answer, but watched his eyes go from Marie's unmade bed to mine and back again.

"Yeah, sorry about that. What did you get up to?" I asked.

"Well," he said, his eyes taking a second or two to return to mine, "after I was abandoned by you two lightweights, I drank rather too much of the ghastly free-fer-a-tip no-brand whisky, and went to this abominable titty bar called Crazy Horse Too. Mimi from the Ukraine was quite a charmer, but I woke up with an empty wallet and a sore

74

crotch from dry-humping."

I winced. I had no sympathy for his lack of release. He edged closer to me, and I realised that his chipper exterior had not been buoyed up by anything as novel as a wash. I could smell sweat, booze, and – I thought – Ukrainian Mimi.

He walked over to the stack of books on Marie's bedside table. He picked one up and flicked through it.

"Look at this dreary feminist hag manual," he said. "Does she actually read this stuff?"

I shrugged.

"I guess."

He put the book down and came over to me.

"I won't maintain this, you know. I can't abide it," he said.

"What?" I said, wondering what the hell he was on about.

"This…. young-person-early-to-bed nonsense. To make the most of our little sojourn I fear your Catholic routines might need to be jettisoned. I can help you out with that later."

He winked, just as the shower went off.

"Well, I'll leave you to get ready. See you downstairs in half an hour."

I sat down on the bed and gave the Casino a bit of a workout. Marie emerged after ten minutes or so.

"Some bint knocked on the door for you here last night," she said, standing at the mirror to put on some earrings.

"Bint? Who?"

"The Budweiser girl. I forget what she said her name was."

Shit. Sam! I had forgotten all about her.

"Did she leave a number or anything?"

"No. I think when she saw me she thought she had the wrong room. Either that or she thought she was the victim of a cruel joke."

"I bet she did. Don't tell me you answered the door like that."

She was all business today – heels, blue jeans that looked as if they had been painted on, and some kind of black sequined top with a flower at the shoulder and her abs winking at me from a slit between the two.

I would slice and dice…

Thank God for the hangover.

She hadn't answered.

"Oh, bollocks," I said, screwing my eyes up.

"Got lucky last night, did we?"

There was an edge to her voice that I recognised, but when I looked up again she was smiling.

"Well, funnily enough…"

"What?" She came over and sat next to me on the bed.

"Let's just say the man upstairs was smiling down upon me last night."

"You won some money, didn't you, you jammy little shit?" she said, nudging me with her elbow.

"Charming."

"How much?"

"Not that much. Offset against my losses, net gain probably… couple hundred dollars?" A conservative estimate never hurt anybody, I thought, wondering if this capacity for minor deception would come back to bite me in later life.

She leaned her head on my shoulder and fluttered her heavily made-up eyelashes. They made me think of tarantulas' legs.

"I'd be an excellent gold digger, you know," she said.

"Wouldn't you just."

"What's that supposed to mean?"

"Nothing."

She squeezed my hand, and held my gaze.

"I didn't want you to pay me for the guitar," she said. "But thank you."

For a horrific second I thought we were going to have another Moment, but then I realised with relief that with the morning's sobriety her libido had shrunk back to more conventional proportions.

"Come on," I said. "I'll buy you a proper breakfast."

The Strip by day just seemed to be white and grey angles, a concrete equation on graph paper, and in the day's triple-figure heat the buildings shimmered like mercury.

We walked to the Stratosphere Tower, the sun a white-hot constant. It was relentless in a way that made it impossible not to think our evolution was fragile, and that the odds of it happening at all should make winning the lottery a breeze.

We crossed at an intersection. Marvin ran excitedly across the road a second before DON'T WALK appeared, apparently sucked towards two tourist shops selling enormous Stetsons and inflatable maps of the state of Nevada.

Marie and I followed him, earning an angry honk from a 1967 Mustang. My gaze was pulled back to a traffic island, where there was a man sitting against a telecom cabinet, a large handwritten cardboard sign leaning against him that said *PLEASE HELP THIS VET.* A battered hat lay at his feet with a sprinkling of coins.

His face was dry and cracked, his opaque sunglasses somehow fossilised into his face like a totem mask, and his legs were swollen with elephantiasis to almost twice the width of his body. They were huge, naked and bulbous like dehydrated, gelatinous black tree trunks. He sat silent and absolutely motionless, the traffic roaring past on both sides, people navigating their way around him as if he were not there.

Marie and Marvin were talking about something and didn't really notice him, but the sight appalled me. How long had he been there? How did he get about? Did he sit there all day and all night? How could he survive this unbearable heat? Why was no one helping him? I wanted to give him some of my winnings, but in the end I compounded my own misery by telling myself I was already across the street, and that it would make no difference anyway.

"Should just put the poor bastard out of his misery," Marvin said, appearing at my shoulder and thrusting a ten-gallon hat into my hand. "Matching pair," he said, pushing up the brim of his own purchase.

"That's a terrible thing to say," Marie said, as we hurried across the street.

"Nonsense. Kindest thing to do. He can't have long to go anyway."

"You're a real humanitarian," I said.

"When I was thirteen, I was attacked by an enormous moth. Size of your palm," he said, holding up Marie's hand. "Tried to kill it with a dart gun, but the bugger refused to die."

"I have dreams like that," I said.

We entered the Stratosphere Tower, and Marvin needled Marie with another comment about mercy killings, and the two of them got into a fervent debate about involuntary euthanasia that spiralled into capital punishment and the treatment of refugees, which continued across the lobby and towards a bank of lifts.

I guess Marvin pegged Marie as some kind of liberal, for it ended with him telling her to shut up, which he rounded off by calling her a big stupid sow – the grin never leaving his face. From my point of view, she was decidedly less bothered about this than she might have been two years ago, but she still made a point of storming off to the lift. Marvin dropped to his knees in the lobby, and followed her – still on his knees – into the lift, watched by a gaggle of passing Japanese tourists who no doubt thought this twisted sideshow was just part of the entertainment.

In the lift he remained on his knees and began an impassioned apology – or so I thought. He was doing quite well, and had even grabbed her hand so it looked like a slightly uncomfortable marriage proposal, but then he closed by telling her that everything she said filled him with contempt.

Marie seethed for the best part of an hour, and at one stage I thought she was going to demand that I take her back to LA and abandon my cretinous associate to the fate he deserved. However,

Marvin continued as if his insultathon had been as inconsequential as the weather forecast, and this almost sociopathic disregard seemed to rub off on us. I somehow knew that if, in a vague effort to defend Marie's honour, I demanded an apology, he would have obliged in sincere droves, and just knowing this somehow made everything alright. It was impossible not to be infected by his exuberance, and his honest appraisal of Marie's social values became unimportant far quicker than it would have done had it been delivered by someone else, somewhere else.

During the day Vegas was on hiatus, everyone clock-watching until the sun disappeared and the neon reigned again. By the time the evening rolled around, my hangover had vanished and I was primed for another evening of success and booze.

Marie had wandered off to the slots, while Marvin got into an emphatic debate with a seasoned veteran from Florida about the realities of beating the house – a conversation that earned him rather more attention from the pit boss than I was comfortable with.

I went to see what Marie was doing, but all her attention was focused on politely feinting and parrying the expert advice of a musclebound college jock in a beanie hat. I thought about going over and rescuing her, but I guessed such advances were an occupational hazard for her these days, and she seemed to be doing just fine on her own.

We reunited later at the Broadway, and had a team talk over more whisky and a buffet breakfast. I didn't have a clue what the time was.

"The thing of it," Marvin said, "is that most people just want closure."

"What are you talking about?" I said.

"The path of justice. On the whole we are pretty soft, but that actually suits a lot of people. Your moral code might bend a bit, but if it stays intact people bounce back from a remarkable level of heinous deeds."

"Are you speaking from experience?" I said.

"Let's say some grossack Serb militia razes your village and cuts down your family with some Luger relic. Or your buddy, the one you've walked to school with every day for seven years, one day brings a military surplus G36 carbine in with his lunch bag and mows down his classmates. If, at the judgment, they are crippled by remorse and beg for forgiveness in the dock, you'd be surprised how many people can come to terms with it. But if they cackle when they go down and say they'd do it again in a headlight flash, that's a lot harder to live with."

Marie and I exchanged glances.

"Think about it. Someone cuts you up in traffic. Your hackles go up and you stab the horn. Maybe shout a bit. If the culprit waves their hand *sorry*, you're probably defused, more or less instantly. But if they flip you the bird, that's going to make your blood boil all day. I mean, you know *para bellum* means 'prepare for war,' right?"

"What are you *on* about?" Marie said.

He leaned over the table.

"You notice there's no windows?" he said, his voice dropping to a whisper.

"Yes," I whispered back in an equally conspiratorial manner.

"They pump these places full of oxygen, so you never get tired. It is actually 3am."

I hadn't realised. I also hadn't realised that his hand was on Marie's thigh.

It was only a twenty-minute walk, but we took a cab to Bellagio's, Marvin continuing to expound theories about crime and punishment. As we disembarked, he slipped a small package into the breast pocket of my shirt.

"What's that?" I said, in a stupid loud voice.

"A little kick start," he said, not looking at me.

Marie caught my eye, but didn't say anything.

To my amazement – and that of my compadres – someone in

a bow tie who looked vaguely important recognised me from the night before and ushered me with utter obsequiousness to the blackjack table. Within minutes a martini, a tumbler of single malt and a king prawn cocktail appeared on a hostess trolley next to me. I wanted to look around for Sam, but, to my chagrin, I wasn't *completely* sure I would recognise her.

I played a couple of hands. Marie and Marvin clapped and applauded, but it was muted, as if they could tell my heart wasn't really in it.

And they were right.

I looked at the drinks and a voice in my brain said *now or never.* As in, if you don't get up and leave now, the fawning floorman will continue to give you reasons to stay. You'll have a couple drinks and think *why not?*, then you'll lose all over again and you'll never get to find Rosco.

So I made my excuses and went to the bathroom, which took me well out of sight of the table, the floorman, Marvin and Marie. In the bathroom, I slipped the pill Marvin had given me under my tongue, took a deep breath, and strode out, unseen, across the gaming floor towards the exit.

How the hell was I going to find Rosco? I couldn't follow my ears, and this was a big city to find one man and his guitar. I had rather foolishly assumed that the information I – or rather Marie – had prised out of the doorman at the Mint would be enough to find him within a day or two.

I needed *information*. Since arriving on this guddam continent I had felt adrift, cut off, struggling for survival, a minnow fighting for clarity in an ocean of strangeness. I craved directories, posters, editorials, classified pages… but more than this, I wanted the familiarity of knowing who to ask and where to find them. Nearly everyone here spoke English, but nobody seemed to talk my language.

I didn't have a watch, but time was meaningless here in any case. Outside the refrigerated casinos, my skin began to feel like a cracked, sun-baked riverbed, and I eventually recalibrated my direction and began a slow-shuffle back to the hotel. In any case, where Rosco was concerned, enquiries with staff back at the *Circus Circus* would probably be a good place to start.

The lights were beginning to hurt my eyes. The thick red carpet in the corridor back to the room was soft and inviting underfoot, the halogens in the ceiling started to smudge, and by the time I slipped my key in the door I was leaning against the frame.

I had no idea what the time was. I sat on the edge of the bed and undid my shirt, tilting my head to read the titles on the spines of the books stacked on Marie's bedside table. *Love in the Time of Cholera, Tom Sawyer,* a new one called *Charlotte Gray* and Germaine Greer's latest – the 'hag manual' that had caught Marvin's eye. I shook my head – until I realised it was going to make me vomit, then I stopped – we were only here a couple of nights. How could she be reading all of them at the same time? Her luggage must have weighed a ton.

Behind the books were a glass of water, a notepad, a mini photo album and a small purple box that I recognised instantly as her birth-control pill.

"Fucking things," my foul bitter-liquor tongue said aloud to the room.

They were a constant motif when we were together. She took them fastidiously, and although I guess that was the point, a night of headspinning passion always seemed to have the rock 'n' roll tempered somewhat by the daylight routine of reaching for the little purple box.

We used condoms as well, and one night the thing split. Marie freaked out – I mean she freaked *out* – and sent me immediately to the nearest pharmacy for the morning-after pill. On a Sunday, no less. Her panic was infectious, but now, in retrospect, there was absolutely no way she was getting pregnant. Not with that little security trifecta. All of which seemed odd, given that the weekend before she had been jotting down baby names in her diary.

Had I been possessed of a little more clarity of thought, I

might have wondered why she was taking them given that her boyfriend was in Canada and she didn't cheat. Then again, I might also have told myself that you don't stop and go with these things – cumulative effect, and all that.

I wasn't quite sure how I'd ended up back at the room. It seemed to indicate a desire to lie down and pass out, but then I saw the Casino standing quietly by the bed. I could practically hear Marvin's dismay. What was I doing going to bed? I was in *Vegas*, for Christ's sake. And now I had a beast.

It was time, I felt, to seize the fucking day.

CHAPTER EIGHT

DUDE RANCH

I picked up the Casino, and slung it across my back, midnight hustler-style, stopping long enough on the casino floor for another drink. I sucked the whisky out of the tumbler, and headed towards the exit. Immersion in the refrigerated air caused my skin to contract, and as I stepped out the midnight air was like a thick blanket of microwaved cotton candy.

I looked up and down the Strip, the rainbow kaleidoscope of neon burning my eyes, the rumble and swish of the huge cars the lifeblood of the city. I felt the whisky start to seep into my legs where it made my muscles throb, and I began to crave another – neat, this time – with an urgency I had not felt before.

As I stood on the roadside, I heard music coming from all directions. 80s stadium rock, hip-hop, Cajun blues, pumping house; from bars, casinos, basements and roadhouses.

I moved down the Strip, the air like warm swirls of horsehair around my skin. The colours were brighter than earlier, of that I was sure. My eyes felt like golf balls in my head; I could *see* the music, strands of yellow staves and notes and bars flowing like golden ribbons in a Disney film. Amongst them was Marvin Gaye's *Trouble Man*, and my fingers began to itch with whisky and a burning to play.

But somehow I got away from the Strip's neon mainstream and found myself rounding warehouses, alleyways, industrial units; great bland blue/grey boxes; the nucleus of Vegas's inner workings away from its twinkling membranes.

Among this network of functional substance were bars and clubs, their dark entrances garnished by neither giant conveyor belts nor spewing faux-Botticelli statues, but dumpsters, fire escapes and roller doors.

Outside one basement club called *Dude Ranch* was a board with OPEN MIC written on it in yellow chalk, and a buzz passed through me. Open mic. Free to all. No pressure. I could do it. I *needed* to do it, before the magic touch of the whisky and the pill left me.

The wooden door was painted matte black, and I got the sudden feeling it was just part of a huge set, a massive fictional toytown where everybody was a player with some director sat somewhere laughing his behind off.

I pushed it open to be confronted by a tiny red booth. Behind the counter was a thin woman with purple hair hanging over one eye, who was engaging in some kind of whispered conversation with a large man in a black rollneck who had hooded eyelids. He was on *this* side of the counter – which meant he was directly in front of me.

"Ten-dollar door fee," he said with a thick Eastern European accent. He peered over my shoulder at the Casino slung across my back. "You playing or just drinking? You playing, it's a four-drink minimum."

"Four drinks? That's not open mic. That's pay-to-play."

The man shrugged, and I handed over forty hard-won dollars.

So I had a three-song set list. I opted for *Malted Milk*, *Country Boy* and an old Lightning Hopkins number. Clapton's renditions were always good to regurgitate, mainly because his stuff sounded incredibly complicated and the work of a virtuoso, but when you got down to the technicalities, it was pretty easy to play, and could elevate a merely average talent considerably.

It's a strange business. One minute you're just one of a sea of heads in the darkness all facing towards the empty stage with its plain matte-black backdrop, happy and invisible and united in anonymity; then you're moving through the crowd, trying not to trip, trying not to bump anyone with your guitar; then you're on the riser and sitting on the chair. You're facing into the crowd like the proverbial lamb, but all you can see are the blinding white spots like oncoming car headlights that pick up the edges of the crowd's hair like burning cotton, and a fine pale blue mist that could be the remnants of dry ice or the crowd's rising sweat vapour.

In fact, you can hear more than you can see. Even in a small place like this, where I was less than ten feet from the nearest punter in a basement that was probably at half its hundred-strong capacity, each face was blank in the darkness, and you had no idea whether they were interested, bored, jealous or so caught up in their own thoughts they hadn't even registered the change of act. The ambient noise seemed clear and amplified – coughs and conversation, glasses clinking, chairs scraping. And above it all, the shuffling of your fingers over the fretboard and the sound of your breathing, both echoing around the basement as the mic, as sensitive as a fresh bruise, picked up every tiny noise you made, ready to bring your output to the masses. Or the gaggle, at least.

The important thing was not to delay. This was open-mic, so everyone was fair game, and a delay of more than about fifteen seconds would mean someone would start heckling and put me off my stroke.

Falling off the stage notwithstanding, there were two major opportunities for a car crash. The first was the opening chord, where you could fluff your note, or get your fat fingers over a fret and hear a dampened throb instead of a clear ring, or realise your guitar was hopelessly out of tune.

If that went okay, the next window for disaster was opening your mouth for that first note. You might sing in a totally different key. You might hear nothing but a hoarse rasp. You might forget the words. So many things could go wrong, and these possibilities always tumbled through my head and meant my openings were never terribly confident.

I'd been doing it a while, though, and had got used to these jitters, not least because in some of the pubs I sang in you were singing for your life. A wrong note, an unfavourable song choice, a dubious shirt – you never knew what could set off a bald, two-ton psychopath.

But the opening fingerpicked notes to *Malted Milk* sounded

86

good on my new beast, and the crowd's murmured conversation faded away to nothing as I began to play, which was simultaneously terrifying and encouraging. I was aware of the metallic odour of someone else's tobacco breath on the mic.

As it was, I needn't have worried about the niceties. This was a pared-back, stripped-raw solo blues number, with plenty of emotive silences and drifting *sotto voce* moments. Perfect, in fact, for a tremendous belch to erupt from somewhere near the back of the room the second I opened my mouth.

Which is exactly what happened.

A low sprinkle of tittering rose and fell around the room, but I strummed a little louder and held the notes a little longer to minimise the windows of opportunity for sabotage.

As the laughter petered out there was the sound of a glass smashing on the deck and a low bawl of frustration, followed by a chair being knocked over. This happened over the *other* side of the room, so I couldn't write it off as being the work of one single idiot fucking yokel; rather, it seemed that isolated pockets of disorder were starting to spring up all over the room.

It was nothing I hadn't experienced before, but I guess some small part of me hoped that in a basement club in the Nevada desert, five thousand miles away from home with a wad of cash so thick I could feel it in my back pocket, things might have been different.

Open mic, it seemed, was universal.

On the upside, I had some well-established coping mechanisms for such eventualities. Allowing yourself to falter was fatal. Then they'd won. You might be playing to a room of twenty people, and while nineteen of them might be contemptuous – or worse, indifferent – towards you, the twentieth person might have been sitting quietly with a drink, just happening to really enjoy your music. So you tell yourself you're playing to them, even though you can't see or hear them in the clamour. If the nineteen put you off your stride to the extent that #20 gets up and leaves, then you may as well give up entirely and post one of those application forms.

So that's what I did. I shut my eyes, thought about the words and the music and sang louder and harder. The blues, fortunately, lend themselves to this kind of situation. So far, such nights were *my* blues.

"I've been drinking malted milk, trying to drive my blues a-way…"

Once I'd got past the start, I found my stride and loosened up. There was enough whisky in my system to quell the anxiety, but not enough to impair my playing, which, given that I legally had no business being anything other than stone cold sober, was a comfortable balance.

For the most part, zoning out was a successful strategy. I even made it to the end of the second song. That was probably a mistake – I should have added a ten-minute coda and let it ring out. The minute I stopped I heard a shouted expletive and saw the silhouette of a fist fly past the bar.

A full-on brawl ensued within seconds. I *think* my part was largely incidental, but when a full beer bottle came flying out of the darkness and tonked me on the head, I decided to curb the analysis.

I got up to leave and climbed off the stage, dragging my guitar behind me, warm beer dripping off the fretboard.

A couple of bouncers were neutralising the brawl fairly efficiently, probably because it was blocking the bar, which was a wooden counter no wider than a telephone box framed in a square of light. I thought it *was* a telephone box until the girl with the purple hair appeared and I realised that the bar was just the back end of the coat-check booth, and the whole thing snaked around in an L-shape.

I shook the guitar off and leaned it carefully against the bar – upside down, so the beer wouldn't drip into the chamber. The width of the bar meant there was a narrow beer fridge with the optics limited to scotch, bourbon, sourmash or rye. A single Miller's draught tap sat in the middle of the counter.

Under the row of liquor bottles was a photographic montage of local talent that had, at one time or another, played the Dude Ranch. One or two big names were up there, and had signed napkins and the like, proclaiming it to be the greatest venue this side of the Mississippi, or words to that effect.

"Got some towels or something?" I said.

She didn't answer, but rummaged around under the bar and handed me a couple of bar towels.

I mopped up the beer as best I could. I could feel the girl watching me.

"Sorry about all that. It happens."

"That was her maiden outing," I said.

"Christened, huh?" she said, unsmiling. "Then you'll have to give her a name."

I stood up and looked at her.

"What's your name?" I said.

"Me? I'm Minnie."

"Minnie?"

"I'm from Texas," she added, as if that explained everything.

"As in 'Mouse?'"

"Oh, I've never heard *that* one before," she said, rolling her eyes.

"Hey, I just want to make sure I've got it right. Minnie, meet Minnie," I said, holding up the guitar that now had that bad-eggs stink of stale beer. As, I imagined, did I.

Nevertheless, we could have a moment, this trifecta of Minnie, Minnie and I, especially when the original opened a beer and slid it across the counter to me.

However, a hand appeared over my shoulder, clutching a ten-dollar bill.

"I'll get this," said a voice.

I turned to see a craggy man, not much taller than the bartop, with teeth like tombstones and a thick beard like a skunk's tail. Oily strands of hair poked out from under a grimy blue baseball cap that I could smell from ten feet. There was an age-faded tattoo of the scales of justice on his forearm.

I had always hoped that Person #20, if they existed, would look more like Minnie and less like a transcontinental trucker who hadn't washed for a month, but I suppose beggars can't be choosers.

"Great set, little man," said the man.

I looked at him sideways. Was he serious?

"Thanks," I said.

"Folk-blues. Love it. Enjoyed that more than kitten-baiting."

"Kitten… what?"

"I'm Randy." He extended a dirty hand.

"Alex," I said, returning the shake. His skin felt like sandpaper. "Thanks. Glad you liked it."

"Hey, are you English?" he said, his handshake becoming more vigorous until it started to give me a friction burn. "I always said nobody does music like the English. Just look at Tom Jones."

He added his other hand to the shake, and continued talking before I could correct him.

"We need more stuff like that in here. Decent music. Not like this non-*sense*," he said, nodding to the stage behind me, where a human beatbox was warming up.

"Well, to each their own, I guess."

"Shit, what a gent you are. You're the second English I've met tonight. What are the odds? Y'all are so guddam *polite*. Now, mon-*shaw*, can I get you anything?"

I looked from him to Minnie, confused.

"Something to, ah, *sustain* you on your heavy touring regime?"

"I'm not on a…" I began, and then the penny dropped.

"Don't start that shit in here again, Randy. You want a lifetime ban? No parole this time," said Minnie, putting his change on the counter.

"Hey, missus," Randy said, putting up his hands. "I'm goin', I'm goin'." And then, to me, out the side of his mouth: "Out back in five if you're looking to score. In the alley."

And off he went.

I looked down at the money on the counter. It was a five-dollar bill and some coins.

"I guess that's for you," I said.

"Thanks," she said.

I squinted at her. "I thought Americans didn't do sarcasm."

She raised an eyebrow.

"Hang on a second," I said, already getting into that mindset that supremely confident people have that anyone who isn't fawning over them must have something wrong with them. "Do you have something against Englishmen, or something?"

She looked genuinely puzzled.

"Look, hon, it's just open mic. It was a good set, but before you there were two performance poets and later Marco the solo tenor will be on. Even if you have a good few nights, no one ever beats the house in the end."

She turned, bent down and began unloading a tiny dishwasher.

"Hey, hang on. Look." After Marvin's advice I was clanking around everywhere with two copies of my demo tape in my pockets. I took one out.

"Do you have a pen?" I said.

She exhaled heavily and straightened up. I took the sleeve out of the tape box and signed it. After a second, I put the date too.

"I don't care if you don't listen to the tape. I know guys like me are ten a penny. But it would mean a lot if you added this to your photoboard, if there's room."

I pressed the tape into her hand. She looked at it. I could feel the moment slipping away from me. I suddenly felt reckless, and put down two hundred-dollar bills on the bar.

"One for you, the rest behind the bar."

"For who?"

"Call it a general line of credit."

"Why would you do that?"

I grinned what I imagined was not a particularly warm grin.

"I want to be a player, I need to pay the toll."

I turned to the crowd and addressed the backs of fifty or so heads, yelling to be heard over the human beatbox, who hadn't taken a breath.

"Hey guys! Hundred bucks behind the bar! First come, first served for a free drink!"

The response was far more energetic than I had imagined. In fact, it was something of a stampede. Chairs scraped, people yelled and glasses went flying as patrons mobbed poor Minnie and I was jostled out of the way. No one even realised who had made the announcement. I guessed in this town, if anything was advertised as free, best grab it before it became too good to be true – irrespective of the product.

It was such a bunfight that Minnie summoned the same bouncers that had broken up the fight during my set not fifteen minutes earlier. She pointed me out over the heads of the scrum, and they advanced, righteous anger in their faces.

As they went to lay hands on me, I saw something on the photoboard behind Minnie's purple hair that I hadn't noticed the first time around.

In the bottom corner of the montage was a tiny black-and-white image of Rosco, in profile, wearing a black shirt with white braces. It was a grainy shot, but there was a sheen of post-gig sweat on his brow and a sour look on his weathered old face. The picture looked to be at least ten years old. His apparently ubiquitous collection of coins and notes formed a footer to the photograph. His signature was scrawled across the bottom, on a white business card that had been stuck on to sidestep the natural issues of black ink on a black background.

I took a step forward. The bouncers took an arm each.

"Hey, wait a minute. That picture…" I began, but the minute they met resistance they propelled me backwards and I was out the side door and on the ground in the alley before I had time to argue.

Minus my guitar.

"My guitar!" I yelled, as the two knuckledraggers stepped back inside without a word. Not a word. Not 'Go home,' or 'Don't come back,' or 'You guddam moron,' or 'Take your charity elsewhere.' Not a word.

One of them did, however, come back with Minnie. The instrumental version, not the human. He didn't throw her, either, but placed her against the brick wall that looked blue in the neon-polluted air.

I picked her up and checked her over. As well as the smell, she now had two broken strings and a huge scuff on the bottom of the body.

"I didn't think you English liked upsetting anybody." The voice came from behind me, and sounded like it had been soaked in petrol and then dried off with a cheese grater.

I turned around. Randy was standing there. His body language was not threatening, but I was suddenly very aware that I was standing facing a self-confessed drug dealer in a Vegas back alley with a large bundle of cash in my pocket, with my only weapon unlikely to withstand much more abuse.

As it was, I needn't have worried. He seemed to be alone. His movements were furtive, and he scurried over to me, urgency galvanising him.

"Quick, quick, I'm carrying. What is it you need?"

"I didn't say I needed *any*thing."

Now he looked vexed, like I'd wasted his time.

"Look, I'm sorry if there's been a misunderstanding, but I do not need to buy drugs."

"Jesus-aitch-fuckin-shit! Will you keep your voice down?" he hissed. "You've put a man in a compromising situation, my English friend. This is not a debate. I should be gone already. You have committed to buy."

"I've *what*? I have not…oh, fuck it. Give me something to, Christ, I don't know. Something to keep me awake."

Randy's eyes crinkled under the peak of his cap and a gummy grin erupted somewhere behind the vegetation that passed for his beard. I barely saw him move, but whereas his handshake had been heavy and rough, I felt a whisper of silk brush my own hand and then there was something hard and cylindrical in my palm.

"Proper chemical, ah, *empowerment*," he said. "As synthetic as you like. Made by scientists. Fifty bucks the roll."

"How do I know they won't kill me? What are they called?"

"Street name's *Cirrhosis*," he said. "Like the clouds. You'll get so high you won't wanna come down."

"Er, isn't that *Cirrus*?" I said.

"It's all blue-sky thinking," he said, and winked.

The roll felt like a stack of five-cent pieces. I gave him seventy dollars.

"Here. There's a twenty-dollar tip there. I need some help."

"Twenty for me to listen, then I decide the rate."

"Fine, fine. Look, behind the bar there's a bunch of photographs."

"Yeah, yeah, I know it."

"Bottom corner there's one of a guy named Rosco Dunhill."

"Never heard of him."

"Maybe not, but someone at the Dude Ranch obviously does. Just find out who and where I can find him, okay? I know he's playing somewhere in Vegas this week."

He shrugged.

"You're a strange little number, sir," he said. "You want me to go now?"

"No, not now. They're still dealing with the goldrush."

"Huh?"

"Never mind. I'm staying at the Circus Circus, room 1850." The minute I said it I regretted it, especially as I was in danger of being showy with my gradually-decreasing billfold. "Come find me when you know."

"Another fifty."

"Fine. Here. That's sixty. I don't mean to be rude, but you're making me nervous. There's an extra ten to leave me alone, okay?"

His eyes glistened in the gloom.

"I take it back. You English are rude fuckin' pricks."

He edged forwards. In the gloom I didn't really register any movement, but there was a sudden cold feeling on the tip of my nose, and it took a second or two for me to realise with horror that it was the end of a revolver. I looked down, going cross-eyed, and saw the black hole at the end of the barrel, like a tunnel leading out of hell, from which a thunderous screaming locomotive would fly, intent only on decimating my body as I lay paralysed on the tracks.

"I've been ripped off by one of your countrymen already tonight, and it's only 'cos of my cosmopolitan outlook that I ain't tarring you all with the same brush. Don't make me revise my position. I need my *rounds*."

His voice was a low growl, his eyes pale and clear.

The only thing I could think of to say was: "Sorry."

He tucked the pistol into the waistband at the small of his back, turned on his heel and stalked off down the alley, swaying like a socialite hostess whose delicate sensibilities I had offended with a breach of some drug-dealers' etiquette.

His shirt had rucked up over the weapon, and as he rounded the corner the neon caught its polished surface, and my hands began to shake uncontrollably.

CHAPTER NINE

LEGEND OF THE DIGITAL JACKHAMMER

When I woke up, Marie was busy packing.

"What happened to *you*?" she said.

"Let's say the Casino broke her cherry. I've named her Minnie."

"What do you mean?"

"And I think… I may have found Rosco."

She came over and sat down. I opened my mouth to tell her the story, but was interrupted by Marvin's customary knock.

I shuffled over and answered the door. The fact of standing/walking caused a whisky/pills hangover to go *whomp* through my system like a torpedo being launched. I braced myself for an exuberant greeting. None was forthcoming. He was quite subdued, which I wasn't sorry for. In fact, he looked rather pale.

"Y'alright?" I said.

"Yeah. Yes, er… Can I… come in?" He looked over his shoulder.

I held the door open.

I sat heavily on the edge of the bed. Marie started flinging things into a bag.

"We need to check out by eleven," she said.

"I might need another night or two," I said. "I think I might be able to find Rosco."

"Oh, really?" she said.

"I… need to get back," Marvin said.

Marie and I both looked over at him. The strain in his voice was palpable.

"What's the matter?" Marie said.

"Just… you know. Work stuff."

Marie and I exchanged glances. This was clearly bollocks, but who were we to question him?

God, my *head*. I couldn't leave just yet, but the hangover was killing my ability to have an intelligent discussion about it.

I went to root around in the bedside drawer and rummaged around for some paracetamol. Instead I saw Randy's roll of pills. I picked them up and tried to read the label. It showed a yellow sun and some foreign language. Nothing even vaguely medical.

Two things struck me. One pill might make me feel a whole lot better, or a whole lot worse. The other was that the tube was remarkably similar to the tube Marvin had palmed off on me the night before.

I stood up, and held out the tube.

"Did you get these from Randy?" I said.

Before he could answer, there was a knock at the door. Not *quite* a fist-pounding we-have-a-warrant knock, but not the super-servile tip-tap of housekeeping either.

I looked from Marvin to Marie, and got up to answer it.

Standing there was Randy, the alleyway drug dealer to whom I had given details of my precise location and accommodation the night before.

"Hey," he said to me, with all of the salesman's good humour. "I found your…"

You couldn't exactly say he looked pleased to see me, but his countenance was a damn sight more agreeable than when he saw Marvin. His eyes flicked to my road-buddy, and darkness crossed his face.

"You…" he said in a low rasp. His body began to shake with anger as tension infused it. "You gud-*dam*, mother-fuckin', cheap, low-life…"

His voice was cut down to a muffled bawl as Marvin marched

over and kicked the door shut.

It didn't end there, however, and after a brief pause a furious hammering began to befall the poor door, accompanied by a rapid-fire tirade of Nevada rage.

"*YOUGODDAMLIMEYPIECEOFSHITOPENTHISFUC KINDOORNOW*!"

The intervals between the pounding grew longer and the weight behind it grew heavier as knocking was superseded by what I took to be shoulder-barging and genuine attempts to enter. The yelling continued unabated, however. The door buckled alarmingly.

I looked at Marvin.

"What the hell?..."

The noise must have jolted Marie from her shock, for she strode over to the door and hammered on it in riposte.

"Go away!" she said. "I am calling the police."

The knocking stopped, as did the yelling.

We all stood frozen. Marie had a faintly triumphant look on her face, but the sudden silence was still a hideous moment of uncertainty. Maybe in his instant and inexplicable rage, Randy had not realised Marie was present, and her no-nonsense female tones had given him pause.

"What the hell?" Marie said to Marvin, echoing me.

"What the hell?!" Marvin cried. "What the hell is right! What the hell is he doing *here*??!"

"Will you shut up?" I said. "He's got a fucking *gun*," I hissed.

"He's *what*?" Marie said.

"Well, he is a drug dealer," Marvin said.

"We have got to get out of here," I said. "Marie, check the spyhole."

She shot me a split-second look that might have been *Who do you think you're bossing about?* but, equally, might have been *Oooh check you bossing me about!* but I was too preoccupied by palm-sweating fear to dwell on it.

In either case, she went. She pressed her eye to the spyhole.

"How long does it take?" Marvin said after five seconds.

"He's gone," she said.

"Right. How long do you need to pack?" he said, more to Marie than I.

"Two minutes," I said. "Right?"

"Sexist pig," she said.

"Huh? What?" I said.

"Come on," Marvin said. "Chuck your stuff in your bags. I'll meet you at the car. You've got ninety seconds. He might come back."

He ran next door to his room while Marie and I did as bidden. Marvin's parting comment was enough for us to focus all our energies on getting out of there, and save the debrief for the desert freeway.

We were probably ready to go in less than a minute, but it felt a hell of a lot longer. Marvin was waiting outside in the corridor, his usual nervous energy amplified a hundredfold. I felt sure that if I touched him I would be instantly electrocuted.

"At last," he said when he saw us. "Come on."

I looked down at the carpet outside our hotel room door. A couple of what looked like fifty-pound notes winked back at me, and the dim bulb of understanding began to slowly come on.

The three of us hurried down the corridor, somewhere between a brisk walk and a run. The garish red-and-pink pattern swirls on the gleaming white walls and carpet felt as though they were going to leap out at us, and I felt suddenly disorientated, a razor-edged pinball bouncing around like a bullet in a machine made of human organs.

"This is ridiculous," Marie said as we bimbled along, three gawky British soul-searchers who had somehow managed to upset the wrong back-alley Vegas street dealer.

Not, however, as ridiculous as the muffled shouting that was coming from somewhere in the hotel. It sounded like it might have been inside one of the rooms, or on the next floor, or somewhere else in the corridor network that traversed the building. It couldn't have been much further than that or we wouldn't have heard a thing.

"Hold up," Marvin said. "We're like sitting ducks here."

He stopped and strained to listen.

"You hear that?" he said.

"Too right I do," I said. "And it's getting closer."

"Sounds like there's more than one of them," Marie said.

"Come on," I said, unable to stand the inertia any longer. "Let's take the stairs."

"Do you *know* what floor we're on?!" Marie said.

"Wait!" Marvin shouted.

I headed off anyway, towards the door at the furthest end of the corridor. The only thing beyond it was a picture window and the shimmering Nevada skyline.

The corridor was so long it stretched away almost to a point, and the concentration required to maintain perspective suddenly seemed to elude me. So when the three men appeared from the door up ahead – the very same one I was heading for – it took me half a second to work out how far away they were.

We had about thirty yards' grace. Barstool-height Randy was flanked on either side by two men who had as much on Randy in height as they did in disagreeable countenance.

I didn't see any weapons, but figured they'd be unlikely to be parading them on display. In any event, the sign of reinforcements was clearly not encouraging. I staggered to a stop and turned to pelt back the other way, an action that, behind me, Marie and Marvin had pre-empted. They were already clattering off down the corridor.

Our collective burst of activity prompted shouts from the three men, who charged down the corridor towards us.

"This isn't happening!" Marie cried. "They can't attack us in broad daylight!"

Even as we ran, I could sense her well-established world-view bristling with outrage.

We thundered down the corridor. I worried that being so

bunched up meant we would collide into each other, so I pulled out in front a bit, while Marvin dropped back slightly. His laboured breathing suggested this wasn't deliberate on his part, but spreading out a bit did wonders for our progress.

"Where are we going?" Marie said as we ran.

"Just run!" Marvin wheezed.

She had a point. Hotel corridors don't offer much in the way of options. Lifts, stairs, other guest rooms. That was about the extent of our escape plans. We'd left one bank of lifts and a staircase behind us, as well as three yelling Nevada drug dealers. I only hoped that a hotel this vast wouldn't just have one bank of lifts per floor.

As it happened, the Japanese saved us. There was a chatter of excited voices up ahead, and we rounded the corner to see a gaggle of about ten of them emerging from a lift.

We shoved past them, barely slowing up, and dived into the lift. They seemed greatly amused by the whole thing. Marvin smacked the 'door close' button repeatedly, but the timing of the Japanese tourists' exit couldn't have been better. The doors were already sliding shut as we barged in. The metal box began to slide downwards just as muffled shouts became audible on the other side of the doors.

Marvin pressed himself against the glass wall and leaned his head back, his breath coming in throaty rasps.

"See your embracing of the Californian lifestyle has been a bit piecemeal," I said.

"Don't be fooled," he gasped. "I don't actually exercise, and I still smoke like a navvy. The natives treat me like a leper. I am so unhealthy there are new strains of watercress growing out of my stools. Goddam 'bines."

Marie grimaced.

"Thank God for the Japanese invasion, huh?" I said.

"Why can't I get that lucky on the gaming floor?" Marvin said.

"We're not out of the hotel yet," Marie said. "And when we are, you two idiots owe me an explanation."

The lift eventually opened out into the cavernous lobby, the huge pillars throughout offering ample cover from fire should it have come to that. I didn't think drug dealers were likely to call the law on us, but it was still a relief to not be met by a cordon of Nevada's finest.

The express checkout option involved us running past the desk and tossing our key cards in the direction of one of the receptionists, and then we were out into the sun-baked car park. We seemed to have shaken Randy and his goons, but that didn't stop us flinging our gear in the boot of the Chrysler and me performing a deft fishtail into the Strip's chaotic traffic and some right turns at a couple of intersections to make doubly sure.

"Nice," Marvin remarked, his more familiar upbeat nature beginning to surface again. "Have you done counter-surveillance training, or something?"

He was in the back, with Marie up front, and he realised that she was glaring at him in the rear view mirror.

"What?" he said.

"You know very well what," she said, as we roared out of Vegas under the noonday sun.

We compared notes, and it transpired that, prior to my procurement of *Cirrhosis* from Randy, Marvin had done much the same. However, and as I had come to suspect, Marvin had indeed thought it a good idea to try to palm off his counterfeit prop-sterling on our diminutive supplier, telling him that it would be a simple matter of changing it up at any casino cage. Randy, clearly, had not been fooled, and Marvin obviously hadn't banked on me leading the defrauded drug dealer directly to our door.

"With luck like that, I've no business coming back here ever again," he said, and then, after a brief pause, he leaned forward and shouted: "Truly a lean bird!" making both Marie and I jump.

With a bit of a buffer behind us, I realised that Marvin's provocation of Randy meant I had never got that fix on Rosco's whereabouts, and I could hardly go back to find out. Not only that, but, now the panic had subsided a bit, I realised that, in the furore, I had left most of my surprise winnings in the room's safe.

Great.

Still, I had more or less broken even.

More or less.

I suddenly realised that I was ruined. My head felt like it was being sat on by a cow, and my mouth was like a carpet of desert sand. Mr Dylan was strumming his laments on the car stereo, blithely informing me that the hanging judge was drunk.

I felt violated, resigned, weary, broke – and strangely complete.

We stopped at a tax-free clothing outlet in Barstow. The heat was like a wall as I stepped out of the car, and I was sure the DTs were coming on. I couldn't even bring myself to enter the store, instead just loitering around by the entrance to get the full force of the aircon and the benefit of a wall to lean against. Marie, meanwhile – her mood having improved somewhat by the discovery of the store – happily skipped from rack to rack with a discerning eye; gathering, examining and returning.

Marvin bought a novelty hat with two fabric breasts that lactated beer, and walked over to me by the entrance. He had a solemn look on his face – although the presence of the hat meant I had to look twice to gauge its sincerity – and I realised he was holding out a bunch of cash.

"Take it, man," he said.

"What for?"

"The cash, the money you left behind. That's my fault. Come on, duderino, just take it." He poked me in the sternum with it.

A number of noble platitudes crossed my mind – you know, the usual kind of thing that friends say to each other in distinctly uncomfortable situations involving money: *Don't be silly* / *Put it away* / *I won't hear of it* / *blah blah blah*.

As it was, I felt too ill to do anything other than take the path of least resistance. Even if I could have summoned the energy to refuse, the memory of his hand on Marie's thigh suddenly appeared in my brain, and I snatched the cash from him.

"Thanks."

He nodded, and went off to find something to fill his hat with.

Marie flung her purchases into the trunk. I tried to make a joke about accidentally locking the keys in there, but it just brought on the shakes again.

We stopped in some dusty forgotten outpost called Baker, and went to a Bun Boy for lunch. It was all I could do to not press my forehead against the Formica tabletop, and I managed to force down half a sandwich and a 7-Up.

I looked up and down the deserted main drag as we walked back to the car, feeling like we were the only ones left after the apocalypse. Fucking Baker, I thought, as we raced south on the freeway in a daze. What was the matter with these people?

Eventually, LA hazed into view, and I got that sinking feeling again – not just because I had nowhere to stay, but because I always feel like that when I get where I'm going.

"What the hell are we going to do now?" I said.

Marvin clicked his tongue against his teeth.

"Let's go to San Francisco," he said.

ACT TWO – SAN FRANCISCO

CHAPTER TEN

PORNOG THE TERRIBLE

Let's be clear about something. I don't want to sound petulant, but this trip was *my* idea. I thought of it first. I'd planned it long before a year in Canada had even occurred to Marie, while the fact that Marvin had got to LA before me was just coincidence. Not only that, but I had factored in a few in-the-event-of-failure days in New York at the end of the trip well before Marie had apparently decided to do the same.

As it happened, I didn't actually know Marvin that well. We only met the year before, at some month-long retreat for wannabe writers in the middle of Brecon, where we'd sat in the drawing room until the small hours – smoking, talking about films and drinking the vintage proceeds of our regular cellar-raids. It was a bit amateurish because there were no drugs, but it was still good fun. We got on famously (I think), probably because most of the people I knew thought Ginsberg was a kind of lager, which set the bar pretty low on the kindred spirit front.

In between hastily-scribbled experimental musings, I'd played some smoky front-porch blues to the twenty or so other bright-eyed hopefuls – of whom I was the youngest by a clear three years – while Marvin had spontaneously improvised rhyming couplets like some haggard old master of ceremonies. He curled his papery tongue around the words with a lusty swagger, and made you feel like the English language was some kind of slutty muse you couldn't resist but didn't want to keep around either.

After the month was up, we returned to our respective dead ends – me to the building trade, Marvin to the dole – with not a lot to show for it besides a near-permanent hangover, a few 'useful' contacts and eager dreams of fame, cash and legacy that seemed to be dangling almost within reach.

I say 'dangling,' but between then and now Marvin's ship, although not quite in, was definitely on the horizon. He'd somehow managed to land a job writing screenplays for Pacific Jetstream, this production company in Santa Monica. He claimed to have been given a company credit card and a $50,000 advance for three completed scripts on a twelve-month contract. This may have been crap, but his extended displays of generosity and digs in Hollywood certainly helped maintain the illusion.

Sabotage seems too strong a word, but – whatever. I thought of it, but Marvin got there first. So when he got wind of my plan – 'literary pilgrimage,' he called it – he'd insisted we hook up when I landed. *He'd* insisted.

The first stop on our arrival back in LA was Marvin's place. He'd already suggested we stay with him, and so we unloaded the Chrysler and collapsed in his front room. The sunlight beamed onto the front garden, filtered through the oaks on the sidewalk, and I marvelled at the peace and tranquillity one could find in the middle of this raging city.

I got up to go to the bathroom and take a shower – which, incidentally, was an exercise in self-abuse. The water powered through the head in such a fine spray that it was like having your skin peppered by razor sharp needles, and by the time I'd lathered up it took me nearly twenty minutes to rinse off.

Anyway, my hangover was fading in favour of the utter lethargy that usually comes in its absence, and I felt a whole lot better once I'd put on some clean clothes.

As I left the bathroom there was a strange, rhythmic hissing noise coming from the front room. I passed the kitchen – noting a brightly-coloured high chair and collection of matching plastic bowls and cups – and returned to the front room, where Marvin was frantically inflating a camping mattress with a foot pump.

"Feel better?" Marie asked.

"Christ, yes. Good siesta and I'll be one hundred per cent again. The shower's for sado-masochists, though."

"Oh yeah, I meant to mention that," Marvin said, not looking up from his task. "Not that there's much one can do about it."

"What do you mean?" Marie said.

"You'll see," I said.

"Maybe I'll wait," she answered.

That suited me. The thought of Marie, naked and soaping up only twenty feet away with just a partition wall between us, was just about more than I could bear, even with the dregs of my hangover taking their sweet time to budge.

I collapsed onto the sofa.

"You got kids?" I asked.

"Me? Christ, no. Why...oh, I see. No, it's a houseshare."

Beside me, Marie gave an almost imperceptible twitch.

"Yeah, my mate Roger rents the house. Him and his wife. They have a small son. He's one, I think. No, eighteen months. He sublet me the room when I flew out here. Roger, that is, not the baby."

The mattress was coming on a treat.

"Where are they?" Marie said.

"Skiing in Colorado. Actually, they'll be home soon. You'll like them."

"Don't you think you should, you know, check with them before we stay here?" Marie said.

"Nonsense. They'll be fine. Besides, we're buzzing off to San Francisco tomorrow, aren't we?"

"Tomorrow?"

The front door opened.

Marvin's housemates were Roger and Zephi. Roger was a 2nd unit director from Enfield, who, as it turned out, had been here three years and was already contracted to Pacific Jetstream. It was he that had persuaded the company to hire his mate Marvin.

Roger had met and married Zephi – a Californication of Jozephine – a slender Los Angeles native with an all-weather tan and sun-bleached hair, who carried a carbon-copy-handsome young chap in her arms.

During the introductions, I was dimly aware of Marie whispering in my ear about making our excuses and finding a hotel. This didn't go unnoticed, and when she realised she'd been heard, she stood up and very politely told Roger and Zephi that we could not impose on them.

"Oh no, you guys can totally crash here," Zephi said. In fact, she wouldn't – the proximity of a drop-dead gorgeous female within her husband's fighting arc notwithstanding – hear of anything else, and in the end Marie capitulated graciously on the understanding it would just be for one night.

Their invitation was a blessing (I say 'their,' but it was really Zephi doing the inviting – Roger sort of shrugged acquiescence in a way that suggested the idea was about as palatable as fisting his grandmother), and so Marvin continued his efforts with the inflatable mattress.

We helped them unload their SUV, and then the householders went off to perform the rigid routines that a baby necessitates, politely sidestepping us as we began our occupation of their front room and enormous, side-of-a-barn home cinema screen. Marvin and Roger went into the kitchen for some kind of serious work- (or possibly houseguest-) related discussion.

I offered to play with the baby – who was actually two, and whose name was Harry – while the grown-ups sorted themselves out, and by the time Zephi emerged from the bedroom in her dressing gown, we had grown kind of attached. I even kept him Zen before bed – there was no wind-'em-up horseplay, and Zephi praised my instincts. Marie kept out of our interplay, but I could feel the warmth of her eyes as I imitated Harry's accent and he mine.

I lay down on the mattress – it was a double, but Marie still took the sofa. Harry went off to sleep, and a wave of quiet exhaustion and unreality descended with the Los Angeles night upon the house. Its occupants did not know each other, but by some bizarre series of events, we had all arrived at the same place at the same time.

In the morning I got up to put gas in the Chrysler with the intention of returning it to Hertz, only to find that Marvin and Roger were already hovering around it, having another earnest discussion.

I returned to the kitchen. Harry was at the table, having a spectacularly colourful breakfast. Zephi was bustling around him. He grinned when he saw me, and waved.

"He likes you," Zephi said. "He's normally very suspicious of men. It was a week before he would go anywhere near Marvin."

"I like kids," I said, walking over and making a show of shaking his hand. He gave me his spoon, wanting me to feed him.

"Do you have brothers and sisters?" She stopped what she was doing and turned to face me, leaning against the counter. A coffee machine spluttered behind her.

"One of each," I said. "Five years between me and my sister. My brother is twelve years younger than me, so I got pretty hands-on when he was born."

She poured two cups of coffee and brought them over to the table. She was wearing a tight green singlet and combat pants. Her feet were bare. She wore bracelets and a silver ring at the top of her ear. Her skin smelled like coconut.

"That's some useful experience," she said, sitting opposite me and passing me a cup. "Babies faze a lot of men."

"They're easy once you know how. Aren't they, bub?" I said, stroking his hair. "Thanks."

"Good practice," she said. "You think you'd like to have kids?"

"Oh, yeah, one day," I said. "A couple, I reckon. I'm from a line of big families. Got to meet the right woman first, though, right?"

"Oh, lots of time," she said, resting her chin on her hand. "You're – what – twenty-three?"

"Nowhere near. Twenty-one in four months," I said, spooning porridge into Harry's mouth.

"Damn. Tough paper route, huh?"

"Ha ha," I said. "I guess now I know why I don't get carded much."

"Well, you look older."

"Too many hours laying felt out in the sun."

"Marvin said you played music?"

"Oh yeah, but, you know…"

"…You gotta make a living. I act a bit, but there's no way it pays the rent. You should play us something. You got a tape?"

"Yeah, in my stuff… hey, you act? That's cool."

"Me and the rest of Los Angeles. What would be cool is if I said I didn't."

Marie appeared in the doorway.

"Morning," she said, looking from me to Zephi and back again.

"Hey," I said.

"Morning," Zephi said. "You sleep okay?"

"Great, thanks. Thank you so much for letting us stay."

"Oh, hey, any time. Stay another night, if you want. Hell, the way Harry here has taken to Alex, stay a month."

"Thank you, but we really can't impose."

"Harry here has smashed his breakfast," I said, standing up and showing him the empty bowl. "Good job, little man." I used the spoon to blob a spot of jam on his nose. He grinned.

"So what's next for you guys?" Zephi said, as I finished my coffee and put the dishes in the sink.

"Oh, you know, get some breakfast, find a motel, hit some bars. Should have fame and fortune cracked by Tuesday."

She smiled. Marie and I gathered up our essentials and took

them out to the car, leaving most of our gear in Marvin's room. We all congregated on the front lawn before leaving. Zephi said again we could stay longer if we needed to, but wasn't terribly convincing this time around – perhaps the result of some overnight pillow talk – and so we thanked her again and climbed aboard.

Roger was at the wheel, and I only found out later that the rental was in his name and he had organised the car from Colorado as Marvin did not have a driving licence. In practical terms, this meant that Marie and I got dropped off somewhere on Ocean, while Roger and Marvin buzzed west into Santa Monica proper, towards the Pacific Jetstream offices and to 'work.' (I kept pretty strict hours in the trade, and the thought of breezing in at 11am on a Monday morning seemed decidedly lo-fi to me.)

I called some hostels from a payphone, but they were all full, and so Marie and I went for a breakfast of eggs and fried potatoes at a diner on the lip of the Pacific while we decided what to do.

We walked for a few more aimless blocks, the sun beating down, the Casino clunking across my back, the few bags we did have getting heavier and heavier. The buoyant, beer-induced good moods of Vegas suddenly seemed a long way away, as did finding Rosco, as did sorting out my life.

Marie had become quiet, and I sensed her stress levels rising. To her credit, the Marie of three years ago would have been crippled by irritability and in the fits of a terminal sulk in this situation.

I turned to her, and smiled.

"You'd better give me some of what you're taking," I said.

She smiled back, not understanding.

I made some more calls from another payphone, the anxiety of the aimless forming again in my stomach. I tried to tell myself that the thirty-eight year-old driving past in his family station wagon on his way to the office – who had to behave himself at every turn to keep his job, wife and mortgage, whose capacity for the spontaneous had been shelved long ago in favour of a vague day thirty years hence when everything would be paid up and he would finally finish his climb to the house on the hill, who *could* come tonight but would need to be away by eight, who could only go to Vegas with his wife's permission and with a year's notice and some strict ground rules, whose life would be plunged into utter chaos should he miss a payment or lose his diary or if interest rates rose – would look at Marie and I standing by the payphone and think: my God, look at them. They have no plans, no demands, no commitments. Look how utterly free they are. They don't even know where they're sleeping tonight. What fun!

I looked at Marie as I slipped the coins in.

"We could sleep on the beach," she said. "Do you think it's warm enough?"

The idea was suddenly appealing, as the station wagon whispered past.

"I'll keep you warm," I said.

The call was picked up, and we finally had some success, landing a room at Carlo's Cotel in Venice Beach. We split the fare for a yellow cab with a manic depressive Bolivian driver to get us there, stat.

It was a four-bunk room with a small cloud of flies buzzing around by the tiny window, from which you could literally climb out onto Venice Beach.

'Functional' was probably pushing it a bit, but it was comfortable, clean, I had paid for it myself and didn't have to worry about upsetting the host or treading on the baby.

I was a little apprehensive as I turned to gauge Marie's reaction to the less-than-five-star accommodation, but she simply skipped past me and sprang onto a top bunk, where she spread her bare arms and legs back and forth on the cool sheets as if making a snow angel. I shook my head slowly.

"Who are you, and what did you do with Marie?" I muttered under my breath.

There was a split-second stand-off when our two roommates appeared, but it evaporated considerably quicker than when we met

Roger and Zephi. The playing field here was, after all, level. Matt was from Birmingham on a two-night stopover before continuing his journey to Fiji where he was going to spend six months building charity shelters for Unicef, while Simon was a Glaswegian doing a summer internship at Sony. He'd bounced from hostel to hostel for eight weeks.

"It's the only way to do it," he said. "You'll have such a blast. Drinks and music with new people every night. Makes staying in a hotel seem like lying on a mortuary slab."

Marie and I went out to get some pizza from a rapidly-cooling Venice beachfront. The tourists were starting to thin out, leaving Muscle Beach diehards and seriously aggressive beggars, whose appeals we parried with the remnants of our box of pizza. We retreated to the hostel, where the atmosphere coming from the ground floor could only be described as electric.

Behind the reception booth was a little lounge area with a tiny bar that appeared to have been hand-whittled from a lump of driftwood. There was pink lighting and plastic palm leaves in the lounge, with a terrace at the back that opened out onto the beach.

It was the antithesis of the Dog and Duck. It was heaving with people drinking cheap bottled beer and homemade cocktails. There was hardly anyone over twenty-five, hardly anyone with less than half their skin on display and hardly anyone that wasn't here for some vaguely thematic reason – people didn't rock up in a place like Carlo's Cotel unless there was some kind of common interest in travelling, drinking, music and generally having a good time. For this reason, you could walk up to anyone – *anyone* – and start a conversation. Everyone just seemed to want to *love*.

I saw our bunkmate Simon, the Sony intern, at the bar. He ordered a couple of extra bottles of Rolling Rock for Marie and I. *The Night They Drove Old Dixie Down* was playing out of a very old pair of Amstrad speakers mounted high on the wall.

I asked Simon if it was sacrilegious to think The Band were actually better than Dylan, and this prompted a very long and fervent discussion about music that must have been boring as hell for Marie. She sloped off to the terrace to be engulfed by a group of people who wanted her in their gang.

"Don't forget San Francisco," she said over her shoulder as she went.

Don't forget it? Meaning what? Don't forget it in some romantically significant way? Difficult, as none of us had been there yet. Don't forget to include it on the itinerary? Don't forget to sort it out?

Ah, yes. That would be it.

Marvin had been the only one to talk San Francisco with any conviction, and yet here he wasn't. We had made no real plans to even see him after work, let alone take in a slice of California coast. I wasn't even sure if he'd taken time off from work, or if it had even occurred to him. In any event, he still apparently thought that it was all on tomorrow. I couldn't help feeling that we were the ones absorbing all the logistical worries.

So I found myself standing by the payphone in Carlo's Cotel, trying to find somewhere that would rent a car to a twenty-year-old. Marvin couldn't drive, Marie had no intention of doing so, so it was down to me. It took half the fucking evening – one of the firms actually laughed at me. A queue of people wanting to use the phone began to form on the stairs.

Eventually Basic Car Rentals in Inglewood agreed to hire me an ancient sedan at astronomical rates. The villain on the phone insisted on a $400 cash deposit and practically the same again for the special insurance premium. Danger money, he called it. With no better offer, I accepted and the guy said he would send someone round in the morning with it, which I supposed was something.

Once the deal was agreed, I hung up and relinquished the phone to a slim woman in a bikini top and shorts who smiled at me. I suggested to Marie – who had reappeared while I was on the phone – that we ought to let Marvin know where we had pitched up and what the plan was for the morning, and so we sat halfway up the staircase to rejoin the queue.

"What about somewhere to stay?" Marie asked.

"Christ, I'm not doing that as well. I'm practically deaf in one ear."

I touched the rough woven hessian walls, and smelled lime and coconut sun tan lotion from somewhere. We only had to wait a few minutes, but when I got up Marie touched my knee.

"I'll call him," she said.

I stared at her for a moment, then passed her Marvin's business card. She dialled the number.

"'Ello," she said when the call was answered. Her voice was half an octave lower than usual, and had a thick Eastern European twang. "May I plees speek with Meester Price plees? Mr Marveen Price?"

The voice on the other end spoke in her ear.

"Yez, you may tell him thees ees Mimi."

Another question.

"Mimi? From the Ukraine? We met in Vegas. At the Crazy Horse Too. I weel be most offended eef hee does not remember me."

The accent was spot on. She beckoned me to the phone while the person on the other end attempted to locate Marvin. We shared the earpiece. There was a rustling and whispering on the other end.

"Er, hello?" It had the hammy virginal awkwardness of an educated Middle-Englander whose boss has just found out he's into swinging. I started to splutter as I stifled my laughter – Marie, on the other hand, was a proper pro. Her capacity for acting certainly hadn't diminished since our school days.

"Marveen! How wonderful to hear your voice again. I do hope you remember me?"

"Well, yes, yes I do. How are you?"

"Oh, wonderful. A little tired of strangers waving their cocks at me, so I was very happy to meet a gentleman like you."

"Oh… really?" I could almost hear him thinking: *I behaved like a gentleman*??

"Yes, you gave me your beezneez card, so I thought I would come to Santa Monica to see you."

"You're…. you're in LA?"

"Of course I am," she said. "I thought I would surprise you. Now, where would you like to take me so we can talk about the future?"

"The future? Well, I'm a little busy right now…." He covered the receiver with something, and I heard him utter a muffled curse to someone: *why the fuck did you put her through to me?*

"Meester Price," she said, turning cold and haughty in a way that made even me feel scared, "…do not be treating me badly. You will regret it. I have many brothers. I am no slut. Now, let us talk about baby names. What do you think of 'Cuthbert?'"

I made the mistake of catching her eye, and that was it. We were both gone. A couple of our fellow travellers came into the corridor to make sure we were okay.

"Very. Fucking. Clever." Marvin's tinny voice rattled out of the receiver in a drawl that somehow managed to be simultaneously relieved, amused and irritated. "I hope that your whimsy is prelude to some kind of news?"

"We have the car," Marie said, the first to compose herself.

"Fucking tremendous."

"Where do you want picking up?"

"Depends where you are."

"Hostel in Venice Beach," I said. I resumed my position next to her, like two backing singers sharing a microphone. It was weird. Our lips were only inches apart, and yet due to the machinery involved the situation was innocuous in a way that it couldn't have been in any other scenario. Well, as far as Marie was concerned, anyway.

"My office, then. It's on the way to the coast. Otherwise we'll have to go back into Hollywood."

"How soon can you finish work?" Marie asked.

"Umm…umm… if I work late tonight you can come for me after lunch."

"Great. See you then."

By the time we'd sorted all that out, the bar had virtually cleared. Apparently that was less a soiree and more an aperitif. Checkout time was early, which gave us time to receive the car and stock up for the road before collecting Marvin, so we went to bed.

We lay there in silence in the half-dark – Marie on the top bunk, me underneath – the waves of Venice Beach and the strains of an unseen party giving me a sense of wonderment as my eyes began to close. I was suddenly and impossibly tired, which was just as well, because Marie's breathing became heavy, and I could smell her skin, and the urge to climb into her bunk and pull her to me was as intense as it was fleeting.

CHAPTER ELEVEN

XANADOO

The rep that delivered the car to us could best be described as brain-dead. Still, he took the money and handed over the keys without too much in the way of nasty surprises, and then loped off into Venice.

It was a white Kia Sephia that I drove away down Santa Monica Boulevard with Marie beside me. It was a piece of shit, but something about driving just eased all my worries away. Plus, cruising LA had decidedly more wonder to it than a five-hour desert haul.

We parked up in Santa Monica and got something to eat in Borders. Afterwards we browsed for maps and stuff, where I met Kevin, a native of San Francisco who was going to Europe in the autumn and wanted to know the best way to do it. I told him that a car was essential, and he gave me his number in San Francisco and told me to call him when he got back there the following week. I suspected we'd already be back in Los Angeles by then, but I just thanked him.

Marie caught the exchange with some degree of amusement.

Marvin's office was a glass-fronted building on 3rd Street, framed by steel girders and orange panels. The reception desk was in a small atrium with the girder theme continuing onto a metal spiral staircase leading to the first floor mezzanine, where all the work was going on. Movie posters showcasing the company's recent efforts – slick, low-end, high-budget summer blockbusters all, with the exception of a Fellini spread – were everywhere, most notably in Marvin's office, which was a glass pod adjacent to the main open-plan bit. It had the healthy modern appeal of a funky, soon-to-be thriving startup, and it certainly did not detract from whatever image he'd been trying to cultivate so far.

We hung around while he finished and took some calls, then we bundled out into Santa Monica Boulevard and headed for the car. Marie raised the accommodation issue again, and so we made some half-hearted calls. All the motels were full and, so, wanting to get on the road, we agreed to find something on arrival.

On the way to the car I revisited the site of my first introduction to Rosco on the Santa Monica Promenade, but he wasn't there. In his spot was some kind of mime artist.

We were chucking stuff in the boot of the Kia when I realised I had left all my tapes at Marvin's place. The thought was sudden and horrific, but my insistence that we go back east into Hollywood to get them was robustly outvoted by Marvin and Marie.

"Dude, you'll add an hour-plus to our journey. The ocean is right *there*."

It was a fair point, given that it was already nearly four and we hadn't left yet, but decent music was so essential to this venture that capitulation felt a bit like losing a limb. However, as I pulled away and headed towards the Pacific, Marvin slipped in a tape of his own. The thunderous opening bars of Hendrix doing *All Along the Watchtower* burst out of the car's – thankfully satisfactory – speakers, and I stopped worrying about the music.

Just the introduction of that song into the mix seemed to change things. To *start* things. Marvin was up front with me, while Marie was sprawled across the back seat, her bare feet hanging out the open window. She was playing with a string of beads, one end wrapped around her fingers, the other around her toes.

The day was moving from overcast to sunny and back again, and Marvin pointed out the homes of the stars on the mountainside as we left Santa Monica and headed into Malibu. My muscles relaxed as I settled into the driving, loving it completely, easing the car about, reacquainting myself with the left-hook.

Marvin and I talked movies and music – Tarantino vs Scorsese, the *White Album* vs *Pepper*. We were still in LA, cruising the narrow road alongside the ocean, whose steady waves, some selected by the sun, would watch us every step of the way and see every change, every new facet of life each would discover about the other.

We finally began to head out of LA. The road widened, the traffic thinned, and dusk began to fall. Route 101 continued inland, but we took Route 1 along the coast, through Santa Barbara, Santa Maria and San Luis Obispo.

Amber streaks lined the sky. I had these fantastic, practically opaque sunglasses, which were so dark I could stare right at the setting sun and see the crisp outline of every hill, tree and road beneath it as they stretched back towards the horizon like cardboard cutouts, growing darker as they did so.

Conversation lulled. Dino sang *You're Nobody Till Somebody Loves You.* I thought the other two were asleep, and then Marvin broke the silence.

"What do you regret most in your life?"

Bang. That moment, watermarked on time. Marvin's third dimension opened up, and I suddenly thought of him as a friend.

I thought about the question honestly, and what I came up with was this: I was ten years old, sitting in my school's lunch hall with my friends, exchanging Penguins for Kit-Kats and the like, when I felt someone touch my elbow. I turned around and saw my five-year-old sister walking past, clutching her pink lunchbox. She gave me a wave and a little smile, but I stopped chewing and just glared at her in some kind of passive-aggressive how-dare-you expression of meanness.

It was her first day.

"You never told me that," Marie said.

"You shattered some illusions for her, eh?" Marvin said, in a thoughtful tone.

"I guess."

"Kids can be cruel."

If I had been given more time to think about it I would no doubt have come up with something else. That this was the first thing I

124

thought of was probably significant. We all lose our innocence one way or another, but, ten years later, the thought that I had materially contributed to hers still caused me to flinch, and I suspected that in another ten, twenty, thirty years, it would continue to do so.

So I moved it on, and asked Marvin for his, which was some sordid tale involving a groom-to-be, industrial clingfilm and a one-way ticket to Inverness. We discussed it further for a while, then got Marie in on the conversation.

We moved onto sexual encounters, embarrassing moments, just shooting the shit, learning something new every second. Insisting on brutal honesty, Marvin strove for more subjects to further what he called the 'corporate bondage.' This should have sterilised the process somehow, but it didn't. In fact, this overt labelling of our efforts made me feel closer to him.

I don't know how we got on to it, but in the openness of the moment I started talking about my trip, my journey, and why this run along the Pacific Coast Highway didn't, well, *feel* like it should.

I think it started in Burger King, where I said that *being* on the road isn't actually like *reading On the Road*. Marvin instantly picked up on who and what I was quoting, making me feel a little sheepish as I hadn't actually offered the reference. However, it did make it easier to explain that when I read that line, I was outraged and determined to prove it wrong. I also rather glumly added that, so far, despite the run to Vegas and the current jag, I had failed to do so.

I wondered aloud just what Kerouac and all that shower did on their trips that was so *different.*

Marvin and I walked out into the parking lot while Marie went to the bathroom. As we approached the car, Marvin piped up. Turnaround began.

"You do know that all Kerouac did was get pissed with his mates and talk shit, right? They got pissed in their front rooms, or they got pissed while driving around, or they got pissed in bars, or they got pissed in the street. But that's pretty much all they did. Shit, we can do that right now."

"He doesn't *read* like that."

"Well, consider. It's a long journey, coast-to-coast. The journey is made up of hours, minutes and seconds."

"Details."

"That's a lot of wonder. You'd be all romanced out by the end of it."

"So what are you saying? It's nothing without hindsight and nostalgia?"

"Well, partly. But you'll put a different slant on it when you come to write it down – or write it up."

I looked at him sideways. He grinned.

"I've seen you scribbling in your diary."

"Have you really?" I said, deadpan.

"Don't get many roofers with diaries, I wouldn't have thought."

"Fuck off. It's a journal, anyway."

"Whatever. What I'm saying is, when you're in the moment, you can't escape reality. It's like a cold, hard concrete block. After the fact, you can choose to include as much or as little of it as you like."

"Huh," I said, pondering it. "I was playing my guitar in a meadow in France a couple of months ago. Dylan stuff. Nobody around, singing as loud as I wanted. It was beautiful, overlooking an orchard – I was in the full glare of the sunset and it lit up the meadow like it was on fire. And then I broke a string. The nearest guitar shop was thirty miles away, and they were closed on Sundays."

"And there's the rub. Life's full of Hamlet cigar moments. Plus, another observation, if I may?"

"Er."

"You're a little uptight."

"What?"

"You worry an awful lot. About logistics, mainly."

"Comes of not having a car."

"I get it. You're out of your back yard, that kind of stuff becomes all-consuming. But, dude, you need to chill out a bit. Relax. Improvise a little more. *Drink* a little more."

I made a sound like a horse exhaling.

Marie left the restaurant and walked out to join us. We hit the road again.

Up ahead in San Simeon, Marvin pointed out William Randolph Hearst's castle, the original Xanadu template, and said it might be worth checking out.

After stopping once to give the windscreen a proper clean after the wipers smeared it and I couldn't see anything against the setting sun, we landed in San Simeon a little after nine.

It became obvious that any idea of getting to San Francisco in one night had petered out around the time we were fannying about actually getting out of Los Angeles, and so we pulled up at a string of motels lining the highway, their lights facing out onto the darkening Pacific in a way that brought the lyrics to *Hotel California* to mind.

We walked from one to the other, window shopping, and eventually plumped for the cheapest in the interests of economy, given that this was an unexpected stopover. The buzzing red neon crucifix was disconcerting to say the least, but the green VACANCY sign underneath meant it was a no-brainer.

Money was tight, and no one really wanted to discuss the sleeping arrangements. We compared currencies in the car and the men figured out that Marie was going to have sign over some traveller's cheques to cover the stay. The old fruitbat on the desk, pleasant in a way that only the truly pious can be, offered to put in an extra bed into the double room for only five bucks and took the decision from us.

"Thanks," I said, turning to go.

"Jesus loves you," she said to my back.

We drove to the room, dumped our stuff and walked to a bar at the end of the lot. It was proper Wild West, catering mainly for hostile-looking Latinos. I blended in pretty much okay, but Marie and

Marvin stuck out like a couple of milk bottles. We took our Dos Equis outside and sat on the empty terrace, taking a table in a corner that seemed to overhang the Pacific on a precipice.

The night was crisp, a lime slice of moon shining on our faces as we talked, the beers sliding down with ease. With rather more candour than I was used to – which I ascribed to the alcohol and the twin mantras of brutal honesty and living for the moment that the three of us seemed to have unconsciously adopted – I started telling Marvin about an idea I had for a film script. It's been done, he said, but as one beer became three I went into it anyway with increasing excitement. It was a feel-good film, I said, all about the *now* and *here*, like on this bar terrace. Marvin indulged me but then there was a pause in the conversation – he got this kind of nonsense from excitable idiots all the time, no doubt. For a moment I thought I could hear the black Pacific scumming in the distance.

Undeterred, I put forward another pitch for a movie about government-enforced euthanasia.

"That's been done, too," Marvin said. "*Logan's Run.*"

I sat back in my seat.

"Fuck it."

This led onto another earnest conversation about euthanasia, which caused Marvin and Marie to butt heads again. The subjects changed – talking, just talking, words coming like giant brush strokes that made each of us broader, brighter, more complete, somehow. Marvin raised his glass in a toast – to what, I can't remember – and then we talked some more, not tempered by embarrassment, fear, social awkwardness, projected images, desired effects – or sobriety.

And then, just as I thought my earlier concerns about romance and wonder had been neutralised as quickly as they'd surfaced, something else happened.

Marvin got up to go and order an upgrade to whiskies, and Marie offered to help. She got up to follow – just a split-second too quick, but it was enough. The penny dropped, only it was a ten-ton penny the size of a Lincoln Town Car that dropped on my chest like a wrecking ball.

As well as the penny, the temperature dropped suddenly. I waited for five minutes on the cold terrace, alone in the dark like an idiot, and then got up to go to the room for a sweater.

I'd taken about five steps towards the room when I changed course and headed for the bar. It was warm, glowing and busy inside – unlike the dark, now cold and suddenly-uninviting terrace. I paused inside the door, for a moment unsure what to do. I opted to make a beeline for the bathroom, and walked past them in the queue for drinks, passing within maybe ten feet of them.

They didn't see me. Marvin had his arm around her shoulders. Marie did not look at all uncomfortable about this.

I made it to the bathroom and leaned on the sink, my arms locked straight, my breath coming in acidic shreds through my mouth. After a moment, I gawped at the mirror, my mouth open like a guppy, willing my reflection to come up with some form of explanation – like, maybe I was hallucinating.

After splashing water on my face, I left the bathroom and walked outside. *Oye Como Va* started playing from somewhere, the traffic-horn *beep-beep* of the Hammond organ and the crybaby guitar echoing out into the night.

Instead of going back to the table I walked around to the side of the building to watch them through the glass doors. I needn't have bothered with the subterfuge. They were necking so ferociously that they didn't see me.

No-one saw me, and the shame only comes now, as pen touches paper. Even so, it's easy to dismiss.

They left the bar after five more minutes or so, and I walked the long way around the back of the building to our table.

They were still kissing as I walked over, and I made a loud comment about the bloody awful Mexican hip-hop as I approached the table. They sprang apart like guilty teenagers being discovered having their first blind fumblings.

"Got you a sourmash, dude," Marvin said.

"I may need it," I said.

We all clinked glasses.

"Where'd you go?" Marie asked, her legs crossed, hands in her lap, the moon pale on her beautiful face.

"To get a sweater," I answered after a pause, giving her enough time to wonder whether she'd been rumbled.

"Where is it?"

"Huh?"

"Your sweater."

"Oh. I couldn't find one."

Conversation dried up thereafter. We drank quickly and quietly, as if intoxication was the only way out of this awkward mess, me staring at the bottom of my glass, wanting to tell it my secrets. I could almost hear them wondering: *does he know? did he see?*

But while they were no doubt consumed by this psychological cold warfare and its attendant hyper-awkwardness, I was distracted by the hideous, nameless sick feeling in my stomach. I had no words for it. I hadn't experienced it before. Jealousy? Betrayal? Rejection? Anger at the bubble we had cultivated between Hollywood and San Simeon having been burst before we were even properly on the road? Or some thick dark undulating wave marking the passage of Marie out of my life and my transition to some grim new chapter of adulthood?

What next? I asked myself. More drink seemed to be the only answer. I got another round in, and started slamming back Jim Beam.

In the end, despite myself, I decided it couldn't have been jealousy, because the feelings of hostility I would have expected to feel towards Marvin and Marie were conspicuously absent.

Despite my alcohol intake, I did, however, lose patience with the increasing cold and the lack of conversation to banish it. I stood up, and announced I was going to turn in.

To my surprise, they both got up to follow.

The old Jesus-beater on the desk – assisted by her six-foot son, no doubt – had indeed put a third bed in the room. Well, it was a cot, lying perpendicular to the two doubles, and one which made it very difficult to walk anywhere. It filled the gap between the foot of the beds and the dressing table, and anyone going to the bathroom was going to brush my teeth with their leg hairs.

I climbed into the cot, half-dressed. I was drunker than I realised, which was a bore, because I was suddenly consumed by a desire to grab the car and go for a drive. A long drive, up and down the coast, maybe ending with a full speed pelt off the bluffs into the Pacific.

I said goodnight in a thick tongue and turned out the light as they took a bed each, and then thought that, actually, my level of drunkenness might bring merciful oblivion pretty quickly.

It didn't.

Instead, I was still wide awake when, after about ten minutes in the darkness, I saw Marvin's dark form move silently across to Marie's bed. He got in. I screwed my eyes shut and lay frozen in the dark, willing myself to pass out.

The breathing became heavier. Marvin started whispering something indiscernible to Marie – whatever it was, she liked it. By contrast, I could hear what she was saying to him – something I tried to instantly forget.

After a while they stopped moving about, and so, in some ridiculously indirect form of protest, I got up to go to the bathroom. When I returned, there was silence. I tried again to sleep.

Then they started again. I suddenly realised with horror that I could have slept if I chose to, but that I was transfixed by things I could barely see but could all too easily imagine. I raged at myself for the helpless hot pulling in my loins.

I heard him instruct her to remove her panties. My eyes gradually grew accustomed to the dark and I was able to make out their entwined white forms – Marie's newly-muscular thighs wrapped themselves around Marvin's carcass about the same time I heard her start to stifle her whimpers. I imagined her biting her lip.

Within about ninety seconds, it was over. I heard Marie say something bilious to Marvin, and I finally coasted into sleep drawing some small comfort from the fact that the pillow talk didn't sound all that. I prayed that I wouldn't have a hangover, but either way, the likelihood of vomiting seemed pretty strong.

CHAPTER TWELVE

POLONECK ASSASSIN

Despite the hangover, by 8am I was sitting in the car with the engine idling and my stuff in the trunk.

I was staring straight ahead, the coffee in my hand cooling rapidly in the paper cup.

The urge to drive off and leave them both there was pretty strong, and was tempered mainly by a blanket of white fog, thicker than anything I had ever seen, that was creeping in from the sea. It was consuming the bluffs and hills of the coastline and made driving something of a challenge – otherwise, I might have been long gone.

The urge to call up my namesake – the professional snowboarder in Vancouver seven years my senior – with the latest instalment of the *This Is The New Marie Show*, was also up there.

The urge to yell in Marie's face was also on the podium. Yell – the boyfriend-in-Canada line was good enough to resist me, but not him? Yell – what the fuck was that?

Just as I was thinking that I needed to act on one of these urges in order to salvage at least a little dignity, the passenger door opened and Marvin got in.

"You're still here," he said.

"You're very perceptive," I said.

"Look, Alex..."

The brief window of opportunity for punching him square in his tanned jaw came and went.

"What?"

"I'm sorry."

"What are you sorry for?"

"For… you know."

"No, I do not know."

"Alex, come on…"

He faltered. I was not going to make it easy. I wasn't even going to confirm his suspicion that I had lain awake in wide-eyed horror while he screwed my ex-girlfriend six feet away from me. I wanted him to wallow in his *does-he-doesn't-he* doubt. I was going to be as passive and dumb as possible. It was a sit-in. I was going to make him *say* it.

Plus, if I confirmed that I knew precisely what fluids had been exchanged – not to mention where and when – I would then be backing myself into a corner that would force me to make a decision. Stuff the coffee cup up his arse and abandon the whole trip before we'd really got going, or simply press on, thereby giving my implicit acceptance. If I did that, then they might happily accept my blessing and throw caution to the wind.

So best, I felt, to fudge, stall and defer – a much maligned and underestimated social and political tactic.

"Come on, we need to get going," I said.

He got out. It was another hour before they got themselves together. When Marie got in the car, she murmured *hello* to me and didn't say much else. To my horror I found that I actually felt a little bit sorry for her, and when the three of us were on the road again my righteous anger began to dissolve, and I felt – bizarrely – that I didn't want the bubble to burst. I wanted to recapture that feeling that had been growing from seed from the moment we left, and which had come on exponentially since Marvin and I had discussed Kerouac at Burger King. Such was this innate desire that I was almost willing to be the mug and tolerate whatever activity was going to be on the menu. Maybe it was just my fucking problem after all.

As if trying to escape the funk of sheets in a San Simeon motel room, I put my foot down and we pulled away on the PCH as much as the conditions would allow, racing past Hearst Castle and north. The fog had lifted a fraction, and the sea was just visible. Under the canopy of cloud, it was a dull grey-blue, like a shark's back.

We drove for a couple of hours straight, and around mid-morning the highway began to twist like coiled vertebrae as we began the run along the peninsulas of the Santa Lucia range, into the Ventana wilderness and the heavy leafy shade of the Los Padres National Forest.

We stopped for gas. Those hoodlums at the rental company gave me a car with no cap on the petrol tank, and the attendant – a one-armed old biker with a braided white beard and prison ink that had faded to the point of being indecipherable – raced off to find one for me.

"How long does the road twist like this for?" I asked when he came back, palming him a couple of bucks. He was wearing a yellow singlet with *Riot Engineering, Oakland 1971* written on it in faded blue lettering.

"All the way to Monterey," he answered, tunefully.

"I'm glad the fog has lifted, then."

"Most mornings in summer it's like that. The north-westerlies sweep the warm water away, and when the cold water wells up in its place, it's like Neptune's beard growing all over the land."

I started to feel better, and managed to share a laugh with Marvin, Marie chipping in with her observations about the journey. We stopped at Big Sur – Henry Miller's place, where Kerouac came to die. In the gift shop I bought a Miles Davis tape, a guitar keyring to hang off the mirror and a bunch of other novelty crap for no good reason – including, bizarrely, a massive Honda bumper pennant that said PARIS-DAKAR 1982.

Marvin continued browsing. I went outside to wait and looked out at the sea. The day had ripened into glorious warmth, the Pacific like royal blue tinfoil. The gift shop was part of a ranger centre perched on an outcrop over the bluffs. There was a sheer drop to the broad tops of a cluster of redwoods, and then a further plummeting descent to the ocean beyond, where green islands and rocks were visible as land met water.

Marie appeared a few feet away. She looked guilty, expectant, toeing the dirt like a child anticipating a fierce telling-off.

I felt a moment's relief. The new sexual independence didn't seem to be synonymous with total disregard for my feelings, which, I supposed, was something.

I walked up to her. She looked up at me, eyes wide. It was a moment before I said anything.

"I was awake last night, if that's what you're wondering."

She looked crestfallen.

"I guessed you probably were."

"Then why did you do it?" I said, trying to keep my voice level. Other questions rose like bile: *did you like it did you come how does he compare did you want him tell me how it felt were you wet how big is he don't you love me were you desperate for him did you forget me…* but I pushed them down.

"I… don't know," she said after a moment, killing my vigour stone dead.

"Cop-out, Marie," I said.

"I've… I've never had a one-night stand before."

What did that mean? That it was the start of some beautiful and lasting union? Or that it was another one ticked off Marie's pre-millennium bucket list?

I was distracted by a shadow moving above me, behind Marie. At first I thought it was a gull or something similar, but I realised the midday shadow was too large, and I looked up to see the sprawling wingspan and magnificent tailfeathers of an enormous bird of prey, circling about fifty feet away.

"Alex…" Marie's voice said.

"Sssh," I whispered. I didn't take my eyes from the beast, but took her gently by the shoulders and spun her around. "Look."

"Oh my…" she said, squeezing my hand, hard.

"What is it? A falcon?" I said.

"I think… I think it might be a condor," she said.

The creature swooped and soared, almost boastful in its grace. It was clearly not hunting, and seemed to be putting on a casual display purely for our benefit. It was a nice thought, anyway.

There was no sound other than the beat of its wings against the air and Marie's breathing beside me. At one stage I couldn't tell one from the other. There might have been the distant rumble of waves and a low hubbub from the gift shop, but I had tuned them out. I just stared, transfixed by this majestic creature.

Marie started to fumble beside me, but by the time her camera was at the ready, the bird had taken flight and dived lazily towards the redwoods, where it was swallowed up by a carpet of green.

"I got it."

We both turned to see Marvin, his face partly shaded by the wooden roof of the gift shop, his camera held aloft.

"Beautiful creature," he said.

We walked back to the car. I took hold of Marie's wrist as she was getting in.

"Just don't throw it in my face, Marie," I said.

She nodded, and offered nothing more. Maybe she thought she'd got off lightly. Maybe she thought I had no business being angry with her. It was, after all, uncommon ground. She'd seldom apologised or backed down when we were together, which was both down to her occasionally obstinate manner, but also the age gap. When you're with someone older than you, it takes a while for the assumption that they know best to wear off.

We got on the road again. Marvin obviously knew Marie and I had exchanged words, and it was awkward again for a little while. Concentrating on the road was a welcome – and, as it turned out, necessary – distraction.

We hit the freeway at Monterey and booted straight into San Francisco. I felt like I was driving into a dream.

Kevin from Borders had mentioned Lombard Street was good for accommodations, and so we cruised up and down for a motel, eventually landing at the Royal, which seemed to fit the vital criteria of half-decent / cheap / not full. I was amazed. To date any attempt on my part to spontaneously wing it had never met all three.

Marvin said he wanted two rooms, and was happy to spring for the extra. Credit to him, he didn't just turn to address the elephant in the room – he ran at it, got it in a headlock and wrestled it to the ground, screaming.

"We'd save money if we just had one," I said, hoping my wanton dumbness made him uncomfortable – and, I supposed, some half-arsed hope that he might be persuaded to keep it in his pants. Marie was silent throughout this debate, and clearly a success where my interminable attempts to induce discomfort were concerned.

Money was exchanged, papers were signed, and then the deal was done. They went off to their room, and I went to mine. They didn't quite go hand in hand – Marie hung back in some kind of indecisive stalemate, but eventually followed, and a more bald statement of intent and exclusion could scarce be found. Standing there, like a lemon, it suddenly seemed like the right path to take had been the stuffing-of-coffee-cups-up-arses after all.

The neatly made bed was huge and empty. I took a shower and lay down, the quilted bedspread cool on my skin, with just Rocky IV on the TV for company, and thought about finding a nice San Franciscan lady for company tonight, in an attempt to cleave some kind of born-again freedom from the – frankly rather surreal – situation.

I was taking some kind of atavistic pleasure in Dolph Lundgren knocking seven bells out of Carl Weathers when there was a knock at the door.

Marvin stood there, alone. He came in and sat on the bed, looking sheepish and embarrassed, and he apologised over and over for 'putting the moves on my lady.' A small part of me wanted to tell him to shove it, a slightly bigger part of me was irritated at the thought that the show of contrition was exactly that, but in the end I opted to be a man about it – or rather, to park my own disquiet in favour of not wrecking what I perceived to be a potentially strong friendship. I mean, hey, if someone can pork your ex and still come through as best mate material, you can overcome anything, right?

"I'm sorry, dude," he said again.

"For fuck's sake, will you stop saying that?"

"I just…"

"Look, Marv, third wheel aspect aside, Marie is not my lady," I heard my voice saying. "We split up years ago. She went to Canada a year ago for kicks, and when she heard I was coming to California to do the same, she wanted to hook up. We're just mates. I haven't seen her in a year, and we broke up years before that. Do what you need to do."

"You're a mug," he said, looking at his feet.

"You misunderstand. I am totally cool with it. Have a bit of tact when I'm around – like you would your mother-in-law – but otherwise, go for it. I'm having too much fun to let it spoil things."

"Me too. I really am."

It was a bit off the terraces, but we shook and hugged, and then it occurred to me that a paraphrased version of this exchange would probably get back to Marie, and so I added a bilious postscript.

"I don't let women spoil good friendships. That's more important than some chick I dated a million years ago. She means nothing to me, mate."

As he released me, Marie arrived, clearly aware we had been talking about her.

"When you two lovebirds are finished, I'm starving."

Marvin clapped me on the shoulder.

"Excellent point. We need to get out and see the city. Get some drinkies into us," he said.

"Good idea."

We filed out, and he turned to me as we left, in order to draw parallels with the weird arrangement between Neal Cassady, Carolyn Cassady and Kerouac.

"She was doing both of them, you know," he said.

"Yeah," I said, looking at Marie. "Reckon I'm missing out on the best part of that comparison, though."

He roared with laughter – to my mind, just a little too hard.

CHAPTER THIRTEEN

ORGAN GRINDER

There was a common saying that Los Angeles was full of beautiful women. I'd been party to the odd glimpse, but the unglamorous circles I'd been moving in to date – riding the bus, fleapit motels – meant they had been far from abundant in my eyes.

San Francisco seemed to be different, however. They were funking everywhere. (I could hear one of my roofer buddies, Ian, in my head, landing ever-expanding social theories that became more earnest with each pint, that the imbalance of homosexual men meant that said gorgeous women would be *desperate* to boot.)

Although, when I thought about it, there had been more than a handful of bright-eyed cute things at the Venice Beach Cotel. And Marvin's flatmate, Zephi, was clearly an A-list model. She was obviously taken, but anyway.

As my thoughts drifted to idle fantasies of Zephi and Marie wrestling in a mudpit, I realised that I simply hadn't noticed the women in LA because I had been glued to Marie – both visually and through some hideous sense of runaway anticipation that was like an outboard motor in its persistence. Alas, it seemed that this dry-mouthed hopefulness had not only been to the exclusion of all else – not least my surroundings – but that in the intervening period certain colours had been nailed to certain masts in a determined fashion.

The net result of this brain-aching self-analysis was that I was now very much seeing the women in San Francisco, and I hoped that the two-guys-and-a-girl thing would not mean they wouldn't see me. If it did, well, I would just have to do something about that.

"You'll find him," Marie said.

"Huh?"

"Rosco. You'll find him. You'll find Camille too."

She had come over to join me at the table I had claimed while she and Marvin went to the bar.

"Take a seat," I said, and moved the chairs round a bit so she could sit. "I won't find Camille. She's long gone. I'm trying to forget about her."

I fixed my gaze on hers as I said it. She didn't miss the fairly clunky meaning.

"You don't need to forget about her. She'll always be yours."

I wanted to make a wisecrack about the analogous jousting, but it fell over in my mouth just as Marvin appeared with three beers on a tray.

"This all you got?" I said.

"A loosener," he said. "We've lots to get through."

"Amen to that."

We had walked down to Fisherman's Wharf, Alcatraz a smudge in the distance between the two bridges, and had parked ourselves in a seafood restaurant with a view of the Bay. The waitress, a pretty young redhead who moved like a cat and didn't make eye contact, sat us down and brought three more beers along with menus and a basket of bread rolls.

"Jesus, look at these prices," I said.

"I don't like seafood," Marie said.

Marvin froze mid-gulp, having virtually emptied his first bottle already.

We were close to the door, the waitress busy behind the counter. The silent agreement passed between us and we hurried out as discreetly as possible.

As we slowed to a walk, fifty metres up the boardwalk, Marvin dished out the six beers he had retained from the table.

"You brought the beers?" I said.

"The bread, too," he said, indicating bulging jacket pockets with the lip of a napkin poking over the top.

"Did you pay for them?" Marie asked.

"Well, I sort of flung a note behind me as we left. I couldn't swear which President's head was on it, though. I worry our waitress might be seeing George Washington grinning up at her from the floor."

Marie and I looked nervously back down towards the restaurant.

"We'd better maintain our pace," he said.

We found a half-decent Chinese restaurant on Pier 39 and positioned ourselves accordingly. Beer in chunky bottles was delivered to the table. I couldn't help but watch Marie drink hers. Some women just look wrong drinking beer. Marie looked hot as hell, effortlessly so.

"Brutal honesty," Marvin reminded the table. His camera was hooked around his neck, and he began snapping his environment, although *documenting* it was probably more accurate.

"Christ, you two," I said. "Give me another beer."

Marvin pushed one across the table to me. The red-and-blue label read *Spitfire*. I idly noted that Marvin had managed to acquire real ale in a garishly lit Chinese restaurant many miles away from the English countryside, but I was too preoccupied to dwell particularly long on the fact.

Our body language, I noted, was largely unchanged. We were equally spaced at the small round table. Marie might even have been sitting slightly closer to me – albeit this was probably because Marvin tended to need a lot of elbow room when he talked.

The point was – she was not sidling up to him, nor were they closing me out. We were equidistant, which was the best way to have a genuine, three-way conversation. We could have been playing poker. I may have been hyper-sensitive to every tic, twitch and gesture, but then so were they, probably. We all seemed to still be pals, we three, and I found myself quietly relieved at the notion. For some idiotic reason, this seemed to be more important than anything at that moment. I wanted to be able to *say* this, but felt far too dry to do so.

As if sensing this, Marvin reached in his pocket and put down a small black item in the centre of the table. For a second I thought it was a chocolate bar, and then I realised what it was, although it was smaller and more discreet than any model I'd ever seen before.

"What… is *that*?" Marie said.

"See your tape recorder, raise you two Duracell and a pair of earphones."

"Social experiment," Marvin explained. "Did it all the time in college."

"How's it work?" I said.

"Very simple. You press record, get progressively more drunk, record everything, replay the whole lot when you're sober, and then again when you're drunk."

"For what purpose?" Marie said.

"Deconstruction and analysis," Marvin said, with a solemn expression. "If you haven't documented *everything*, how do you know you've lived?"

"This is a tape recorder?" she said, picking it up and examining it. "It's tiny."

Marvin caught my eye for a fraction of a second.

"Strictly speaking, it's not a tape recorder, because there's no tape," he said.

"What's it record onto, then?" I said.

"It's digital – records directly onto a little memory card. Got it from a mate in the biz. He gets all the new prototypes first. He's the one that put me onto those DVDs I was telling you about."

"Divvy… what?" Marie said.

"Tell you later," I said.

"Not only that," Marvin said, "but I just signed up to a new website that lets you download music for free. No discs, no tapes, no records – you just log on and go. You can have the entire Willie Nelson back catalogue beamed from cyberspace into your living room in an instant, a bit like that scene in Willy Wonka where they transmit the chocolate bar from the television set into the factory. The Napster, I think it's called. I tell you, the world is going places. Assuming we survive the millennium bug, of course."

"Is that legal?" Marie asked.

Marvin frowned at his glass, as if the idea hadn't really occurred to him.

"So if there's battery life to consider, three ales are not going to get us very far, no matter how real they are. We'd better get cracking," I said.

"Time to get spitfaced," Marvin said, waving his bottle at me.

I stood up and made for the bar. As I did so, I felt a sudden wave of paranoia wash over me. Expecting to see the pair of them fly together like magnets the moment my back was turned, I chanced a look back over my shoulder.

They were not canoodling. They did not even look like they were consumed by an urge to do so and were only resisting out of courtesy to me. In fact, the picture was exactly as I would have expected had they not fucked less than thirty-six hours and ten feet from me – Marvin was talking earnestly, his hands flying about all over the place – possibly lecturing on the DVD revolution – while Marie sipped her beer, her eyes flicking to me as she put her bottle back on the table.

I ordered more ale, and then we switched to sweet lager like fizzy pop when the food arrived. It was a good meal, spread out across every inch of the table, and the smell awakened the appetite I had worried might become utterly dormant.

My legs felt heavy when we left, and yet again my hunger for music was commensurate with my alcohol intake. We walked on up the boardwalk to Jack's, a bar boasting an array of 110 draught beers – Marvin and I made an impossible pact to try all of them. Our table was undisturbed by too much in the way of passing foot traffic, and with a view of the Bay out of the window. I had a feeling we were going to hole up here for the night.

"We need to be systematic about this," said Marvin.

Marvin and I ordered half-pints of the first three beers on tap. Marie had tired of beer, and opted for a cocktail of some sort.

In the corner was a portly Mexican guy with an acoustic guitar playing sad Spanish songs. A placard leaning against his amp said his name was Skinny Pedro. He was pretty damn good, but the urge to go up and kick his fat ass off the stage was nevertheless rather strong.

Marvin clinked his glass against mine, and we both drained Beer #1 of 110 together.

"It's okay," I said. "A bit pissy, perhaps."

"An occupational hazard where pale ale is concerned, I guess." Marvin said. He slid both forearms across the table towards me, palms down. Marie watched, chewing the olive from her cocktail glass.

"You," he said, making fists and then straightening both his index fingers, "have suffered the unmitigated agony of unrequited teenage love. Am I right?"

"You bet your backside I have," I said.

"I knew it. Another shared experience, old boy. I'd know a brother anywhere. Whereas you…" he said, rotating his left arm across the table towards Marie – "…have not. Correct?"

"If, by unrequited love, you mean pining like a lovesick puppy for someone who either cannot or will not acknowledge you exist, then no, I most certainly have not," Marie said.

"That is what I thought," Marvin said, resting his forehead momentarily on the table.

"In my experience it is the preserve of fourteen-year-old boys," she said.

Marvin stretched an arm around my shoulders.

"An inescapably shared experience for us both, I'm afraid," Marvin said. "You first," he said, releasing me. "Brutal honesty," he added.

I didn't know where to start. Most – in fact, nearly all – of the women I had encountered in my life since hitting double figures had involved some form of dry-mouthed hormone-wrapped fascination –

classmates, co-stars, neighbours, mother's friends. So I tried telling them a spontaneous composite of several experiences, which was mired in self-consciousness induced by Marie's presence. It wasn't very good.

Marvin noticed. He sat back in his chair, an unimpressed look on his face. It felt like some of my job interviews, and whatever Marvin meant by brutal honesty, I wasn't getting it.

"You're not quite getting it," he said. "That will not cut the mustard with *this*," he said, tapping the dictaphone. "Let me school you."

And he did. His story, to my surprise, was only a couple of months old. He'd met some aspiring starlet at a launch party. Things had followed a fairly conventional route for several weeks – movies, walks, dinner – and had been going rather well until she ended things rather abruptly – just as Marvin's *corazon* had been opened and primed for something more. You'd never know it to hear him tell the story, but she seemed to have really knocked him for six.

"What happened?" I asked.

"It was one of four things," he said. "It was my drinking, my smoking, my sexual tastes, or the fact that I'm not far enough up the ladder to assist her career. Or all of the above," he added.

"Just not Hollywood enough, eh?" I said. I had tried to catch Marie's eye at the mention of sexual tastes, but she deliberately avoided it.

"Well, I went to see a shrink after she chucked me. I thought that was a pretty good concession."

"Really? You needed *counselling*?"

"She cut me up bad, man," he said, and made a show of plunging a butter knife into his heart. "Besides, every other prick here is in therapy. It's very fashionable."

"I'm sorry, but you two are just sad," Marie said, finishing her cocktail.

I went to the bar and ordered Beers #4 through #9, and a gin and tonic for Marie. As I slipped my fingers into my wallet, I realised that the thickness of dollar bills under my hand was not particularly reassuring, but I did the mature thing by totally ignoring the worry and sense of responsibility, and duly handed my money over.

The girl busied herself with my order. A small television mounted behind the bar caught my eye while I waited, and the muted opening credits to *NYPD Blue* were playing. It got me thinking - and the idea only partly filled me with horror. The rest of it was a curious kind of excitement. Responsibility, security, respect. A salary. The unknown. Action. The guys in these shows, they loved coming to work. They might have been grim-faced and dramatic in their angst, but they'd rather be on the streets than pacing up and down their pea-green windowless brownstone apartments.

Because they were in charge. Not of their colleagues, or the criminals, but of themselves. They knew their stuff. They weren't *rookies*. The foremen on my roofing crew were bullish, rough, union men, who didn't give a hoot about how they spoke to people. The police detectives wouldn't have to take that. I was only twenty, but I was already tired of being kicked around like a skivvy.

As the 'L' train thundered past in a flash of red and yellow light and the camera jerked between the skyscrapers, I got a strange feeling in the back of my head, and I realised I was grinding my teeth. I thought: when the partying is over and it's time for Life to get Serious – is that where I'm going to end up?

CHAPTER FOURTEEN

IMMATURE STUDENT

"Drinking game," Marvin announced when I returned to the table with the tray. "'I've never…' Ready?"

"Like a coiled spring," I said. "I'll start, if you like. I've never… crashed a car."

Marvin and Marie both took a drink.

"You said you can't drive," Marie said to Marvin.

"Probably why I crashed it. Okay, lady, you next."

Marie stuck out her lower lip while she thought.

"I've never… shoplifted."

Marvin and I took a drink. Marie shook her head in mock-disgust – at least, I think it was mock – and looked to me.

"Your turn, pumpkin," she said.

"Thank you, honey-bunny," I said.

Marvin's eyes were flicking between us like a Wimbledon spectator.

"*Pulp Fiction* tribute," I explained. "There's a photo kicking about somewhere that I took of Marie recreating the Uma Thurman cover pose."

"No, there isn't," she interrupted. "My dad threw it away after he found it and saw me holding the cigarette."

"He *did?*" I said. "That's terrible. Your cleavage shot knocked spots off Uma's."

"What a dreadful shame," Marvin said to his glass. "Okay, back to business. I've never… scabbled."

Marie looked at him. I was the only one to drink.

"Say… what?" Marie said.

I stretched out in the chair, steepled my fingers and adopted the theatrical countenance of a seasoned lecturer.

"Scabbling is a process whereby a layer is skimmed off concrete, usually to prepare the surface for some form of treatment. When I first joined the trade, one of my first glamorous jobs was to scabble the flat roof of a high-rise – after picking up all the loose rubble and stones first, of course. Two hundred square metres of hardcore lawnmowing, fifty metres up, in the middle of February. Shockwaves up my arms like they were in a blender, but it was the only thing keeping the blood flowing. To this day I don't think the feeling has ever completely returned to my hands. It's a wonder I can play at all."

"Jesus," Marie said, quietly, looking at her glass. I couldn't read her meaning.

Marvin swigged his beer.

"What, now you realise you've actually done it?" I said.

"No, but it sounds so utterly joyless I had to drink," he said.

"It's good, honest work," I said, in a gruff Louisiana voice. "How do *you* know about it, anyway?"

"Old man used to dig roads. I heard him mention it. I never really knew what it was, though – just wanted to chuck in a low-baller. But it sounds like you're the expert."

"I'm lucky they kept me on. I broke three scabblers just doing that one roof. That was a record, apparently."

"That really is the blues."

"Okay, my turn," I said. "I've never cheated on an exam."

Marvin drank alone.

"Me now," he said, "or you two will fall behind. I've never killed an animal."

Nobody drank.

"Brutal honesty," Marvin said.

Marie slowly took a drink. We both turned to look at her.

"I hit a fox once," she said in a small voice. "In my Citroen."

"Did you stop?" Marvin said.

She shook her head.

"So how do you know it was dead?"

Marie said nothing, but she looked very unhappy.

"What about you?" I said to Marvin, moving it along. "That giant moth."

"Ah, that was an attempt only. I told you: it refused to die."

"Your turn, Marie," I said.

She gave a big sigh, shaking off the memory. "I've never... been arrested."

Marvin took a drink. Marie and I looked at him.

"It was a stitch-up," he said, shrugging. "Come on, Alex."

"Hang on, I want to hear about this," Marie said.

"All in good time," Marvin said. "The idea is that you save the interrogations and confessions for later."

"You mean, when we're all paralytic?" Marie said.

"Exactly. Alex, the floor is yours."

"Okay," I said, thinking. "I've never... had a homosexual experience."

Marie licked her lips and frowned, then presumably decided there was no point in playing a game like this by halves, and so she took a drink.

"Holy shit!" Marvin said, spilling half his drink in excitement.

"You still want to save the confessions for later?" I said.

He coughed and held up his index finger.

"Why? You *know* about this?"

I shrugged.

"Christ. But yes," he said. "Rules of the road. Okay, back to me," Marvin said. "I've never... had a relationship with someone older than me."

Both Marvin and I took a drink.

"Hang on a minute," Marie said. "If it's your turn and you've done the thing you're saying you've never done, then you've not never done it."

"Succinctly put," Marvin said. "Two answers to that. One: I like to drink. Two: I've done an awful lot."

For some reason, this comment irritated me, and so in a flash of one-upmanship, I said:

"Seventeen *years* older than you?"

I looked at Marvin, feeling Marie's stare boring into me. She didn't say anything, but I could feel the questions bubbling to the surface like a tidal wave.

"Save it for later," Marvin said, smirking like he'd *planned* to entrap me. "Your turn, lady."

Marie didn't take her eyes from me, but picked up her glass and emptied it – apparently without realising.

"Okay," she said. "I've never paid for sex."

I grimaced, and took a drink. So did Marvin. Marie's eyes widened like saucers.

"I'm not sure I can play this game much longer," she said.

"Precisely!" Marvin said. "That's why you drink. To allow the lava-flow of honesty to melt away your discomfort. Ultimately you'll find it very liberating."

"What in hell are you talking about?" I said.

"No, I mean, my glass is empty," Marie said.

"Of course!" Marvin said, leaping to his feet. "I shall pop to the little boys' room, and be right back."

Behind us, Skinny Pedro moved into a pretty slick rendition of *Pieces of a Man*. Marie stood up, and held out her hand. Her abs were at eye level, and I had to stand just to get them out of my mind.

"Dance, mister?"

There wasn't a dance floor as such, just a small space in front of Pedro. She led me to it and put her arms around my neck.

"The human noose," I said.

She raised an eyebrow.

"So how exactly does one achieve a stomach you can cut your finger on?"

152

"You don't even want to know. The sit-up is the most revolting thing the human race has ever created," she said.

"Hmm. As I recall, you always hated the story of *The Ugly Duckling*."

"Well, it *would* have been much more rock 'n' roll if John Travolta had turned into a studious bookworm at the conclusion of *Grease*. But your illicit Mrs Robinson affair is a *far* more interesting subject."

I stumbled slightly as we moved, and caught her toe under my heel.

"Oh, I see. Well, I don't think that's really fair. You hearing about it before Marvin, I mean."

"Are you kidding? You're about to make some kind of earth-shattering disclosure about your sex life and I get to hear about it along with the rest of the audience?"

"Maybe you should get used to it. I mean, when I start doing talk shows and interviews, all kinds of personal questions will get asked, and you'll just have to listen with the rest of America."

"That mean you're not planning on coming home?"

"Shit, I'd rather hang myself. What about you?"

"I thought we were going to New York together. Come on, who was she?"

She moved forwards, and rubbed her lower lip against mine. I pulled away.

"No fucking way," I said. Maybe she was more intoxicated than I thought. Or maybe I was intoxicated by the sudden, fleeting, inverse power of rejection. She stepped back and swung her fist into my gut, laughing. I think she was fooling around, but it winded me nonetheless.

Marvin came back as I was doubled over, and he must have wondered what he had missed. He went back to the table via the bar, where Marie and I joined him once I had recovered. The dancing made me realise that I was pretty well oiled. I was fortunate not to have thrown up.

Both of them were staring at me expectantly as I sat down.

"Wait. We've got a lesbian experiment and a criminal history between us as well. Why do I have to go first?"

"There is no criminal history," Marvin said. "I just told you it was a fit-up. Besides, you're outvoted."

I sighed, and told them the story of Karen Phillips.

She was my GCSE English teacher, and, later on, my 'A' Level tutor. My 'A' Level had necessitated additional one-on-one tuition after hours – not, I hastened to add to the table, due to any academic shortfalls on my part, but because I was trying to cram a two-year course into one year, the consequence of putting the binary tedium of Computer Science in the bin after a couple of terms.

Nothing happened while I was actually a student – and I became too preoccupied with the intensive work schedule to notice the frisson of sexual tension that grew steadily over nine months – but thanks to her, I smashed it and got an 'A.'

She sent me a card congratulating me after I got my results, and I sent her one back with a bunch of flowers thanking her for all her commitment and for believing in me. She wrote back, in more general terms. She used this expensive scented paper and envelopes, and she often included postcards of obscure art and French movies. She had the most incredible handwriting – my roofer's scrawl must have seemed like bloody cave drawings to her. Maybe she liked that. Then again, she had seen the evolution of my writing from my first wittering attempts to deconstruct Wilfred Owen to something supposedly approaching a cogent argument. Maybe she believed I would be more than a roofer.

I replied again, giving her an overview of my life plans, which included attempting a novel. She replied with various encouraging sentiments, signing off with a couple of kisses. I replied, with more kisses. She invited me to hers for dinner. I didn't need to tell Marvin and Marie much more than that.

Karen lived alone in a very large Victorian apartment in the middle of the city. It had varnished wooden floors and high ceilings and Tiffany lamps. It had dark wood furniture and large sofas and Twenties art-deco stuff all over the place. It had been tremendously exciting. I felt like I was playing at being a grown-up. She had a turntable and seemed to only ever play Billie Holliday records. She smoked. I smoked. We cooked and drank wine and made love practically everywhere. Like I said, this all happened only *after* I left college, but when she first kissed me she said:

"I've been wanting to do that for years."

Marie, having been taught by the same woman a year or two earlier, was utterly stunned. She had no idea. She verbalised the chronology and worked out that although Karen – Marie still referred to her as Miss Phillips, which I thought was hilarious – had tutored me before Marie and I got together, we started seeing each other the year after Marie and I split up.

"You never said," she said.

"Wasn't any of your business," I replied, after a moment. It came out more sharply than intended, which I put down to the drink, but it was already too late to do anything about it.

She went very quiet.

"Now *that* is brutal honesty," Marvin said. "So, hold on, what did you say the age gap was?"

"Seventeen years," I said. "I was eighteen, she was thirty-five."

"*Ouch*." He clapped me on the back and proffered respect with a Labatt's.

I could have sugar-coated the pill a bit – if indeed, there was a pill to swallow at all. I could have said that it fizzled out pretty quickly. I could have said Karen started to want things that I clearly couldn't give her. I could have said that towards the end, she actually went a little bit psycho. I *could* have said that I never felt about her the way I did about Marie.

But I didn't.

The Jim Beam continued flowing while Marie and Marvin shared their own stories. Marie's I'd heard and did not want to hear again, but she definitely sexed it up on a number of levels – for whose benefit, I wasn't sure. Marvin's arrest story continues to be incriminating to this day.

Around 2am we fell out of Jack's and headed vaguely back towards the motel. We were utterly plastered by now, and I continued details of my sexual encounters in increasingly sanguine detail, including a garish – and only half-true – story about an S&M prostitute in Amsterdam.

Marvin talked incessantly on the way back, in a way that made me think he'd popped a little something in the bathroom. If he had, he didn't share.

My motel room began to spin like an astronaut's training simulator the moment I lay down, and so I stood up again to hold it at bay.

I walked over to the wall and pressed my ear against it, straining to hear the sounds of sexual gratification. I thought I heard some kind of high-pitched whimper, but I could just as easily have imagined it.

I couldn't go to sleep yet. It would be disastrous.

I went out onto the balcony, and, after a moment, walked down to the reception office. I got a Mountain Dew from the vending machine, its lone, pale green glow like a beacon in the gloom.

Next to the ice chest was a payphone. In a moment of drunken madness, I thought it would be a good idea to call Zephi, see if anyone had called about Camille. Some distant part of my brain told me it was the middle of the night, that I would wake the baby, but I rationalised it by telling myself that these Hollywood types didn't keep regular hours.

Nobody answered, which was probably fortunate all round. It clicked through to voicemail and I hung up. I wandered the streets for a while, looking for somewhere I could check my email, then eventually decided it could probably wait till the morning.

When I got back I stopped in the car park and stared at the car. I thought – briefly – about taking it for a spin, but I wasn't so drunk to think that this would be a good idea.

A plain white Kia sedan rental. A more nondescript car was hard to imagine. Here I was, trying – supposedly – to get noticed, but it was never going to happen all the time I was driving around one of the world's most vibrant cities in a car that was about as interesting as a tax return.

Something had to be done about it.

CHAPTER FIFTEEN

THE DIRE LOG

"Jesus."

"What the hell happened?"

The voices were the first thing I was aware of. The rough velour of the back seat on my cheek was the next. The sun burning my legs through the glass was the next. It had apparently done a fine job of burning up the fog, and it felt well past mid-morning.

I had fallen asleep on the back seat in a position that no sober person could have fallen asleep in.

"Alex, what did you do to the *car*?" Marie's voice was incredulous.

I hauled myself out and joined Marvin and Marie in front of the car.

"I kinda like it," Marvin said.

"Oh, fuck," I said.

The car was no longer a plain white boring sedan. In my inebriated state I had apparently got the idea to, well, make it a bit more… interesting.

The PARIS-DAKAR rally sticker took pride of place above the grille. Above it, on the hood, I had sprayed BABY-FACED BLUES in blue and red bubble letters. Using white sticky labels I had pasted the word 'LUV' on the top of the windscreen above the passenger side, and 'HAIGHT' above the driver's side.

On the driver's door I had written "*Want the blues? …*" with a marker pen. Then, on the rear passenger door I had written "… *Tune a harp*." On the rear bumper I had written '*Babies + motorbikes = world peace*.' The roof aerial was decorated with Bay seashells. The front offside tyre

I had painted red. The rear nearside tyre had white stripes painted at intervals, so it looked like a zebra. A fake raccoon tail hung from the exhaust. Two sets of those joke fingers that look as though someone's trapped in the trunk were stuck to the lid. The headlights had been turned into great big eyes. There was a huge treble clef painted on the roof. It was a bit amateurish, but it *did* stand out.

"Well, if you wanted to attract attention, that's one way of doing it," Marie said. "What are the people from the rental company going to say?"

"I… I don't know," I mumbled, genuinely flabbergasted by my own endeavours. Where the hell had I got a marker pen and spray paint?

We drove through the city to an underground car park on Columbus Avenue, where we paid a Mexican guy $5 to watch the car all day. The sign said $10, but he was apparently most enamoured of the décor job.

City Lights Bookstore was intoxicating. We soaked up Beats all day, hours spent rooted to the floor, drinking in words that just made me want to sing. I bought *Howl*. Marvin bought Kerouac's *Big Sur*.

"That's how I'm going out," he said. Marie got upset at the morbid – and probably accurate – prediction.

"Get a fucking life," I said, clapping him on the shoulder.

The book became a marker on him, the lettering of the title forever poking out of the pocket of his trademark coarse sport coat every time I looked at him.

From a payphone on Cooper and Jackson I called home. It was a fumbled conversation. The first thing they asked about was Camille, naturally. I glossed over the negative answers and instead repackaged my being sluiced by Vegas into a quaint, entertaining story. Dad was still aghast, but he was half-cut, which made me wish I was.

The call brought forth a wave of homesickness – the kiss of inertia and lethargy for someone trying to think about eking out an existence in another country. Marie saw my face as I hung up, and squeezed my hand, which made me feel worse.

We went for coffee at Coppola's café, and a syrupy espresso fired me up no end. Christ, it was better than speed, and I pranced around outside with Marvin trying to decide if it was THE Zoetrope building.

In Market Street I relaxed a little among the canyon of skyscrapers – something conspicuously absent in Hollywood – and got a pang for the fierce wonder of NYC, the contingency endgame of my trip. I had never seen the place, and the sudden urge to drop everything and bolt across the continent to take refuge in Manhattan was extraordinarily powerful. The rate I was going, 'endgame' was going to be around sooner than I thought.

Marvin got into an argument with some crusty virgin wearing a sandwich board proclaiming the ills of all kinds of sex.

I nudged Marie.

"I hope you're paying attention."

A man with shoe polish on his face who was wrapped from head to foot in Bacofoil walked past us, shouting "It was Adam and EVE, not Adam and STEVE!"

Nearby was a queue of people waiting to get into a cinema, and he began to stalk up and down it, yelling at the customers. Marvin's attention turned from the crusty to the foil-wrapped homophobe, and he engaged him head-on in a fierce debate – much, I guessed, to the relief of the bemused bunch who just wanted to see *Austin Powers*.

After a frank exchange of views the man began to scream incoherently; a guttural, high-pitched sound. When Marvin started to match him for volume, it became apparent that the guy was starting to freak right out, so Marie and I coaxed Marvin away.

We walked miles, getting off the tourist trail onto back streets with adobe warehouses, wire-fenced compounds, clapboard liquor stores and grimy working wharves. This was at Marvin's insistence, to find the REAL San Francisco. We gave it up after he asked a couple of psychos to take our picture, and we ended up legging it. To this day I'm not entirely sure why – maybe it's just that Marvin had the kind of face people liked to hit.

We holed up in the aerial bar of the Marriott, drinking thick beer and recounting stories of drunken exploits which somehow morphed into impressions of various cartoon characters. Marvin and I were pretty evenly matched on this score, and had Marie in fits of laughter as we took in the sprawling sight of the city below, stitched out like a robot's close-up.

At the motel we changed and took the car over to Haight-Ashbury. To the astonishment of Marvin and I, Marie had never seen *Bullitt*, and so for her benefit I attempted to emulate the car chase on the hills of San Francisco, something that did little to endear me to my fellow motorists.

Tattoo parlours, porn, music – it was beatnik central, but it was like Haight-Ashbury™. As I tried to photograph the famous sign, a cute blonde girl with a gold chain link belt and tight white jeans flipped me the bird. I adjusted the shot to include her, so she grinned and held the pose.

"You bloody cheeky cow," I said, and she blew me a kiss.

I lowered the camera and grinned at her, suddenly feeling rather pleased with myself, and then saw Marie watching with one eyebrow raised. I cocked my head.

The Asqew Grill provided the best meal of the trip so far. With simple straight-back wooden chairs, small counter and whitewashed walls it looked like somebody's kitchen.

The absence of an alcohol licence only added to this – doubtless entirely deliberate – image, and so we obeyed the BYOB instruction on the door and dashed off to buy a bottle, leaving the attentive waiter to bring us glasses. He uncorked it for us and poured, so, when added to the square no-nonsense food, it was all rather neat.

Marvin had picked the wine – a rather inviting-looking Napa Valley cabernet that immediately induced me to start calculating walking distances back to Lombard. As designated driver for the entirety of this

West Coast weirdness, I watched Marie and Marvin imbibe for about thirty seconds before I drained my highball glass of mineral water and poured myself a glass of the wine.

Marie looked at me.

"Just one. Well, one and a bit. We can come back for the car tomorrow if we need to."

It went beautifully with what essentially amounted to a nouveau version of pie 'n' mash, and I got to thinking about my flash-love affair with the girl wearing the chain-link belt, whom I would never see again, but whose grinning middle-digit would forever be preserved on my camera.

Between courses I noticed a small booth in the corner of the room with a phone in it, and I stood up suddenly.

"I'm going to check in about Camille."

"Okay," Marvin said. "I might have to slip out for another bottle in a sec. All that beer has rather improved the taste of a fine wine."

I dialled the number, and butterflies suddenly started to ping-pong off my insides. How to introduce myself? 'Alex' might result in 'Alex who?' which would be disastrous, but entirely possible. I'd only met her once, and she was a jobbing actress with a husband in the biz – her social circles were doubtless huge. 'Alex Gray' might not fare any better – it sounded ridiculously formal, and in any event I had no idea whether Marvin had even told her my surname. I knew I hadn't. What about 'Alex, Marvin's friend?'

What about: why not save your blathering? Her husband might answer.

What about: why the hell are you worried about how you come across to a married woman with a young child?

What about: are they even aware that their housemate kindly offered up their phone number for public display across the Los Angeles metropolitan area?

Too late. She picked up.

"Hi, Zephi? It's Alex here – er, Harry's new best mate? We

stayed with you a couple of nights ago?"

"Oh, hi, Alex. Don't worry, I remember you. 'Mate' isn't yet a typical California colloquialism."

"Ah, we're working on it. Between me, Marvin and Roger I'm sure we'll get it settled into the lexicon."

"I doubt it. Roger's English accent disappeared the minute he passed over Nova Scotia."

I chuckled.

"But anyway," she said, "…how are you? How's San Francisco?"

"Foggy."

"Yeah, I bet. Best time to go to Alcatraz is when it's foggy. Really adds to the atmosphere. Anyway, what's up?"

"Well, I don't know if Marvin told you, but I wondered if you'd had any messages for me? My guitar got stolen, you see, and I put out a reward ad. Marvin said I could put his number down – except now I realise he was actually volunteering *your* number."

"That's okay. I'm afraid there's been nothing, though."

"No problem, thanks."

"What a lousy thing to happen to someone. How did it happen?"

"Don't ask. It's a bit like letting the winning lottery ticket blow away in a storm. I'm such an idiot."

"Ah, it happens. You never know, it might turn up."

"Yeah, maybe. Hey, how is Harry?"

"He's good. He's here, if you want to talk to him?"

"Well…"

"Harry, honey," she said, calling away from the phone. "Remember the crazy Englishman who fed you breakfast? He's on the phone – do you want to speak?"

He apparently did. There followed a minute or two of fairly juvenile conversation – on both sides, it has to be said – before he got bored and ran off. The sound of the receiver hitting the laminate flooring bumped in my ear.

"Sorry about that," she said. "He loves talking on the phone. Thinks it's very grown-up."

"Not after speaking to me, he doesn't," I said.

She laughed.

"Good luck," she said. "I really hope your guitar turns up. Enjoy the rest of your trip – and if you do end up doing the Alcatraz tour, take off the headphones. Listen to everyone shuffling around like zombies. Makes you realise just how creepy the place is."

"Thanks, Zephi."

I hung up and went back to the table.

"What? Is there news?" Marie asked.

"News?"

"On Camille?" she said slowly, like I'd taken a blow to the head or something, and only then did I become aware of the residual grin on my face as I sat down.

"Oh. No, nothing, unfortunately. I've got to check my email yet, though. Where's Marvin?"

"He went out to get another bottle," she said. "You shouldn't flirt with married women, Alex."

"I don't know what you mean," I said. "Besides, how do you know it wasn't Roger?"

She pulled a face, but Marvin walked in clutching another Napa red under his arm, and she didn't labour the point.

"It occurs to me," he said as he sat down, "that, for someone here to conquer the States, as it were, we've heard precious little out of you. In terms of angst-ridden output, I mean."

I shrugged. I knew exactly what he meant. I'd experienced it before, when I was signing on and frantically jobless. With every failed day of phoning up for interviews and application forms, the imagination went into overdrive at the prospect of actually having to *work* one of these thankless occupations, to the extent that rejection brought a degree of relief.

So while, through necessity, the shortlist of tinpot situations vacant became ever longer, the incentive to continue became less. The inertia was self-perpetuating. Discouragement became dismay, which in turn became a thick wave of depression.

I realised Marvin was looking at me.

"What?" I said.

"You with us?" he said.

"Sorry," I said, and paraphrased my own take on the muck-spreading *ennui* that comes with trying to find work.

"Well, why don't you write a song about it?" he said.

I thought about it.

"You think?"

"Mate, you are preaching to the converted. Before I came here, I was a classically-trained dole scrounger. If there's one thing suited to the blues, it's being unemployed and skint. But shit, you can make it your own. Personalise all those horrible feelings you had when you were going through the Friday-Ad with your highlighter pen on a wet Wednesday morning with Richard-and-fucking-Judy on in the background. Then get out there and sing it."

"It's not a bad idea."

"You could pen it now. Look, I got some extra paper napkins. You could be done by the time we get to coffee and mints."

"I don't have my guitar."

He opened his mouth, but the waiter came over to open the wine, and so he exhaled loudly through his nose instead.

The waiter was a muscular guy with waves of yellow hair and a jaw sprinkled with sun-bleached stubble, and he looked from Marie to Marvin to me while he opened the bottle.

Marie leaned in after he'd gone, a huge grin on her face.

"He was giving you the eye."

"Don't be stupid."

"He *was*. He was trying to work out whether or not you're with me."

"And am I?"

She stopped smiling.

"What I was going to *say*…" Marvin said, leaning forward on his elbows, "…was that you are in the nerve centre of Sixties counterculture. Jerry Garcia cut his teeth over *there*, Janis Joplin lived over *there*, Dylan went electric over *there*. Can't you feel their energy?"

"Actually, I think Dylan went electric in Rhode Island."

But he wasn't listening.

"… you can practically still hear the fading first licks of Santana and CCR. The point is, we are toasting each other in the middle of Haight-sodding-Ashbury. We are not fucking tourists. We want to suck their footprints right out the concrete. There is nothing to stop you, Monsieur Gray, writing a song, borrowing a guitar from some crusty and going and sitting down right in the middle of the fucking street and singing your heart out until the cops come and remove you. Yes, you might spend the night in jail, but what a fucking story. You've already glitzed the car. There's no such thing as bad publicity. You will be *memorable*."

"I'm thinking about joining the police," I said.

A stunned silence descended over the table. No heads had turned during Marvin's rising monologue, but they did now he had stopped.

"You… what? You fucking what?" he said after a moment, in utter disbelief.

"You are?" Marie said. "You can't."

"And why's that?"

"You're a loose cannon."

"I'm a what?"

"All the rules and discipline. You'll hate it."

"It might be just what I need."

"Please, please," Marvin said. "Don't decide that now. Don't give up. Not here. It's sacrilegious."

"I said I was thinking about it."

"Are you sure? Are you so sure? Pulling up kerbside with your light bar strobing over the battered face of some poor dead debutante? All those horrendous brutal acts you'll seldom see but will be forced to imagine?"

"No, I'm not sure. For the third time, I'm thinking about it. The idea of a regular salary gets more appealing by the day."

"Christ, we need to get another bottle."

"Look, I'm bleeding money, I've barely played a note, and after eight days here all I've got is some casual invitation from a three-hundred-pound pimp who probably won't even remember me but who I'm clutching onto like a mail-order bride whose visa is about to expire."

Marvin twitched.

"I've got four application forms under my bed. One for the army, one for the navy, one for the Metropolitan Police and one for a management consultancy. They're all complete."

Marvin was shaking his head slowly.

"I made myself a promise. This trip was a deal breaker. Progress my music, or put them all in the fucking mail box."

"What does 'progress' mean?" Marie asked.

"Fuck, anything," I said. "A weekly slot in a semi-decent blues club with expenses covered would be a start. Actually, not ending the night in A&E would be a start."

"Hit bottom, the only way is up, I guess," Marvin said.

"But, shit, there are so many variables. Talent isn't enough. Contacts aren't enough. A self-built following isn't enough. You have to come along at the right time and tap into some consciousness, some niche, something that people don't know they want on a collective basis until it happens. And *that* is just random, but you can't bottle it. Why do you think huge studios with massive stars still manage to make flops? Image, sound, lyrics, even the tone of your bloody voice. And I'm just not sure I'm it. Since when have you heard of a nation subconsciously craving an ethnic minority labourer who plays the blues in his short pants?"

"Are you *kidding* me? What about Phil Lynott? Or Slash? Or that geezer from Rage Against The Machine?" Marvin said. "Or even Shirley bloody Bassey? I don't know about short pants, but you have to start young to work on your slow burn. And what about….. hang on."

He got up and ran out of the restaurant.

"He keeps doing that, they're gonna make us pay in advance," I said.

"Where's he gone now?" Marie said.

He was back in five minutes, clutching a rolled-up newspaper. It was some kind of cheaply-produced underground music rag, called *The Dire Log*. The cover featured a recent photograph of Jimmy Page onstage, in the midst of a grinding solo. He just looked like a decrepit science teacher to me, one of those old men whose lower lips are always glistening with wetness.

"Where'd you get that?" I said.

"Amoeba Music. I was reading it earlier," he said, smoothing out the pages on the table. "Check out *this* guy. He's a second-generation Mexican construction worker singing folk and blues in Detroit when Detroit was only interested in Motown. He played a few clubs, cut a couple of cheap records, kept on with the manual labour, then faded into obscurity. Rumour was that he'd topped himself."

"He didn't?" Marie said.

"He did not. One of his records found its way to South Africa and became *the* soundtrack of the anti-apartheid protests. He became huge in South Africa, but the guy had no idea – mainly because his label fleeced him. He kept carrying his hod and strumming in his front room, blissfully unaware that he was becoming a political legend on the other side of the world."

"Shit," I said, picking up the paper and leaning back in my chair. "So what happened?"

"That's the best bit," Marvin said. "After about twenty years some Springbok journalist tracked him down, told him he was a star, and he flew out to find more people waiting on the tarmac than when

168

the Beatles landed at JFK. He played a couple of huge gigs over there last year."

I absorbed the piece, which was, in the main, a review of the Cape Town gigs Marvin mentioned. The guy's name was Sixto Rodriguez. The main photo was of him onstage at the Belville Velodrome. He was a tall, slender man with Mexican blood, dressed entirely in black, with a shock of long black hair and opaque sunglasses, casting an enigma all around him.

"Don't tell me that isn't the best fucking story you've ever heard," Marvin said when I looked up. "Imagine being able to break the news to someone that they're a superstar."

I started off agreeing with him, that it was a great story, but then thought – if I had to work as a skint roofer into middle age with hands so beaten and scarred and riddled with iron shrapnel that they had no feeling, and only *then* found out that, ten thousand miles across the ocean, I'd been a superstar for years, I'd probably top myself. This guy was obviously blessed with more grace than I.

I suddenly wanted to know what a Rodriguez record sounded like.

"Come on, let's settle up and get out of here," I said. "Let's go and bother Amoeba Music. Bring the wine."

We finished our meal and headed back out onto Haight Street. Consideration of whether or not to leave the car was fast becoming a moot point, unless I wanted to chance making the acquaintance of San Francisco's finest.

As luck would have it, Amoeba Music was closing as I rushed up to the doors. Sorry, we're closing, said the douche with the ponytail and chin ringlets, but yeah, we probably have that Rodriguez album. Thanks, pal.

We had more luck at Reckless Records, where we bought a stack of second-hand tapes – not only did I find *Cold Fact* by the man Rodriguez, but I also picked up *Blood on the Tracks* for two dollars, and an early demo called *Bad Susie* by one Rosco Dunhill.

The only pisser was that it was on vinyl, which meant I couldn't play it in the car, but I turned the record over in my hands, lightly fingering the smooth sleeve. The cover vaguely resembled a Munch painting, but there was an inset panel with that same strange assortment of dollar bills and coins that I had seen before.

"One day, I'm gonna ask him about this," I said aloud.

A couple of people turned to look at me.

Back out on the street, Marvin was wired again – "Look at that guy! He's taking a piss! Fantastic!" – and so I pointed him in the direction of a guy with a tattoo on his face eating out of a bin.

Our attention was further diverted by some geezer on a soapbox declaring that the FBI kill WOMEN and CHILDREN.

Marvin caught my eye.

"You still considering, officer?" he said.

I don't know, I thought. *I really don't know.*

CHAPTER SIXTEEN

STRESSED DESSERTS

The lunchtime boozing and heavy walk back to Lombard led me to propose a siesta, which drew immediate consensus. Like a sleep-deprived idiot, I didn't twig the myriad hidden agendas and connotations, spontaneous or otherwise, that this suggestion could invite until I was back in my room. It was tantamount to saying: "Hey, I'm beat. Why don't you two go fuck like rabbits?"

What.

A.

Mug.

So, with a view to deflecting my attention from one depressing barrel of shit to another, I decided to stick my headphones on and do some forensic accounting.

I wished I hadn't.

Three hundred and seventy-four dollars. That was precisely what I had left. I flicked through the television channels to work out the date, and from there established that I still had another thirty-four nights to survive before my scheduled return flight – I was only eight or nine days into the trip, but it already seemed inevitable I would be using it. That meant a daily budget of about eleven dollars, which had to include food and accommodation.

The numbers didn't really fit. Had I really spent it all on booze? Even with my stroke of Vegas fortune?

Stress and worry have a curiously soporific effect on me, and I stretched out on the bed, thanking the wine for numbing the edges of my anxiety.

When I awoke it was getting dark. I had no idea of the time.

I must have set my body-clock adjustment back several days.

I called the airline – changing the date of my return would cost seventy-five dollars; changing my departure city from Los Angeles to San Francisco would be another hundred dollars on top of that.

'Administration charges,' the woman called them. It didn't really matter to me whether they called them administration charges, handling fees or booking levies – to me they were nothing but meaningless, arbitrarily imposed generators of bureaucratic revenue.

It occurred to me that, if you were the one providing the service, you could charge whatever the hell you liked for, well, whatever the hell you liked.

With this in mind, I hauled myself off the bed, picked up the Casino and the remainder of a bottle of Wild Turkey that seemed to have found its way into my room, and wandered out onto the balcony. I knocked carelessly a few times on Marvin and Marie's door, not really expecting an answer.

My room was on the third floor. I went down to the square, empty pool and sprawled on a lounger. The night was warm and still, the lamps in the pool casting a torpid, milky glow over everything. I stretched my neck back and the four sides of the motel rose up around me, with the purple sky beyond it. I felt like I was at the bottom of an elevator shaft, and any minute something would come plummeting towards me.

I sang *Five Long Years*. After a few generous helpings of the bourbon I was drunk enough that I cared not a fig for whether my expressive impulses were welcome or not – at worst, I would get into a fight; at best, someone might pay me to keep going. Either would have jolted me from my turgid navel-gazing, and I probably would have welcomed the opportunity to spar.

But the faint hubbub and sounds of life from Lombard gave me encouragement, and I took a swig from the bottle and went into *When The Levee Breaks*.

I started to feel better. Music, booze and the unwinding

feeling I got whenever I sang came together under a San Francisco sky, confined as it was by the four balconies of the motel's rooms.

Marvin came out onto the balcony, bare-chested. He was threading marshmallows onto a long stick. In the split-second before I realised it was him, I had an end-to-end fantasy about the mistress of a record exec coming out of the room they shared whenever he was here on business. She was all smiles, dressed for bed in a man's white business shirt, only half the buttons done up, her backside only just about covered. She brought whisky and sat on the timber deck beside me and offered to play one of my tapes to her cuckolding executive boyfriend.

But it was just Marvin.

"You ever had an epiphany?" he asked, as he arrived poolside.

"I did, once," I said, not looking at him. "But I traded it in for a Strat."

He snorted with amusement.

"You got a band?" he said.

"Just me," I said. "Guitar and voice, that's all you need."

"Worked for Robert Johnson. *Come Into My Kitchen?*" he said, offering me a marshmallow.

I looked at him.

"Is there anything you're not an expert on?"

"There is one way to guarantee success."

"Oh yeah?"

"You could die."

"What?"

"Yeah, yeah. You're – what – twenty? Shit, crack on for another seven years, cark it, join the 27 club, instant legacy."

Marie came out. She was wearing the T-shirt Marvin had been wearing earlier in the day.

I stood up.

"I'm going for a walk."

"Well, hold on. We'll all go."

"You can catch me up. I'll be down the Wharf somewhere."

"Oh, wait for us, Alex," Marie said.

I didn't say anything, but turned and walked off towards the street.

After rather more reflection than was healthy, I realised that the gossamer thread connecting Marie and I had torn, with bleating inevitability. Many men – although not all, by any stretch – will, once in a lifetime, land a woman whom they know, deep down, is way, way out of their league. It creates a very uncomfortable elation, a kind of urgent constant that one day you know she's going to wake up, realise someone's switched the light on, and then when *you* wake up, she's gone.

It had taken a good few years and one hell of a makeover, but I finally asked myself the questions that blind infatuation, drink and stupid teenage self-confidence had kept at bay all those years we'd been rolling around on riverbanks: what, exactly, had she seen in me?

Marvin just exacerbated this, of course. The prick was only five years older than me, but we were poles apart. I was just a kid to him, and he an irritatingly paternal figure to me. He was knowledgeable, well-informed, talented, gregarious, witty, intelligent, brimming with energy and confidence and had the kind of life-affirming outlook that comes to the precious few who land the job of their dreams. Moreover, he was loaded. Without blowing my own trumpet too hard I might have pegged myself ahead of him in the looks department, but that went out the window the minute he arrived in LA and got Californified. Driving skills were neutral, no pun intended, which left fighting ability and penis size. This was admittedly pretty pathetic and so I kept it well and truly internalised (but just for the record, I put money on myself for the former, and I guessed that Marie would have to be the final arbiter of the other).

Fisherman's Wharf was alive with an amber umbrella of light, warm air spiced with the smell of salt and frying, and a collective murmur that indicated the vibe was generally good. Crowds of all ages peopled the boardwalk, taking in the assortment of street entertainment, suggesting to me that it was still relatively early.

I found a space between a mime artist and a lady painted entirely silver, and sat down.

The Casino had a humming, golden sound that somehow found a decent acoustic arc in the spaces between the small buildings dotted along the pier around me, and from the moment I picked out the opening bars to *Three O'Clock Blues,* people turned to watch. A few stopped to listen, and one guy even sat down. He had a ponytail and spectacles and looked like the kind of middle-aged person that lectured in cultural studies, or had some kind of sideways niche in professional music – like writing scores for school musicals or something – but I didn't hold it against him.

I was fairly encouraged by the standard of applause from my American cousins – which included the odd whoop – as the best you could really hope for from a British busking audience was muted approval.

I delayed rather too long between my third and fourth song – which, as it happened, was as a result of realising that silver paint was, in fact, the only thing that the lady next to me was wearing – and in this interval I was approached by a man in a suit.

"How you doing there?" he said.

He was friendly enough. Myriad possibilities caromed around my stomach.

"I'm very well, thank you. And you?"

His eyebrows went up.

"You British?"

"I certainly am."

"You got some Asian in you, there?"

"Maybe," I said, smiling without teeth.

"I like your playing," he said. "Got some guts to it. Your voice is pretty heavy."

"Thanks very much."

So convinced was I that this was the MOMENT – a prelude to a watermarked contract being thrust towards me in one hand and a gold-plated fountain pen in the other – that I missed what he said next.

"I'm sorry. Beg your pardon?"

He grinned, showing uneven teeth.

"'Beg your pardon,'" he repeated to himself. "Love it. I said: Do you have a permit?"

The contract evaporated in a puff of smoke, while the fountain pen sank to the bottom of the Bay.

I looked him up and down. The suit did not look especially expensive. It looked, in fact, like the kind of suit a low-end public official might wear.

"No, I do not have a permit. Do I need one?"

"Well, not exactly. But if you don't have one, then you have to make way for someone who does."

He poked a thumb back over his shoulder. About ten feet behind him was a fat man in a hessian smock with a string of coloured balls around his neck. He carried a bongo drum under one arm and a ukulele under the other. There was a catapult tucked into his belt.

"And I'm guessing serf's up?"

He grinned again and cleared his throat, not understanding.

"It's not normally a problem," he said. "Just come back when it's not quite so busy. You're pretty good."

I gathered up my stuff. It wasn't quite as rock 'n' roll as Marvin's idea of being hauled off by the cops for obstructing the highway while playing protest songs, but I supposed it was on the same set of liner notes.

I made a cursory inventory of my spoils. I'd netted about thirty dollars for twenty minutes' work. Not bad, *pro rata*, although it probably wouldn't cover my bar tab for the evening. I looked up as my usurper started his routine, which appeared to be an odd blend of music, jokes and medieval conjuring. I watched for a moment or two, wondering if I should recruit him, and then picked up the Casino and carried on walking.

At the very end of the boardwalk was a short line of people

queuing to get into a club. There was nothing beyond the doorway but a staircase; a mournful guitar, heavy, meaningful rhythm section and a bumbling piano drifted out over the Bay from the top floor.

I joined the queue, willing myself not to think ahead or second guess anything. Guitar in hand, I would sit at the bar and order a drink. Depending on what happened thereafter, I would take the guitar out and start to strum, right there at the bar. That might provoke a reaction of sorts – at best, I might get invited up; at worst, I'd get a shoeing, which I was kind of used to.

So much for not thinking ahead, goddammit. Maybe Marvin was right. I needed to chill out, but alcohol being the sole catalyst for this could hardly be healthy. Moreover, all this depended on being permitted entry with a fuck-off great flight case, and my track record with door staff was hardly compelling.

"ID," said one, eyeing me in a way that suggested he remembered me from somewhere. He was built like a barrel of sprats, with a blonde stripe across an otherwise black thatch of hair and a tattoo of a spider on his neck.

My luck to date with the too-young-to-drink thing – coupled with the liberal attitude towards alcohol age restriction in the Chinese restaurant – had led me to almost forget that it existed. A cold shudder went through me as I reached with a distinct lack of confidence for my fake driving licence. I handed it over, feeling like a persecuted refugee handing over papers of dubious origin to the secret police.

However, failure to satisfy did not, fortunately, result in immediate incarceration in some altitudinal gulag. He simply handed it back with a slow and unimpressed shake of the head.

I turned and started to trudge back down the boardwalk.

"Hey."

I looked up. I couldn't see the voice's owner, nor who it was directed at, and so I resumed looking at my feet.

"Hey, you."

I chanced a look back over my shoulder. Heads were turning

in my direction, and I got that strange ratchety feeling of fingers sliding down my rubbery insides. Heads followed heads, like a series of doors opening, and they all turned in my direction.

"He was in here last night, with two others. They didn't pay their check."

I stopped and turned, scanning the crowd furiously to try to locate my accuser, but by now the three cement-mixing bouncers were also looking my way.

"Stop him!"

Careers and other things flashed before my eyes, and, wrapping my arms around the guitar case like I was rescuing a drowning victim, I spun gracelessly on my heels and bolted back along the boardwalk.

"Hey, stop him. He didn't pay his *check*!"

Introspection was proving costly. In my fug of navel-gazing I had failed to notice that the blues club abutted the same seafood restaurant that Marie, Marvin and I had bilked only twenty-four hours or so earlier.

Idiot.

My footsteps thundered on the wooden boards, and people took evasive action with gasps and tuts. I pelted back past the medieval jester, whose slide whistle froze on a high note. To my dismay the sound of pursuing footsteps was still plainly audible, and I started giving some thought to dropping the case behind me, not only as ballast but also in the hope it might effectively impede my pursuers.

The thought of losing *another* guitar in idiotic circumstances was really not appealing, however, and I chanced a look over my shoulder with a view to some kind of informed decision-making.

When I did, I juddered to an immediate halt.

There was no army of public-spirited tourists, nor a mob of leathery bouncers. In fact, the only one chasing me was the waitress, who couldn't have been any older than me and who looked as though a strong gust would have blown her into the Bay.

Despite this, she reacted to my sudden stopping with dubious reflexes, and clattered into me so hard that we both tumbled over. I landed on my back, but she somehow kept going, rolling over and landing in *front* of me, like a cyclist going over the handlebars.

"Christ, are you all right?" I said, pulling myself up. She was staring at the sky, eyes wide, hands clawing the boardwalk, winded beyond speech.

A couple of people ambled over with expressions of concern and suspicion, and I took advantage of my enforcer's sudden lack of vocals by exhorting a tale of horseplay-gone-wrong 'twixt my silly girlfriend and I.

It wasn't massively convincing, but she couldn't protest to the contrary, and the concerned citizens wandered off, apparently relieved to have got the wrong end of the stick.

"Here, let me help you," I said, and bent down to help lift her. She didn't resist, but she was practically dead weight, and didn't exactly help, either. I slung an arm – briefly noting a sprinkling of freckles and a soft but muscular tone – around my neck and helped her to a bench.

She sat forward, her arms locked straight on the bench either side of her, and got her breathing under control. I stood in front of her, and scanned around again. It really had been a single-handed pursuit. There wasn't a colleague in sight.

Her chest rose and fell as she took giant breaths, and I couldn't help but notice – I *couldn't* – that she was in remarkably good shape, with strong shoulders, a narrow waist and shapely calves. A few yards further and she probably would have caught *and* subdued me. Not that I would have protested much – the balmy evening, salt air and a curious aroma that was like flowers and peaches and cream all conspired to induce me to look down upon my would-be custodian with a warm kind of fondness.

Her breathing began to resume normal service, and she pulled herself up off the bench to face me, still panting, the brown-and-white fabric of her waitress's dress heaving as she fixed me with her stare.

I chanced a nervous look back over her shoulder, in case this was some elaborate stunt and the muscle of her operation was poised around the corner, waiting to pounce. In any case, she had a grim look on her face, and I held up my hands in surrender in case she decided to start screaming.

"Look," I said hurriedly, "I didn't realise my mate had taken the beer until after we'd left. Or the rolls, for that matter. I just thought we'd just decided to eat elsewhere." I felt slightly shamefaced for dropping Marvin in it so readily, but then I thought of Marie gasping in ecstasy and it quickly passed.

I looked around again.

"What are you doing, chasing me alone anyway? Suppose I decided to turn around and deck you? Suppose I had a knife? Are you simple?"

"Do you know how many tourists leave without paying?" she said. Her voice was soft and whispery, and made me think of Joni Mitchell and lemon cake frosting.

"Well. No." I hadn't given it any thought. "I hadn't given it any thought."

"Let me tell you: it's a lot. And they dock it from my wages. On a bad week I go home with half-pay."

"I'm not sure they're allowed to do that."

"Are *you* gonna tell that to the boss?"

She put her hands on her hips and pouted when she said this, and guilt and courage and the sound of the Bay and that what-the-hell feeling you get when you know moments are going to be indelibly marked on your life all came together and I said:

"I'll make it up to you. How about I buy you a drink?"

CHAPTER SEVENTEEN

DIRTY BLUES

Her name was Rosanna. She was nineteen; as such, the only woman I'd ever been on a date with who was younger than me. She had red hair and a fearless countenance that continued long after her technically-fruitful pursuit.

I walked with her back to the fish shack and strummed idly outside until she finished her shift an hour or so later.

I'm not sure where we went, but it was a large building in the city that reminded me of a vacant department store, with each of the display windows framed by sticks of red neon. It was seven or eight clubs in one, spread around different corners and elevated platforms and VIP booths and darker corners, with bars dotted around the various levels like stairways in an Escher painting.

I was mildly concerned that my admission successes to date had largely relied on trailing around after Marvin, but Rosanna knew a few people there, and it didn't pose a problem. Plus the whole place said *underground* to me, and such mainstream bourgeois worries needn't have troubled me.

I made her calculate, with tedious accuracy, exactly how much we'd skipped out on. It worked out at twenty-one dollars fifty-five. The bread rolls were technically complimentary, so I rounded up to twenty-five, adding a tip and something for her inconvenience, and pressed the cash into her hand.

She was a native of California who had struck out for San Francisco from Santa Clara the previous year. She had a blue-collar edge to her that made my soul-searching sojourn from across the Atlantic seem a little trite when I told her about it. In her view, such things were the privilege of the, well, privileged, but I must have sounded sincere, for she gave me credit for not being a buck-a-plate tourist.

This conversation inevitably got around to the guitar I was hulking around with me, and I told her the whole sorry tale to date of Marvin, Marie and Rosco.

She went over to speak to someone at the bar. The radio was suddenly silenced, tables and chairs were cleared, and before I knew it I was playing to an enthusiastic audience of about fifty. It was totally impromptu – no mic, amp or anything – but the sound carried pretty well.

Then something incredible happened. As I played, the band – or rather, *a* band – came in behind me. I couldn't see them, but presumed the sound was carrying from one of the other stages. It was a fairly basic twelve-bar blues structure, and thus hardly difficult to pick up, but the music suddenly stopped belonging to me and took on a life of its own.

It carried from the basements over the rooftops of San Francisco and out into the night. It suddenly became real; in the same way that a symphony is far more than the sum of the parts of the orchestra, it became something tangible that people could pack up and take home with them and say 'Hey! I was *there* with *him* on *this* night.'

And people started to move. They closed their eyes and waved their arms and touched each other. I could smell them, feel them; I wanted them. I wanted them to want each other. They got up on tables and tapped their feet and held each other as they danced. Some of them were people that had never met before tonight; some had been coming every night since forever, and although I was just another lonely musician, the only other people playing right here, right now were playing along to *my* tune. I could suddenly see my own life played out in front of me, and whoever was going to write the obituary would need to talk about the San Francisco Domino Ballroom on June 20th, 1999.

Rosanna watched me as I played, more or less impassive throughout, but her eyes gleamed in the red half-light, and I thought

Look at me. Look at what's happening. I need someone like this by my side, if anything is ever going to come of anything.

After I'd finished I went to sit back down, but she steered me to the bar.

"Christ," I said, as we sat down on a couple of stools. "I have to get a band."

The next twenty minutes were taken up with handshakes, backslaps and complimentary drinks from my impromptu audience. By the time the well-wishing abated, there was a sea of full glasses in front of us.

"Well, this ought to keep us going," I said. "We may need a doggy bag. Or, er, crate."

I looked around the cavernous bar, then my eyes settled on her again.

"I feel so high," I said. "Who *are* you?"

She said nothing, but smiled as her lips touched the glass, her eyes unfocused on a spot behind the bar as William DeVaughn sang *Be Thankful For What You've Got* around us.

She moved closer to me, and slipped the tip of her tongue between my teeth. I responded, tensing slightly when I felt something small and hard inside my mouth, but she squeezed my hand and whispered *take a drink*, her lips still against mine.

I swallowed the pill and she kissed me again.

There was more music, but I was watching myself play. There was dancing, light beaming around the ceiling like yellow comets, syrupy cocktails and a hot airless kaleidoscopic press of bodies that was simultaneously intoxicating and claustrophobic.

My leg muscles twisted inside me like ropes being spun tight, while sweat erupted over my body like an army of tiny men with freezing feet marching in waves from my neck to my forearms to my toes. I could *see* my heartbeat, pumping at the edges of my eyes like a kick drum, while my loins were this roaring red furnace that was heavy and hard and aching.

The only memory with any focus was the change of temperature from inside to out; then there was a tangle of sheets and slick skin pressing up against mine; heavy moaning and whimpering that soared over the Bay like notes from a saxophone, the moon a sentinel and a door back home; arms holding me tight; hot breath in my ear; whispering my name, over and over.

CHAPTER EIGHTEEN

VOICES FROM THE BACK SEAT

Unlike many other people of my age, heavy drinking did not go hand in hand with sleeping late. Quite the contrary, in fact – the more I drank, the earlier I awoke. That's not to say this physiological quirk meant I avoided hangovers – far from it. But instead of ducking my head and waiting for the locomotive to thunder past, I usually woke up in its path, seconds before impact. I never got used to it, either – it was like a kind of horrific, inverse narcolepsy.

On this particular morning, and with a degree of horror that experience had not diluted, I was wide awake by five-thirty. A small part of this may have been the final adjustments of my stuttering body clock, but in the main it was my consumption levels – supplemented as they were by whatever it was Rosanna slipped me. The net result of this was that my head was pounding, my mouth was like a strip of Velcro and my stomach felt like a particularly unpleasant Balearic maelstrom.

The fact that she was gone when I finally woke up seemed to be a fitting coda. I was quietly thankful that we had somehow made it back to my motel and that I wasn't lost somewhere in the desert. Her smell lingered throughout the room.

I got up to go to the bathroom. I don't know what she had slipped me, but I had to sit down before I got there. I sank to the carpet, the rough pile itchy against my bare backside, and let out a primal groan.

Once the room had stopped simulating bad direct hits on the *Starship Enterprise*, I made it to the bathroom. My urine was at least a normal colour – ish – but when I picked up my crumpled jeans from a corner of the floor, I found that they were soaked through, and there was a large, foul brown stripe down the inside of one leg.

"Oh, my God," I muttered.

I made myself shower, and then collapsed back on the bed, soaking wet and naked.

I don't know if I slept for thirty minutes or thirty hours. There was a definite break in the continuity, but it was apparently still early when I woke up.

I sat up, feeling fractionally closer to a normal state of being. I rubbed my face and took another shower. By the time I'd got dressed and chucked my soiled jeans in the bin, I felt relief that she had walked out on me. Not only that, but the whole night was such a hazy dreamy half-truth that I was glad – had it happened with more clarity I would have undoubtedly fallen in love with her overnight, no doubt going on to make a pining arse of myself down on the Wharf. But the drugs numbed that.

I sat on the edge of the bed and took deep breaths, which is when I saw Marvin's voice recorder on the little round table by the window. There was a yellow post-it note stuck to it, in Marie's unmistakably immaculate hand.

DID YOU SLEEP WITH KAREN WHEN WE WERE TOGETHER???

I pressed PLAY, and heard the bawdy slurring sound of my own voice telling the story of Karen, with a slightly insufferable gloating edge.

I looked up. My motel door was slightly ajar. Clearly I'd been in no state to shut it. Had Marie stolen in here, left the gift, and crept out again? Had she seen Rosanna lying next to me?

I wound the tape on a bit.

Marvin's voice, over the indistinct ambience of some bar and what might have been Skinny Pedro:

"…..*So, let me guess – you're not worried about money and accommodations now, right?….."*

"…...*Very right. Not worried in the least. In the LEAST….."*

"……*Just remember, if anxiety is your problem, sobriety will only bring it back twice as loud….."*

I wound it on some more.

"……..What is your earliest memory?….." said Marvin's voice. In the background were waves and gulls.

There was a shuffling sound, and then, my drunk voice, clear and vexed.

"………First day at primary school. I had lace-up shoes and hadn't learned to tie them properly yet. I asked one of the cloakroom monitors – a bigger girl, must have been nine or ten – to help me. She gave me the filthiest look you've ever seen and told me to do it myself. I remember, even at four, being totally shocked. That was my first ever experience of how nasty people can be. Up until that point I had just assumed everyone I met wanted desperately to make my life nice in some way. That was an eye-opener. What a horrible fucking bitch……."

Then just the sound of the gulls, with Marie talking faintly in the background.

"……….asking for help?…….."

…………it could be. That school playground had a pavement running around the outside, with a four inch concrete kerb. That same term I saw a friend of mine one break time, and went pelting over to see him. I tripped over and cracked the bridge of my nose on that kerb. I put my hood up and hid in the corner of the playground, tears and blood pissing down my face, while all these other kids queued up at the first aid station to get plasters for their grazes and splinters pulled out their fingers……….."

The gulls again. Traffic noise and sirens. Maybe some waves in the distance. Somebody coughed.

"……….no, wait!" I heard myself cry out. *"There's an earlier one. I skinned my knee in the car park at Disney World. Must have been about three. The rental car was pale blue, with red leather seats that burned my legs when I got in………"*

I clicked the tape off. I realised Marvin was right, and I got a sudden sharp pang for a drink, like a slice of rock tumbling off a mountain and leaving a trench in the dust. I didn't want to think about what this meant, as Mick Jagger sang to a mournful steel guitar about a girl with faraway eyes.

I picked up the post-it note and wrote the date on the back, then stuck it carefully to the inside of my guitar case and walked back up to Haight-Ashbury to collect the car. The morning was still and grey, and coils of wetness wrapped themselves around my legs from the younger brother of the fog we had seen at Big Sur, which now appeared to have taken San Francisco.

I tried to find the place Rosanna had taken me, but an hour of fruitless cruising around the back streets of the city got me no more than the kind of suspicious stares that preempt calls to the local police, so I abandoned it. I couldn't *completely* swear that it actually existed.

Instead, I drove to the Wharf. At that silent time of the morning, the fish shack was closed, and so I scribbled a message on a postcard for her and slipped it under the door. The message was strictly logistical – essentially that I would meet her after work if she was up for it – had I known I would not be seeing her ever again I might have opted for something a bit more lyrical.

There were hardly any signs of life in the streets as I drove down towards the Bay, following the signs for the Golden Gate Bridge. I supposed on some level I should have been worried about cops, but all I could think about was how the perfect intoxication of last night was fading quickly in favour of an unhealthy preoccupation with what Marie and Marvin had no doubt done last night, and would continue to do again this morning – if, indeed, they were not doing so right this minute. Ah well, maybe this cavalier attitude just meant I was taking Marvin's advice at long last.

The car accelerated in tandem with my thoughts, and wisps of fog shredded around the car like so many silently screeching ghosts. Only when I got to the bridge and burst out of the city, soaring above the water, did I realise I was twenty miles an hour over the speed limit.

Bringing my concentration back to the car did not mean a return to careful driving, however. Thinking that, if I had all my stuff in the trunk right now, I would tank it back to Los Angeles and leave the two of them to it, I put my foot down and raced across the bridge at dangerous speeds.

I switched on the radio, thinking: I left my goddam tapes behind again. I didn't want to listen to Marvin's stuff. Fiddling around with the radio in search of a suitable tune was *contrived*, and did not allow you to get a handle on the moment. But planning ahead, killing the spontaneity – *that* was contrived too. So we were fucked all ways, really.

But by some stroke of fortune there was no asinine DJ, no brainaching commercials, just some blue-eyed soul thing with a steady rhythm and a one-hit mono bassline that was perfect in a way only complete happenstance can be. You can't force these things. Whatever this guy was singing about, it was the ideal counterpoint to my kinetic rumination.

Lose the 'm,' and it's 'ruination,' I thought.

I stamped the pedal to the floor and gripped the wheel. I wanted to fly. I wanted the air on my face. I wanted rid of the metal box keeping me from feeling the road. I wanted to run like a cheetah. I wanted my eyes to tear from the rush. I wanted to bend my mind with whatever chemical I could find.

However, the car was a dog, and any thoughts of reaching some kind of speed-fuelled crescendo evaporated with the fact that it had no guts whatsoever.

Just over the bridge was a sign that said *Vista Point*. I pulled over into a small gravel apron and sat on a low wall, looking out at the fingers of ocean fog as they whispered over the city. I set the timer on my camera and took a grim-faced self-portrait, with the city over my left shoulder.

Here I was. San Francisco Bay. Freshly arrived from Santa Monica. Homeward bound via New York City – maybe sooner than I'd planned. Even before I arrived, I sang in pubs about the Mississippi Delta and working on the railroad tracks and sleeping in boxcars and going to the city. But the people that conceived all these themes *lived* them, of course. My current vista was as close as I'd ever got to the

Delta. I felt like a big fraud. But what the hell was I going to sing about? [*Marie.*] Used condoms and shopping trolleys in the storm drain that overflowed from the sewer running through the council estate? If you drove sixty miles north and kissed the lip of London, you could find an 'American-Style Diner' next to a Little Chef at Clacket Lane Services, complete with stars-and-stripes décor, 1950s rock 'n' roll and popping neon bulbs. Here, of course, they just called them diners. Who was the fraud, really?

Jazz was the counterpoint to the shenanigans of Kerouac and all his lot. It was contemporary then – rebel music, the music of the underground, of the anti-establishment, the counterculture – now you couldn't read about the Beats without seeing 'postwar' in the same sentence. It's a museum piece, reserved for chin-stroking professors with tortoiseshell spectacles and elbow pads. What was I meant to do? Listen to house music? Fuck that.

And Marvin said to me that Kerouac couldn't possibly have *lived* all that wonder and romance he was blathering about – that only came when the words hit the page. Real life held too much tedium. That was all well and good – and if the sight of your ex-girlfriend crawling into bed with your new best mate didn't give you something to channel into prose or music then nothing would – but I wanted to feel it NOW.

I drove back, at a fraction of my earlier pace. My good fortune with the radio ended with a commercial about novelty plumbing and a segue into Soft Cell, so I switched it off.

It was still early and quiet by the time I arrived back at the motel. I'd been gone about an hour. I parked up in the same space, mildly perturbed that probably no one would even realise I had gone out and come back again. They'd get a bloody shock to find me gone for good.

There must have been another break in the film reel, because the next thing I knew I was on the bed, being woken by a heavy knocking at the door.

I staggered over to it. Marie stood there with three cups of coffee in a cardboard tray, the morning sun like a halo around her. I blinked, because, like some nymph of the Sixties morning, my eyes were telling me there was dew on her skin, flowers in her hair and bluebirds tweeting on her bare shoulder.

I blinked again. There definitely weren't any of those things, but at least she was smiling.

"Hey," she said. "Rough night?"

"I'm not sure," I said, opening the door. She came in and sat on the bed. "What time is it?"

"7-ish."

I looked at her.

"Is it really?"

"Yeah. Marvin needs to be in work by 3."

I didn't say anything.

"I brought coffee," she said, holding up a cup.

I sat down next to her. She smelled glorious, like a summer's day, and the heady traces of Rosanna melted away on the breeze, like the funk of the past.

"I might need more than that."

"I got these too," she said, holding up a white blister pack.

I took them from her.

"Are they, er, legal?"

"Relax. They're just stay-awakes. Sorry you've got all the driving, honey."

She was still smiling, leading me to conclude there was no way that she had crept in here while I was curled up next to Rosanna. She clearly had no idea. It must have been after she left – or even before she arrived. I wasn't even sure how many days I'd lost.

Come to think of it, was her name even Rosanna? Like the traces of a dream, her name was slipping from my mind as the sun came up. I was also aware, on some dim level of self-loathing, that I was faintly disappointed that Marie *didn't* know, and telling her about it after the fact just wouldn't be the same.

Thoroughly jacked-up on the caffeine pills and a second espresso, I put gas in the car and supplemented the coffee with OJ while Marie hauled Marvin out of bed. It was a great team effort, and I couldn't decide if there was some post-Darwin plane of reality where we could all get the best of being three friends. The psychological significance of Marvin sitting up front next to me and Marie stretched out on the back seat was like a huge block of melting ice sitting in the middle of the car. Some kind of sympathy rota they were indulging in to just take the edge off me feeling like complete shit, or a genuine attempt by Marvin to have his cake and eat it?

We were on the road by 7.30am, heading out onto Van Ness and onto the freeway. We belted out of San Francisco to the San Mateo bridge. It was only seven miles from the city, but they were both asleep by the time we got there. Only then, and with a sudden start, did I remember the note I had left for Rosanna, and got a strange feeling that I did not like, a feeling of windows of opportunity rattling closed for no reason other than my own indolence.

We shot through Modesto, George Lucas's home and a practically infinite stretch of sprawling, desolate desert that must have inspired his *Star Wars* landscapes. This particular phase of being on the road was strictly utilitarian – there were no scenic ruminations, dreamy reflections or sun-drenched philosophising – this was Route 5. Four hundred miles of straight, flat nothing at two thirds the PCH journey time. Even if the environs had lent themselves to romantic interludes, the dusty-eyed, grime-smeared, tired-and-grumpy outlook of the three travellers would have put paid to it.

We stopped at a gas station. It was only about half a mile off the main highway, but the land was so flat that you couldn't see anything other than desert. Still, there was a bus stop, which I took as at least some indication of civilisation.

I filled up the car and went in to pay. The only sound anywhere was the rickety whirr of the air conditioning. I was convinced that the only people in the store would be dead ones, so I got a surprise when I was greeted by a three hundred-pound woman behind the counter with a growth on her eyelid the size of a golf ball, and a damp patch on her chest like a sweat bib.

I paid for the gas, half expecting her to have flippers for hands or something. Despite being inside for only a couple of minutes, the sun was blinding as it consumed the white sands, and I had to shield my eyes even *with* my superpowered sunglasses.

When my vision adjusted itself, I saw Marvin standing at the bus stop, arguing with what looked like a tall, muscular woman wearing a picture hat, fishnet tights and carrying a red vinyl handbag. The woman was being aggressive, but Marvin was not backing down, and it looked like it might get physical, even though she had a good three inches on him.

I hurried over, wondering if I was hallucinating. I had popped some more ProPlus in the shop and was feeling faintly hysterical. Marie was still asleep in the car, and I checked she hadn't been roasted alive as I rushed past.

As I approached I saw the woman had a tattoo of a scorpion on her neck, a lantern jaw, and that her tights were filled with some extremely solid calves. The Adam's apple bobbing up and down in her neck seemed to have a life of its own.

I was now convinced I was imagining it all, and so with a strength of persuasion that I did not really feel, I uttered some pacifying remarks to both and dragged Marvin off to the car. His version of events was that the transvestite had hit on him, and had reacted badly when Marvin had spurned the claw-like advances.

"Jesus, you're lucky you weren't raped to death. That was prison ink," I said as we roared back onto the highway.

"Well, your umpiring was profound. I take it back – you'd be an ace cop. Just don't be."

Images have a way of gripping the mind, especially when yours is delicately unsure which planet it's currently on.

"If you'd carried on walking that way," I said. "… how long before you'd find a hollowed-out cattle carcass??"

"Twenty, maybe *thirty* paces," he murmured, and then he shouted, in a hammed up redneck accent: "Opposable thumbs! You come in here with your opposable thumbs! Bessie! Bring me the shotgun! These city folk don't be respectin' our ways!"

Marie awoke with a start.

We highballed it through the desert, and eventually swept into the LA basin. Marvin spoke, in somewhat melancholy tones, of a third act. How will it end, he wondered – an explosive climax, *a la Easy Rider*? A violent act? Slow fade-out? Or would the endless trundling of the wheels through the desert and the mere fact of an ending be pathos enough?

"Or maybe," he said, "one of us will have to die."

I could feel him looking at me.

"I don't know," I said, deliberately avoiding his gaze, instead catching Marie's eye in the rear-view, "but I need to get laid."

The Hollywood Freeway was thick with sunshine and smog, like a skillet about to seethe over, and the traffic engulfed us like a long-lost friend. It was heavy, but moving.

An object in the road caught my eye, about two hundred yards ahead. At first I thought it was an animal, but as we got closer I saw that it was what appeared to be a Christmas or birthday present – it was about the size of a small fridge, wrapped in shiny purple paper and adorned with a green ribbon.

Cars were avoiding it, albeit not especially carefully – it was shunted this way and that as fenders glanced off it, and I steered around it, at pains not to collect it or one of my fellow road users.

"Did anybody see that?" I said, looking in my rear-view.

"See what?" Marie asked.

"That thing in the road. Looked like a… present."

"A present?"

I heard a distant screech and thud, and in my rear-view, now about fifty yards behind us, I saw an explosion of what looked like soft toy stuffing burst up into the air amidst the bumper-to-bumper scenery, while a green bow floated delicately onto the blacktop.

"Never mind," I said, rubbing my eyes.

We got to Marvin's editing room in Venice bang on 3pm. He kissed Marie goodbye – peck on the cheek, four feet from me – and I helped him with his stuff out of the trunk. We made tentative plans to see him after work, but, for all my sharp disregarding of his third-act talk, it did feel like an ending.

I shook his hand, and he pulled me to him in a fierce hug. When he released me he handed me a brown paper bag, ink-stamped with the City Lights Bookstore logo.

Inside was a first edition of Bukowski's *Post Office*. On the title page was an inscription:

ALEX,

HERE'S TO FINDING ROMANCE IN EVERY SORRY SORDID MOMENT.

YOUR FRIEND,

MARVIN

21ST JUNE 1999

I didn't know what to say.

ACT THREE – SAN DIEGO

CHAPTER NINETEEN

DICTAPHONE MONOLOGUES #1

EXT. PIER 39, SAN FRANCISCO - VERY EARLY MORNING

                    ALEX
        I worked in a chemist shop for a year.
        It was a twelve-mile commute through
        the countryside and I used to get the
        bus. Every morning at 7am, on this fast
        main road that cut through the
        countryside and had no pavements, I
        used to see a man running.

                    MARVIN
        Press the… is it recording?

                    MARIE
        Yes, look, the light is on.

                    ALEX
        [interrupted briefly by a horn from out
                    on the Bay]
        Anyway, the guy was about thirty. He
        didn't look like a runner. He always
        wore combat shorts and a vest, and
        these black plimsolls.

                    MARVIN
        No sponsors, huh?

                    ALEX

Definitely not. He had an enormous
green rucksack that was almost as big
as him. I wondered if he was training
for the Army - he had these huge ruddy
redbone arms - but he had monstrously
long hair piled on his head in a bun,
and a thick shipwreck beard. There was
nothing else around at all - just the
cars and the fields and the cows, and
he would hug the verge as the cars
whizzed past him. Rain or shine, summer
or winter, he would run that road; his
feet were like a drumbeat, his eyes
fixed on some point in the distance,
like he was in a trance…

And so it went. Marvin didn't want me around, that much was becoming
obvious. Given half a chance he would pay me to disappear – I could
feel it. And in any case, I was by now getting sick of being the spare part.
But Marie wanted both of us. She wanted to have her cake and eat it,
wrap it and sell it.

Logistically, the whole thing had become political. Clearly
Marvin wanted Marie to stay with him, but the urgency of his going to
work meant that the inevitable three-way conversation about just who
was staying with who was limited to Marie and I. I opted not to broach
the subject first, but to my surprise Marie clearly had it in mind that she
and I would stay together somewhere, with Marvin remaining ensconced
at his own pad.

I didn't know if this was through guilt, sympathy, a continued
discomfort at imposing on Roger and Zephi, or some bloody-minded
determination to salvage whatever was left between us. This last point
struck me as unlikely. Maybe it was because even she couldn't bring
herself to issue the final insult of dumping me in a fleapit hostel in skank
central while she scurried back to the relative comfort of West

Hollywood and the smooth tanned arms of my mate Marvin.

So we drove to Hollywood, tangled up in bittersweet blue. There was nowhere to park, so I stopped by the kerb while Marie went to find out about rooms on Hollywood Boulevard.

The prospect of returning to marathon hikes and public transport made me feel a little bit desperate, and so I opted to hang on to the car for a bit longer, given that my sense of responsibility over money died somewhere back in the Modesto desert.

A bus pulled alongside me and belched diesel fumes through the window. *Buckets of Rain* started on the stereo – I leaned my head against the doorframe, the five o'clock sun pouring through the grime-caked windscreen, and wondered, really, if this was meant to be.

As it happened, Marie found half-decent digs at the Millennium Hostel on Santa Monica and Vine – with parking, of all things. A huge, airy, whitewashed room on the top floor, with its own bathroom.

And only one bed.

Given that matters of social etiquette were now completely beyond me, I again opted for being totally reactive and let Marie touch upon this thorny issue first.

After freshening up we took the rental car down to Santa Monica. The majority of the decorative garnish had survived the desert battering of the Santa Ana winds, and avoiding the freeway earned us more than the odd appreciative whoop.

"Fame has found you at last, Alex," Marie giggled over her sunglasses as a cluster of college kids congregated outside Fatburger cheered us on towards West Hollywood. Her legs were stretched out on the dash; I smiled back at her, and suddenly desperately wanted to say: *let's go out, let's have dinner, just you and me, no Marvin,* but wasn't sure how to phrase it, and our itinerary seemed destined to orbit around his work schedule as a consequence.

We met him in Santa Monica and, now back on his patch, he flexed his host-with-the-most muscles. We pitched up at Ye Olde King's

Head in Santa Monica, a proper pub serving steak and Guinness pie, with rows and rows of signed pictures of matinee idols lining the walls. I took up position next to Cary Grant, which gave me a curious kind of home comfort. A first-generation Brit boy done good, naturally, but also because his birth namesake featured as a character in *A Fish Called Wanda*, mine and Marie's favourite movie. The film had been a game-changer – our first ever arranged date, conducted by daylight and with none of the romantic spontaneity of the post-school play celebrations, had felt formal and a little awkward. But our mutual fondness of *AFCW* had surfaced during a seafront walk, and everything suddenly slotted into place.

After we ate we had a quick beer at the Brewhouse, then walked to the Santa Monica pier. Marvin and Marie went on the big wheel, while I walked to the end of the pier and regarded the fishermen. A cool breeze blew on the day's dusty remnants, and I found it remarkably peaceful.

A police car was parked at the end of the boardwalk. I slowed my step as I approached it. It was an enormous thing, a black-and-white Ford Crown Victoria waxed like glass. I couldn't conceive how anyone could actually *drive* it; it was bigger than any car I had ever seen.

There was nobody with it. It was a massive predator lying in wait, silently taunting me, so I took a closer look through the glass.

It had a tan interior, and with the radio set and the bank of controls on the dashboard I found myself drifting off into serious contemplation. Was this really something I could do? Was I kidding myself? The structure and adventure and independence it would bring were a million miles from anything I was used to, but, by the same token, maybe it was something I secretly craved.

Hanging off the rear-view was a purple air-freshener in the shape of a treble clef, which set the fear and nervousness booting around my stomach again. Maybe the twenty-year vet would come back to the car, and maybe once upon a time he was a stupid kid like me, and maybe he wanted to be a musician, and maybe the cops soaked him up for life and he forgot all that as institutionalisation took hold, and now it was too late to do anything other than strum in his front room and play in the odd police bar.

Maybe, actually, that wouldn't be so bad in the long run, but right then, the idea scared me half to death.

One thing I did know – I had precisely thirty-two days left within which to do something about it, and sightseeing and trailing around after Marie were not going to achieve anything.

"Jesus, look at the size of this car," Marvin said as he appeared at my shoulder. "I need to get you away from this, bud. You getting a proper job would seriously burst my bubble."

"I need to get my act together," I said, still looking at the car.

"Of course you do," he said. "But there's time, dude. Don't rush into anything."

"There's no time. The window is closing," I muttered.

"He needs to get his act together," Marvin said to Marie, as she approached and passed around ice creams.

"See, this is what I'm talking about," I said, holding the ice cream in one hand and pointing at it accusingly with the other. "Sightseeing and getting leathered and ice creams and bullshit. I'm just wasting time and money."

"You don't want it?" Marvin said, and I allowed him to take it from me.

Marie looked at me dolefully. I exhaled through my nose.

"Sorry," I said. "I just feel like... the crossroads is getting closer, you know?"

"Why do you put yourself under so much pressure?" Marvin said. "One, you're in the right place. Two, we'll help you. Three, you need a drink. Come on."

We drank Dos Equis at the Mariasol. A flamenco trio, whose sound could best be described as incessant, was playing outside. There was a large hole in the wooden boardwalk next to our table – I peered into it and saw nothing beneath it but a thirty-foot drop straight down to the sea; mocking, undiluted horror.

I thanked Marvin again for the book.

"You're welcome. I was actually doing the inscription when you knocked for us in San Francisco."

"And there was me thinking you were just fucking," I said. Despite my louche tongue – which I blamed on the drink – I nevertheless felt a wave of relief at Marvin's assertion that they *hadn't* been fucking when I knocked on the door of their San Francisco motel room. Which, when you thought about it, was stupid, really.

They both looked slightly uncomfortable at my crass observation, and so I held up a twenty-dollar bill and ordered more drinks. Anywhere else, a twenty-year-old might feel stupid holding up cash to summon the waiter, but here, it was the most natural thing in the world.

Marvin toasted the benign marvel of short, ugly, pointless lives, and then described in detail a very complicated – if apparently plausible – series of events that would need to transpire for him to meet and perhaps even work with Scorsese.

The late afternoon sun continued to relentlessly bake our corner of California, in such a way that the air pressure was palpable. It had to break soon. I could feel the storm building in the air.

And so after the sheer drop to the ocean got too much, we ordered a bunch more Dos Equis and a brightly coloured ball to go, and took them down to the beach, where the salt breeze was a little more bearable. We walked half a mile northwest up the beach towards Pacific Palisades, the already thin crowd becoming ever thinner as we moved away from the pier. The flat expanse of sand was warm and free, the sky like a blue canvas stretched taut over the world.

With my killer sunglasses I could stare right at the late afternoon sun, a huge white globe cutting misty beams down through the clouds over the clifftop homes on Malibu like divine inspiration.

"Look at that," Marvin said, holding up his hands to frame the skyline. "My opening shot."

Marvin and I indulged in a mirthsome riot of chasing and being chased by waves. In our drunken state this was fairly challenging, and we ended up face down in the sand on several occasions. I was dimly aware of Marie in the periphery, chuckling and photographing the two gallivanting men, and many months later, when the adventure was all over, she would frame one of these shots of the two of us and put it on her bedside table.

"Christ, it's hot," I said, choosing, in a brief interlude, to pause for breath and give her my full attention.

At which point I happened to notice, in an oxygen-starved moment of thrill and horror, that she was stark naked.

I had pulled up after a deft outrunning of one particularly troubling swell, and Marvin clattered into the back of me.

"Come on, boys," she said, with a huge grin and a wink that no doubt reflected the dual gaping of both Marvin and myself. "Life's too warm for clothes."

And she waded in. I watched her go, the waves kissing her buttocks as she got further in, an outbreak of goosebumps sweeping up her back.

When she was in up to the neck she turned and wiggled a finger at us.

"Clothes," she said. "If I'm still the only one naked in thirty seconds I'm taking the next flight home."

Marvin turned to me and shrugged.

"She's seen us both naked, mate," he said, and began stripping off.

I could feel, deep inside me, a hot wave of anger and upset growing that I could quite easily have succumbed to. It was the big brother of how I felt when I found out Marie had been canoodling with her sister chambermaids on her gap year. It was a similar feeling, I imagined, that a man gets when he comes home early to find his wife deliriously riding the window cleaner in the marital bed.

But I made a noble – and, I have to say, fairly impressive –

effort to quash it, assisted by necking my two remaining beers without drawing breath, and began to peel off my own clothes.

"Come on in, the water's fine!" Marie yelled.

I sprinted in while they applauded.

And the water *was* fine. It was refreshingly cool after the heat of the afternoon, but warm and clean in a way British waters never could be, and being unencumbered by fabric was a curiously complete feeling.

"Swim that way for a few days, we might get to Hawaii!" Marvin shouted.

We cackled and laughed in the ocean and tossed the ball around, and I tried not to notice when Marie leapt so high her breasts cleared the water. Instead I scanned the shore for any invasion of our private moment, but our nearest beach neighbours were hundreds of yards away, little black jellybabies being fried by the sun.

"Marie, help me find his eyes. They've fallen out of his head!" Marvin shouted.

I was just glad nobody had proposed applying sun cream to one another.

We larked around in the water for what seemed like hours, before the merest nip crept into the air and we finally realised it was beginning to get dark.

Any worries about shrunken pride after being in the sea for such a long time were nullified by both the fading daylight and the fact that Marie got out first. Not only that, but as I went to pick up my clothes she caught my eye, held up her two index fingers opposite each other a certain distance apart, and winked.

We ambled back towards Santa Monica, the sky like burning coal as dusk fell proper, every nerve ending alive, somehow hot and cold at the same time, the salt caking on my skin.

3rd Street was far busier by night than day, with all manner of shoppers, stealers, tourists and street entertainment. I developed an all-too-familiar misanthropic introspective mood.

Two wired student geeks were arguing religion. One had a mic and was standing on a soap box, which kind of gave him the edge over the other guy.

"These guys are completely fucking nuts," Marvin said.

"Fifty bucks if you kick over the box," I said, and he laughed.

"You don't like people much, do you?"

I didn't say anything. He laughed again, and genuflected in my direction.

"Don't worry, me neither. It's not uncommon – just you, me and every other sensitive liberal pseudo-intellectual college student that secretly craves adulation but doesn't have the confidence to actually *do* anything."

I stared at him, derailed by his apparent insight. He shrugged.

"Hell *is* other people," he said.

"Sartre," I said.

"Spot on."

"But all his mates were French."

"Oh, WHAT a great thing to say!" he said, roaring so loudly he even put the soapbox diva off his stride.

He was wild, on paper more like Dean Moriarty than Cassady could have ever hoped for. For this reason – and maybe because I couldn't be sure he wasn't just kissing up to me through guilt – I didn't admit until much later that I had shamelessly lifted this line from a well-known author entity.

We made a point to again go via the spot on the Promenade where I had seen Rosco. There was no street entertainment of any kind in this particular section of the Promenade, just the relentless footfall of tourists. I found myself thinking of Rosanna from Santa Clara, and suddenly I wondered just how many opportunities I had missed in life.

We took the night bus back to Hollywood, rumbling through the night like the ferry across the Styx. Marvin and Marie dozed off, but I remained awake, staring out of the window, playing word association games with the neon on Santa Monica Boulevard, scaring myself with where my brain ended up.

I kept an eye on them, to check they weren't robbed while sleeping – thinking, maybe protector is the best role I can hope for within our little trifecta. Maybe it was necessary for survival. Maybe I should have been getting the practice in.

At the next stop a huge Gen-X punk bull that I initially mistook for Dennis Franz boarded the bus along with a couple of friends. *Too Drunk to Fuck* was emblazoned on her T-shirt. Not to mention, I thought, too ugly to comprehend and too fat to do anything except roll down a hill. The three of them were smoking weed and singing some bastardisation of an old Faith No More song, only with less irony and more anger:

> '*WE HATE THE DEMOCRATS THE DOLLAR THE TV*
> *FUCK THE KKK*
> *FUCK THE ACADEMY*
> *AND FUCK LAPD…*'

They lumbered off at Fairfax and a security guard boarded. He looked like he had just finished a shift, but he was still in full uniform. I couldn't take my eyes from the array of kit on his belt – including a nightstick, Mace can and Glock sidearm. He sat near the front and swayed with the bus, eyes fixed dead ahead, in an exhausted kind of trance.

"What you staring at, hon?"

I turned. Marie had woken up and was giving me a sleepy smile.

"Nothing. Go back to sleep."

We disembarked at Pico and walked back to Marvin's house via an all-night supermarket. Marvin branched off in search of something, while Marie and I focused on the snack situation.

Something made Marie look back as we passed the baby aisle, a finger in her mouth. I followed her wide-eyed gaze and saw, halfway down the aisle, a black-clad man with a scrub of sweaty blond hair, brow furrowed with determination. He held a crash helmet in one hand, a box of formula in the other and a bumper pack of Pampers under one arm.

"There's something so sexy about a man in leathers buying nappies," she murmured. "Especially at this time of night."

It's always a little sobering when an extremely attractive woman waxes enthusiastic about other men, particularly when you used to be (without sounding like a fathead) the centre of said woman's world. Still, the feeling that someone was scraping the inside of my stomach with twenty toothbrushes was offset by the fact that, while sprogs were theoretically a considerable number of years from my radar, I had – in fact – recently acquired a rather well-preserved 1986 snow-white Honda VFR-750F. At that moment, the beast was under cover six thousand miles away, and Marie had no idea about it, much less that I knew how to ride. I decided there and then to bank that little nugget for when I really needed it.

I guess you'd call it a Margate two-step, or something, but their disappearing act when we got back to the house was something to behold. One minute we were all piling in through the front door in a cyclone of drunken laughter; then, as I was shrugging off the carrier bags filled with beers and Doritos, I heard Marvin's bedroom door close and suddenly I was alone in the lounge.

Arriving at the decision to stay was an untidy journey, but it was cemented by the TV screen that was wider than the car and Marvin's unopened bottle of rare malt, which I clocked on the sideboard.

I made myself comfortable in front of the home cinema, and worked my way – with headphones – through *Kundun*, *The Asphalt Jungle* and *Swimming to Cambodia* on laser disc. The volume was up, but I could not resist taking the headphones off periodically to listen to Marvin and Marie fucking.

Jesus, they'd been at it forever. And it didn't matter how you dressed it up – etiquette, manners, consideration of another's feelings, whatever – the simple truth was she never made noises like that when we were together.

I don't care I don't care I don't care I don't care… And I didn't, not really. But who wants to listen to two people in another room achieving sexual ecstasy – two people who *know you're out there* – while the best you can do is stroke your empty beer bottle?

By the time the triple-bill ended, it was nearly 5am, the bottle was nearly empty, and I was very, very drunk.

She staggered out in a T-shirt, reeking of sex.

"Can I 'elp you?" I slurred in a French accent.

She sat beside me.

"Do you think Marvin will mind if I smoke in here?" I said, picking up a pack from the table.

"Yes, I do."

I put the cigarettes down again.

"So, can I interest you in spending the night with me here on the sofa?" I said.

She was silent. I sat up, suddenly serious.

"Yeah, come on, lie with me. I'll cuddle you, sing to you, it'll be good. Like old times."

"Okay then."

I leaned towards her, a sudden movement.

"Are you serious?"

"Yes… why so surprised?"

"Well, I just thought…. Hang on, what did you say? Did you say you're going to sleep here with me or you're going back to Marvin?"

"Marvin." She looked uncomfortable.

"*Ah!*" My mistake. Apparently I'd misheard her. I fell backwards, tipped the remainder of the whisky down my throat and covered my head with a blanket. "Good night, then."

I thought humiliated drunk thoughts for approximately eight seconds, before the black canvas of sleep sank over me like a spent parachute settling over the ground.

CHAPTER TWENTY

VIENNESE FINGER

I dreamed of a newly-built motor racing track set in the undulating sprawl of a pristine garden city. There were only two cars on the track – one driven by Marvin, the other by me, and we whizzed around the empty grandstands and deserted paddocks.

Marie was at the finish line in a pink bikini and heels, waiting to unfurl the chequered flag for the eventual victor. There was a magnum of champagne at her feet and a winner's garland around her neck. She looked bored, and examined her nails while she waited.

I thrashed that little car, wringing every last ounce of horsepower out of it. Marvin was a hopeless driver, but had the better car, and so we were neck-and-neck for most of it.

It was just a question of who would yield first…

The sound of chattering female voices and a boiling kettle penetrated the fug of unconsciousness, but it was being tonked on the head by the two-year-old wielding a toy fire truck that really brought me round.

Zephi had come home with Harry at some point during the morning, having stayed at her mother's. Roger was off scouting on location somewhere in the Midwest. She and Marie were chatting like bosom buds in the kitchen. Marvin had gone off to work well before any of this.

Embarrassed, I rose and tidied the sofa and played with Harry for a bit, still not really with it. Marie brought two mugs of coffee through to the lounge.

"Hey," she said. "You hungover?"

"Biblically," I said. "You?"

"A bit."

"Where's Marvin?"

"He went to work early. Zephi's just getting changed."

"I must look a state," I said, as Harry's fire truck answered an emergency call with tremendous speed into my groin.

Zephi emerged, putting her hair up. She was clad in trainers and a blue-and-black Lycra outfit.

"Morning," she said.

"Hi," I said. "I'm sorry about the mess. You must love walking into refugees in your front room."

"Hey, don't be silly. Make yourselves at home. I only stopped in, anyway. I'm going to the gym. You want to come?"

I stared at her for a second.

"Who, me?"

"Might perk you up."

"Well, tempting though it is," I said – and it *was,* "I don't think I'm quite up to it. What will you do with Harry?"

"My gym has great day care. He loves it, and mommy doesn't miss her workout."

"Cool. I was going to say you could leave him with us, if you wanted."

"Ah, he'd like that. Another time, huh?"

"Okay. Enjoy your workout," I said, mildly relieved.

She smiled, scooped up Harry and a bundle of bags, and they were gone.

"I can't see why anyone with a child under five would *need* to go to the gym," Marie said.

After hauling myself to the shower and finishing the coffee, I felt slightly less horrendous, and we drove into Santa Monica.

The car began to clank and rattle as we progressed west, and I stopped outside a 7-11 to investigate. I couldn't diagnose the problem, and carried on cautiously.

"I need to get this back to them before it gets any worse," I said.

"Why don't you, then?" Marie said.

"I'm a bit worried they'll blame me and steal my deposit."

"It isn't your fault they've rented you a deathtrap."

I hadn't thought of it like that – a vaguely roadworthy car did not seem like an unreasonable expectation, but at that age you tend to feel most things like that are probably your fault. And besides, beggars can't choose anything.

While we drove we somehow got into the analysis and review of our first sexual encounters. We already knew most of it anyway – and most of mine were with Marie – and so without Marvin the concept of brutal honesty was a little tame. It was still funny, however, especially since we both personally knew most of the other's prior conquests and the scant regard we afforded them. She remained in disbelief about Karen, though.

"Still can't believe you did that."

We walked to Abercrombie and Fitch where she tried on some new clothes. On the way I bought a dog-eared copy of *Fear and Loathing in Las Vegas*, which turned out to be a canny move – she took bloody ages.

I sat in the waiting area in front of the changing cubicles and read (I nearly put 'bored boyfriends' area, but that would have been QUITE inaccurate).

She emerged periodically.

"What do you think?"

I still couldn't get over the new body, and she was attracting more than a few stares, but I kept it cool and buried my nose in the book before I was lured into a sex crime.

"Shouldn't Marvin be giving you his opinion?"

She frowned in a way that I read far, far too much into. Like, *I value your opinion more*, or *Why would he? We're not together* or maybe just general puzzlement over the way I had forensically deconstructed our *ménage à trois* in a way that suggested she had not at any point stepped back and thought seriously about how you would label it. Maybe she just thought it was the most natural thing in the world.

"Do you think he will like it?"

Or maybe not.

I shrugged, just as some dude walked up to me and said: "That book is my absolute and total favourite book of all time!"

"Mate, she's taken," I said, and he scurried off, confused.

You'd never get away with a book like that in this day and age. It was important because it Meant Something. But today, the tight-lipped pious conservative bleeding-hearts are too loud and too powerful. Leave it to the accountants to take the fun out of a wild funeral.

We met Marvin for lunch at the Midnight Special. A bitch of a day, apparently. The rewrites for his latest project were not going as well as he'd hoped. Not only that, but he'd finished *Big Sur*.

"It's fantastic," he muttered, dejected. "Why bother writing anything after that?"

"I thought good writing should inspire you?" I said. "Don't forget – it was 1951. Everything was easier then. Put a '90s slant on it."

"It will be contrived."

"Hang on, didn't *you* tell *me* that Kerouac *was* contrived? That he consciously wanted the image of a lonesome traveller? That didn't mean he didn't have moments of doubt and spirit-crushing boredom. But that didn't put the stoppers on his output, for Christ's sake. That didn't detract from the sheer bloody romance on those pages."

"You should listen to yourself," he said.

Marvin was in work mode, and drunken concepts of romance and wonder and life seemed a long way from his preoccupied state; by turns, talking in such a way seemed self-indulgent and foolish.

As it turned out, Pacific Jetstream were on the cusp of the big time. A Very Important Hollywood Player – I believe they are meritoriously referred to as A-listers – had apparently voiced an interest in getting involved in one of their projects. (In an earlier draft I referred to said A-lister by name, which I hurriedly redacted after an unfortunate midnight encounter with two men in dark suits inside a Lincoln Town Car in the parking lot of K-Mart.)

The project – a European World War Two transvestite comedy that seemed to me to be a bad cross between *Some Like It Hot* and *The Heroes of Telemark*, but what did I know? – had been bimbling along quite happily until this unexpected phone call, and it had caused all manner of frenetic activity within the production company. This could make them. All systems were go. They were going to:

Get.

It.

Right.

This meant a hell of a lot more work for Marvin, but the pressure of his other script deadlines had not eased. They just wanted him to work more. After all, they were paying him, were they not? This was Hollywood, for Christ's sake. As Marvin put it: "Not only do you not bite the hand that feeds you the dream, but you kiss it very very deferentially."

The working title was *Viennese Finger*.

As if to hammer the point home, Roger – to my dismay – joined us for lunch. He remained as cold and aloof in the restaurant as he did in his own domicile. Maybe he'd have been different if we didn't keep crashing at his house. Marie made a laudable effort to be warm and pleasant and inclusive in what amounted to holiday-related small talk, but what was noticeable – and vaguely amusing – was Marvin's own level of deference.

In fact, as we got up to go, Roger leaned in towards Marvin and whispered:

"Get it delivered. No excuses. I'll see you at the office."

It was only meant for Marvin's ears, but Marvin caught my eye, and then Roger looked to see where he was looking, and they both knew I'd caught it.

Roger went ahead while we exchanged pleasantries with Marvin. We agreed to meet him in the evening for a movie, and then he trudged back to the office. We watched him go.

"Look at him. He's living his life's dream. Why the fuck can't he be a little more up for it?"

"His step doesn't have its usual spring," Marie agreed. "And you sound like a tobacco-chewing Hollywood mogul."

"Maybe I'm in the wrong job. Shit, Marie, if someone paid me shitloads in advance to play the guitar on the understanding that there was a bit of hard work in the pipeline, you wouldn't hear me bitching."

She turned to look at me.

"He wasn't bitching."

I kept quiet. This was heading directly towards a pile-up, and I had plenty to say when *that* finally happened, so I decided not to bait the issue.

Despite an afternoon of lazing on the beach and drinking sweating Desperados at the Mariasol bar, the slice of tension remained wedged between us throughout the afternoon. I made some cursory enquiries at a number of bars about open spots for playing, but my heart wasn't in it, and I sensed – although I could have imagined it – Marie growing impatient with me.

There was no sign of Rosco anywhere.

We hung around the 3rd Street Prom until Marvin finished work. When he emerged I rushed at him and yelled "Oooh, Mr Marvin! Please sign my autograph, thank you!" and we took the bus back to his place.

It was pretty frenetic *chez* Marvin – Harry was causing mayhem in the front room, while Zephi and Roger appeared to be having strained words in the kitchen – so Marie and I walked down to the Beverly Center to get the tickets to *Wild Wild West* and told Marvin to catch us up.

Marie and I had seen countless movies together – as a couple, and with friends – and I knew the drill. She did not like sitting right at the front. I, however, did – as did Marvin – but naturally always compromised and sat somewhere in the middle.

Marvin joined us as we entered the auditorium. The slice of tension grew barbs. I made for the front, and felt her hand on my arm.

"Aren't we sitting together?" she said.

"I want to sit down the front," I said.

She tilted her head as if to say *But you know I don't like that.*

I shrugged and pointed at Marvin.

"I believe seating sacrifices are the remit of boyfriends," I said, and resumed my journey to the front.

I didn't look back, but knew – *knew* – she would go and sit in the middle. I could feel her glare from ten rows back.

To my surprise, however, Marvin came and sat next to me.

"Got to be front and centre," he said, elbowing me in the ribs so hard I spilled some of my popcorn.

And after about fifteen minutes, Marie, to my surprise and abject dismay, followed us down to the front and sat the other side of Marvin.

I seethed into my popcorn at the enormous symbolism of this simple series of movements. No way would she have done that for me. No *way*.

Time heals all, however, and most of it was forgotten by the time the end credits rolled around. In any event, it was usurped by the sheer terribleness of the movie, a fact that Marvin seemed to take as a personal affront on a number of levels. It appeared he hadn't quite got over the shock of the *Star Wars* prequel a couple of months beforehand, and was finding the state of the industry rather upsetting.

We avoided Marvin's house and instead made for the Millennium Hostel, scooping up a box of beers on the way. We shot pool for a bit and worked our way through the box, and then went up on to the roof and looked out at the trawler net of lights spread over Hollywood. I took my guitar and interspersed old-school blues with long, languorous conversations about the road and the millennium until 4am and the sun started to wink on the edge of the world. Around us, the old deckchairs and empty beer bottle sculptures and jam jars of cigarette ends and cold, scorched garbage-can barbecues suggested similar dreamy conversations had taken place a thousand times before.

Back in the bedroom Marvin said: "I love you both. You are wonderful wonderful people. I have had the best time."

I put in my earphones, hit PLAY and turned out the light before he finished speaking.

CHAPTER TWENTY-ONE

YOUTH HOSTILE

With a roaring – and probably not really legal – hangover, I drove Marvin into work. Marie sat in the back, watching the City of Angels go by. I eyed her in the mirror, thinking that when this all ended, I'd probably never see her in my rear-view again. And, happy or sad, I had a feeling back seats in the future would only ever seem drab in comparison. They might be loaded with shopping, kids, furniture, dead bodies or car parts, but I didn't think Marie would ever be on my back seat again, prone or otherwise. She was like a ghost, an ephemeral being that I couldn't touch and could only just about see, and the future would either hold her settling into the front seat alongside me, or evaporating out of the sunroof altogether.

The car started to groan and clank again, and while the driving didn't seem unduly affected, we were somewhere between Beverly Hills and Century City, and I didn't want to break down in a plume of smoke where the cast of *Melrose Place* were having a celebratory goodbye latte or something. This might have seemed at odds with the way the car looked, but my ignominy threshold was pretty much maxed out.

I pulled over near a functional looking mini-mart and started a perfunctory examination under the hood. There was nothing immediately obvious, and so I lay down on the deck and started poking about with the front axle.

Other than the fact that this bloody thing would never have passed an MOT back home, it suddenly occurred to me that a failure to diagnose when I resurfaced might lead to helpful suggestions and additional foraging from my companions. If this morphed into a suggestion – from Marie, most likely – that I didn't possess the wit to get underneath a car, then I could very well end up killing someone.

The prayers of the sadist – for that is surely what I was – must have been answered.

My head was somewhere between the kerb and the front suspension bushes when I heard what sounded like a jeer coming from the mini-mart. It made me jump, and I cut my finger on a sticking-out bit of metal that shouldn't have been sticking out of anywhere.

I crawled out from under the deathtrap and stood up. The first thing I saw were the heads of Marie and Marvin poking out of their respective windows, like a couple of spaniels enjoying the breeze. They were looking at a gaggle of youths outside the mini-mart.

At first I thought the kids were just being boisterous, in a way that the proximity of convenience stores just seemed to cultivate; then, as I watched, the tableau unfolded a little more clearly.

There were six or seven of them, aged about fifteen. Some wore bandanas, and death-metal T-shirts. They were smoking, and passing round an expensive-looking tennis racquet.

In their midst was a fat kid. He was younger than them – maybe about eleven or twelve – and he was dressed in tennis whites. I guessed he was the owner of the racquet, as he was running this way and that like a cornered rodent to try to reclaim his item.

The game appeared to be: throw the racquet to your mate, then smack the fat kid on the backside before he could turn around. They were quite good at this, and they were indeed hitting him.

Hard.

He was miserable. He was babbling and crying and snot was smeared across his red, sweaty face. Every time they whacked him he let out a squeal.

They had a distinctly white-rich-kid look about them. Had we been back in Inglewood, it might have given me pause. But as I looked down at the blood pulsing through the grime on my finger, the cocktail of heat, hangover, sexual gooseberry and jarred moral compass caused my adrenaline to bubble over. Add to this a general disquiet about Life that was probably tied to some deep-seated reason for my empathy – that Marie, as the psychology graduate, would have doubtless loved to dissect – and you had a fairly potent combination.

I marched over.

I went straight for the biggest – who, as it happened, was holding the racquet at the time. His bravado made him seem bigger than he actually was, although he flinched ever so slightly when he tossed the racquet to his left and I still kept coming for him. I clearly wasn't going into the shop.

"What the fuck do you want…" he began.

My hand shot out and clamped him round the throat. His hands flew up and started frantically trying to pull mine off. His eyes bulged and it became apparent I had a good grip on his windpipe.

"Leave… the kid… alone…" I growled through clenched teeth.

This was not me speaking. This was not the ruminating, introspective, wondering, wandering, romantic, bewildered Alex. This was a red square of righteous anger bouncing like a hot iguana across California.

I released him after twenty seconds or so, with a final squeeze before I did so. He sank to the floor and began to cough and wheeze uncontrollably. I turned around. The gang had circled around me. They were wide-eyed and afraid, but they were not backing down.

I heard car doors close – it could have been cops, parents or my shagging compadres. I didn't care at that point.

"Give him his damn racquet back," I said.

They didn't say anything, but continued to stare, flitting between me and their leader. I couldn't see the fat kid.

There was a wheezing sound from behind me as the kid got to his feet – to his credit, fairly quickly.

"Oh, you in trouble now," he said. His voice was close. He was right behind me.

My money would have been on him saying *My father's going to bring a monster of a suit against you* as opposed to producing a gun or something, but I never found out.

With my back still to him, I turned my head and elbowed him sharply in the face. It connected with a crunch and a shriek, and he collapsed again, blood spewing from his nose. He looked like he had grown a bright red goatee.

That did for the rest of them. This had got proper, nasty violent now, the kind of violent that meant things would get worse before they got better. It suddenly didn't matter who their parents were – survival had to come first, retribution later.

They were frozen to the spot. The racquet was dropped on the floor.

"Get the fuck out of here," I said, and they ran off, helping their fallen mate as they went, who was crying tears of blood down his Dogg Pound T-shirt.

I picked up the racquet and looked around for the fat kid. He was behind me, over by the shaded doorway of the shop. He was just as wide-eyed and just as scared, and he flinched as I walked over. Suddenly the anger and adrenaline vanished and I felt horrendous guilt, fear and sadness.

"Here," I said, passing him the racquet. "Doesn't matter how old or how successful you get, pricks like that are everywhere. Be safe."

He didn't say anything, but he at least took the racquet from me. I hoped I hadn't made things worse for him.

An enormous woman clad in white with billowing sleeves approached the store. She had her hand wrapped around something small and black at her breast; as she got closer I saw that it was a tiny baby. The only visible part of it was its pink head; no bigger than a tennis ball, it was covered in fine dark hair that made it look like a baby chimp.

I suddenly felt horrible. It was clear from the woman's expression and gait that she had no idea about what had just happened, but Christ. Sixty seconds earlier and she would have seen the whole thing.

I walked back to the car. Marie and Marvin had got out and walked forward about ten paces, and their hesitation had kept them there. They were equally wide-eyed. It was like *Day of the Bug-Eyed Aliens*.

"What?" I said, turning sulky. "Come on, you're going to be late for work."

I didn't feel exhilarated, I felt shitty, but as I glanced in the mirrors and saw no cops, no writ-wielding lawyers and no triple-size gang pursuing me, I did feel a trifle relieved.

We drove in silence for five minutes or so. Marvin tended to meet events head-on, however, and he spoke first.

"That... that was truly Robin Hood, sir."

"It was horrible," Marie said.

"A little harsh, perhaps, but you stuck up for that poor young doughball. You will not be out of place in the cop world. You may wish to keep an eye on your complaints record, however."

Nobody said anything.

"So.... How are you guys spending the afternoon?" Marvin said.

"I'm going to prostitute myself around the bars again," I said. "I brought some copies of the demo this time."

"You have some on you?" Marvin said. "Stick one on, old boy, for heaven's sake!"

I obliged, and passed Marvin a copy of my demo, an EP entitled *Frets to Kill*. He read aloud from the track listing, which contained a mix of covers and originals.

"Look at these titles: *Tingle/Swell... Yeah, You... 5am Sam...* these are great, dude!"

He sat back in the seat and there was quiet as we enjoyed the – frankly bizarre – experience of my voice and guitar filling the car.

When I dropped him off outside the Pacific Jetstream offices, Marie got out as well. The sound of her car door slamming couldn't have been louder; it was the sound of her leaving my life, the summation of my petulance and jealousy and anger, all rounded off with a display of violence that had driven her away from me once and for all. I wanted to run after her and plead for her forgiveness.

But she had gone.

"Meet me after work, guy," Marvin said, hovering by my window. "Here."

He passed me a rolled up manuscript, printed on yellow paper. I took it and dropped it on the passenger seat.

I should have researched my target demographic or something, but instead I spent two hours going into every bar I came across, leaving a copy of *Frets to Kill* and Marvin's phone number, my sudden focus motivated purely by a desire to occupy my brain and keep me from thinking about how I had fucked things up with Marie.

I quickly depleted my supply of tapes, however, which left me with precious little to do, and so I took my guitar and Marvin's script down to the beach and mixed playing with reading.

As it turned out, I did rather more reading than playing. Unlike '*Finger*, the cover said this was Marvin's work and Marvin's alone. Despite myself, I had to admit it was good. It was some epic drama about the fortunes of the postwar Mercedes F1 team, and it had me hooked from beginning to end. I'd always thought of screenplays as purely functional works; just blueprints, instruction manuals for directors to help bring their concepts to life. But Marvin's story had comedy, tragedy, drama, love and adventure, all wrapped around man's quest to push himself to the limit and the bonus zing of *Based on a true story* for double kudos.

It was late afternoon by the time I finished it, and I could see the movie playing out in my head as I watched the horizon and idly strummed *Dust My Broom*. The script had given me pause. Just how much good stuff – scripts, demo tapes, whatever – was lying around this city in drawers, all ignored in favour of the big-budget tripe we put ourselves through last night? How many talents would remain undiscovered until some future people excavated them as part of an archaeological dig, if ever?

The thought made me shudder.

If you have talent, you need dogged persistence. If you manage dogged persistence, you need luck. If you have luck, you need hits. If you have hits, you need honesty. If you have honesty, you need to know the business, if only to keep from getting screwed. If you know the business, you need unwavering self-belief, so you know when not to care.

Talent is the unspoken assumed prerequisite – like when the surgeon strides into theatre and snaps on their gloves, people just assume he or she knows what they're doing. Sure, you can obtain degrees in this, that and the other, but academia is no guarantee of anything, and actually might even be counter-productive when compared with those rags-to-riches tales where the off-their-heads pass out in the dole queue and are then woken up backstage at Barrowlands by a 2,000-strong curtain call.

There was no romance in my failures – I didn't live in a basement flat opposite the Gaslight circa 1961 – I lived with my parents and the closest drinking establishment served double-strength cider and had a senior citizen discount on Thursdays.

I had no religion, no cause, no cultural fabric or extended ethnic family I could call upon to explain my place in the world, no pluralist traits that would lend themselves to stereotyping – the pride of the hometown, the pessimism of the Empire, the luck of the Irish – none of it applied to me. Even the raw blue-collar ebb and flow of the people I worked with – work, eat, drink, gamble – I couldn't define myself in that way. Politicians liked to pigeonhole people into 'communities' – the Sikh community, the business community, the gay community, the sports science community, the smoking community, the disabled community and so on. Although it was a banality I never understood, they were all part of their own team, and I wasn't in any of them.

CHAPTER TWENTY-TWO

BUMPIN' GUM BLUES

Marvin and Marie were leaving the office as I arrived. One of the recipient establishments of *Frets to Kill* was the Pacific Jetstream local, a little place off 3rd Street called The Stovepipe, where Marvin had apparently negotiated a half-hour slot for me to play. It was a simple enough arrangement – Marvin went there often enough to be on first name terms with the landlord, and had apparently brought a bunch of Pacific Jetstream staff along – but I was grateful for the thought, and it was a fun enough set. There was no money, naturally, but Marvin and his gang bought enough drinks to mean that I didn't have to pay for any of mine.

The bar was cool and dark, with bright neon beer signs dotted around the place – perfect for some slow blues. I decided to give them one of my own, a heavy, stomping number called *Bumpin' Gum Blues.*

> *Mackie drove to work down in Birmingham*
> *Parked his car in the middle of a traffic jam*
> *Walked barefoot 'cross the field past the hanging birch*
> *Met the girl with red hair by the old stone church*
>
> *She wore a purple skirt and some bobby sox*
> *She offered him a toot of her Entonox*
> *He took a hit and sailed off to the fourth dimension*
> *But he couldn't shake the worry 'bout his shrinking pension*
>
> *The reformation wine just got stuck inside my joints*
> *My shoulder's getting colder; I'm so far behind on points*

She stroked his Wall Street haircut and consoled him with her sex
Then she laughed and broke his arm to get at his Rolex

Every road I take, I see a damn black cat
There's 'Private Property' on my gate, 'Welcome' on my doormat
I saw the cop break the robber out his prison cell
And I wondered if, maybe, I'd be better off in hell...

"I like your stuff the more I hear it," Marvin winked when I'd finished. "And now they'll tell their mates, and then you invite them to the next one. It'll be like a snowball rolling down a hill."

Despite myself, I felt encouraged; his tone suggested that it really would be that simple.

Suitably inebriated by the atmosphere, Marvin insisted we soak up the ambience of 1950s Hollywood glamour, and so after I finished playing we drove back into Hollywood and to the Musso and Frank Grill on Hollywood for gin gimlets. It was within walking distance from the hostel, which was handy, because although the gimlets tasted fairly innocuous, after four I was utterly wankered.

We sat at the bar, a row of softly-lit orbs stretching away down the room, the music, dark panels and red leather booths somehow capturing a moment in time.

"The problem with this place," Marvin said, apropos nothing except our slightly stilted conversation, "is that when fortune comes knocking, you don't turn it down. You get your reward up front, but if you ever say no, you can guarantee you won't be asked again. And there are thousands more who would gladly take your place for half the fee."

"That doesn't sound very healthy," Marie said.

He shook his head emphatically as he glugged his cocktail and put the glass down.

"It's like driving thirty miles an hour over the limit for the whole journey and wondering how long you can get away with it. The same tension and apprehension, but *constant*. When I first got here, I thought FIFO stood for 'first in, first out.' How wrong I was."

I was still buzzing from the earlier set, and so clattered over his maudlin musings by launching into a drunken monologue about how the movie of my life was going to open.

"It starts, okay, with a wide aerial shot of the desert. High, high shot, maybe wisps of cloud tickling the lens as it descends towards the ground. Then, as it gets lower, there's a car gleaming in the distance, just a speck as it cruises along the thin strip of blacktop.

"While this is happening, *Bloody Well Right* by Supertramp starts to play. You know, the opening bars, that solo electric piano? When you hear that, man, you have to listen to the silence. You know, what's *behind* the piano. That's the most crucial bit. You can't listen to that tune while sitting in a traffic jam, you know what I mean?

"Anyway, so, every time there's one of those crashing whole-band accents – bah-BUM – they punctuate the opening credits onscreen. I'm talking big red letters, Seventies road movie-style. So – crash! – So-and-so Films Present – crash! – A Doorstep Loaf Production – and so on.

"Then, when the song starts proper, drum beats and guitar solo and all, close up on the front wheel as it speeds along the highway, all mirror chrome, spaghetti spokes and whitewall tyres. Cue voice-over, just as the vocals start, then cut to the interior of the car."

"Where we find?" Marvin said.

"Well, shit, I don't know yet. I guess we'll find the people in the car."

"Two Brit bad boys and a drop-dead gorgeous girl?" Marie offered.

"Yeah… maybe."

The waiter heard our accents while he was shaking another round of gimlets. He had thick, black hair and a ruddy Cajun complexion.

"You a long way from home," he said to me.

"Wanderlust." Gin and joy were spinning end-over-end in my

veins, making me stupid and confident. "I want adventure."

"I am from New Orleans," he said, although he pronounced it *N'awlins*. "The French got a word for you – *clochard*."

"What's it mean?"

"Means you too proud for worldly possessions. Means you want to see the world, have it as your back garden. Means you want to travel light, and drink slow. Means you want to marry every woman you meet, and take home stories that will last long after you gone."

The romance of *this* notion struck my drunken brain as pure epiphany, a concise yet eloquent summary of my design. In an instant, it seemed to erase all my bleating about what the Beats had that we didn't.

He laughed at the stunned look on my face, and poured my cocktail. I took what I thought was a tasteful sip, but it was gone inside thirty seconds.

"You keep on them like that, you'll be carried out." The waiter shook his head, and resumed drying glasses.

"Did you *hear* that? Did you hear what he *said*?" I said to Marvin and Marie. "That man… he knows. He knows why I'm *here*."

"He certainly does," Marvin said, nodding sagely. "This ain't no goddamned Mardi Gras, that's for damn sure."

"I don't have a pen. Marie, can I borrow your lipstick?"

I grabbed a Musso & Frank napkin and scribbled CLOCHARD on it in big red letters. I still have that napkin, somewhere.

While the barman dried his glasses, I thought about what he had said. As I did so, I remembered the time I let the woman out of the junction, not long after I'd passed my test. She'd obviously been waiting there ages, her kid strapped in the back, and when I slowed to let her out she blew me a grateful kiss. I guessed she was about forty, but I was just a stupid eighteen-year-old with no idea about that kind of thing, but in any case I'd have married her on the spot.

"Do you *realise* how many arses of legend have occupied these paunchy bar stools? You can almost feel their stale breath in the air," Marvin said, puncturing my thoughts. "So tell me, lady, while our friend orgasms over his moment of enlightenment, tell me why *you* are here."

He leaned forward and rested his chin on his fist.

"What?" She looked uncomfortable.

"This is important. I must have *brutal honesty*."

"I… I just came here to see my friend, and, you know, have some fun."

"That's it?"

"What more do you want? That's what people do after sweating at uni for five years. I think I've earned it. I want to see the world."

"Better, but I want you to really *plumb* the *depths*. Honesty."

"I guess I… hang on, this is stupid. I feel like you're interviewing me."

"The thing is, my wonderful friends, is that you won't get romance from no goddam fly-drive vacation. One of those hideous guided all-inclusive things with itineraries more rigid than a snapper's backbone. Yosemite – Yellowstone – the Grand Canyon – photos, hotel, bad shirts and saddlebags, then home to talk about how it was too hot and how the food is odd and how duty-free isn't what it once was."

He became increasingly animated, and bounced on his stool. He was half-sitting, half standing.

"That's death on a stick. If you're going to hit the road and look inside yourself, you need at least some *joylessness*. Some *purpose*. An EDGE. Driving to a funeral three hundred miles away when you know you should have made more of when they were alive. Driving home after getting out of prison. Driving to see someone you love knowing it's slowly fading away. Shit, even driving to a job interview. Otherwise you may as well be goddam comatose. But it's the only way to find the wonder."

He sat back down again. A few heads had turned our way. I took Marie's lipstick back off her and started writing down some of what he said on another napkin, figuring there were some lyrics there. Then, to my surprise and mild amusement, it deteriorated into a tiff of some sort.

"So, Miss Clement, try again," he said, giving her surname its original Gallic inflection – *cluh-maw*. "And remember – brutal honesty."

"So you keep saying. Five days every month, mate, and you'll get more honesty than you can handle. I don't know what the fuck you want from me."

I ordered another round. Floor seats.

"All I want, Marie, is to know you. I need to see the inside of your head. Just tell me you're not here on some anodyne bucket-list vacation."

"So what if I am?"

"But don't tell me you're here to find yourself, either. That's just as bad."

"For Christ's sake, what are you on about?"

Then, while they were arguing, Marie looked at me for help. I shrugged. Then, to my surprise, she mouthed *I love you*. She must have been drunker than I was, but the feeling was still blissful. Like getting into a February bed when the electric blanket's been on for half an hour.

Marvin noticed.

"More of the fucking conspiracy," he cried.

"You know he was awake in San Simeon?" she said, a bilious edge to her voice.

"Of course I do," he answered, and stomped out.

We went to find him in the parking lot, where a speed freak called Kenny was selling him a golf ball for five bucks.

"Now you can do anything," Kenny said.

Marvin simply applauded and gave him a boiled sweet. Kenny sauntered off, muttering about love, then Marvin and Marie resumed the argument. I'm normally a fairly relaxed drunk, but the gimlets had invoked some kind of aggressive bravado in me, and so I went over to some scaffolding and channelled my listless desire into a series of chin-ups while I waited for them to finish.

"I'm sorry, Miss Marie," he said. "Forgive me. I was merely

projecting my current trough of shite onto you."

"Meaning?"

"Pressure, baby. Crazy, tectonic work pressure. Projects and pitches and punishments for my romantic quests to find you in Vegas and Frisco. I've been finding love on the company's dime. They're making me eat it."

I think what he was saying was that he was stressed out because work was busy. I guessed this was right because Marie had her arms folded with a kind of *So why take it out on me?* look about her.

But his bald contrition continued unabated, and eventually the argument petered out and she softened up. We mooched our merry way along Hollywood Boulevard to Frolic, a cocktail bar that featured briefly in *L.A. Confidential*. It was tiny – much smaller than it looked onscreen. Perks of the wide angle lens, I guessed.

It was Rolling Rock for three, caricatures of the Rat Pack on the walls. By now, Marie and Marvin had definitely reconciled; she sat astride his lap, looking recklessly sexy, flushed, her top hanging off one bare white shoulder while he told her about a project that he was working on, the historical motor racing drama that I'd just read.

Jesus, how badly did I want her? My lust was now actually trying to kill me – if it had been an overflowing dustbin in Vegas, now it was a seething, heaving landfill site that even the most apocalyptic of marauding machines couldn't keep in check.

I wanted to know what they were talking about. What they had already accumulated in the way of shared experiences. I wanted to know every sordid agonising detail, just because knowing was better – marginally – than wondering. I wanted to interrogate her, to get her to admit *I-want-him-more-than-I-want-you*, because I knew she wouldn't and because I wanted her to realise that's what she had been saying all along. I wanted to deconstruct her thoughts on going from *there* to *here*, to compare and contrast all the foibles and features that set Marvin and I apart. For all I could fathom, we were worlds apart – not least because it felt a little bit like she was sleeping with my big brother.

Coming back to LA again had felt a little like coming home, inasmuch as it was stripped of the sightseeing and drinkfucking of our Vegas and Frisco excursions. To use Marvin's diatribe, this was the joyless bit. This was where I was meant to get my shit together. This was *work*. I had made a sort of unspoken promise to myself that I would try to be a bit more focused and make a bit more of an effort once we got back. If that meant distancing myself slightly from the two of them, then so be it – I didn't think they would notice, let alone mind. But here I was – yet again – shitfaced, hanging around like a bad smell, and going nowhere.

Just for a moment I allowed my head to rest on the bar.

There was a sudden jolt of pain as my arm was wrenched up behind my back and I was yanked bodily off the stool.

"Hey. Hey!" I yelled.

"None of that here, pal," came an unseen voice as I was pushed towards the exit.

I couldn't see my assailant, but simple logic hadn't completely deserted me, and suggested that I was, in fact, being frogmarched out by the bouncers.

"I didn't do anything," I said. I heard Marie squealing.

I was launched bodily onto the sidewalk, and just about managed to keep my balance.

Marie was protesting loudly, getting right in the bouncer's face. At one stage she grabbed his arm, and he shoved her after me.

"Hey, you fucker!" I threw myself at him, thinking about a right hook but opting last-minute for a double-handed shove to the chest. "Big man, hitting a woman."

It was quite a thump, going in low and driving up from the hips. He lost his balance and tumbled over, but as backup arrived in the form of more tuxedos I recognised the imbalance of odds. I grabbed Marie.

"Let's run," I said, and we hared off down the street.

"Marvin!" she cried.

We hid in an alley and looked back.

"Where *is* he?!" I said.

And then he appeared, strolling out, whistling, hands in pockets, sidestepping the advancing melee of bouncers with a look of bemusement. They didn't notice him.

He walked towards us, as nonchalant as possible.

"Psst! Marvin!" I hissed. "Over here."

"Hasty exit?" he said.

I grabbed him and the three of us ran across the road. We hurried down Vine. I chanced a look back, and saw, thankfully, that there was no pursuit.

"What happened to you?" I asked.

"Ahem. Never much cop in a fight," he said, embarrassed.

I shrugged. Marie looked nonplussed.

"Turn off the monkey music!" he suddenly shouted.

I looked at him.

"Bill Bendix," he explained, pointing down at the star at our feet. We'd ended up on the Walk of Fame. I hadn't noticed.

The next one belonged to Sabu.

"*I want to be a sailor…*" I sang.

"*Sailing out to sea…*" Marvin finished.

"Fuck, I've never met anyone that knows that song," I said. "I first saw that film when I was six. No one I know has ever heard of it."

"Thanks for sticking up for me, hero," Marie said, grabbing my arm.

"Pleasure, m'lady," I said as casually as possible, trying to stifle the rather juvenile euphoria that being back in her good books elicited.

Marvin strolled off ahead of us, hands in pockets.

We followed for a bit, and then Marie stopped and faced me.

"You know you'll always be my boy, don't you? I'll always come back to you."

She touched my face. The elation was suddenly displaced by

red, and I pushed her hand away.

"What am I, your bargain basement deal?" I said. "You think I'm going to wait around while you shag half the southern hemisphere on this little voyage of self-discovery?"

She looked genuinely hurt, but I couldn't hold it. She was remarkably patient with my self-righteous indignation – just about the only avenue to the few scraps of dignity that I had left.

"Let's be clear. This little triangle is unfortunate, because three's a crowd. But that's all there is to it. It isn't like I *feel* anything for you. You think I'd still be here if I did? I'm pissed off because you've hijacked my trip. You've sabotaged my friendship with Marvin. We're not even *together*."

I pulled her to me, and kissed her hard on the mouth. Then I turned and walked off towards the hostel before she could say anything.

CHAPTER TWENTY-THREE

DICTAPHONE MONOLOGUES #2

INT. THE GNASH LOUNGE, SAN DIEGO, CA - NIGHT

ROSCO DUNHILL III
[to crowd]
Someone once asked me what the blues
were. I told him: you start with a
gonorrhea swab and work your way down...

Marie and I met at the raggedy, grime-caked comprehensive that we both attended back in the day. It was a horrifying, rough place, and I was exposed overnight to the desperation of drugs, violence and the thin line of self-destruction that seemed to separate those who had some vague idea about what they wanted their future to hold and those that were just hell-bent on surviving until the next day. Curiously, where I was concerned, the two categories seemed to be interchangeable.

The one beacon of hope in the bleak trenches of this bleak institution was my discovery of the school drama club. Twice a year – at Christmas and at the end of the summer term – a full bells-and-whistles production would be staged.

Marie was into it as well – but then, of course she was. My maiden outing in a speaking part was in *The Voyage of the Dawn Treader* – I was Caspian to Marie's Lucy. That was when I was 13, and she was 15. By the time we'd gone through *Dick Tracy*, *The Box of Delights*, *Cinderella* and had progressed to Molière, at the ages of 16 and 18 respectively, I was desperately, hopelessly in love. In love in that almost-ethereal, totally-unattainable, never-gonna-happen, she's-way-out-of-your-league kind of way.

We had co-starred in a summer production of *Le Médecin malgré lui* – Marie as Martine to my Sganarelle – and I was acutely and painfully aware that, following the final show, Marie would be leaving school and heading to university after the summer break.

The final night of *Le Médecin malgré lui* coincided with the last day of term before the summer holidays. It was a hot and sticky July evening, and the heavy topcoat, wig and thickly-caked foundation of my French aristocrat's costume proved decidedly uncomfortable.

By the time we had finished the bows – Marie hanging off my arm like the dutiful wife she was portraying – there was a kind of electric euphoria in the air. The run was over. The tension that had built steadily since the first audition had dissipated, and we were alive with the satisfaction of a job well done and an unrelenting urge to celebrate.

The director led us all en masse to a pub way, way out in the sticks – which might have explained the tolerance of babbling artisans – and the garden at the back tapered away down a grass verge to a riverbank where, in the summer, kayaks and small fishing boats would idle lazily downstream towards the sea. On the other side of the pub was a disused railway line sprinkled with bluebells and forget-me-nots that hadn't been operational for thirty years.

It was there, lying on the grass in the dark, listening to the ripple of the water, the strains of *Liars' Bar* and *Rotterdam* drifting outdoors from the pub band, the evening still warm from a day incubating in the July sun, that the virginal, sixteen-year-old Alex Gray found himself. Lying on his back, looking at the clear navy blue sky, wondering at the intoxicating smell of the eighteen-year-old woman beside him, whose head was resting on his chest.

I don't remember what we talked about, other than it was everything. I do remember, however, Marie lifting her head to look at me. Her face was in shadow, the edges of her hair like electric filaments in the glow of the outdoor terrace lights. She touched me on the cheek, said "You've still got some make-up on your ear," and pushed her lips against mine. She touched my tongue with hers, and I might have lost her forever, lost her to a yawning summer cut free from the social network of school to hold us together, lost her to university and adulthood and the big world beyond this one, but I didn't. From this magical night onwards, she was mine, and I hers.

"Jesus, that's… that's beautiful, man," Marvin said, looking a little crestfallen. "If I'd known…" His voice tailed off. "I thought you were just fuck buddies, or something. Did the pub really burn down?"

"It certainly did. It was called The Restful Orange. Played my first gig in that pub. It's still just a pile of rubble, even now."

"That's when you know your past is just that," he said, shaking his head. "Proust may have had his madeleine infusions, but nothing kills your memories deader than the building they were locked in being razed for retirement flats or a drive-thru."

He got up to harangue the waiter for more wine, and then disappeared to the bathroom.

We were in a curry house on La Cienega, and had somehow got around to the story of Marie and I. I had started it, but then Marie had joined in. It had come over as pretty intense, which, for an outsider looking in, I guess it was.

Dinner was on Marvin, celebrating some work-related cause that I didn't quite get, coupled with what he perceived to be my breaching the fortifications of the Hollywood music biz.

Marvin returned at the same time as the food. We drank white wine and discussed the third act, maybe unaware it was already unfolding around us. I had been thinking seriously about trying to find some cash-in-hand labour work, just to take the pressure off a bit, with a view to renting a room somewhere. Hostels were all well and good and cheap, but they were still intended for the temporary visitor. I had started perusing the classifieds; there were a few houseshare options in the Hollywood Hills – bunking in with wide-eyed hopefuls had a certain amount of appeal. Failing that there were residential motels that offered weekly or monthly rates. They weren't quite…

"So, we need to go to San Diego," Marie said, derailing my train of thought completely.

Marvin and I exchanged glances. I put down my glass.

"We do?" I said. Maybe part of me was thinking *oh no not this again*, but it was Marie, not Marvin, that suggested it. A longer pause in the conversation and I might have thought *she can't stand it things are finally starting to happen and she wants to hold me back* but I didn't think those things because she said:

"That's where Rosco is."

"Pardon?" I said.

"Rosco. Is. In. San. Diego."

"How do you know that?" Marvin said.

"I applied some lateral thinking. And some lippy."

"Meaning?"

"Meaning: you bought his CD. On his CD is the address of his record label. Said address triangulates with our hostel and the Capitol building – it's about a fifteen-minute walk. I went in, said Rosco hadn't been at the Mint for a while and where could I catch him next."

"And they told you?"

"Why wouldn't they? Well, they actually directed me to his agent, but I still got an answer."

"Were you…. wearing that?" I said.

She had on some summer combo that was 40% fabric, 60% skin.

"More or less."

"And where is he?" Marvin said.

"San *Diego*," I said.

"Some sort of mini-tour, temporary residency thing," she said. "Short notice, apparently. That's why he's been one step ahead of you."

I wanted to gush *you did all this for me?* But it came out as:

"That's what you were doing all day?"

"What, did you think I just spent it bare-arsed on Marvin's desk?"

The displacement of expressions from Marvin to me and back again must have resembled a hydraulic press.

"So, I need to go to San Diego."

"It's business, Alex," she said.

"You're coming too, yes?"

"Of course we are," she said.

"We should take the train. It'll be a fantastic experience," Marvin said. "We are a band of merry blatherers, after all."

"Well alright," I said. "I'll drink to that shit."

CHAPTER TWENTY-FOUR

DICTAPHONE MONOLOGUES #3

INT. MUSSO & FRANK GRILL, HOLLYWOOD - NIGHT

                    MARVIN
     Okay, I got one. Would you rather be
     deaf or blind?

                    MARIE
     Oh, deaf, I think.

                    MARVIN
     Why deaf?

                    MARIE
     I just think you'd be more lost without
     your sight than anything else. I mean,
     if it were to suddenly happen to you
     mid-life. I think it would be harder to
     adjust. But I think if you'd been born
     with it...

                    ALEX
               [*interrupting*]
     Blind. Hundred per cent.

                    MARVIN
     No hesitation, sir. And your reason?

                    ALEX
     I couldn't live in a world where I

So on the last Saturday in June we took a cab to big and beautiful Union Station and got the 9:40am Amtrak. Maybe it was against our better judgment, but soon we were having fun again – and it was the simple fact of being on the road.

Marie and I got the tickets while Marvin got into a deep conversation with a baglady. Our preliminary phone enquiries had suggested they would be $25, but to our pleasant surprise they were only thirteen bucks. Nothing starts the day better than a bargain.

Huge and sleek and shiny, the Amtrak was like no train I'd ever been on before. I felt like I was in *North by Northwest*. Eva Marie Saint could have been just around the corner. I felt like a suitably rolling Henry Mancini soundtrack was going to start any minute out of the platform tannoy.

We dosed up on cream cheese bagels and half-bottles of Californian chardonnay and juddered through the sprawling industrial wasteland of South LA. Marvin made friends with a helpful guard, and I suddenly wondered if I saw the same thing in him that Marie did. Marie wanted to be with him, but so did I. Didn't I? Didn't everyone? He'd made friends with nearly every stranger he'd encountered, people that I and most other people would have just walked on past without a second look.

Or maybe it was just semantics. The helpful guard was actually, politely, pointing out that we had only paid for passage as far as San Juan Capistrano. My bargain bubble was instantly punctured, and the thought of spending more money was irksome.

We briefly debated what we should do. The guard, seeing our dilemma, made a brave attempt at extolling the virtues of San Juan Capistrano.

"Nixon ate there once," he said.

This kind of cemented it. No, the plan was for San Diego. You don't cure wanderlust by shooting yourself in the foot, or something. Plus, even if Marie and I had voted to spend a day in San Juan Capistrano and then head back to LA, both of us were aware of the public outrage Marvin would no doubt create with this decision.

So we paid the extra and continued to shoot south past countless Pacific beaches and hot freeway networks, sheets of sunlight flooding through the window. Half bottles weren't really cutting it, and Marvin went to the buffet car for more wine.

As we passed a seemingly endless orange grove, Marie, quite without warning, kissed me on the mouth. She was a little summer drunk, and I could smell the wine on her breath. She lingered there, her eyes meeting mine, and I tasted her tongue. Warmth and excitement flooded through me.

She suddenly sat upright, and looked away.

"Gosh," she said quietly, pressing her knees together.

Marvin returned with the wine, oblivious, and began a lengthy diatribe about the merits of the Impressionists.

"Didn't your mother ever tell you not to discuss politics, religion or art in polite company?" I asked, opening my bottle and feeling really rather good.

"Oh, you are SO cool!" he said, shooting me with double gun fingers.

We were all pretty steaming by the time we reached Santa Fe, and failed to notice both that we'd stopped and that the train had emptied. In the end we were kicked off by a trash collector who told us we'd arrived in San Diego.

We stepped off the train, feeling pretty good. The air was clear, the sun warm and fresh, and then Marvin started telling a story about his college days, about a Spanish girl so wretched that she sat patiently while he and his mates played poker to see who got to fuck her first. Marvin had a high hand and described his shock at discovering that her brown body was criss-crossed with great swathes of hard scarring. He passed on the encounter and gave the girl to his mate instead.

Marie, who had been holding Marvin's hand in her right and

mine in her left, suddenly disengaged from us.

"Why… why do you *say* these things?" she cried.

She got upset. Proper, run-off-into-the-concourse upset.

Marvin followed and caught up with her in the middle of the concourse, and as I watched his attempts at impassioned reassurance, I started to wonder a little more about the whole have-your-cake-and-eat-it thing.

Eventually he went down on one knee, and they kissed like sated lovers in a concrete Eden. I walked over to the information desk.

"Alex!" he yelled from twenty yards away, his voice echoing around the cavernous station. He was beaming. "Get over here for a group hug!"

I slowly shook my head, pretending not to know them.

We took the $1 Orange Line trolley to the Gaslamp Quarter and started lugging our bags through the streets, looking for a bed. The streets were modern, and über-clean, like a film set, and I was taken with the pristine beauty of the place. Marvin bounded in and out of various stores, and only one proprietor threatened us with the police. One jolly guy, sweeping the walk outside his record store, guffawed and said:

"Whatever he's on, I want some!"

"Oh my god!" Marvin said as he rejoined us. "I think I'm getting sober."

He was right. Sobriety was indeed starting to kick in and the bags were getting heavy. We stopped for a beer at a Mexican café to regroup, and then found a backpacker hostel around the corner.

They had rooms and dorms. My now-familiar hyper-sensitivity at how the accommodations etiquette was going to fall was sidelined a bit by Cheyenne, the girl on the desk. She was friendly with me, and I started to enjoy myself.

Which was just as well, because Marvin immediately paid for a room for him and Marie, while I said I was happy with a dorm.

"I might meet some people," I said to Cheyenne, looking her dead in the eye.

"Dear boy, they have private rooms. Let me pay for one for you."

Had snogging Marie on the train and flirting with Cheyenne not taken the edge off my sobering mood, I might have told him to fuck off. The generosity-through-guilt thing was becoming pretty obvious now.

"We could all bunk in together," I said. "Is that allowed?" I said to Cheyenne, while Marvin twitched.

Cheyenne laughed, and I paid my own way for a dorm.

We bopped out into a humming Quarter and ate at Kenny's Steak Pub, where I wrestled with a giant filet mignon. We were outside on the terrace, under the watchful eye of a statue of the Duke.

While I was thinking that the arrival of the bill was going to be a bit like getting a parking ticket – totally unwanted and best dealt with by paying-and-instantly-forgetting – Marvin was negotiating the purchase of a giant plastic monkey called Bobo off a greasy street urchin. He spent nearly ten minutes haggling with him, but in the end settled on a sale price of ten dollars.

I couldn't concentrate on the food in any case. Marie's information was that Rosco could be found at the Clarion Hotel. We took a cab through the Quarter and then went decidedly third-rate as it made a series of turns to where the lights grew less and the tourists grew conspicuously absent. Darkness had the upper hand here.

We passed a white stretch limo that seemed to be longer than some British trains, and then the cab pulled into the forecourt of the hotel, some huge white tooth that stuck up from the land for about twenty floors.

I paid the cab driver and we made straight for the hotel lounge – a huge, sterile, whitewashed square box of a place with enormously high ceilings. It was practically empty, utterly soulless and somehow wonderful as a result.

"Rosco's here?" I said.

"That's what they said."

"I'll go make some enquiries."

"Want us to come with you?" Marie asked.

"That's ok, I'll only be a minute. I'll come find you if there's news."

Behind the bar was a tall man with a shaved head and a soul patch. He was drying glasses and had a contented smile on his face that I presumed came from being the font of all knowledge – which of course any good bartender should be.

I approached, bumping the guitar against a stool as I did so. It made a *bong* sound that echoed around the room.

"Give me a beer, please," I said, sliding across a twenty. "I'm looking for Rosco Dunhill."

He gave me the beer and change. I already knew what he was going to say.

"That's for you," I said. "For information."

"That's okay. It's in the public domain, I think."

"Huh?"

"You just missed him. He finished here last night."

"Tell me you're kidding."

"Flew back to LA this morning."

I was somehow not surprised – albeit I had half expected him to say he'd ridden the boxcar back – but, equally, it seemed strangely fitting. Increasingly the guy was becoming my embodiment of the road, always one step ahead, leaving a trail of spectral staves in his wake.

"So he was playing here?"

"You could call it that. He plays, he works, he hosts, he transacts. He'll be back in a few weeks. Are you a friend?"

"Not really. Well, sort of. Hey, listen, this place seems a little, er, conservative for someone like him."

He put down the glass and came around from behind the bar. Instinctively I took a step back.

"Come this way," he said.

I followed him around the bar back down to the entrance

lobby. There was a reception desk opposite the bar, with the lift and an incongruously grand staircase further along.

We walked past the lift bank and up a set of stairs to a deserted mezzanine. There was a set of white inlaid double doors with brass handles. Rosco's framed photograph was outside. The barman opened the doors.

He flicked on some lights and led me into a circular auditorium that would have held five hundred people, easily. The seating descended from our position down to a round black stage with a single chair on it. The barman flicked a few more switches and the place was bathed in spotlights.

"Wow," I said.

"The best kept secret in San Diego," he said. "Real music, real people and not a gift shop in sight."

"Do you mind if I… just for a moment?"

"I'll wait outside," he smiled.

I slowly took the steps down past the rows of seating to the stage. I sat down and looked up at the rows and rows of empty seats on all sides. I unslung the guitar from my back and strummed a single chord, which echoed right up into the rafters.

Imagine… just imagine.

The barman was indeed waiting outside. As I closed the doors I noticed, again, Rosco's dollar bills and coins at the bottom of his photograph.

"What's with the money?" I asked. "I keep seeing it."

"His master's blues," the barman said.

"You seem to know him," I said.

"Everybody knows him, one way or another."

I felt strangely reassured by this. It was only Monday. That gave me the best part of a week to get back to LA and try the Mint one more time. I walked slowly back to the lounge.

"What happened?" Marie asked as I approached.

"I missed him."

"You're *kidding*."

"No, but it's okay. He's here often. The guy knows him…" I jerked my thumb in the direction of the bar, but when I looked, it was a different guy serving. "Anyway, he's gone back to LA. He said I'll be able to catch him there."

"In your own back yard," Marvin said.

"More or less."

"Oh, Alex. I'm so sorry," Marie said.

"What for?"

"The wasted trip."

"I'm far from wasted yet," I said, and winked.

"I shall take my cue," said Marvin, and got up to fetch drinks.

We drank bad scotch until midnight, with only a hysterical troupe of Chinese conference delegates for company.

The drink got to Marie, and she curled up on a sofa. Pretty soon she was sound asleep.

"I tell you, I am decidedly taken with the lady," Marvin said after a while.

"She's a find, no doubt," I said, looking at her sleeping form.

He held my gaze, and I knew we were about to get into some deep conversation about our history and what this all meant and what now and maybe some apologies, but…

"Hey! Hey, you there," called a voice.

We looked round. A small white man with the Chinese delegation was calling over to Marvin.

"Speak English?" he yelled.

"I am English, old boy," Marvin said.

"Well, don't you know kissing is bad for you?"

This chrome dome midget was bevied in the extreme – more so even than us – and so we ignored him and turned back to resume our conversation.

"As I was saying…" Marvin said.

"Yeah, yeah, kissing that lovely little lady there, is bad for you!

It makes your heart speed up and your brain spin! Hey, are you *listening*?"

"Excuse me," I said, and stood up.

I walked over to him, pushed my way past a couple of Chinamen – who didn't even notice – and squared up to the idiot.

"Why don't you mind your own fucking business?" I said.

"Now listen…" he said, trying to put his arm around my neck in a gesture of comradeship.

"Either shut up, or come outside with me and we'll talk it over," I said, removing the arm.

Something filtered through his drunken fog, and he just nodded and sat down again quietly.

I returned to the table. Marvin was grinning.

"You see," he said. "It just goes to show: everything is relative."

"What do you mean?" I said, grimacing as I took a large gulp of nasty scotch.

"What I *mean* is: You probably think you're the Baudelaire of roofers. And compared with your colleagues, you probably are. But compared with us – well, me: a self-confessed, bona fide pansy – you're a hard, nasty bastard."

"Hardly."

Georgia on my Mind played over the hotel's sound system more than once, and so we gently woke Marie and returned to the Quarter in search of jazz. Marie had a headache and was making noises about going to bed early – even though *early* was a moot point – but we propped her up on either side and made our way to Jimmy Love's club.

Things started to fall into place – from fruitless searching for a *moment*, and contriving everything as a consequence, we got a table near the stage without effort, and ordered Rolling Rock as a nice, light counterpoint to the heavy scotch. In fact, the only thing missing was that the whole scene should have been shot in black-and-white.

Onstage was the Wendy Lee Quintet. The eponymous Wendy Lee was white, but sounded remarkably like Billie Holliday. She was also utterly stunning. The whole countenance was carefully crafted in the name of image – soft curves and a soulful voice promising you your wildest dreams with nothing required in return but a little love for the girl next door. Calculated or not, Marvin and I were transfixed.

"She's incredible," I said.

"She's pretty fucking good," Marvin agreed. "Damn."

"She *sounds* like she's singing with a dick in her mouth," Marie said.

We both turned to look at her.

"You should get up there and jam," Marvin said, nudging me. "Be a great opening. Show her the Viennese Finger and you could hit on her."

"Don't be ridiculous. These guys are a decent outfit. They're probably getting *paid*. You can't just get up onstage without being invited."

"Well, let me see what I can do."

"No, don't. Please don't. Don't be disrupting things with your blue collar ways."

He looked ready for the challenge, but Marie was fidgeting and wanting us to take her home to bed.

At the hostel we said goodnight. They went off to their room, and I went to my dorm.

There were three other guys staying in the room with me – Allen from Doncaster, who was your regulation backpacker; Federico, who was a native of San Diego but had lost his job as a night janitor at the Convention Center and hadn't quite worked up the *cojones* to tell his wife; and Russ, a New Jersey workhorse who'd retired only three weeks before being widowed. An eclectic mix, but Russ had whisky, and so we chewed the fat. Jeez, it was nice to talk to people without having to worry over whether they'd secretly wish you'd fuck off.

Dear old lonely Russ, with his drool-encrusted pillow, phlegmy old man's snore and his frequent trips to the toilet in the night, which had him moving sideways across the floor like a hermit crab in an effort not to wake us.

By the morning it became apparent that Russ had latched onto a new bunch of friends. Allen and Federico slept in, while I went down to the breezy front lounge that looked out onto the Quarter. There was a wicker bench, a coffee machine and a sprawling palm plant, and so I sat down with the newspapers. There was a piece about a plane that had overshot the runway at an airport in Little Rock, Arkansas a few weeks previously, killing the captain and ten passengers.

"Now *that* is what you call a receding airline," said a voice from behind me.

I put the paper down. Marvin – by coincidence or otherwise – had joined me in the reception area. I saw over his shoulder that Russ was hovering around the doorway.

"Should we ditch him?" I said.

"Certainly not. This is the path that Life has selected. Resistance would be futile, as they say."

"If we're going to be a foursome I'd prefer someone with a slightly different set of chromosomes," I said.

Russ had a car, which kind of sealed the deal, and so the four of us ate breakfast and made for the San Diego Zoo. He regaled us with tales of the New Jersey Lions' Club, and his sadness and pointless pan-American searching went from our cruel amusement to a genuine happiness and muted pontification when it became apparent just how much he loved his dead wife. Even to us strangers, he was like a shell, a man who had been drained by loss and who knew his own time on Earth was limited as a consequence. He had no heirs or other family to speak of, and so it seemed that cruising a sun-baked Park Boulevard with three new friends in his Chevy station wagon was his legacy, his way of making sure that at least someone on the planet would remember him.

The zoo was as impressive as we had been led to believe, but in the heat the animals were lethargic and wouldn't cooperate. Our fractured disappointment led us to the open-top bus tour, which was a generally more agreeable and restful way to tour the place. (That is, until a woman riding up front decided to hold on to the branch of a tree as we passed it, bending it back until she let it go and it flew back; we all ducked apart from poor Russ, and it collected him right in the kisser.)

"You have to wonder who the suckers are," Marvin remarked, watching a trio of bawdy apes scratching their genitals in front of horrified pre-adolescents. "Who's really in captivity?"

"Man, you are so *deep*," I yawned.

I acquired a rather natty porkpie hat from the zoo gift shop, which I was very pleased with, and then we had a makeshift picnic at a table shaded by a cluster of trees. Russ had a hip flask that he passed round, and Marie went out of her way to be kind to him, but it was becoming apparent that the old boy was struggling to keep step with our brand of humour.

We headed back to the Quarter and shot some pool in an empty, black-bricked underground bar near the hostel. Marie and Marvin teamed up against me – they ended up soundly thrashed. We did end up ditching Russ. Not deliberately – we went to a bar while he parked his car. He never showed up, but no one was quite sure whether we went in the bar we said we were going to go in. We didn't sweat it, figuring we'd see him at the hostel, although Marie said we should go and find him.

We were thrown out around midnight and headed back to the hostel. A beggar asked me for change, to which I replied: "Don't speak to me. I'm wearing a hat." Marie was unimpressed by my sharp tongue towards the homeless man.

"What's he ever done to you?" she said, and suddenly she was sixteen again and I was fourteen and she was telling me off and I didn't know her but desperately wanted to.

At the hostel we disappeared off to our respective rooms. I was by now used to the significance of these separations, and they no longer seemed quite so pointed. Plus I was drunk and tired enough not to care anyway.

That said, when I got to my dorm I found both a snoring Russ and Marvin's overnight bag. I couldn't resist a peek, but other than a soiled-looking copy of the screenplay for *Viennese Finger*, printed on pink paper, the contents were surprisingly mundane. Figuring he would probably need the bag, I walked down the corridor to their room.

I knocked on the door, and heard them both laugh. Not a laugh directed at one of Marvin's latest witticisms, but a laugh aimed at the door. The kind of laugh that is usually followed by a comment like *I bloody knew it!* or *Told you!* I dropped his bag carelessly outside the door and walked back to my dorm.

I'd gone about six paces when I stopped and went back to the bag. I knelt down and unzipped it, removed the screenplay, then zipped it up again and went to bed.

I stuck my earphones in to drown out Russ's old-man snoring, and settled down with the script.

This was the trans-European project that everyone was so on edge about. *VIENNESE FINGER* was block printed on the front page, with the sole credit going to a name I thought I vaguely recognised from the BBC sitcom crowd.

It was fucking dreadful.

I lay on my back and stared at the ceiling, allowing my mind to wander to the strains of Rory Gallagher's *Lonesome Highway*, but then the batteries in my Walkman died and Russ's pneumatic snore penetrated any kind of wanton navel-gazing. I climbed down off the bunk and rifled around his stuff, finding his hip flask in a coat pocket. I drank the contents and went back to bed.

I awoke before any of my fellow bunkers. I sat on the edge of the bed for a moment and then traipsed down the hallway for some water. Some girl walked past me.

"Morning, fulla," she said – breezy, playful. "It's a hot one."

I took a punt on the accent – New Zealand.

"Morning, Kiwi," I fired back.

She raised an eyebrow, which I read as meaning I had placed

it correctly.

"Ten points for you," she said as we passed. "See you in the bar later?"

I grinned. And that was it. But fuck, it felt good. Fresh. Made me realise just how claustrophobic this Californian love triangle thing was. For some reason I thought of that Dylan song, *Shelter from the Storm*.

As if to reinforce the point, when I reached the water cooler I saw Marie standing there. She had ventured out without Marvin. Moreover, she had witnessed the little exchange with the Kiwi girl.

"Who was she?" Marie asked, with naked contempt.

My grin got wider.

"Are you… *jealous*?" I said. "Fuck, Marie, you've got a nerve. Where's Marvin?"

"He had to go."

"Go? Back to LA?"

"Work. Rocco called him early this morning."

"Who the hell's Rocco?"

"His boss." She looked at me like I was stupid. "They needed to see the script urgently."

I felt a moment's panic rise in my gullet. I swallowed it back down. He'd have another copy, surely.

Surely?

"Why didn't you go with him?" I said, stuttering for a change of subject in case I looked hopelessly guilty.

She didn't answer.

"Come on. Let's get some breakfast."

I discreetly moved my stuff into her bedroom, both to avoid Russ and so the staff wouldn't think she was a hooker or anything. We ate in the hostel café and then caught the lunchtime Amtrak back to LA.

We drank wine on the train, and I pointed out the orange grove as we raced past it. Marie didn't recognise it, and in any event she was preoccupied by a huge dude staring at her.

"I wonder if he's the train serial killer Zephi told us about," she said.

She was sitting opposite me; I had my back to the serial killer, so she came and sat next to me. She pressed up against me and my heart and loins began to thump. But the wine made me sleepy, and we both woke up suddenly as we were pulling into Union Station.

CHAPTER TWENTY-FIVE

DICTAPHONE MONOLOGUES #4

INT. AMTRAK TRAIN, SAN JUAN CAPISTRANO - DAY

MARVIN

[*to himself*]

A curious creature is language

Not least our beloved English

I made one brave attempt to comb honey

But I've no idea how to mong fish...

Marvin was busy, trying to shoot a pop video at the Marriott. We didn't see him for several days after getting back – not even for a beer after his dawn-till-dusk tours of Hollywood duty.

Marie didn't seem unduly perturbed by this, and so we had a few days alone in each other's company. We went piggybacking round the La Brea Tar Pits, drank sweating Desperados in Tom Bergin's tavern and took in a couple of movies at the Beverly Center – alternating, in some tacit mutual compromise, between the front and the middle of the auditorium.

We took the subway to Hollywood and went for dinner at Miceli's. Toni, the ancient-but-glamorous waitress, put us in the 'romantic corner' by the stage. While we were being seated I saw clips of Mario Puzo in his huge spectacles on the muted TV behind the bar – I sat up straight when I saw him being served in Miceli's by our very own Toni in some weird doppelganger homage to alternative dimensions. Only then did I realise it was a video obituary – he died that very day.

"Do you remember the magazine?" Marie said.

"You betcha arse I do," I said.

When we were going out Marie had written to one of her post-adolescent glossy magazines to nominate me as Boyfriend of the Month. It was a quarter-page spread, with a colour photo and a bullet-point list of why she thought I deserved such an accolade.

"It was overshadowed a bit by the problem page, as I recall," I said.

She nearly choked with laughter. She knew exactly what I was talking about. Adjacent to the magazine feature on yours truly had been the letters page. One was from some simpering goggle-eyed teenager – actually, I think they *all* were – who had written in to say how special and loved she felt that her boyfriend willingly agreed to perform oral sex on her during her menstrual cycle. At the time I had said that I couldn't shake the image of him appearing once he'd finished, knackered and beaming, looking like a zombie or a cannibal after a particularly savage meal. This description had caused us both to nearly haemorrhage with hysterics, and we were dangerously close to doing so again.

"I mean, that was just a *little* wrong, wasn't it?" I said. "Surely."

All she could do was nod. She was starting to lose it a little, and she had to put her fork down. Her body shook as she guffawed.

"Thank goodness," I said. "I remember feeling quite inadequate."

She inhaled water and began to cough, which set me off, and we started attracting stares.

"I wasn't sure you'd remember," she said, when we finally began to recover. "I was so chuffed when they picked you."

"Are you kidding? That's my only claim to fame. Did you not know I have 'As Seen In The August 1995 Edition Of *Hormonal Confusion*' on the cover of my demo? Hell, it's on my *CV*."

The food was great, the wine was better, and the Oscar Peterson trio in the background was the perfect counterpoint. Before I knew it she had moved around to me and her lips were pressed against mine. I felt elation and confusion and a jealous crazy longing for the simplicity of when she was the only one in my world and I likewise, thinking – I let her drive away from me to catch that plane that day and maybe I shouldn't have.

"You'll get there," Marie said. "This is the land of dreams."

"Maybe."

"Come on. If you were an animal, you know what you'd be?" she said.

"What?"

"An ant."

"Oh, *cheers*. And there was me feeling inadequate about the ravenous carnivore."

"That's gross. What I *mean* is, you don't let things get in your way. Most people, when life deals them a bad hand they use half their energy bitching and moaning and complaining. You don't."

"I don't?"

"Nope. You step back, size it up and work a way round it. You adapt. In a very detached way. It's very sexy. It's one of the things I love about you."

Note to self on preferred choice of tenses.

"So what would I be?" she said.

"Huh?"

"What *animal?*"

"A beaver."

She doubled over again. When she got her breath back she wiped the tears from her eyes, took a drink and held my stare.

"What is it?" I said, eagerness and anticipation manifesting themselves in a stupid sort of half-smirk as I waited for whatever disclosure that was forthcoming.

"I missed my period."

Feeling your face fall is a curious experience.

I didn't know what to say. There was too much fighting to go first.

How is that even possible?

What does that mean?

Why are you telling me?

In the end I made a joke out of it, pitying the poor offspring that would result from such a genetic combination. I may have even gone a bit over the top, just to conceal my horror. Which was daft, because any kids they had would undoubtedly be gorgeous, gifted and serene.

She frowned at me.

"I'm not that worried. It could just be a thing," she said. "He also said he wants to fuck me with a steak knife."

I sprayed water across the table.

"He said *what*? How are you so calm about that?"

"Oh, it's pretty typical. Sex and death. Freud would call him a classic case."

"I'll take your word for it," I said, calling for the bill as I marvelled over her redoubtable nature.

The check arrived as I mentally did the sums. Things were now redlining. Mum would probably tide me over until my return ticket, but I was almost definitely going to be using it at this rate.

Thinking laterally, if music didn't start generating an income soon – and, by soon, I meant yesterday – there would surely be some other way of getting some money – preferably something that wasn't going to trouble the INS. Or the IRS, for that matter. Even out the breadline, something to keep me around longer.

I thought about Marie's ant analogy. The sexual minutiae notwithstanding, it had given me a surprising boost. Not just the analogy, but the fact she had thought about it. Thought about me.

We hopped a bus back to the hostel. We got off at Vine and ran around the corner to change to another one that would drop us right outside – only when I saw the same fat passenger in the orange jumper and the driver with skin like ebony did I realise it was the same bus. The implicit competition that had arisen between Marvin and I meant that, ordinarily, this kind of demonstrable idiocy would have had me seething at myself for hours. But tonight it was just Marie and I, and we laughed with proper amusement at the joke. When we got off Marie told the lady sitting next to her that we were rehearsing for a show where the aim is to beat the bus to the next stop.

"We're stunt passengers," she said.

In the hostel reception we were greeted warmly by the girl on the desk. She was cute, but the spread of acne on her chest and shoulders had a way of making eye contact difficult.

"How you guys doing tonight?" she said.

"We're just fine, thank you," I said, smiling.

"Well great. There's a party on the rooftop at 9pm, if you get bored," she said. "Bring a bottle."

"I reckon she was checking you out," Marie said as we climbed the stairs.

Confusion took the lead again in the three-emotion race, as I thought *is she trying to get herself off the hook again? Despite what's been happening?*

"Hey, guys," said a fat guy on the landing stapling posters onto a noticeboard. "Party on the roof tonight."

"Yeah, we know," I said as we passed.

"Christ, I thought you were going to punch him out," said Marie when we were out of earshot.

Maybe I wasn't as relaxed as I was trying to convey.

We walked back to the room.

"What's Marvin up to?" I said. "Are we seeing him?"

"I called him earlier. He's still busy."

"What about the script?" I said, wondering why I was sticking my head above the parapet.

"Okay. Still needs work, apparently."

I relaxed. Clearly he did have other copies. Or maybe he'd been summoned back to talk about another project entirely. Although the fact remained that, motivated by pique, I had shoplifted his script from his bag, and he hadn't mentioned that it was missing. Maybe he'd been in a rush. Maybe he hadn't unpacked yet.

"I'm taking a shower," she said.

I said nothing, and sat on the bed with the classifieds, scanning for work. Cash in hand stuff. Labouring, roofing, removals. Anything that might stop the cash from haemorrhaging out of my pocket.

The idea had appeal. At the very least it would relieve some of the pressure. Marvin and Marie's romance had interfered with my plans for greatness, or at least semi-solvency. I couldn't face that journey home, that ten-hour admission of failure, and as I read, I realised that it was because I didn't want to miss anything. I couldn't bear the thought of not being on hand should things develop between them, I couldn't face missing an opportunity to pick up the pieces, and I still, like an idiot, wanted to build my apparently-plateaued friendship with Marvin.

Ten minutes later Marie was out, holding the towel around her.

"Rub my back?"

"Christ, this again? I'm not so sure that's a good idea, Marie," I said, trying not to look up from the paper. "You became a butterfly in Canada, and you are the hottest thing I've ever seen, okay? Exactly how many men do you need to have flocking around you? Have I got 'mug' written on my forehead, or something?"

She let the towel drop.

I swallowed.

"Rub my back," she said again, only this time it was an instruction, and her voice was half an octave lower.

She lay down on the bed, the contours of her pale backside like the smooth, fragile curve of an eggshell against the darkening contrast of the evening outside.

I sat astride her back.

"We still going to New York?" she asked.

"We?"

"Yes, 'we.' Don't tell me you'd forgotten."

I hadn't forgotten, but needless to say, I was surprised that she appeared to still be working to this game plan. The germ of going alone – and unannounced – had formed some time ago.

"Not exactly," I said.

"So when are we going?" she said.

"You still want to come?"

"Always," she giggled.

"That's not what I meant."

"I want a picture taken of me in front of the World Trade Center," she said. "Then I can say one of the towers is Alex, and the other one is Marvin.

"I thought you and Marvin were… well, what *are* you and Marvin?"

"In love."

"So why aren't you staying here with him? And why are you allowing me to do this?"

She didn't answer, but a little moan escaped her. The massage was slow, deep, and before long I was pressing my chest against her back, touching her neck with my lips, and moving my hands over hers, our fingers interlocking.

She wasn't resisting, and this fact alone was turning me on, big time.

We were interrupted by a sharp knock at the door.

"Come on, let me in, there's fish to catch!" Marvin's voice was hoarse. Marie ran into the bathroom and I stretched out on the bed with my newspaper.

He tumbled in.

"Who needs five Chihuahuas? Seriously," he said.

"You look tired, dear," I said. "Long day?"

"The worst. Four weeks I've spent trying to resuscitate that screenplay, round the clock. The bastards still hate it. You read it, right?"

I nodded.

"And?"

I just shrugged.

"Thirty-six grand Devlin got for that, all up front."

That made me sit up.

"Thirty-six *thousand*? Dollars?"

"Sterling, my love. He did it all from the front room of his fetid Slough maisonette."

"Wow."

"The spotty little chancer. And I'm left clearing up his mess. Where is little lady?"

A quip died on the tip of my tongue, and I just nodded towards the bathroom. He got up and knocked on the door.

"Darling?" he said.

"Shut up, you wanker," I said.

It's okay to be smug if you don't let on, right?

"Anyway, I must apologise for neglecting my duties as a host. What have you been up to?"

"Not much," I said, fishing around for a can of Budweiser from the cool bag by the bed. "Bit of sightseeing."

I tossed the can across the room. He caught it gratefully and sat down.

"You should come over. Roger and Zephi are going away for the bank holiday weekend. To San Diego, bizarrely." His eyes kept flitting to the bathroom door.

"Bank holiday?"

"Fourth of July, young 'un. We're going to party like it's 1999."

"Sounds good. The only concrete thing in my itinerary is catching Rosco at the Mint tomorrow, which I intend to do even if it kills me."

"Don't you worry about that."

"He's probably forgotten all about me. Which reminds me…" As nonchalantly as possible, I dug around in my stuff for the pink copy of *Viennese Finger.* "You left this in my room. In San Diego."

He slowly extended a hand and took it. He met my eyes – and, to my surprise, looked as guilty as I felt.

"I guess you didn't need it, huh?"

"Thankfully not," he said. "This was my… backup copy."

"Well, that's a relief."

"Indeed. Did you read it?"

"Yes."

"And?"

I shrugged. "Wouldn't wipe my backside with it."

He nodded. "Can't disagree with you there."

Marvin demolished his beer and exercised a slightly stilted – by their standards, anyway – reunion with Marie. After a few more beers we began our usual trick of contemplating our collective navels in the sun, when Marvin suddenly stood up and announced:

"Let us hit the road, young 'uns. The Mint beckons. Tomorrow is going to be your night, Mr Alex, and your place in history should not be sideswiped by idle meanderings on life, liberty and the scripted effluence that I am expected to spin into gold."

He booted his can across the room, and – like some self-titled healer of the sick coaxing believers to stand up before the flock – held a hand out to each of us.

CHAPTER TWENTY-SIX

DICTAPHONE MONOLOGUES #5

EXT. MILLENNIUM HOSTEL ROOFTOP - NIGHT

                    MARVIN
        This band I'm shooting the video for?
        Called The Platelets. Indie four-piece
        from Bristol. They're having difficulty
        settling in LA. Today they told me you
        have a choice here: you either make
        your own luck or rake your own muck…

It turned out that Roger and Zephi were not going to San Diego after all. It made no odds to me, but Marie and Marvin's collective disappointment when we arrived the following day was palpable. I wasn't quite sure why – it seemed okay to fuck like rabbits when I was around.

They went out in any case, and we spent a hot, heavy day sprawled in the lounge with the air-conditioning on, working our way through *Glengarry Glen Ross*, *Swimming to Cambodia* and *The Killing*.

I couldn't relax, however, and as the evening rolled closer I grew into a twitching ball of nervous tension. Tonight was the night. I was finally going to pin down Rosco Dunhill III and get him to make good on the promise he made me when I stopped a couple of young oiks from stealing his livelihood several weeks ago. It seemed like a lifetime. That I had no idea exactly what said promise had been seemed irrelevant. I wasn't even sure I could recall it accurately. I certainly couldn't be sure he would remember it.

Marvin put on a James Bond soundtrack at full volume before

we left the house.

"John Barry – keeps the burgies out," he said with a wink, and then we bopped east on Pico and found ourselves outside the doors of the Mint, the green neon sign etched onto the Los Angeles sky.

He was here all right. The poster said so, the assortment of coinage now a constant association. I took a deep breath as we attempted to penetrate the two tuxedo-clad apes on the door, but once we coughed up the entrance fee, we found ourselves in a small, low-ceilinged night club whose gloomy corners, it seemed, Californian anti-smoking hysteria had yet to penetrate.

It was filling up fast, but we found a table right in the middle with relative ease. A waitress was upon us in seconds, and, bolstered by the confidence of gaining entry, and spurred on by the anonymity offered by the low lighting, I ordered double Jim Beam with Corona chasers for three, and a pack of Lucky Strikes. The order was delivered with little ado – the dubious fake ID stayed resolutely in my back pocket – and as I lit up a smoke and took a large gulp of the whisky, I felt my worries slide off my shoulders like a snake shedding its skin, in a way that was becoming all too familiar.

At this point I identified a problem. A table in the middle hemmed us in pretty well, and, a little like a traffic jam, we could only move as far and as fast as those in front of us wanted to. There certainly wasn't any turning back. It was small, but not so small that I was going to be able to attract the attention of the big lug from where I was. I couldn't see him in any case.

I tried to relax. Maybe I could catch him later, at the bar. Music quietly piped out of a stereo system, over the murmur of the collective assembled – then the room suddenly hushed. I craned my neck to see a small, craggy white man in clothes far too big for him step up to the microphone. He stood, impassive, and looked at his feet while someone hung a Telecaster around his blue checked buttoned-up neck.

"Christ, that's… that's Harry Dean Stanton," I said.

Marvin looked at me like I'd said something obvious, and

turned back to the stage, and I sat in awe while serrated-edge country blues emanated from the haunted guitar.

He played for about forty minutes, without a break, and then he put down his guitar and left the stage without a word. There were huge cheers as he made his way to the bar – passing, in fact, within a foot of our table.

It was a brief interlude, and just as I was about to complain to the others about the logistics of actually trying to proactively intercept anyone, the huge man I knew as Rosco appeared from a door at the side of the stage, crammed into a white tuxedo.

He took the stage, and the crowd erupted with delight as the band opened with *Blue Train*, while waitresses in short skirts glided between the tables delivering seafood, wine, beer and cigars.

And then life ended and dreams took over. Halfway through the set, Rosco set his guitar down and walked to the stage door. I watched him go, then he turned and nodded vaguely in my direction.

I didn't think anything of it to start with, but then I became aware that I was being ushered out of my seat, with some gusto, by Marvin and Marie, like they knew something I didn't. Both of them stood up and started clapping wildly, just as the band resumed with *So What*, and the ripple of applause spread throughout the club. I walked like a prat towards the stage, clutching the Casino like I might fall over if I let go.

I climbed onto the stage, the alcohol firing through my system like quicksilver, duelling with adrenaline as I tried to tune the guitar with shaking hands.

Rosco had swapped his beat-up guitar for a trumpet, and the lilting horn drifted out into the Los Angeles night. I stared out over the heads of the audience, pink spotlights misting my vision as the beams collected the smoke from a hundred cigarettes.

I just about managed to keep up with the pared-down jazz riffs, but when HDS returned to the stage to join Rosco's band for *You Done Lost Your Good Thing Now*, I found my feet. I improvised a twelve-bar solo that, although simple, earned approving looks from my newly-acquainted bandmates and a couple of whoops from the crowd. Heavy blue notes like pieces of broken slate dripped off the fretboard like sparks from a forge. My martini glass rested on my amp, and every time I looked at it, someone had filled it up.

When we'd finished, I didn't wait for them. I started solo on *The Thrill Is Gone*, the mournful notes echoing in the darkness, then the piano, hi-hat and muted crybaby electric came in behind me.

Spurred on by waves of positive energy, I played on. The music tore my heart from its stanchions. Feelings of love, awe and sheer exhilaration flooded through my body as I played. I felt an almost ethereal bliss, as if this moment in a dark Los Angeles blues club was stamped on time.

Fifty minutes disappeared in a heartbeat, and the set was done. The band disembarked from the stage as the stereo system took over and the lights came up, and I returned to the table in a daze. Marvin and Marie were on their feet, clapping.

We moved to the bar amongst a throng of post-set appreciators. I looked around for Rosco, but couldn't see him.

It was gin gimlets again – this time supplemented with Manhattans – and before long I was utterly trolleyed.

Marvin and Marie went off to dance, and I drank in the heady blend of back slaps and handshakes, thinking: this could end at any moment.

And while it did evaporate pretty quickly, a pretty girl with black hair, wearing a pink shirt and black cowboy jeans with a huge industrial buckle, spun around on her stool.

She crossed her legs, and held up her drink. Then she smiled, and slid another across the bar towards me. A big full martini glass on a paper napkin. I wanted to take a picture of it.

I smiled back, some big cocky no-one-can-touch-me grin, and laid my jacket across the stool next to her. She mouthed *Hello*, and was about to slide off her stool to talk, dance or maybe something else.

I didn't find out what, though, because I felt pressure on my arm, pulling me the other way.

It was Marie.

"Do you want to dance?" she asked.

But she wasn't looking at me. She was looking at the girl in the pink shirt. Marvin stood about six feet away, looking a little nonplussed.

I pulled my arm away, as if it were a very real restraint from this world to the next.

"For fuck's sake, Marie. You either want me, or you don't. If you don't want me, then go be with Marvin and leave me alone."

She didn't say anything. I turned back to the girl on the stool, but she had already turned her back on me. Marie went to put her glass on the bar, and knocked my drink over. It spilled across my jacket. It was an accident, but hot waves of anger and frustration made me petulant and stupid. I grabbed the cocktail-sodden jacket and shook it in her face.

"Do you know how much this cost me? Do you *know*? A hundred and fifty bloody pounds!"

Then Marvin was there and we were nose to nose. His chest was rising and falling, his nostrils flared, his jaw set. I felt a peculiar calm.

"You're up, chief," I said, indicating Marie with my chin.

He turned. Some red-faced musclebound football jock had seized his opportunity and was talking earnestly to Marie. She looked uncomfortable.

Marvin turned back to me and swallowed, his eyes wide.

"Don't go in soft. Go in high, then you can come back down," I said, and walked out with my guitar and soaked jacket.

Cocktails are only cocktails when they're in the glass. The rest of the time, it's just dregs going down the drain.

I stood for a moment outside the club, my jacket dripping over my arm, unaware of how heavy my breathing was. I put down the guitar case and laid the jacket on top of it. The air was warm, and away down Pico I could see the lights of downtown Los Angeles condensing on the maroon sky, indelibly marking this moment on my life.

A bouncer came out. Crap. I raised my hands in universal surrender.

"No trouble," I said. "I'm going home."

"Don't worry, dude," he said, offering me a Lucky Strike. "Nice gig. Don't be mad."

I took the cigarette. "Thanks."

"Not often in your life chicks will fight over you."

I turned to look at him. His name badge read Le Touquet.

"Are you French?" I asked.

He shrugged as he lit my cigarette.

"What does 'clochard' mean?" I asked.

He frowned.

"It means 'tramp,'" he said.

I drew on my cigarette and looked away down Pico again.

"Figures."

A hubbub of people suddenly appeared from the side door, the nucleus of which was Rosco in his massive white suit.

They milled around him on the sidewalk. I picked up my guitar and walked over.

"That was fantastic," I mumbled, my voice thick with intoxication. "Thanks."

"You play pretty well, little man. We square now?"

"You could say that."

He just nodded.

"Listen, can I ask you something?" I said. "On your posters, your album covers, there's the same picture of coins and bills. What does it mean?"

He grinned, two gold teeth glinting at me.

"Okay, okay, little man. I'll tell you. When I was a boy, my daddy gave me a watch. A nice watch. It had been his daddy's, and his granddaddy's, and his daddy's before him. My daddy wanted me to give it to my boy. You get the idea."

"And you never had kids?"

He frowned at the interruption. I winced and told myself to shut up.

"Many years later, when I was all grown up, I got into some trouble. I owed some people a lot of money. I asked my daddy to lend me the money.

"And he done gave me that loan, and I got out of trouble. But I couldn't pay him back. So I hocked the watch he'd already given me and settled up. There was exactly one hundred seventy-two dollars left over, and I put it everywhere so's I never forget. My daddy died not knowing his son was a fraud."

His face was solemn. I tried to speak, but the words wouldn't come. I was drunker than I thought.

A huge black stretch limo pulled up to the kerb. The back door opened automatically and a little party of warm lights and a mini-bar beckoned from inside. Rosco's entourage moved towards it in a single mass. I tilted my head and frowned, wondering which side of Rosco was the act.

"Hey, how do you beat the heat in that suit?" I said.

Rosco simply grinned.

"It's cheap, this town. But it ain't free," he said.

I was aware of the blow, but I didn't feel it. I just sensed the impact on the right side of my head. I felt the curious sensation of my legs giving way, and then I was on my back on the warm tarmac, staring up at the tangle of clouds in the sky, my fingers still on the handle of my guitar case.

The world appeared as if underwater, but through my damaged vision I could just about make out the shape of a man buzzing about in my field of vision – a small, ginger man wearing a white string vest and stars-and-stripes pantaloons. I felt my unresisting fingers being uncurled from my guitar case, and hands in my pockets, while my frenetic brain screamed *Please, not again! I don't believe it!* Then there was a second blow, and Los Angeles turned to night.

CHAPTER TWENTY-SEVEN

DICTAPHONE MONOLOGUES #6

INT. THE HOME OF ROCCO LANG, PACIFIC JETSTREAM
PRINCIPAL PRODUCER - HOLLYWOOD HILLS - NIGHT

                    ROCCO
        Of course movies! Everything is movies.
        You go and lie down in the middle of
        the Mojave, it's movies...

On Independence Day I awoke on Marvin's sofa with some trepidation. My head hurt, but this could have been as much to do with the booze as the alleyway assault.

I got up and shuffled to the bathroom. I had a bruise on the side of my face, and the skin was tender, but to me it looked like just another day at the office. In the scheme of post-gig pastings, it wasn't even in the top ten.

I collapsed back on the sofa, sunlight streaming into the lounge. Marvin appeared and started bustling in the kitchen. Marie followed him out and did a bedside triage.

"That was a night," I said as she approached.

"How's your head?"

"Fine."

"You need to go to the hospital. You need to tell the police."

"I just want to forget about it."

"Alex, you were mugged. You lost *consciousness*."

"Only for a second or two."

She made an exasperated noise and went to the kitchen.

Marvin scrambled some eggs and served them up with cream cheese and bagels. We even sat at the table.

"Happy Independence Day," he said. "You had a full night."

"At least I kept my clothes," I said, but he was right. Despite the insalubrious end, all I could think about was being on stage, and how it felt afterwards, and how flat everything seemed now.

"And you're making some progress, now, bud. Real progress."

"That's the careerist view," I said. "I'm still skint."

"I can't believe you lost your guitar again," Marie said.

"I didn't *lose* it," I said. "It was *stolen*. I'm getting used to it, anyway."

"Are you going to mount another campaign?" Marvin said.

"It seems pretty idiotic. Someone will think it's an insurance fraud. By the way, what happened with the idiot at the bar? The jock?"

"Well, you were right," Marvin said, pouring coffee. "I went in hard – verbals only, you understand – and asked him what the *hell* he was doing with my *woman*. Incredibly, he backed down and was very apologetic. Mate, I felt like John Wayne after that."

I smiled.

Roger and Zephi came home around lunchtime in a whirlwind of bank holiday chaos, and the house suddenly seemed to come to life. Zephi seemed thrilled and then genuinely shocked and upset when she heard the end-to-end Mint story. Roger went off to unpack.

"You should tell the police," she said.

"So I gather," I said. "They'll probably arrest me for wasting more paper on Lost Guitar posters."

The phone rang. Roger came out of the bedroom to answer it.

"So, what are you guys up to today?" she said.

"Buying aspirin, probably. But I'm not spending the Fourth of July in a police station."

"Where are you off to?" she said to Marie, who came over with her bag slung over her shoulder.

"We're going to head back to the hostel," Marie said.

"You don't need to do that," Zephi said. "Come on, stay around a while."

"Thank you, but you don't want us getting under your feet," Marie said. "We'll be in your way."

"Stay here," she said. "We're going to a party later. You guys should come."

Marie looked at me.

"Yes, come *on*," she said. "Please don't feel you have to leave. You're coming, right?" she said to Marvin.

"I don't think so," Roger said as he hung up the phone. "Rocco wants him to work."

"Today?" Zephi said.

"*Viennese Finger* needs urgent rewrites," he said. "He needs them done today."

"What's wrong with it?" Marvin said.

"The dialogue, the structure, the characters – everything," Roger said.

"I tweaked the dialogue when I got back from San Diego," Marvin said.

Roger shrugged. I wanted to know where the BBC's Devlin featured in this fervent defibrillation – the script was shite and dialogue tweaks were not going to save it.

"Well, you've got all afternoon," Zephi said. "You guys can go and drink cold coffee and wait for the *Eureka* moment to strike, then we can all go to the party together."

So Marie and I did end up going to the hostel to facilitate the panic-rewrites, but only under Zephi's strict instructions that we return in the evening to go out to this party.

We took a slow walk to the bus stop. Marie was quiet, and despite Zephi's careful orchestration, I knew she was feeling like a child who had been paid to go and play in the garden so the parents could argue in peace. We had another twenty minutes to wait for a bus, so we decided to walk up to the next stop.

"You feel kind of lost without a guitar, huh?" she said.

"Like I've lost a limb," I said.

"You can tell. Just by the way you're walking."

When we finally got back to the hostel, my head was hurting again. I took some painkillers and lay down.

I didn't remember falling asleep, much less Marie leaving, but when I woke up she was grinning at me.

I sat up. She was holding a battered old acoustic with a UCLA pennant stuck to the body.

"Don't tell me you bought me *another* guitar," I said.

"It was only twenty bucks."

I took it from her. "Where'd you get it?"

She shrugged.

"Garage sale."

I took it from her and tuned it up as best I could. It made a surprisingly decent sound.

"I'm gonna run out of names," I said, lying back down and staring at the ceiling. "Thank you."

She blew me a kiss and headed for the bathroom.

"We've got a party to go to," she said.

I almost didn't recognise Zephi. Her natural athletic beauty was apparent in her daytime mommy outfits with bare arms and wavy half-dry just-out-the shower hair. But tonight she should have been on the red carpet. Her California blonde hair was up, showcasing a rather expensive-looking pair of earrings. There was a black cocktail dress, eye-watering heels and a heady scent that reminded me of the ocean.

About the same time, I noticed that she actually had an inch or two on Roger, although that might have been the shoes. I also noticed that his tan wasn't anywhere near as good as hers, and that he was actually a little soft around the edges. He wasn't unpleasant to look at, and he had great hair, but alongside his fender-bender-inducing wife, he looked just a tiny bit uncomfortable.

The Ambassador Hotel was packed. I wasn't sure what the party was in aid of, but it was some kind of industry celebration that Pacific Jetstream were on the fringes of. It was also an opportunity to *network*, whatever that meant.

Influence-wise, I couldn't work out whether Roger was a leg-up to Zephi or vice versa. Or maybe it was a mutually beneficial relationship. In any case, it was Zephi that said to me:

"I got you a playing spot."

There was a live band called The Love Germs playing in the ballroom; Zephi knew someone who knew someone, and they had agreed to let me join them for a couple of songs. I could borrow a guitar. I wanted to say *I can only play left-handed and my head hurts* but I was acutely aware of how churlish that would have sounded – Marvin and Marie had obviously pre-negotiated the thing with Rosco and now here was Zephi doing the same thing, for no good reason that I could see other than trying to help out. I suddenly felt like I had parents all over the place.

So I got on stage and played a couple of numbers with the aforementioned 'Germs. My protestation that I could only play left-handed wasn't technically true – I had taught myself to play upside down on my dad's right-handed guitar at the age of fourteen, but it was passable at best. Still, they loaned me a rather nice Les Paul which was forgiving enough to play upside down, sideways, or back to front.

I freeloaded the applause meant for them, but it still made me realise that this was being alive. Anything in between climbing on and offstage just seemed like lethargic filler.

I put the Les Paul down, nodded thanks to the band and stepped off the stage, very aware that my upside-down playing was not nearly as fluid as it had been when I was cradling Camille, or even the Casino. The casual listener would probably not have noticed, and I used to think such fine distinctions and superstitions – along with embargoed song titles and lucky underpants – were the preserve of the prima donna, but, whatever. I could feel it, and it wasn't quite right.

The Love Germs played on, the crowd in their grasp. Unlike the night before at the Mint, there was no clamour around me as I stood off to the side of the stage. I stood in the wings, alone in the dark, watching the band and trying not to dwell on the fact that the heady euphoria of the Mint was rendered trifling and obsolete in light of tonight's gig. In a narcissistic way, it was easy to see how anything other than unfettered adulation could be deemed a failure. You're only as good as your last show, etcetera.

I sloped out of the ballroom and into the reception area. The hotel had a public computer, so I paid the receptionist five dollars and logged into my email, wondering if maybe I should at least make an effort to get the Casino back. Marie had bought it for me, after all.

As it happened, there were no public-spirited messages telling me Camille was in the safe custody of the sender – and I hadn't really expected any – but there was a very brief one from my mum asking me to call home as soon as possible.

Naturally, panic and worry rose in my chest like a geyser. Dad's had a heart attack, or Jen's pregnant, or Aidan's been arrested. I didn't fanny about with my usual clumsy distended attempts at resourcefulness – scraping around for change, searching for a public phone – and instead borrowed the reception's phone.

After some jousting with the operator, Mum accepted the charges and I was connected.

"Hey, ma."

"Hi, son. Oh, it's so good to hear from you. How's it going?"

"Not too bad. I'm having a good time. What's up?"

"What time is it there?"

"Ten pm. Ma, what's going on?"

"It's two in the afternoon here."

"Yeah, I know. Ma, please."

"Oh, dear. I don't know how to tell you. You got a letter."

"Okay."

"Yes, I'm… I'm afraid you've been… been…"

"What?" She was obviously searching for the least painful choice of words, but as she faltered, I half-guessed anyway.

"Laid off."

I didn't say anything.

"It's true," she said. "I'm so sorry."

"Has dad been opening my mail again?"

"What? No, no, your supervisor called."

"Brian?"

"Yes. They were calling people in to tell them before the letter arrived, but he knew you were abroad and so he phoned."

I bet Mum liked the idea of being able to tell people I was abroad. It would have made me seem important. I bet she added *on business* for effect.

"….having to make savings, profit margins too narrow, work drying up, run of bad weather, he said… they're having to let people go all over."

"He just called to tell you that?"

"He was really apologetic about it. Oh, Alex, I'm so sorry. Your dad said not to tell you, that it would spoil your holiday, but, well, I thought you'd want to know."

He still thought it was a holiday. Still thought I was coming back. Still thought I would fail.

"That's okay. Thanks, ma."

"You don't have to worry about anything, okay? You'll stay with us still. There'll be lots of other opportunities."

"It's okay, ma. There might be a little bit of severance."

There would be no such thing, of course, but my mother clearly felt worse than I did. But it wasn't like I had a mortgage or kids or worries about eviction. Sure, I threw my mum some housekeeping money each month, but I still lived at home. This was like screwing up, only with stabilisers.

And in the scheme of things, it was nothing as bad as I was expecting, and so I felt relieved. I even felt a little exhilarated. I felt the release of pressure that inevitability brings, when free will and choice only serve to create anxiety.

Opportunity. Potential. The future. All these things had been chucked my way before, by teachers, other parents, friends. They put you on a pedestal – he'll be a lawyer, or a doctor, or he'll follow in his father's footsteps – then when you decide to lay brick and follow music, there's a thinly-stretched veneer of people politely holding back their views. My parents would now, no doubt, be saying *well maybe now he'll get serious.*

The trouble with a word like 'potential' is that it's like a road sign. One moment it's far off in the distance while you hurtle towards it, unaware of just how quickly you are gaining, then all of a sudden you are racing past it and it's behind you and it's very quickly out of sight.

The reception had an ATM. I had been afraid of the damn things for the best part of a fortnight, but I just felt a kind of strange, resigned inevitability about the whole thing. I asked it for fifty dollars. It said no way.

I went to a huge bathroom off the main foyer, with wood panelling and brass fixtures. I kept asking myself *what now?* But the answer wouldn't come.

Marvin was standing against the furthest of a line of ten or so stalls, facing me, but he was pretty much totally obscured by another man, who was facing Marvin, his back to me. They were standing very close. They performed what looked like a very brief handshake, and then the man turned to go. I ducked into the nearest cubicle so I wouldn't have to make eye contact with either of them.

"Alex? You in here?" Marvin's voice, from outside the cubicle.

"Yeah, I'm here."

"Thought I saw you come in. You need some privacy?"

No, I came into a toilet and locked myself in a cubicle because I really

really want to share.

"No, you're fine."

"Some digs, huh? This has to be the finest public water closet I have ever been in. I feel quite out of place."

I could hear him urinating.

"Marv…you got any more of those smiley pills? The ones we had in Vegas?"

"Why do you think I'm in here? I'll sort you out, my son, don't you worry."

The sound of a zip. The sound of a tap running.

"*Hoooot… soa-py waaa-ter*," he sang, in a Deep Purple refrain. "*Bam-bam-bam, bam-bam-ba-dam.* You know, it occurs to me that what you're missing is a *movement.*"

"Don't I know it. You're distracting me."

"Ha ha. We should change your stage name to Wry Cooder. What I mean is, a *cultural shift*, a blues bandwagon you can piggyback onto. You know, like grunge, or the swing revival. We need heavy British blues to come back with a big bang, and that could be the hook upon which you hang your hat. Cream, The Yardbirds, Hendrix, all that coke-snorting Sixties shower – if we can get a Nineties resuscitation along the same lines, man – pun totally intended – you're halfway there."

"And if we don't?"

"Well, that's the more sobering alternative. Don't get me wrong, man, I think you're pretty dynamite for a young 'un, but I worry that just might not be enough in this town. The place is literally *heaving* with talent. You can ride the wave, but you've got to wait for it to rise. And you sure as fuck don't miss it. It's all about the *timing.*"

"Well, seeing as you're talking like my manager again, got any ideas how one might give said wave a bit of a nudge?"

"That, my dear, is the sixty-four thousand-dollar question."

"Presumably one has to start somewhere?"

"Well, there's always some clown in the stands who starts waving their arms up and down in the hope that people will follow.

Sometimes it catches, other times 84,000 people just look at him like he's an idiot.

"But you start by playing. Then you keep playing. You play the right places. Then you keep at it, and keep your ears to the ground and go where the people are listening. Then you keep at it some more. Don't join the cops. This is Hollywood, baby."

I hadn't even lifted the lid, but I flushed for effect anyway, and opened the door. He was drying his hands on a paper towel – thick, watermarked, but paper nonetheless – and he was beaming.

"I think you need some drugs."

CHAPTER TWENTY-EIGHT

DICTAPHONE MONOLOGUES #7

INT. AMBASSADOR HOTEL - NIGHT

MARVIN

Where I'm from everybody loses sleep
about foot-and-mouth disease. In this
goddam town you need to be more careful
about geeks infected with the human
strain of bovine endeavour…

I rejoined the party. Well, inasmuch as I reentered the ballroom and hovered somewhere at the edge of the stage and the double doors that led out onto a terrace. My heart was drumming in my ribcage and I was aware of every single major organ. My breaths were sharp and pinched and I could *feel* that my pupils were huge and black.

There was a huge half-moon mahogany table pushed up against the wall. It was littered with empty and half-finished glasses and bottles. I wondered, if you collected the smeared saliva from the edge of each one, could you combine all the DNA to create the recipe for ultimate, unassailable, never-ending success? Could you grow the world's biggest superstar in a test tube?

The reason I asked mum about dad opening my mail was: Before taking the roofing job I had drifted from one nondescript deadender to another. One of these was as a trainee IT engineer – a gig my aspiring capitalist mate Barry had engineered for me in some supposedly-altruistic attempt to get me on the corporate ladder.

For reasons too tedious to recount, the company and I were

incompatible, and they let me go. There was a significant amount of skulduggery on their part in executing this – namely, that they invited me to company headquarters for 'a chat,' and only later did I realise that enticing me to make the hundred-mile journey was the only way they were going to get me to return their company car. After making the journey home (driving up in their pissant Ford Fiesta took two hours; coming home by buses and trains and long walks between the two took five), I found the termination letter on the mat, which meant they must have sent it after inviting me in for a first-thing appointment, meaning I'd miss the postman but find the letter when I got back. Sneaky fuckers.

The reason I thought of my dad was, I didn't actually find it on the mat. *He'd* found it, held it up to the light, read 'gross misconduct' through the envelope, and tore it open. Unbeknownst to me, he'd been having a shouting match with the regional boss while I'd been thumbing a lift home.

I was pissed off that he'd opened my mail; less so about the shouting match. Sometimes – whatever your age – it's nice for someone to go to bat for you in such a way. I, however, was trying to find my way as a man, and dad's actions just made me feel like a ten-year-old again.

Marvin had been starting to make me feel the same way for a while now, and we didn't have the benefit of being a generation apart.

Giving up suddenly seemed like a pointless, and no longer available, avenue. What did I have to go back for? Losing my job felt a bit like losing the anchor. I was here. Why not make the most of it? What the hell did I have to lose? I now had nothing at all. Why not start there?

I looked around the room. It was full of talent, charisma, sex appeal, staggering self-belief, Hollywood business acumen and a general sense of *knowing*. I wondered how the hell it was possible to penetrate this particular circle of wagons. My sphere of influence was about the size of a golf ball.

As I was musing, a friendly face arrived and punctured my self-doubt. Zephi's timing seemed like the silver lining to the whole deal. She smiled a smile that I suddenly, badly wanted to kiss.

"Hey," I said. "What's going on?"

"Not much."

"You look bored."

"Just a bit tired. The illusion of Hollywood glamour is kind of hard to maintain when the baby's had you up all night."

"Can I just say, then, that you pull it off extremely well."

She smiled.

"Where's the gang?" I said.

"Over there," she said, pointing vaguely at a sea of heads. "A night like tonight, if you get it right, can be useful credit later on. Get you a few rungs up the ladder. Etcetera. I believe they call it networking."

"I can't help but detect a note of disdain in your voice."

"Disdain? Moi?"

"Oh Christ, don't tell me you speak French as well. I'm doomed if you do."

She picked up a glass and sipped from it.

"What, exactly, is the story between you, Marvin and the gorgeous girl?"

"Now THAT is a long story. Just trying to recreate some Beat-era love dynamics."

"I hope you boys aren't fighting over her. Although it wouldn't be hard to understand if you were. She's stunning."

I didn't say anything, but held her gaze.

"Do you know something, I might go home. I can barely keep my eyes open," she said.

"Well, I'll go and get the others."

"No, no, they're ok. It's way too early by their standards."

"If you're tired, I'll drive you."

"No, that's really kind of you. You don't have do that."

"I really don't mind. It's the least I can do for you getting me a spot onstage. I've kind of peaked, anyway."

She thought about it.

"If you don't mind? I don't want to spoil your evening."

"I'll forgive you if you do."

She smiled again.

"Well, okay then. Thank you. I suppose I should go and let them know, at least."

"I can do that."

"Okay. I'll meet you by the car. It's the dark blue Mustang."

"Great. Er, where is it?"

"The valet will bring it round."

"Ah."

I wandered off. I found Marvin, Roger and Marie forming a triumvirate around two very large, ebullient characters with German accents who were, in turn, apparently schmoozing three more guys who had 'big shots' written all over their faces. The ego vibe was fascinating, but suffocating. It was clearly business, and Marie, hanging off Marvin's arm, was nicely sugar-coating whatever pitch was going down. I didn't want to interrupt, so I hung back for a moment.

They hadn't noticed me. In a brief aside, Marvin and Roger shared a joke about The Royal Standard. For just a second I thought they were reminiscing about their favourite pub back home, but it only took me a second or two to realise they were talking about Zephi.

I turned and disappeared back into the crowd. They didn't notice.

The California air hit me in a balmy wave of light pollution and moisture. I smelled frying and smog; every sense was tickled with the unfamiliarity of a dream and unspoken promise.

Zephi was waiting outside, next to a marble pillar at the hotel's entrance. She had taken one of her shoes off and was bending down to rub her foot. She stood up when I approached. There was a brilliantly-lit canopy covering the walk from the kerb to the revolving door, and her face tilted upwards towards the lights.

She didn't say anything, but she met my eyes. Her dark blue Mustang appeared from around the corner before I could speak, and a tall, muscular valet with an earring and a beard hopped out.

"Your keys, ma'am," he said.

She didn't answer, but pointed towards me, and the outstretched hand with the keys in rotated ninety degrees to my waiting palm. He was professional throughout, but as he dropped the keys in my hand he held my stare for just a little longer than was necessary.

"You haven't been drinking, have you?" Zephi said, smiling.

I smiled back and shook my head. It was technically true; she hadn't said anything about little smiley pills.

I pulled out onto Wilshire, my senses doing a strange cocktail of pure excitement and the chilled-out bliss of night cruising. Those times in my life when I had encountered worry or stress, driving just seemed to take it away, replacing it instead with a curious confidence about life. Had we taken a cab or walked, the night might have played a different tune.

She pressed a button, and *Oxford Gray* started on the stereo.

"I didn't know you liked Shuggie Otis," I said.

"Excuse me, person I've just met who's crashed on my couch a handful of times, I would wager there's a lot about me you don't know," she said. The street lights of the boulevard bathed her face as she turned to look at me, making her seem part of the city. "Figured this is your kind of thing, though."

"Hey, anyone who can turn down an offer from the Rolling Stones is okay by me."

The car swished over the tarmac, and she lit a cigarette. Her window moaned as she slid it down.

"I thought that was banned everywhere now," I said.

"Practically. Watch out for the smoking police."

"You're a rebel, huh?"

"Not really, but something in that place just brings it out in me. I should have lit up in there. Can you imagine?"

She lit another one, and passed it to me. I tasted her lipstick.

"Well, you'd have certainly made an impression."

"I know. Cheap, sensational and forgotten by the morning, like so many cute tricks in this town."

"Don't they call that the casting couch?"

"Couch, desk, staircase, whatever."

"You sound a little jaded."

"Do I? Don't get me wrong. I don't need to be on a billboard, I don't need to make millions, I just want to do a little bit of something that I enjoy and maybe make a few bucks doing it. But I don't want to trample over my friends or blow the producer to do it."

"You only have to do that if you're trying to cover a distinct lack of talent. That isn't something you have to worry about."

"Oh yeah? You been watching my screen tests?"

I cleared my throat and turned onto Fairfax. Shuggie gave way to Grover Washington Jr's *Mister Magic*.

"No, but you can just tell. It's in the way you carry yourself. You know, your confidence. Your charisma."

I deliberately didn't take my eyes off the road.

"I wasn't fishing. But you're sweet."

"Hey, I'm not blowing smoke. I mean it."

"Well, what about you? Don't you get frustrated by the lack of breaks?"

"I just need time. The world will be mine, you wait and see." I gave a baritone laugh and twirled my imaginary moustache. "They will all come to fear the handiwork of the dreaded.... Viennese Finger!"

She spluttered a laugh.

"Seriously, it's baby steps. You just got to keep on the ladder. Keep on keeping on, whatever that means."

"I hope it works out the way you want it. I really do. You've got that... fearless thing about you. Nothing seems to faze you. You've come all the way out here with your guitar and a plan, and you just kind of know it's going to happen for you. That's so cool. Hey, Marvin said you were joining the cops."

"He did?"

"He did."

"Application's already done. It was gonna be Hollywood or bust."

"That's pretty black and white. You're what, twenty? Bit young for last chances. But, respect. Just don't give up quite yet, huh?"

"Deal. And same to you."

"I'm twenty-eight. *My* Hollywood clock is winding down."

"Ah, that's bullshit. That's all the more reason, if you ask me. Don't give up because the industry's fucked. It probably needs more people like you. I tell you, you knocked spots off every other bug-eyed starlet there tonight."

She didn't say anything. I turned to her. She was smiling at me, and I suddenly felt lightheaded.

"Listen, thank you again for getting me onstage," I said, clearing my throat again for the third time in as many minutes. "I really appreciate it."

"Hey, no problem. Did you enjoy it?"

I stared at the road.

"I loved it."

"Feels good."

"Too good. It's like gambling. I thought I'd be happy with a weekly spot. You know, drinks covered, enough to meet the rent, but you just want more. Bigger crowds, bigger clubs."

"You crave that applause, huh?"

"Like you wouldn't believe."

"It's addictive, baby. You're never satisfied, even if you end up selling out the Civic Auditorium," she said.

"If that ever happens I'll give it all up and go be a farmer."

"That would be about the most rock 'n' roll thing you could do," she said. "Maybe that's why dreams should stay just that." She looked out of the window, and then turned back to me. "So, what you doing for the millennium?"

The question threw me. The last four or five New Years had

been a grotesque medley of warm tongues, warmer ale, sweaty flesh in airless pubs and wretched unconsciousness. Waking up somewhere that wasn't going to get the cops called was considered a bonus.

"I don't know. I suppose I ought to do something a bit... momentous."

"We're supposed to be going to Times Square, but it's going to be a zoo. Plus I'll need a second mortgage to get a sitter for Harry."

"I don't imagine New Year's in Santa Monica will be too shabby."

She gave a derisory snort.

"Knowing my luck I'll probably break down on the way to wherever I'm headed. Spend the millennium in a layby."

It was meant for a laugh, but she twisted in her seat and looked at me intently.

"You might do," she said. "But if you did, you know what? I bet you'd still have a good time. You're that kind of guy."

"I am?"

I followed her directions onto West 6th and Beverly, and then we were pulling up onto the driveway of the house on La Jolla.

I killed the engine and we sat there in the silence for a moment, listening to the tick-tick-tick of the engine. The moon fought its way through the thick canopy of night smog for a moment, and filtered through the trees onto her face.

"Come on, then," she said, and got out of the car.

The house was in darkness.

"Where's little man?" I whispered as she opened the front door.

"Oh, my mom's got him. She lives in Crescent Heights. I'll go and get him in the morning."

She went into the kitchen, dumped her bag on the counter and switched the lights on. I hesitated in the lounge. Suddenly it was her house again and I was a guest she hardly knew and we were back to the politeness and small talk of strangers.

The light in the kitchen went out. She came out holding two glasses of water.

"You good?" she said, putting one on the coffee table.

"Good," I said. "Thanks."

"Okay. Good night."

And she disappeared into her bedroom.

I stood there for a moment in the darkness. I found the light switch and looked around the lounge. The hostel room was still technically mine. The car was still there, but I could maybe scrape together enough change for a cab.

My eyes settled on the garage-sale guitar that I had lumbered around with me and dumped at the house before poncing off to the party. I switched the light off and sat down on the sofa. My eyes adjusted quickly, and the lounge became filtered with a blend of light pollution and moonlight.

I was halfway through *Ain't No Sunshine* when her bedroom door opened.

The open door cast a rectangle of light across the dark lounge, framing her in silhouette at the end of the kitchen counter. The edges of her hair were like glowing filaments, and I could see she had changed into nightwear – which, with the light from behind her, wasn't concealing much.

I paused as she stood there.

"That's beautiful," she said. Her voice was a whisper.

I continued playing.

She moved across the room; her eyes, gleaming in the darkness, didn't move from mine.

She stood in front of me. I could smell coconut and jasmine and a hint of alcohol. I could feel her warmth. She cradled my head and pressed it against her belly.

I put the guitar down and she straddled my lap. She had just brushed her teeth, and her mouth was warm and cold at the same time, her slender, muscular arms strong around my neck. Whatever she was wearing was shed in a single movement, and I was struck by this sudden, incredible sense of intimacy – I hardly knew her, we'd exchanged little more than the pleasantries of friends of friends who are practically strangers, and yet here I was breathing her in and feeling hot, wet flesh and inhaling her scent, her *want*.

In fact, it was too weird. A car passed outside. Its headlights lit up the room momentarily, and caught the glass of a framed family picture of Zephi, Roger and Harry.

I broke away.

"No," I said. "We can't."

"What? Yes, we can," she said, her breath hot on my neck.

"Harry."

"He isn't here."

"That isn't what I mean."

She got the message, and slowed down. Eventually she stood up.

"I'm sorry. It isn't that I don't want to," I said. "I mean, I *really* want to. But you have a family."

I thought she might be angry. Maybe packaged little side-fucks were all part of Californian monogamy, and it was all perfectly acceptable and just how weird was I?

She didn't say anything, but collected her nightie, touched my lips with her finger and walked naked back to her bedroom.

She shut the door without a word.

I picked up my guitar and the pack of Lucky Strikes she had left on the counter, opened the door, and stepped out into the warm balmy promise of the Hollywood night, for a long, long walk.

CHAPTER TWENTY-NINE

DICTAPHONE MONOLOGUES #8

INT. PACIFIC JETSTREAM OFFICES, SANTA MONICA – DAY

                    MARVIN
                  [*on phone*]
        Don't be ridiculous. Everybody in the
        world has a boss.
                    [*beat*]
        Except maybe Noel Gallagher...

You forget that America doesn't have the same depth of history as England, but once upon a time the hostel was a grand hotel, or a trading post, or some kind of municipal building. The whole place was thickly whitewashed, and the huge, heavy, bedroom window was caked in white gloss. I didn't think it would open, but it slid upwards without protest.

I climbed out onto the fire escape and lit a cigarette from the pack I had taken to save Zephi some embarrassing questions, watching the Vine Street lights glow, her scent and hot breath still circling my brain.

On the corner of the street a woman and a man were arguing. He was a pot-bellied guy with a crumpled suit. She was about four inches taller than him, with a pink leather jacket and bright blue heels. She was squawking and pointing in a way that would have had me backing down, but he was fuelled by the righteous indignation of the recently defrauded, and he was giving as good as he got.

A police cruiser rolled past. She ran over, waving her arms, and it slowed down. She bent down to the driver's window and began an animated complaint, gesticulating periodically at the small man. I couldn't hear exactly what she was saying, but I got the gist. He was standing defiant with his arms folded, clearly waiting for his turn.

The cops got out. One tried to calm the woman, while the other went to speak with the man. He began a similarly excited complaint; unlike the woman, however, he apparently didn't like the answer he got. He rechannelled his disquiet into the cops, at one point taking a step forward and pointing his finger right in the cop's face. Then the finger travelled south, and poked the cop in the chest.

Big mistake.

The cop stepped off to the side and twisted the man's arm up behind him, causing him to double over. The second cop ran over, unclipping his nightstick as he did so. He swung it out with a flourish, and brought it up into the man's belly.

I sucked on the cigarette.

This startled the woman, and the soundtrack of squealing and wailing was suddenly silenced. It just became the sound of breathing and whimpering as the cops laid into the man. She broke something under her nose and inhaled deeply.

The beating only lasted a matter of seconds. Then they got in the cruiser and drove away. The man lay in a crumpled heap in his crumpled suit, twitching and moaning. The woman was confused – she took a step towards him, and then away, and then just walked in circles like a shuffling zombie.

A third figure entered the tableau. He looked at the woman, then at the man, then took out a camera and started photographing the whole sorry scene.

He was small, with ginger hair, a string vest and stars-and-stripes pantaloons, and in a bizarre moment that made me think that maybe I was more at home than I thought, I realised I recognised him. It was Marcello, the improbable shoplifter I had met at Venice Beach shortly after arriving all those eons ago.

He looked worse than I remembered, skinny and grey and

kind of shadowy. His clothes looked wet and were hanging off his thin frame.

He continued snapping away, and then, when he was apparently satisfied, he crouched down by the man and started going through his pockets. He pulled out his wallet and started investigating the contents.

That was when I remembered I had seen his stupid pantaloons more recently than Venice Beach. He'd been at the Mint. He was there when the Casino was taken off me.

I was suddenly galvanised into action. I flicked the cigarette and sprinted down to the street, but by the time I got there, the little prick had vanished.

"Dammit!" I yelled. He was obviously just a parasite, feeding off the scraps of other kills.

The man had rolled onto his back. He was crying and swearing, one arm over his eyes. There was a white line where his wedding ring had been. I went towards him, intending to do something, maybe check his wallet, but there was no way he wouldn't have misinterpreted it, and I hesitated. He clearly wasn't dead, at least.

"Suck your cock, baby?"

I turned. The woman was addressing me. I hadn't quite shrugged off the cloak of arousal from messing around with Zephi, and for just a tiny second I considered it. But she was looking through me – her eyes were hollow and glazed, her teeth were bad, her cheeks sunken. It seemed likely that inviting her to my bedroom would have resulted in my ending up in a similarly ignominious state to the man at my feet, figuratively or otherwise.

As it turned out, it would have been a crowded old affair anyway. I went back to the room via an all-night store for water and supplies, but when I got back, I was surprised to find the door locked. It was an old-fashioned key-and-mortice affair – I had left it open, and Marie had the only other key.

Fortunately, my key was in my pocket. I opened the door a

fraction, and froze. The unmistakable sound of giggling and rustling sheets greeted me. Through the crack I saw writhing bodies and Marvin's bare arse as he scrambled for the covers.

"Could... could you give us a minute?" Marie giggled.

I flung the door open and threw the shopping bag and donuts on the bed. One of the water bottles must have collided somewhere delicate, for Marvin let out a pained squeak.

"What the fuck is this?"

"Sorry, honey, just let me..."

"This is *my* fucking room, which I paid for with *my* fucking money," I shouted, the camel's back finally giving way. "You've been rubbing my nose in your fucking naked arses for a month, and now you can't even fuck off and do it at his house?"

"Alex..."

"Get the fuck out, the pair of you."

"Christ, will you pass my jeans, or something?"

"Actually, fuck it. Stay. Enjoy yourselves. I'm out of here."

"Alex..."

I grabbed the car keys and stormed off, raw anger flooding through me, silently hoping Marvin would follow me so I could put him on his backside. I wasn't even drunk.

But the hand pulling at me was Marie's. I spun round. She was wrapped in a sheet. I pulled her into the pool room.

"Alex, please. I'm so sorry."

"Oh, save it, will you. What do you want?"

"Where are you going?"

"I'm going to New York. On my own."

Her eyes widened with genuine... something.

"You can't. Please don't. Please wait for me. We'll go together."

"You must be joking. Look, don't let me get in your way. It's best this way. You two get to do what you like without worrying about my feelings, and I finally get to salvage a little dignity."

"I *do* care about your feelings."

"You must think I'm stupid."

She sank to the floor in a drunken mess. The sheet started to unravel around her modesty. A nipple winked at me.

"Please don't go. I didn't know… I love both of you. You know that's possible, right?"

"I'm out of here."

I ran down to the car, trying desperately to outrun the snapping jaws of three rabid Furies called Guilt, Fear and Anger.

CHAPTER THIRTY

DICTAPHONE MONOLOGUES #9

INT. CAR/TRAFFIC JAM, SANTA MONICA FREEWAY - NIGHT

MARVIN

[*going nowhere fast*]

You want to know the most dangerous
person in Hollywood? The guy who works
in the photocopy shop...

I tore out onto Hollywood Boulevard, the back of the car fishtailing across the lanes. A taxi hooted at me. I pushed the throttle down, and the automatic transmission blipped through the gears as I floored it along the long, straight road. The engine sounded like an old man gargling.

It was 2am, and the few cars that did impede my progress were rapidly overtaken. I belted east, towards downtown, not realising until the rising skyline of gleaming tower blocks had practically enveloped me that I was, in all probability, going away from San Francisco, not towards it.

There was a strange comfort in being surrounded by the skyscrapers. The wash of light over the city was like a net – red and amber and green and blue and gold, with no real darkness anywhere.

I continued to speed through the streets, running red lights, driving like a maniac, the only sound the thump of the tyres and the howl of the engine, my only thought some vague idea of getting onto a freeway and heading north.

I rounded a corner at speed, and suddenly the light was gone. I was on a flat stretch of black road with dumpsters and warehouses and boarded up windows.

I saw the man at the intersection. He was little more than a silhouette, but he was smoking, and the green light from the traffic signal reflected off the gun in his hand.

He looked up at the light as it turned red, and stepped off the kerb, clearly expecting me to slow for the stop light. He brought the gun up, a snarling crazy wanting to jack my car and lunch on my innards.

"Bring it, you prick," I said, and pressed my foot down harder.

I leaned the car in towards the kerb. His eyes widened as he realised I was both speeding up and heading straight for him.

I opened the door as I got closer to him. In a panic he brought the gun up to aim, but he was too slow, and I slammed the door into him as I sailed past. All I heard was a crunch, and then I was out onto the boulevard again with my friend the light.

The car fishtailed again – it didn't spin, but it veered so far out into the middle of the road that it caught the edge of the central reservation.

Suddenly the car was no longer in my control. It spun across the road, and I had the curious sensation of travelling backwards at speed, then it caught something else and flipped over. It rolled only the once, but with a deafening crash of twisted metal. I had instinctively put my seatbelt on before embarking on this ill-advised journey, but I was still bounced around like a soft boiled egg in a tin can.

It came to rest the right way up, steam hissing from the engine bay. There was an unpleasant metallic smell, which, I realised, was the blood pouring from a gash in my head. There was a dull ache in my ribs, which became a sharp, pointed prong of agony as I shifted in the seat.

I got the crazy idea that I was being called across the ocean, that invisible forces were trying to pull me home, and the only thing holding me here was the seatbelt. I fumbled and poked at the buckle, but there was something wrong with my arms. They were incredibly heavy, like I had slept all night with them trapped underneath me. I suddenly felt tired, and wanted to close my eyes.

I admired the Los Angeles sky from flat on my back in the middle of the street for the second time in as many nights. It was beautiful, and *huge*. It was like a palette of purple, gold and blue, the lights from the street pulsing through the floating mist and smoke like an electrical current through a jellyfish, the supercharged thermonuclear atmosphere of some post-apocalyptic world. The towers of the business district pointed away from me to the sky like suggestive fingers, and I realised that the sky was more enchanting than usual because the driver's door was missing and the roof of the car had been partially ripped off, the twisted rod of the fractured A-frame arching off the car like a scorpion's tail.

I thumped at the belt buckle again, and it suddenly sprang free. I hadn't realised quite how much I had been relying on it to keep me upright; as soon as it released me I tumbled out of the car and landed heavily in the road. A spike of pain that made me think of rusty scissors cutting through soft powdery cushion stuffing raced through my body, and I wished I'd left the sodding belt alone.

Salty wetness dripped into my mouth, and my nose began to make gurgling sucking noises. I realised I was crying.

It began to rain, great fat fingers of it hurling themselves down from the sky. It was warm, and the residual smell of dust and dirt and oil and rubber that was released felt like it hadn't rained in a long time.

The surface of the road was surprisingly soft against my cheek. I wondered how many footprints and tyre tracks had been fossilised into the tarmac over the years, how many glass shards and bone fragments had been unceremoniously swept to the kerb, how many yards of blood had been hosed down without mercy; imprints of momentum, all in the name of keeping everything *moving*.

The raccoon tail had survived the crash. It hung off the exhaust like a piece of bedraggled roadkill. BABY FACED BLUES began to drip red and blue paint onto the road. The great jazz-fuelled

Beat journeys of the 1950s and the Fillmore motorcycle acid wave of Kesey's 1960s and the Gonzo longhair rock hangover of 1971 suddenly seemed to be some great big lie, some great big piece of propaganda and made-up history.

I pushed myself up onto my arms in some vague parody of half a press-up, and my existential meandering, fuelled by the pills on one side and pain-induced semi-consciousness on the other, continued. Seeing the road, stationary and up close, seemed to me to be a great opportunity to have some regard to its wonder. What would life be without roads? A series of islands dotted all over the earth; they might be a handful of miles apart, but each would be totally isolated from the other. It linked cities, economies and whole worlds. It created trade routes, bound cultures and connected lovers. The umbrella of light created by the street lights and traffic signals and buildings seemed to me to be an indication of its greatness – no celebrity or landmark or classic painting anywhere in the world got this much of a light show. I looked down at my static patch of tarmac and imagined all the cars and trucks thundering over it, sucking up the miles like vacuum cleaners over an endless ribbon of practicality, not giving any thought to the wonder of its existence.

I think I passed out.

I became dimly aware of sirens in the distance about the same time that I was commenting, inwardly, on how remarkably *quiet* it was. They seemed a long way off, and then in an instant I was surrounded by flashing red and white strobes and the air horn of a fire truck. Paramedics bustled around me, and a blade sliced through the belt.

"Just take it easy, sir. You're gonna be okay," said a bright Californian voice, then there was a draught as a cold blade slit through my clothing, and darkness.

I awoke on a trolley in a brightly-lit emergency room somewhere on West Olympia. A black nurse with a misty face wrote something on a clipboard. When she saw me she smiled and touched a hand to my brow. The world shook, and I knew my pockets were empty.

"You been playing with that cotton candy?" she asked in singsong Creole.

I opened my mouth. It felt like it had been glued shut.

"You'll be just fine," she said. "But we need to know who you are."

"I don't think… I don't think I'm ever leaving this place," I said to her.

She removed the hand from my brow and went back to writing on the clipboard, a puzzled look on her face, and the world shook again.

Then I dreamed of Marvin, his tanned, kind face peering over me with concern. He was wearing a black T-shirt that said WHEN DOES MIST BECOME FOG in big white letters. I tried to lift my arm to sock him one, but it felt like lead.

"You'll be alright, you boob," he said. "They found the carjacker. You're not in any trouble. Just get better."

I wanted to say *Where's Marie?* but my mouth was like tree bark. I dreamed of a yellow cab journey with a Bolivian driver, who drove me to a hotel room on Hollywood Boulevard and wheeled me into the room with his brothers, while I floated on a wave of painkillers.

As it turned out, the pain was like a storm that passed over pretty quickly, and my eventual diagnosis was a cracked rib, cuts, bruises and a query concussion. I made a joke to a pretty nurse about the concussion being due to my whisky intake, but she seemed to turn her nose up. After two nights – most of which was spent as high as a kite – they turned me loose.

Marie had not visited, but she came with Marvin to get me, wide-eyed with concern and worry. The story seemed to have unfolded with me as the fortunate near-victim of a vicious robbery, not as an idiot that had rolled his car in a tantrum-induced loss of control. I was too much of a coward and too craving of Marie's attention to burst that particular bubble.

"Gently, dearest, gently," I said as she enveloped me in a tight hug. I didn't want a wheelchair, but they gave me a cane, which I thought was pretty cool, as I hobbled out through the white sliding doors into the blinding sunshine of West Olympia. I blinked in the baking California sun, the air hot and dry, and the place felt, suddenly and curiously, like home.

Paradoxically, the other thing that was pretty cool was being able to say *just bill my insurance company* when that thorny issue surfaced. Yes, I had travel insurance. Not very Kerouac – maybe it would have been more romantic to allow a natural healing process stretched out on a park bench or something – but then half the Beats didn't see fifty, of course. God bless you, dad.

I convalesced at the hostel. I was privy to some talk about stretching out on Marvin's sofa, but Marie seemed adamant that the hustle-bustle of a busy family household – not to mention the marauding toddler – would be prejudicial to my recovery. I was quietly relieved; as they spoke, the sudden – albeit not altogether unwelcome – memory of Zephi's soft touch suddenly appeared in my brain. It was a secret as far as I was concerned, but I had no idea if she'd confessed all to Roger in a moment of guilty madness, and I had no desire to find out. Even if she hadn't, facing her wouldn't have been exactly comfortable.

So I stretched out on the crisp white sheets, and allowed Marie to make a fuss.

"I called your folks," she said. "I hope that's okay."

"You did? Are they okay?"

"They were worried, of course. Your mum wanted you to come straight home, but I said you were just bruised. I told them they caught the carjacker, which helped, I think."

She shook her head.

"What were you thinking?" she said. "That guy could have shot you. He could have *killed* you. And for what?"

I suddenly felt a huge wave of sadness. It must have shown.

"What is it?" she said, looking concerned. "Do you need some more painkillers?"

"You called my folks," I said.

"Should I not have done?"

"If you hadn't, there'd have been no one else to do it."

She saw where I was going with it.

"Well, Marvin…" she said, weakly.

"He doesn't know my folks. He doesn't know me well enough to call them without reference to me. He doesn't know the *number*."

She didn't say anything.

"We've got *history*, Marie. You can't change that."

She looked towards the window.

"You bastard, driving off like that," she said. "Don't you know how worried I was? I could have *lost you*."

She squeezed my hand. Her eyes were glistening.

"I still love you, goddammit," I said.

She pulled me to her, and kissed my forehead, her breasts warm against my chest.

"Ssh," she said. "Sssh."

CHAPTER THIRTY-ONE

DICTAPHONE MONOLOGUES #10

INT. FROLIC BAR, HOLLYWOOD - NIGHT

ALEX

Listen, the script. Silver Arrows. I
liked it. I mean, I really liked it.

MARVIN

[*glasses chink, ambient bar noise*]
Thanks, man. That means a lot. Editing
has always been more my thing, you
know?

ALEX

The characters were… I could *feel* them,
you know?

MARVIN

Listen, it's no great shakes. Trust me.
I have a list I work through when I'm
drawing up characters. First of all: if
your character has a bumper sticker on
their car, what would it say? If indeed
they are the type to sport bumper
stickers.

Second: what does it say on the front of
your T-shirt? 'Fuck The Police?' 'Don't
Bomb The Snowdrops?' Or 'Stanford: Class
of 1986?'

```
Third: Who do you vote for?

Fourth: If the CIA wanted to kill you,
how would they describe you at the
briefing?

Fifth: Are you the kind of person who
wears a hi-vis jacket while walking the
dog?

Finally: you've had a steady friendship
with a guy for twenty years. Then one
day, you go to him for money. Obviously,
you're a little desperate. Or maybe
you're not. Maybe you have no shame.
Maybe that's part of YOUR character
development. Anyway, what does the
friend do? Refuse? Charge you massive
interest? Turn up to collect once a month
without fail? Or does he say: don't
worry, pay me when you can. Or maybe he
says that to begin with, then after three
months he's turning up the heat. Like
Bobby Womack said: you don't know what a
man will do until he's put under
pressure. You see, things are only
constant while the surroundings are.
When things change, people change…
```

After a few days convalescing – which I milked, frankly, to the *nth* degree – during which Marie and I barely ventured out, I felt quite significantly better. Not just physically, but about myself, about Life, prospects, the whole thing. Maybe I felt there was now a bit more parity in the trifecta. It was probably the drugs. Whatever, I had the idea that the three of us should hang out again – my idea, not Marie's. So Marie and I hopped the bus and headed west to Marvin's.

We walked up the path to Marvin's house. We were sharing a joke about something and so we were practically at the front door before I realised I could hear raised voices from within. I slowed my step. I thought about doing a U-turn altogether, but that would have invited more questions from Marie than I was prepared to answer. Besides, she was already knocking on the door.

It wasn't Marvin that opened it.

It was Roger.

This was not completely unexpected – it was his house, after all – but he opened it so quickly that it looked like he might have been on his way out anyway.

And he looked like shit. He was red-eyed and still in his dressing gown at two in the afternoon. At first I thought maybe the coke had caught up with him, but then I realised he had been crying.

He knows, I thought. *Oh shit, he knows about me and Zephi and I've destroyed his family and it's all going to come out and I'm going to get thumped for the third time in as many days…*

"Oh," he said. "It's you two."

"Um, hi, Roger…" Marie started. "Is Marvin… is everything okay?"

He looked from Marie to me and back again, with a look of such haughty disapproval that it made me feel like I did the time my dad finally opened the front door to my hammering at 4am after I had missed the last train and staggered home plastered.

"It's Marvin," he said, blowing air out of his nostrils in a way that suggested even speaking to us was a tremendous effort, an honour that us mere mortals were not worthy of.

"What about him?" I said, thinking *he's dead, isn't he? Some fucker's gone and killed him. I was in a car crash and he had to go and top that so now he'll forever be Marie's legend.*

"For Christ's sake, Roger. Let them in, will you," came Zephi's voice from inside the house.

Roger pushed the door slowly open and moved to the side, his eyes burrowing into mine as I passed.

He shut the door and turned to face us. Zephi was pacing up and down in the kitchen. She didn't make eye contact. We sat meekly down on the sofa like we'd never been there before, as if Marvin's absence had rewound us back through time by the best part of two months.

Marie was tense beside me, silently demanding an explanation, while I just hung my head and waited for a smug self-righteous telling off from a man older, wiser and richer than me. I didn't think he would hit me.

"*So tell me, young man, how does my wife taste?*"

But nothing happened. The tension in the air was like the LA smog.

"So what's going on?" Marie finally said.

Roger folded his arms and sulked.

"Go on, Roger. Tell them," Zephi said, from the other side of the kitchen counter.

His shoulders slumped a little.

"They came for him. They took him."

"Roger... what are you talking about?" I said, finding my voice as it became slowly apparent the issue of the day might actually have nothing to do with me.

And he told us the story.

It seemed that Marvin's employment with Pacific Jetstream had actually been terminated some six months previously. His work visa had only been temporary, and when it came up for renewal, he no longer had a job to give the INS any kind of reason to show an interest in his application. Roger had tried to keep him on as some sort of freelance script editor, and the urgency to complete *Viennese Finger* had supposedly been so they had a tangible product to wave under the noses of the bureaucrats (and, I wondered, to make sure they got their money's worth). But it hadn't cut the mustard, and the visa had been rejected.

Marvin had been living as an illegal overstayer for the past four and a half months, and the enforcement arm of the INS had come to the house to scoop him up that very morning.

"But… the job. The meetings. The video shoots," I said, my lack of understanding sounding totally fatuous.

Roger didn't say anything, and he didn't need to. Clearly it had all been one big lie.

"What about his money?" Marie said. There were tears in her eyes.

"That's the good news," Zephi said from the kitchen. "At least he was already gone when the men from the credit card company came."

"Oh, Jesus," I said.

"You've missed out the part about how he was able to get away with it so long," Zephi said.

"We don't need to talk about that now," Roger said, looking at Marie, mustering a hollow smile intended to reassure that all was well in the marital bed.

"I think we should," Zephi said. She was extremely busy in the kitchen, and when I chanced a quick look, I realised she was packing Harry's bowls and beakers into a holdall. "I think they deserve to know that you were complicit in Marvin's fraud."

He got up and headed for the kitchen, and I caught a wave of whisky fumes. There followed an urgent exchange between the two of them, Zephi far less concerned about being heard than he was.

"Roger… where is he?" I said, standing. "Is he back in England?"

He turned to me.

"You don't need to worry about it," he said, the remaining shreds of the façade evaporating as he realised any attempts to stay the row between him and Zephi were futile. "It's all under control. My lawyer has it in hand. It really doesn't concern you."

"You goddam sanctimonious asshole," Zephi said.

"Where *is* he?" Marie echoed.

"I said..."

"Roger, can you stop being a prick for five seconds and answer her?" I said, his petulance causing a spectacular headache to form.

"He's at the Adelanto Detention Center," Zephi said.

There was a moment when nobody spoke. Then Roger turned on me, a snide grin on his face.

"Did you really think you could come out here for a couple of months and compete? You need to *commit*, boy. Acts like you are a dime a dozen. And you're not half as good as you think you are. You will never make it."

"That's it. I've had enough of this shit," Zephi said, and hauled a bunch of bags to the front door. She opened it and wedged it with her foot as she pushed the bags onto the path.

"He's right, Roger. You really are a prick."

CHAPTER THIRTY-TWO

DICTAPHONE MONOLOGUES #11

```
EXT. LAS VEGAS BOULEVARD - NIGHT

                    MARIE
      When you think about it, there's
      nothing quite as incredible as a
      bubble. The perfection, the fragility,
      the incredible beauty. Most people
      don't deserve to be anywhere near one…
```

The Adelanto Detention Center was a massive white concrete cube one hundred miles northeast of Los Angeles, and a three-hour bus ride through the sweltering California desert.

Marvin was unshaven, and dressed in an orange jumpsuit with the collar of a white vest forming a triangle at his neck. He wore a large pair of dark glasses – presumably to cover the bruising underneath – but they still gave him the air of a star having fallen from grace.

I wanted to laugh with horror. It was every prison movie I'd ever seen. The whole thing was just stupid, like he was in fancy dress or playing an extra in one of his movies. It couldn't be *real*.

"When you mentioned the Man bursting our bubble, this isn't what I had in mind. Something like a parking ticket would have been a bit easier to absorb."

I meant it, as well. Kerouac and his cronies often stuck their collective thumb on the nerve endings of the establishment – that was kind of the point – but it never seemed to derail their cause, their spirit.

This was different.

"Don't you believe it," Marvin said. "You want a real example of the Man sticking his beak in? Go along to one of Led Zeppelin's plagiarism trials – I think they're pretty much biennial – and listen to one of the musicologists give expert evidence. Now that, my friend, is how to kill romance."

"Marvin – *look at you*."

"Roger says his lawyer is on it," Marie said. There were tears in her eyes, but her voice was steady. "He's going to get you out."

"I think… I would just like to go home," Marvin said. "I will open a pub called *The Naked Bandit*. Fighting it is all well and good, but it will slow everything down interminably. I'm not actually sure how long I will last in here, if I'm honest."

"Don't say that!" Marie said.

"Besides, it's not exactly the kind of job that requires me being in the office," he said. "I can still do script edits for them, and with email they'll get them instantly, more or less. Then if things pick up I can always look to come back. Although I think that if you leave in a jumpsuit on a chartered INS flight, it tends to cast a dim light over your hopes of ever coming back."

"There are plenty of other places with year-round sun," I said. "The whole place will fall into the sea one day, anyway."

"Marvin… will you please take your sunglasses off," Marie said.

"Trust me, you don't want to see what's under here," he said.

"Marvin, listen," I said, getting a sudden cold feeling that this was it, that I wasn't going to see him again. "I just wanted to say… thanks."

"You're welcome."

"No, I mean… thanks for helping me out. For helping me see things differently. For helping me be easier on myself. For… helping me realise most things I want are on my doorstep."

I looked at Marie out of the corner of my eye. It sounded trite, and he didn't let me off the hook.

"Tut, tut, tut. I expected more of you than ripping off Judy Garland."

"I wasn't…"

"Don't be telling me you had an epiphany, my friend. You just stopped caring about the future for a while because you were drunk and having a good time."

"But…"

"Alex, you need to forget all that shit I told you. All that stuff about hope and dreams and the lottery being within Tantalus's grasp. It was a lie. You'll never make it here."

He pressed his palm to the glass, a sudden note of urgency in his voice.

"Take care of your futures, my friends. There will be fortifications going up at every border. The prehistoric landmass will continue to disintegrate and fragment, while millions of refugees stagger across the land like sidelong antibodies without a host. They'll be glad they kept the pieces of the Berlin Wall.

"I worry that our place in history is still facing backwards. You think things like Columbine and Copeland won't happen again? Like hell – that shit will just become fashionable. We only got a peace deal in Kosovo because NATO pummelled the refugee convoys and the embassies that had nothing to do with it. We may be on the cusp of the millennium, but future peoples will still look back on us and see nothing but hateful savages."

Marie was crying properly now. Marvin's speech had caught the ear of some huge dude a few booths down, who was looking at him with a sideways smirk – the kind of smirk that suggested he felt some fun was in the offing later on.

"So safe journey, my friends. I'll see you on the flipside."

He got up and ambled off without looking back, the phone receiver dangling, his sweaty palm print smeared on the glass.

Marie and I couldn't adjust. Even our semi-reconciliations had been, I now realised, conducted with the knowledge that Marvin was still around. I took no comfort in the fact that, technically, I now had her all to myself. You can't recreate the past, and all that.

That we had booked our respective flights home on different days from different airports now seemed like a huge deal, but it was too expensive to move them around, so we agreed to fly home separately and hook up again on the other side of the ocean.

Marie's flight was out of San Francisco in a couple of days; mine from LAX a week later. With a heavy, numb feeling and a lack of motivation to do anything else – and, I guess, a freezing fear of being alone again – I went with her to San Francisco to see her off.

Having a few days to spare ended up being sound planning – we took a cab to Union Station, but the servicing schedule meant we had to get a bus to Bakersfield to catch the Amtrak. The train broke down after twenty miles, meaning we had to wait two hours for the 6.45 to come along to rescue us. Needless to say, it was standing room only. Marie called ahead to tell the hostel in San Francisco we were running late – only to be told we would lose the reservation and the deposit after midnight.

We got off the train at Merced and took a bus to Oakland where we changed to another bus to take us the rest of the way to San Francisco.

"If we lose this dorm then I am going to *make* the first Amtrak official we see put us up in his front room," Marie seethed.

Needless to say, the prospect of having her all to myself had not exactly got off to a smouldering start.

We finally arrived at the San Francisco Amtrak depot at 1am – the place was deserted, apart from a blank-looking night security guy with a stutter who got it from Marie with both barrels. He was sympathetic but useless – Marie quickly ran out of steam and ended up feeling pretty guilty. The guy gave us a number for tomorrow's day supervisor, and we realised this was all we were going to accomplish tonight. We stretched out on some hard metal benches on the empty concourse of the ferry building, dull blue arc lights above us and the black hissing of the Bay outside the plate glass windows, and tried to sleep.

The following day I had something of an identity crisis meltdown. I told Marie, but she already knew, and I wish I'd kept quiet.

We got a dorm at the Globe Hostel and then ate at Lori's, a cheap, tacky, perfect Fifties diner. A waitress called Georgie paid me an unusual amount of attention and insisted on trying to deconstruct my ethnic heritage with forensic accuracy, to the extent that she completely forgot our order. Marie looked on with bemusement.

We walked down to see an exhibition at the Ansel Adams Center on 4th at Howard. I thought it was all pretty good, with the usual surfeit of pretentious bollocks, but Marie was inspired.

"I guess the rest of my life starts when I get home," she said, touching the glass case of a Frida Kahlo portrait.

I left a cigarette packet and a soft drink cup on a bench and labelled it *Blues with Ice*, with a $30,000 price tag.

"You never know," I said to Marie.

Marie bought a couple of prints and we walked to the post office in Macy's to send them home. I waited for her on Market, outside Starbucks, where I got chatting to a retired engineer from Newark with thighs like girders. She had retired to Mesquite, and commented that my teeth were far too good for my bloodline to be *only* English.

The hostel computer was lousy, so we went to Club-i, an internet café on Folsom, for bagels and coffee. Marie's internet time expired while she was getting a refill – and somehow this was my fault. I got it in the neck and we exchanged a short, sharp volley of expletives. We were both tired, and Marie was not particularly looking forward to going home, and so it was quickly forgotten, but I wondered if the tide was just starting to creep onto the shore.

Marie had a redeye flight to NYC, where she was going to

hook up with Alex the snowboarder from Canada before getting a connecting flight to London. This particular reunion had been pencilled in way before this crazy couple of months in California, and she didn't seem to know what to do about it. She certainly didn't seem to be relishing the prospect.

So we showered at the hostel, checked out and dumped her luggage in the hostel's reception, and went to Biscuits & Blues for dinner. The food was good, the live band good, the drinks cheap, and yet the whole thing felt as if I were seeing it in a fishbowl. I didn't know why I was back in San Francisco. Marie kept checking her watch.

We walked back to the hostel, arriving just as the shuttle pulled up outside. Loading Marie's bags onto the bus nearly caused my ribs to break all over again, but I swatted away her offer of help. The sensible thing to do would have been to put my shoulder bag down first, but I didn't and it swung forwards as I bent to pick up her case. Everything spilled out of it.

"Oh, for Christ's sake," I said, as Marie started gathering bits off the ground. "What an oaf."

"Don't worry, I've got it. You should really be taking it easy. I'm not sure coming all the way to San Francisco was such a good idea."

"I'm fine."

"Are you even well enough to fly?"

"I said…"

"Holy shit! That's you!" Marie said.

"Huh? What are you talking about?"

Amongst the contents of my bag had been the rolled up copy of *The Dire Log* we had acquired on our first visit to San Francisco. Marie had been about to put it back into the bag, but now her eyes were fixed to it.

She thrust it towards me.

"*You.*"

I looked at where she was pointing with a neon fingernail – dwelling for only a second on where it had been and what it had scratched – and saw a small inset panel on the back page. The headline – such as it was – read:

Brit Blues Fingers Bruised in Vegas Open Mic Brawl

'Open mic nights at the Dude Ranch are not known for their good behavior, but this most recent event was notable for two reasons. First, the physical antics were higher up the scale than usual; second, there were one or two little gems on the set list, including a folk-funk duo called Boss and Nova and Johnny No-Name, a solo blues act whose rawbones sourmash style belied the tender years and cut-glass British accent, which caught this correspondent off-guard a bit when he was mumbling between songs. Unperturbed by the chaos in the bar, this sly British blues boy sang like a youthful Tom Waits, with wit, guile and a self-deprecating finger-pointing that you stopped hearing in the mainstream about the last time we had a Republican president…"

The piece went on for a few lines more – mainly about the fight, with thankfully nothing attributing the cause to my show of generosity – but underneath was a smudgy photograph. It had as much in the way of silhouetted heads as stage activity, but despite the grainy newspaper quality, it was clearly me; fingers stretched across the fretboard, mouth open mid-howl, begging the mic for some kind of salvation.

I turned the magazine over in my hands, a curious feeling in my stomach. Did this mean something? Was it the kind of moment I might look back on to pinpoint the line in the sand between *here* and *there*?

I could hear, with remarkable clarity, Marvin's voice in my head.

"Life is nothing without posterity. And this is far more flattering than you lined up on parade with a hundred other uniformed Agents of the State. This could be your fork in the road, son."

How ridiculous. He wasn't *dead*. But I wanted to tell him. Really badly.

"'Johnny No-Name,'" said Marie, squeezing my arm. "That's

awesome. And Tom Waits. She compared you to Tom *Waits*! You should ring her up. Tell her you claim the prize of mystery Vegas crooner."

"How do you know it's a she?"

"How do you know it isn't?"

Fair point. The byline belonged to someone called Bernie Snow. But in either case, calling her wasn't a bad idea. At the very least I now had something to put in my scrapbook besides the Dog and Duck's postage-stamp size adverts in the local classified pages, whose happy hour promos took up most of said postage stamp.

"Don't fly. Not just yet," Marie was saying. "This could be the start of something."

I dared not imagine.

"You could stay."

"I can't."

"I'm not sure I can do it on my own."

"You, beautiful boy, will be fine."

She kissed me.

"See you on the flipside, I guess," she said.

"Safe journey," I said, and hugged her in a stilted, awkward way, and not just because of the pain.

I released her.

"It wouldn't have been so bad, would it?" I said. "Having kids with me?"

She smiled a smile so tender I wanted to love and hate and forgive and forget her, all at once.

"Your kids will be beautiful, Alex."

She turned to go.

"Marie…"

She turned back.

"Just tell me one thing. Was it me? Did I… trap you?"

She touched my cheek.

"You just don't get it, do you?" she said softly, and climbed onto the shuttle. Besides the driver, she was the only one on it.

"Maybe we'll get back together when we're fifty," she said.

The door slid shut. I waved listlessly as the shuttle pulled away east down Folsom, but couldn't see her through the tinted windows. Then the city night engulfed her; I heard Bob Seger's *Night Moves* from somewhere, that bridge of silence before the murmuring acoustic guitar and thunder in the night, and she was gone.

"Goodbye, Marie Melanie Clement," I said to myself.

When I was very young, my dad told me I had artist's hands. I guess I only found half of what I was looking for, but I was buggered if I was going to die with worker's hands.

CHAPTER THIRTY-THREE

DICTAPHONE MONOLOGUES #12

INT. THE STOVEPIPE - NIGHT

                    MARVIN
     Let me tell you a story. There was once
     a man, who lived in a tiny little hut
     on a cliff far above the sea. He lived
     a simple life, and every day he would
     sit and watch the hands of his clock,
     always checking that they wouldn't
     catch him out.

     But then a storm came, and battered his
     little hut, and the man had to rally in
     the storm to secure the hut with ropes
     and joists. Then, after the storm, a
     blazing sun threatened to scorch his
     crop, and the man had to fashion a
     protective shade. After the heatwave,
     the rains came and washed away the
     shade, and the man had to dig drainage
     ditches to keep his crops from
     drowning.

     Eventually, the man returned to his
     hut, and found to his horror that the
     hands of the clock, ever crafty, had
     moved faster while his back was turned.
     This threw the man into a panic, and he
     forced himself to remain at the clock

```
even when his wife left and his animals
grew ill, to be sure that the crafty
hands would stay at their same steady
pace and not catch him out again.

But anyway, that's enough from me.
Ladies and gentlemen, let me introduce
you to a very prodigious blues
talent... my good friend... Alex Gray!
```

In the early morning the San Francisco buildings were swathed in fog. I took a bus to the ferry building and was reassured that the Amtrak was running fine.

On the train I showed *The Dire Log* to Casey, a Mexican actress, and Veronica, an author from Fresno who had a serene countenance and kept a diary and reminded me of Maya Angelou. They wanted to hear a song.

My dad, a graduate professional – by which I mean, the sort of person that can sign your passport photographs – reached a certain degree of localised eminence in his career around the time I started learning to drive. One manifestation of this was doing a late phone-in radio talk show on a Friday night. To get some practice in, I would drive him to the studio and park in the multi-storey, then wait for his show to finish. Sometimes I would get fish and chips and listen to the show in the car, but – apart from the time I saw the two middle-aged cheaters meet up and fly into each other's arms like magnets – an empty multi-storey is pretty boring.

The studio was in the city centre – a stone's throw from Karen Phillips's apartment, as it happened. It was nothing to look at from the outside – a grey porch in a council building – but it was surrounded on all sides by a network of interesting shops, and I would quite often take a stroll, peering through the windows while the city emptied of the day's workers.

There was one shop – a kind of treasure trove that sold art

and trinkets and ancient furniture and ornate birdcages. In the window was a painting of a French maid bending over with a feather duster, looking back at the viewer with an expression of coquettish surprise. I don't know what it was, but I loved that painting. It was done in some kind of retro pop art style, like the old Schweppes ads, and it somehow managed to strike just the right balance between porn and romance, between sex and love, between enchantment and titillation. I would gaze at it for hours, week after week, thinking *I must have that* in a way I never had about any material possessions other than Camille, and possibly my motorbike.

I didn't have any cause to visit the city during business hours until I started seeing Karen many months later, by which time the painting had, of course, been sold. I was gutted if not surprised, and tried to tell myself that it was a motif for something else. Maybe I didn't love it. Maybe I was so ready for *something* that I foisted my desire for magic and meaning onto a beguiling-yet-inanimate object.

The whole journey back to Los Angeles took nine hours. I had to take a bus to Emeryville, pick up another Amtrak to Bakersfield and then take another bus to Union Station. Apparently it wasn't running fine after all.

There was a burning car on the Hollywood Freeway. The already-baking air shimmered with incredible heat. I could feel it through the window of the bus as we passed, the flames scorching the twisted metal skeleton. Behind us the deafening air horn of a fire truck sounded.

I took the subway to Vine and checked back into the Millennium Hostel. Bizarrely they gave me the same room that I had shared with Marie, but in the few days we had been away they had turned it from a double room into a six-bunk dorm. Now the brilliant whitewashed walls made me think of the barracks in that movie *Full Metal Jacket*, and I thought about what Marvin said about memories dying with a lick of paint or a demolition crew.

I took a shower. The bulb blew as I stepped in and I soaped up in the dark. I managed to fix it after I'd got dressed and wished I hadn't – in a few days the bathroom had gone from the dainty aspect of Marie's oils and lotions to the full-on occupation of five other gorillas. The rope of hair around the tiled skirting looked like a whole-room draught excluder.

The journey to Marvin's was slow and painful – the bus was packed and airless, while the route seemed littered with the pneumatic juddering of endless roadworks.

Zephi answered the door in her running gear. Her face was flushed.

"How are you doing?" she said.

"I'm good, thank you. How about you?"

"To be honest, I'm not entirely sure."

"I'm sorry to disturb you. I left a few bits here. I just came to get them out of your hair. The guitar, some tapes, not much."

"Of course. I was just… tidying up."

She pushed the door open and let me in.

I stood in the lounge for a moment. It was clear there was no one else home. I didn't ask whether she had moved back in, and I didn't really want to know. There probably wasn't a clean way to label it, anyway. My eyes turned to the sofa. For a second, I couldn't pull them away.

"I think they're in Marvin's room," she said. "Can I get you anything?"

"Actually, a glass of water would be great, if you don't mind."

She disappeared to the kitchen. As I followed her and continued down the short hallway to Marvin's room, I revised my assessment that Zephi was home alone. I could hear the sounds of voices – a conversation – coming from his room.

Marvin's room, in a short space of time, appeared to have become the storeroom. His bed was still there, but most of his stuff was in boxes, along with a load of old baby toys and camping gear. I thought I could smell the sex of another era.

But the room was empty. The voices, I realised, were on

Marvin's television, which was opposite the bed on a small desk. I spotted my (latest) guitar and a small bag with my other bits at the foot of the bed. I picked it up as Zephi appeared in the doorway with my water. She put down my glass on the desk and folded her arms, leaning her head on the doorframe.

"Bad times, huh?" she said.

"I guess," I said, and showed her the piece in the *Dire Log* with a muted kind of pride.

"This is fantastic. You so deserve it."

"It might not amount to anything. But it could be a start."

"So, you gonna stick around?"

"I don't really know."

"I'm sorry about Roger being such a dick. You can't let people like that get you down."

"You don't have to apologise for him," I said. "He was right, anyway. I do need to commit."

She said nothing for a moment, and then moved a little closer.

"Listen, whatever happens... I just want to say thanks. For being so nice. For being... a man."

I smiled.

"I'll leave you in peace," she said, and left.

As she did so, my senses retuned to the background voices on the television.

Mainly because I realised one of them was mine.

"Marvin! What are you doing? Get in the car!"

At first glance it could have been any old home movie. There was my stupid grinning face, sitting in a convertible on the desert highway to Vegas, while Marvin ran alongside the queue of traffic, shooting his movie from the verge.

Then other things I recognised – the Bay Bridge, the Desert Inn at 4am, the condor at Big Sur – but then things I didn't, even though I knew they had happened.

Drunken conversations on Fisherman's Wharf.

Arguments in the dark lot behind the Musso & Frank Grill.

My semi-conscious face in a hospital bed.

Marvin had waxed enthusiastic about DVDs, the World Wide Web and the advent of technology generally. It didn't seem a stretch to imagine that he would be front and centre when God was dishing out tiny buttonhole super-discreet pen spy cameras, or something.

I moved a little closer, realising that it was not just a random selection of home movie clips. It had been stitched together in a narrative order. To prove the point, he had overdubbed our rambling dictaphone conversations onto the video – again, conversations I knew we'd had, but also his own observations as well:

"Clearly, there was a spare female at the table. I was being especially charming, telling all sorts of interesting details about my recent excursions into strip clubs and the pants of frightened strangers. She lapped it all up.

'It thus became a doddle to perform the old Jedi mind trick. Two ingredients are needed to ensure success in such cases. Firstly, a scalding honesty about one's own shortcomings and neurotic sexual pathology. This makes them feel like you are just one of the girls, a crucial disguise that becomes invaluable later. Secondly, a blisteringly personal psychic attack. This is an essential part of gearing up to bed the average reader of post-feminist books. They have such low self-esteem that a few well-placed and terrible insults drastically reduce their ability to withstand even the most lame drunken pass. In fact, they find it utterly irresistible without ever quite knowing why.

"So I put my plan into action in the middle of the casino, throwing a relentless tirade of insults and withering put-downs her way. Naturally, she was upset, but the coup de grace *was my apology. I went down on one knee in a crowded lift, left a dramatic pause and then said, 'I'm sorry. It's just that everything you say fills me with contempt."*

'Half an hour later, she was looking over my shoulder, helping me play the fruity and stroking my leg with surprising tenderness.

"She honestly could not help herself…"

I stared at nothing, all my concentration focused on listening. But before I could spend too long contemplating the weight – and potential consequences – of this morally significant thorn in Marvin and Marie's flowering relationship, the subject of the dictaphone conversations moved on. This time, to yours truly:

"At first I thought he was joking, or telling a line from a film like he often does and in fact does too much, but then I saw, in a moment's dawning realisation, that he was actually upset. Upset real bad with wounded pride like a person never would be over a spilled drink and I saw with cold clarity what I already knew. That I had won Marie from him, a competition effortless and immediate, and in so doing had wounded him badly, and that his indifferent display of bravado and male ennui was exactly that, and I had been too focused on the prize to care..."

The dictaphone was lying next to the television, hooked up to some other gadget that looked like a four-track. Underneath that was a sketch pad, comprising thick, decent quality artist's paper.

I picked it up, and recognised it instantly, even though it had only ever existed in my brain and, once, verbalised after half a dozen gin gimlets on Hollywood Boulevard.

It was a storyboard – pretty well drawn, actually – with scene directions underneath:

```
OPENING - EXT. MOJAVE DESERT - DAY
Wide aerial shot of the desert. A high, high shot,
maybe wisps of cloud tickling the lens as it
descends towards the ground. Then, as it gets
lower, there's a car gleaming in the distance, just
a speck as it cruises along the thin strip of
blacktop.
        While this is happening, Bloody Well Right
by Supertramp starts to play over the opening
credits, which appear in time to the those crashing
whole-band accents as they punctuate the solo
electric piano intro, big red Seventies road movie
lettering:

        Naked Bandit Films Present
```

A Pacific Jetstream Production

Etc.

EXT. FORD MUSTANG - MOJAVE DESERT - DAY

Close up on the front wheel as it speeds along the
highway, all mirror chrome, spaghetti spokes and
whitewall tyres. Cue voice-over and music fade
down, just as the vocals start proper. Manny is
rambling, talking mainly to himself, and is only
just audible above the music.

                    MANNY
                   [V.O.]

        So, I figure, surrender the counterfeit
        dollars quickly - you know, make a show
        of contrition - then we'll be over the
        state line before they realise the real
        loot is gone. Of course, I wouldn't
        have the first idea where to get hold
        of a gun, but you can only ask, right?

Pan up past the wing, the hood, the windshield,
where we see two men through the glass.

Cut to:

INT. FORD MUSTANG - MOJAVE DESERT - DAY

In the car we find two Brit bad boys and a drop-
dead gorgeous girl. Twenty-year-old Alvin Gainham
is driving; a handsome, weather-beaten labourer
with maybe a touch of Inuit in him, his guitar and
old life in the trunk. Louche, lithe, lecherous
Manny Palmer is in the passenger seat, rolling a
dope cigarette and muttering Beat poetry under his
breath while nervous sexual tension grips his body.
Curled up asleep on the back seat is the beautiful

Maya Calley, her perfect bare legs smooth against the leather. There are big dreams and big love in this car, the destination just another job to do.

MANNY
[*soft, reflective*]
What do you regret most in your life?

ALVIN
Honestly? Meeting you.

I put down the storyboard. His soft, deep, BBC naturalist voiceover continued its comforting observations on the television, narrating my exploits on the gaming floor, the tar pits and myriad Hollywood bars.

"The guy is insistent on punishing himself at every turn for not living up to the expectations of his forebears. He's only twenty, but he acts like someone dropped adulthood in his lap like a steaming pile of shit, told him to work it out, and then fucked off. He's a kid in the dressing-up box, playing at being a grown-up, and because of that he thinks his future is 'now or never.'"

I gripped the headstock of the guitar to stop my hands from shaking.

"The thing is, Alex doesn't realise how the loss of his innocence has affected him, and he projects it onto others' kids like a Jesuit missionary or a reformed addict. I mean, how do you help someone like that? How can you reasonably help someone who won't forgive himself for growing up…"

I lifted the garage sale guitar and, in a sideways homage to the stage shenanigans of punk, rammed the end of it through the television. It exploded with a bang and flash of light.

Zephi came running, her eyes wide.

"What was that? Are you…"

She found me staring at the fractured television, my chest heaving like a spent triathlete. I turned to look at her while she took in the scene before her.

I dug in my pocket and – carelessly, in a way I had never done before – fished out my last few dirty dollar bills. I walked past, squeezing right past her in the doorway, and thrust the money into her hand as she continued to stare.

"Sorry about the mess," I said, and left, slamming the door on my way out.

CHAPTER THIRTY-FOUR

BABY FACED BLUES

I sat down at the bus stop, feeling the heat burning through the soles of my trainers from the white concrete. Two buses came along and stopped for me, but I barely noticed, and they moved on again.

Eventually my brain slowed down enough for me to realise I no longer had any money for the fare anyway. I stood up, picked up the guitar, and realised the head was hanging off the broken neck, just about held on by what was left of the strings.

I left it at the bus stop and began the hour-plus walk back to Hollywood Boulevard.

CHAPTER THIRTY-FIVE

DICTAPHONE MONOLOGUES #13

```
INT. ADELANTO DETENTION CENTER - NIGHT

                    MARVIN
                    [v.o.]
     This isn't real. Sitting at your
     kitchen table waiting to go to work
     during an English winter with only the
     skeletons of the trees for company,
     that's real. This heat and sea and neon
     and the smell of sun cream on skin and
     frying and dope in the air is not…
```

In the end, it took me most of the afternoon. I don't remember where I went, but it was turning to dusk when I finally got back to the Millennium.

I nearly tripped over Marcello, even though you couldn't really miss him in his stars-and-stripes pantaloons – and, today, Dixieland vest. He was sitting on the steps of the hostel, his camera dangling from his neck, and as I backed up to move around him, I realised he was waiting for me.

"*There* you are," he said. "It's been a hell of a thing trying to find you…"

Like a man who comes back to catch someone in the act of keying his car, I grabbed him by his stupid vest in a surge of blissful righteous outrage, and slammed him up against the wall of the building that had once been a grand hotel or a municipal headquarters.

"You fucking vulture," I hissed at him. "You dirty, thieving little parasite."

"Let go of me!"

"I ought to break your head against this wall. What are you doing here? Come to steal the rest of my stuff? Well, there's a broken guitar on Pico you could scrounge."

"Steal? *Steal?*" he squealed. "I never stole a goddam thing in my life!"

"You can tell the cops that. It'll take them a week to stop laughing. I've been through half the guitars in Hollywood, thanks to you."

"I didn't *steal* your guitar. I came to give it *back*."

It was as if someone had sucked the air out of my lungs. I turned to see where he was pointing.

And there, leaning against the wall next to where he had been sitting, was Camille.

CHAPTER THIRTY-SIX

DICTAPHONE MONOLOGUES #14

EXT. 3rd ST PROMENADE, SANTA MONICA – NIGHT

                    MARVIN
        Cherish decent conversations, because
        when you're a grown-up all you'll do is
        talk about your mortgage, your kids,
        your car, your job and your retirement
        plans. When you're drunk you'll
        reminisce a bit, but that's about it.
        You'll find your grip on your own
        destiny loosening as you get older.
        You'll never have those conversations
        about Life that you'll have now.
        Especially not when those same
        conversations can give you choices
        about tomorrow you can actually act on…

I don't know what you'd call him. Some kind of public-spirited Samaritan recovery agent, maybe. In any case, Marcello was a relative constant in Los Angeles, buzzing around with his camera, obsessively documenting life, his snaps useful by turns to the cops and the travel guides in equal measure, depending on what happened to pop up in front of his lens. It wasn't uncommon for him to be at the Mint – nor, for that matter, the Marriott, Santa Monica pier or the Wells Fargo downtown.

      I climbed the stairs to my room, Camille clutched in my grip, thinking: whoever's got the Casino, they're welcome to it. I desperately wanted to tell Marie, but she was probably only just flying over Greenland.

The faint strains of music indicated yet another rooftop barbecue, and so I went up for a quick nightcap. The music was terrible, however, and there was only a cluster of three or four geeky looking guys huddled around the garbage-can-cum-grill. I necked a vodka and lime slammer and a Bud, and climbed back down to my floor.

The room was on the top floor of the building, at the end of the corridor. Recessed in the enormous landing, by the banister, was a carefully stacked arrangement of junk, the centrepiece of which was an ancient upright piano, shrouded in polythene dust sheets. Between the last visit and this one, so anxious had I been not to let Marie out of my sight that I had failed to notice it.

I hid Camille in the bedroom, and, after pulling away the plastic, opened the lid of the piano. It had the wobbly double-tone of a very old instrument, but it was more or less in tune. I upended a tea chest as a makeshift stool, and started to play.

It sounded okay. My guitar skills far outstretched my abilities on the ivories, but it could have been worse. Pianos dig the blues, anyway. Or should that be the other way around?

Maybe I should change instruments, I thought. *You're unlikely to get mugged on the street for your piano.*

I started with *Big Legged Woman* and then had a punt at *Night Train.* By the time I got to *The Sky Is Crying* and started singing, a girl had come out of her room. In another time and place, I might have expected a kicking, or at least a complaint, but this was Hollywood. She came and stood right by the piano, leaning on the upright and listening.

Then two guys came up the stairs. They headed for my dorm – *note to self, meet roommates* – but then changed direction and stood near the girl.

Then the four geeks from the rooftop came down, carefully negotiating the carriage of the remainder of a massive bucket of beers.

They may have been about to call it a night, but instead the two guys and the girl beckoned them over and dived into the bucket. One got placed next to the keyboard for me, with a folded dollar bill underneath it to act as a coaster.

When I finished *Night Train*, they started clapping. So I started *Sweet Home Chicago*, and by the time that finished there were twenty people gathered around the piano. One of the geeks had been eating from a box of fried chicken – he got rid of the bones, wiped it out and placed it next to my beer. Only later would I realise he had put a five-dollar bill inside it, which, over the next hour or so, got lost beneath others.

I am Sal Paradise. I am Paul Kemp. I am Raoul Duke. I am Henry Chinaski. I am Holden Caulfield. I am Humphrey van Weyden. I am John Barleycorn. I am Tyler Durden.

The headaches and the drink and the painkillers were like soup on my brain. By the time I went to bed, the chicken box of tips in my hand, fog was swirling in the Los Angeles basin as I swept up and down the Pacific Coast Highway like mercury on a hot day, the jungle music loud in my ears, the headaches a constant pressure, the dry Santa Ana winds blowing the hot dust of my past. From the Yamashiro, high in the Hollywood Hills, I looked down on the patchwork of Los Angeles, where the mounting pile of my discarded days was an indistinguishable mass of orange and white, like so many broken tiles.

I lay on the bunk, alone in the room, staring at the circling flies, my thoughts not quite taking shape. Outside, Hollywood Boulevard was cold and empty, save for the most diehard street hustlers and the silently flashing neon steadily regulating the heartbeat of the city.

I drifted into sleep, but was awoken at some nameless witching hour by a lone male voice screaming "LA! LA! LA!" followed by a high-pitched whistle. There was a pause, and the screaming began again, followed by the whistle. It happened again and again, each time louder as he moved towards my open window.

After a while, I realised he wasn't screaming "LA!" at all, but just calling for his dog, whatever its name was.

THE END

34409342R00197

Printed in Great Britain
by Amazon